Shojo Beat

La Corda d'Oro

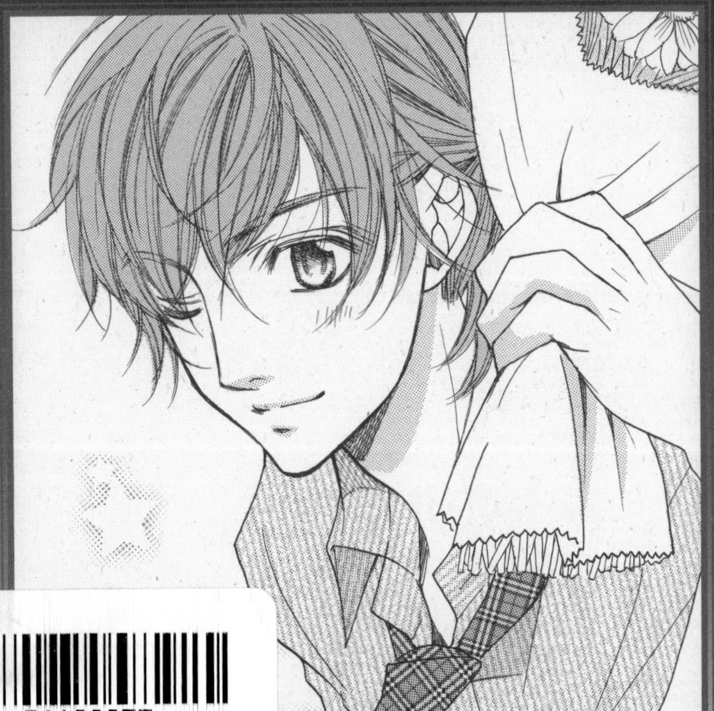

12

Story & Art by Yuki Kure

La Corda d'Oro

CONTENTS
Volume 12

Characters

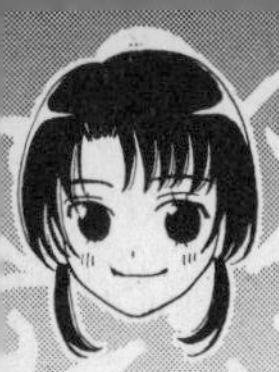

Kahoko Hino
(General Education School, 2nd year)
The heroine. She knows nothing about music, but she finds herself participating in the school music competition equipped with a magic violin.

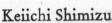

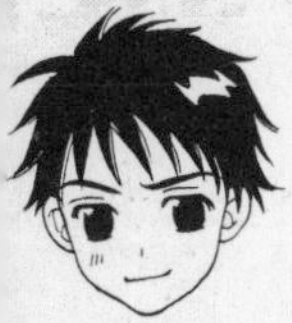

Ryotaro Tsuchiura
(General Education School, 2nd year)
A soccer player and talented pianist who seems to be looking after Kahoko.

Len Tsukimori
(Music School, 2nd year)
A violin major and a cold perfectionist from a musical family of unquestionable talent.

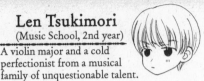

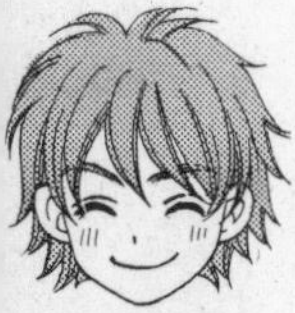

Kazuki Hihara
(Music School, 3rd year)
An energetic and friendly trumpet major and a fan of anything fun.

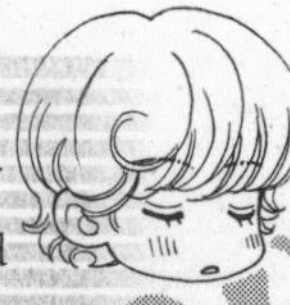

Keiichi Shimizu
(Music School, 1st year)
A cello major who walks to the beat of his own drum and is often lost in the world of music. He is also often asleep.

Azuma Yunoki
(Music School, 3rd year)
A flute major from an ultra-traditional family who's very popular with girls. Only Kahoko knows that he has a dark side!

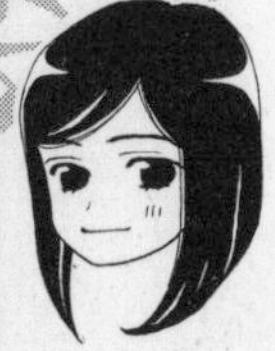

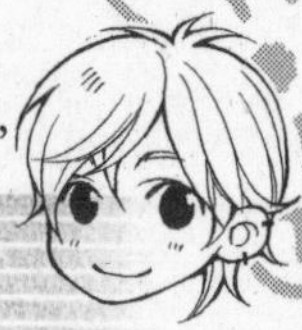

Aoi Kaji
(General Education School, 2nd year)
A handsome guy who just transferred to Seisou. It seems like he's always hanging around Kahoko.

Story

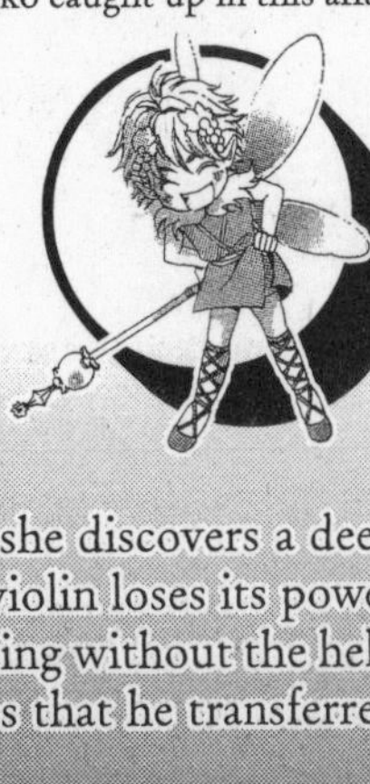

The music fairy, Lili, who got Kahoko caught up in this affair.

Our story is set at Seisou Academy, which is split into the General Education School and the Music School. Kahoko, a Gen Ed student, encounters a music fairy named Lili who gives her a magic violin that anyone can play. Suddenly Kahoko finds herself in the school's music competition, with good-looking, quirky Music School students as her fellow contestants! Along the way she discovers a deep love for music. At the end of the competition the violin loses its power and disappears, but Kahoko decides to keep practicing without the help of magic. Meanwhile, a new student, Aoi, confesses that he transferred to Seisou just to be near Kahoko...

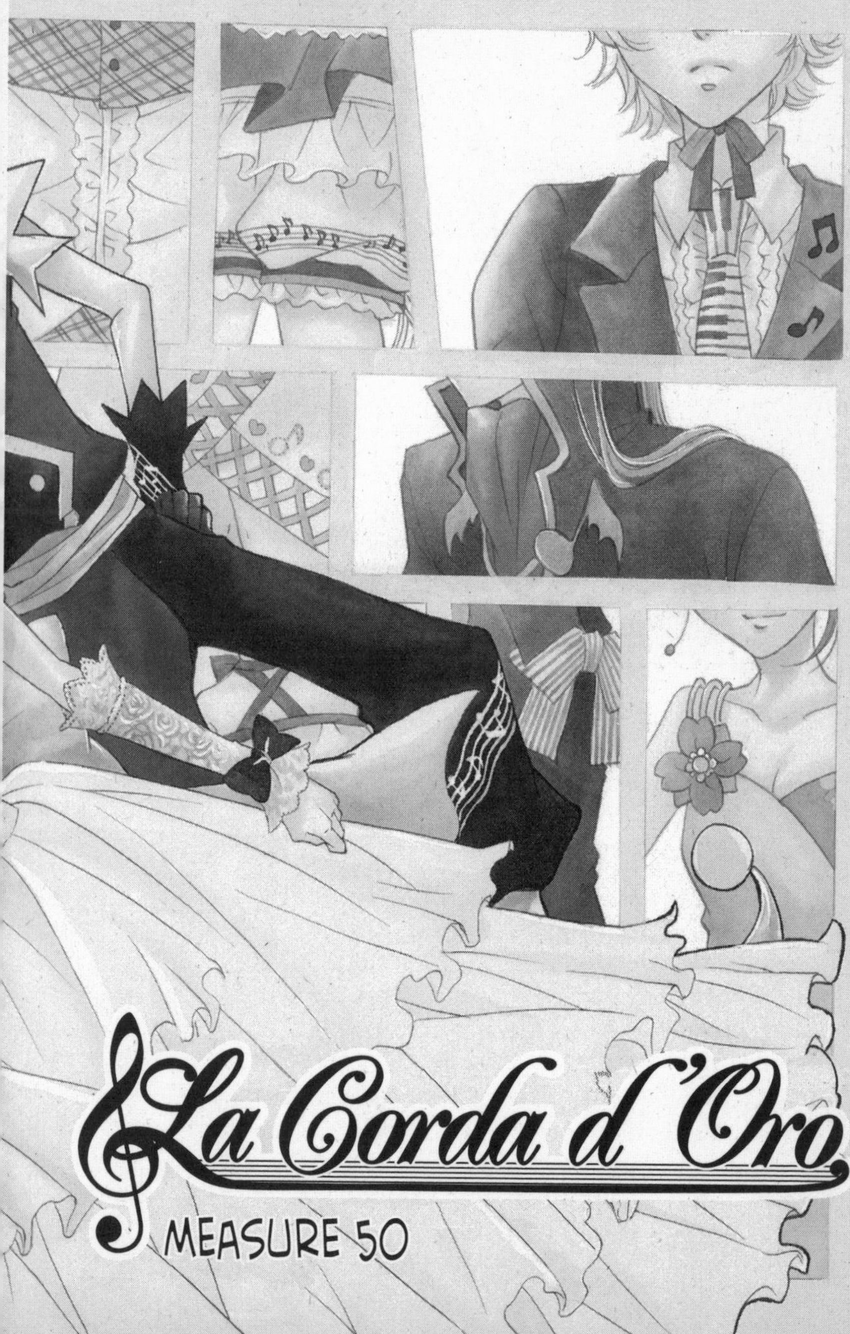
La Corda d'Oro
MEASURE 50

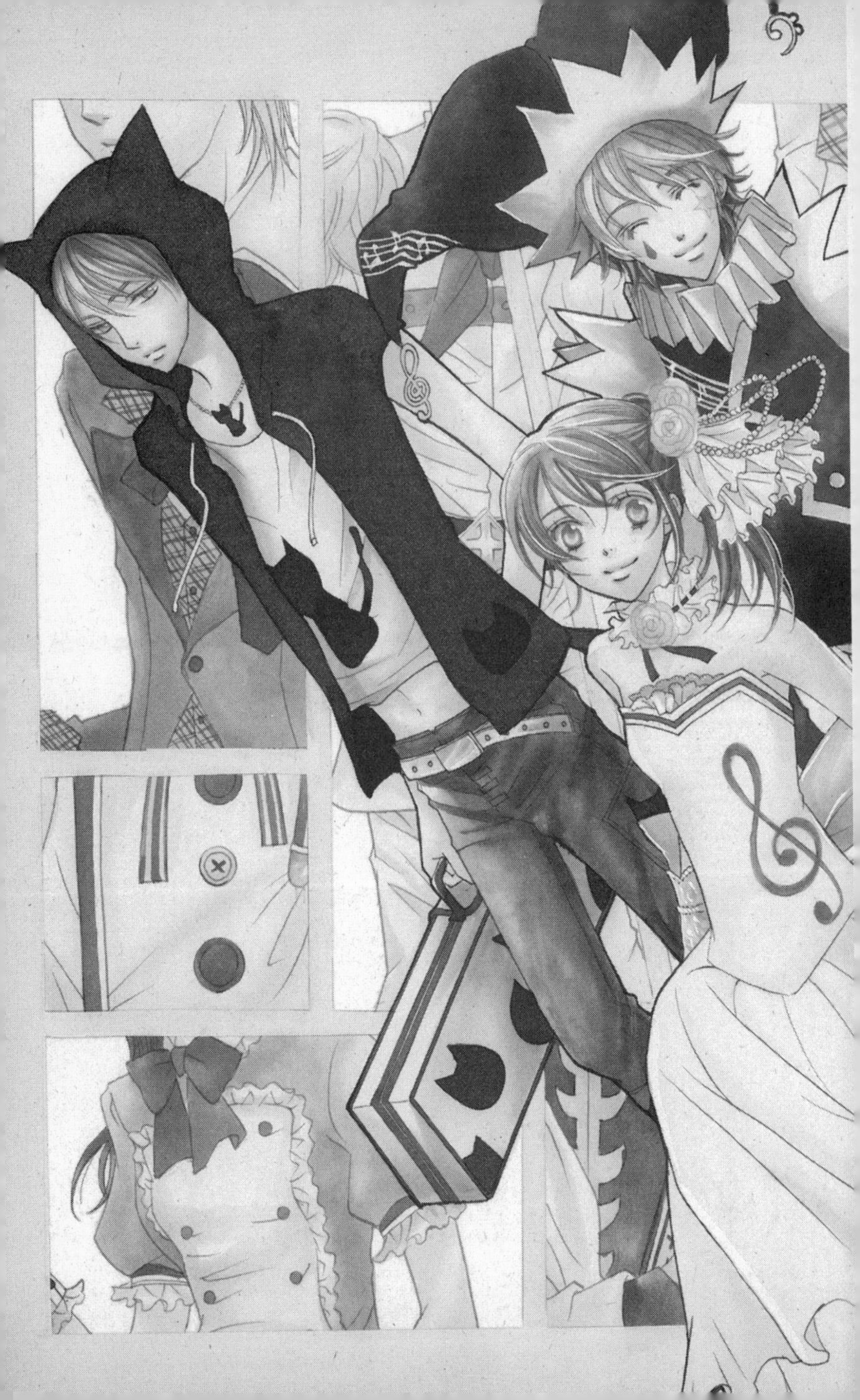

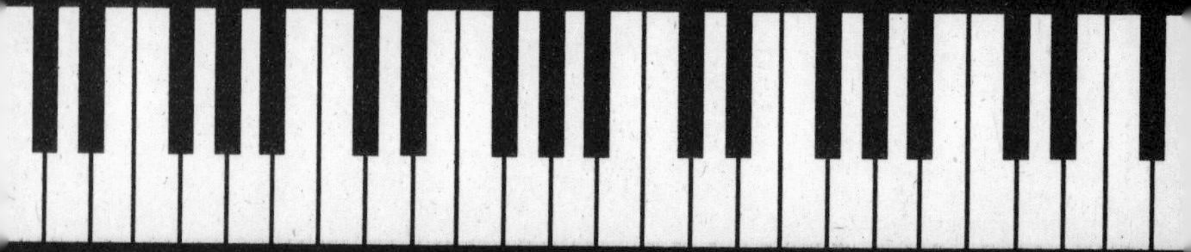

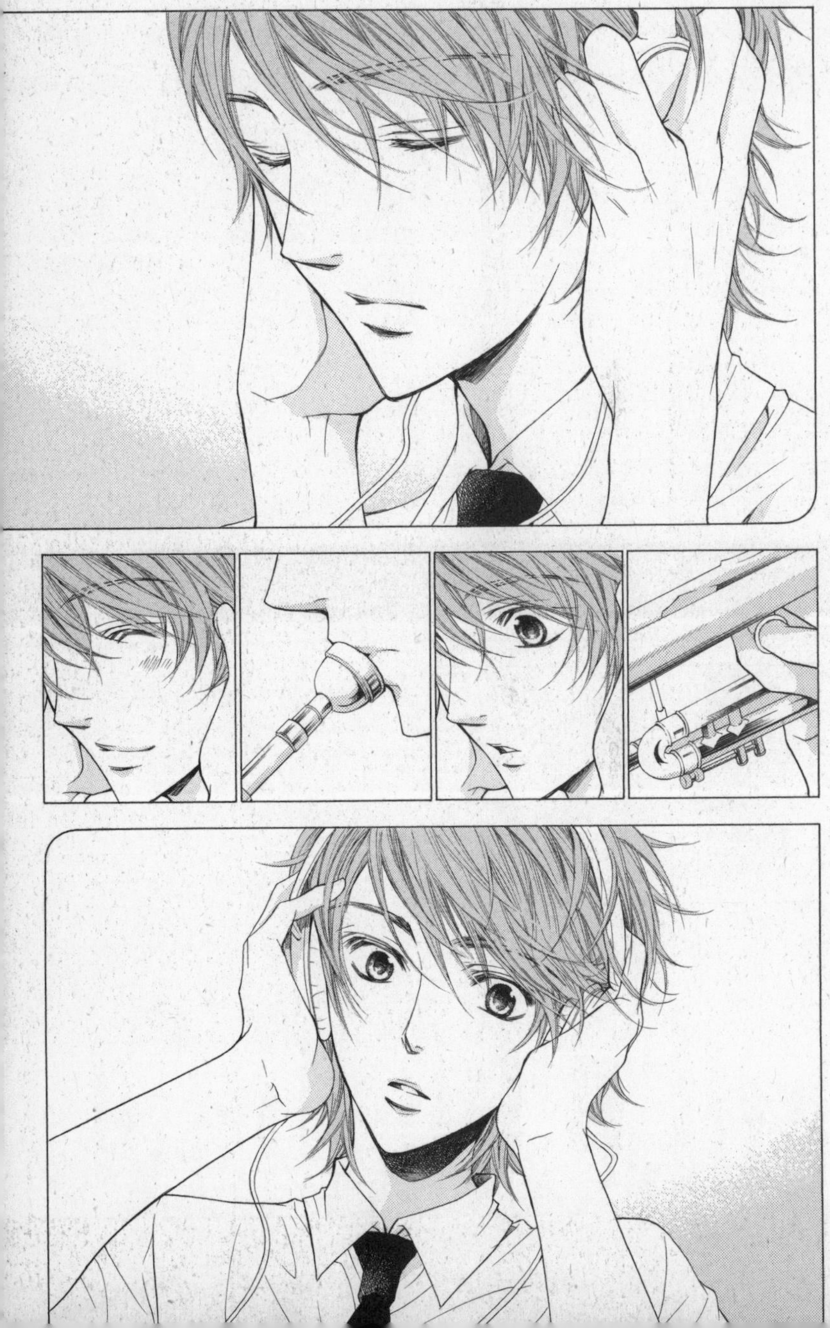

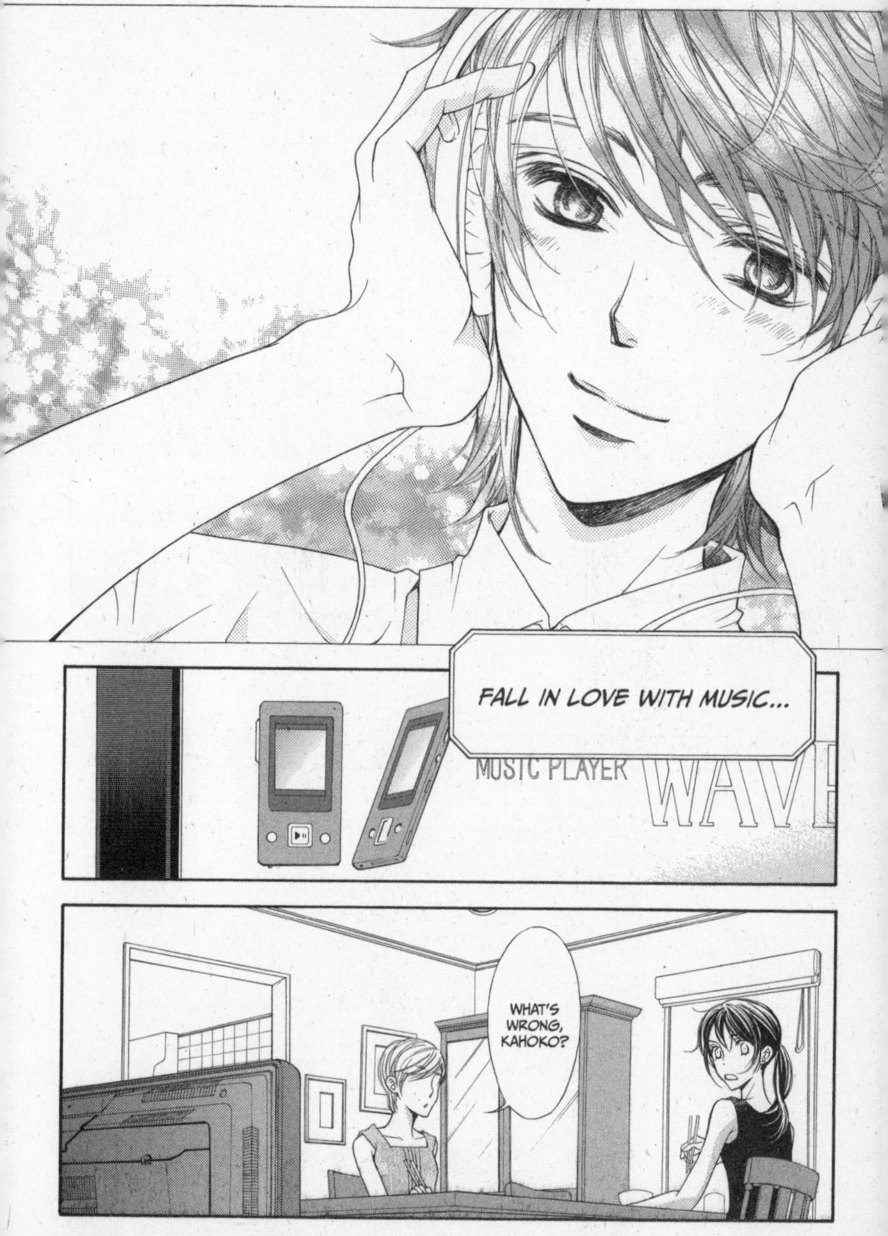
FALL IN LOVE WITH MUSIC...
MUSIC PLAYER
WAVE
WHAT'S WRONG, KAHOKO?

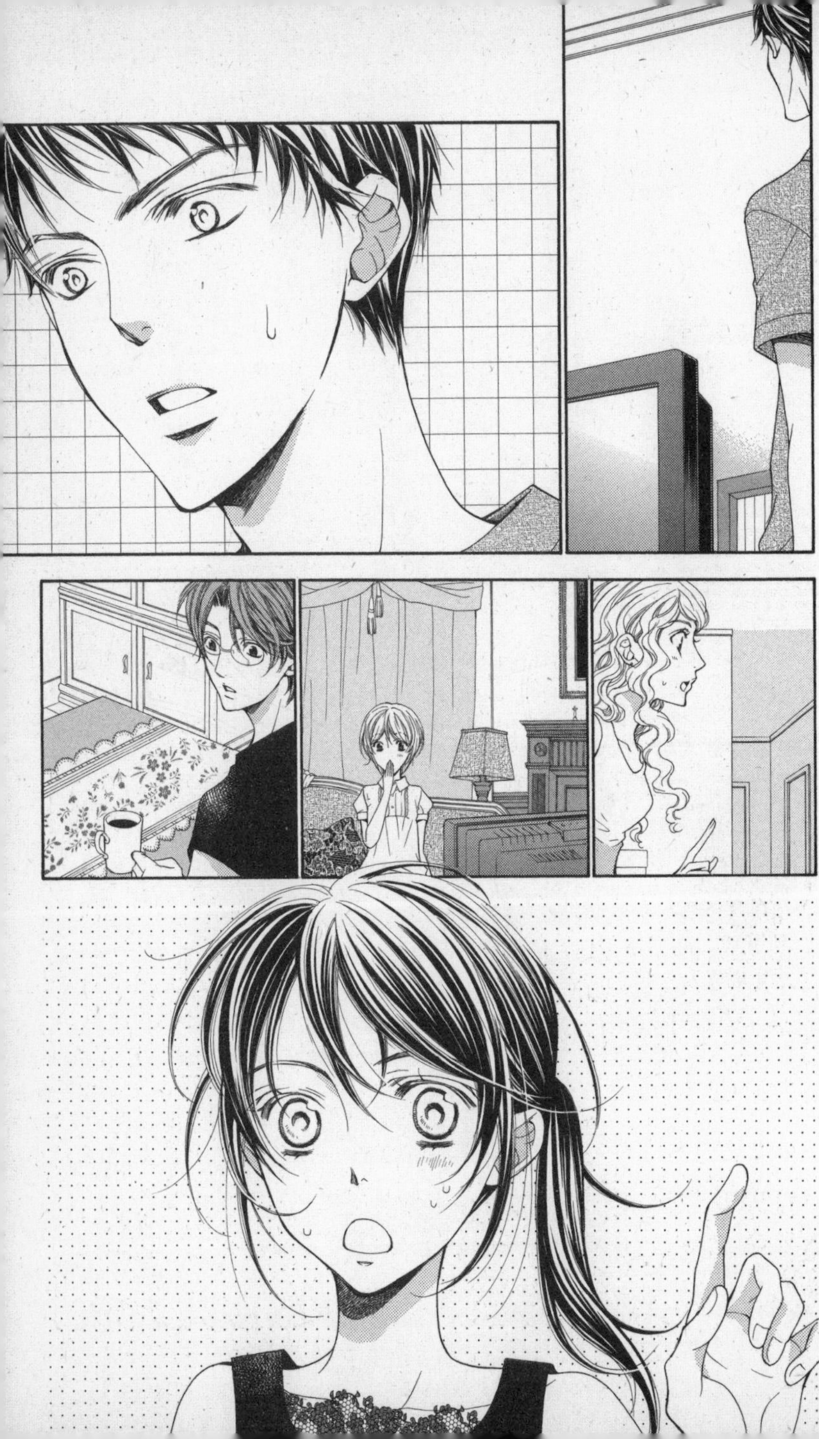

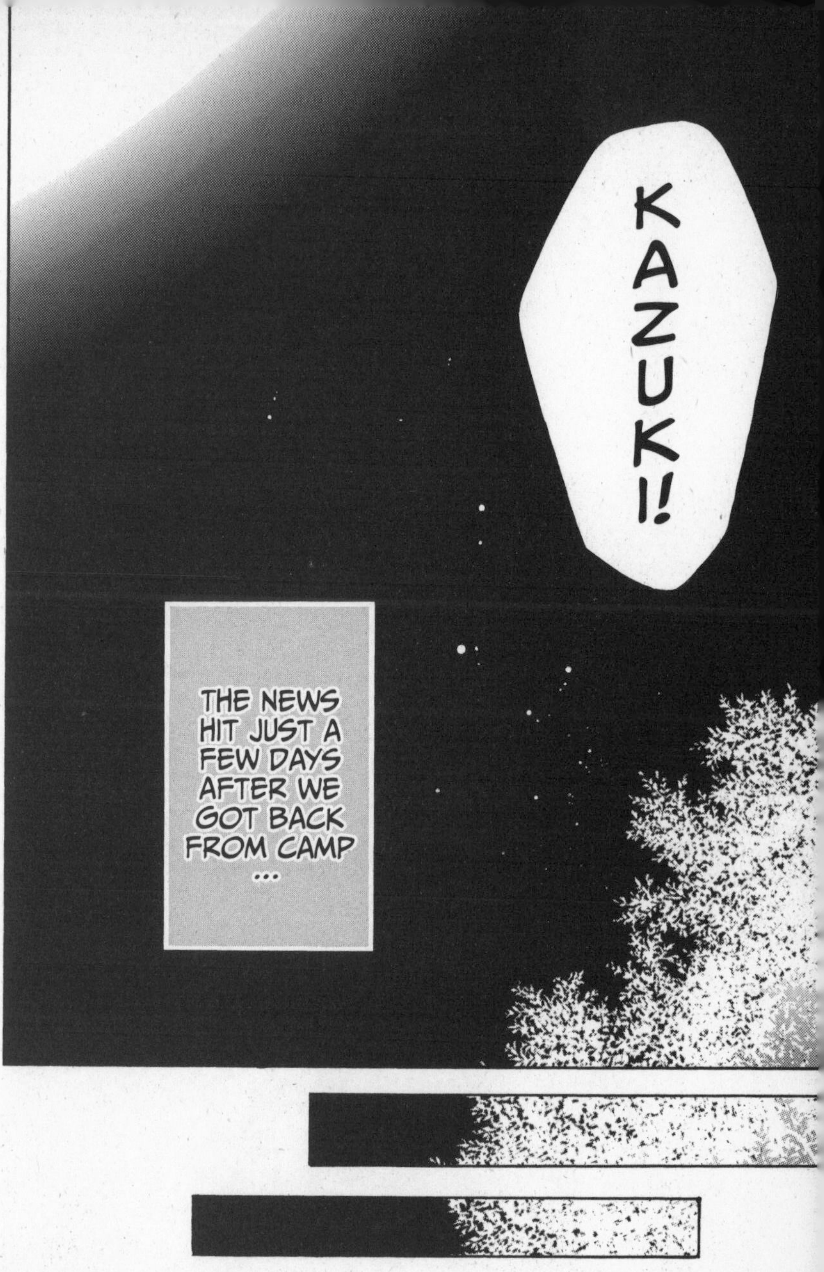
KAZUKI!!
THE NEWS HIT JUST A FEW DAYS AFTER WE GOT BACK FROM CAMP ...

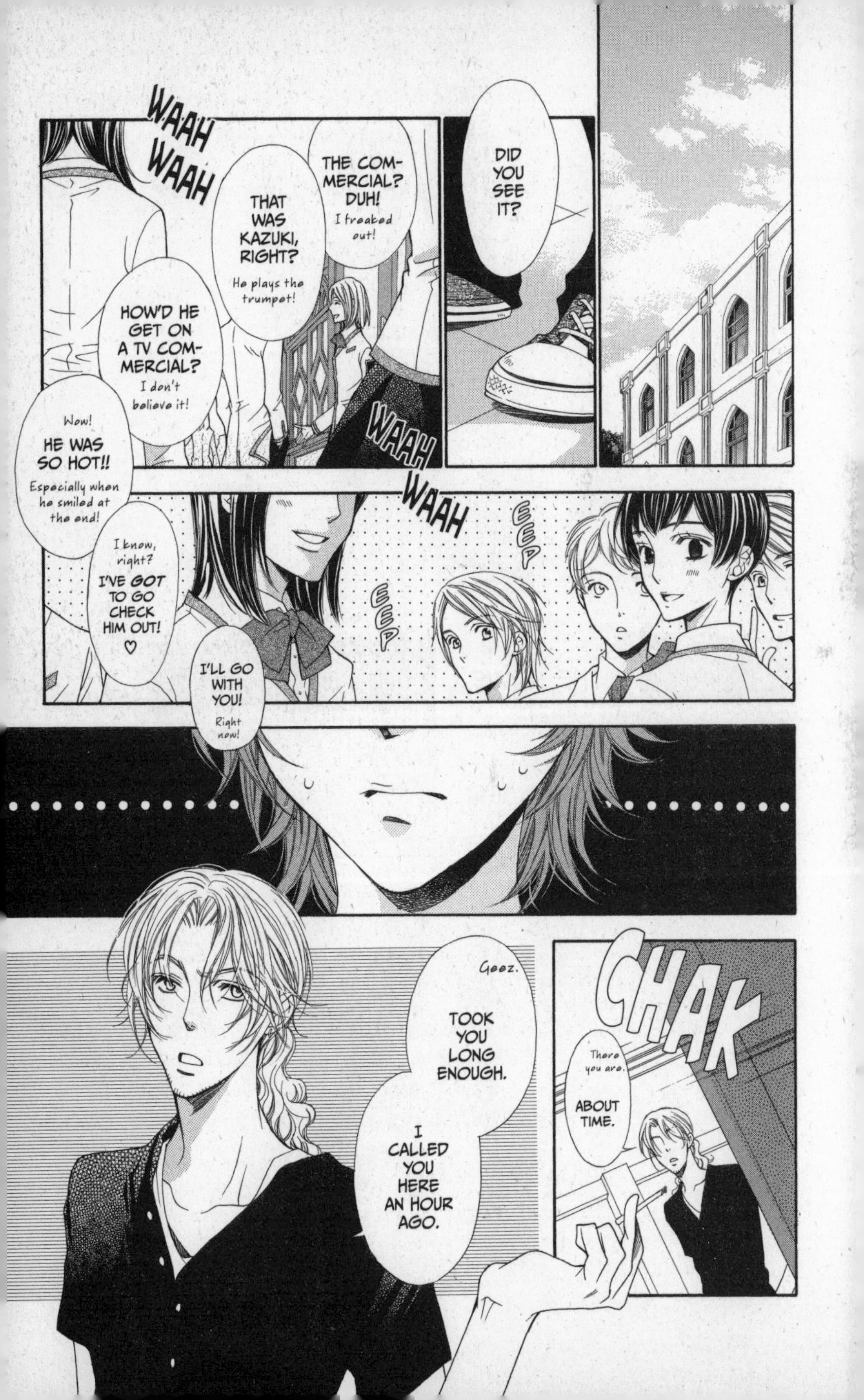
DID YOU SEE IT?
WAAH WAAH
THE COM-MERCIAL? DUH! I freaked out!
THAT WAS KAZUKI, RIGHT? He plays the trumpet!
HOW'D HE GET ON A TV COM-MERCIAL? I don't believe it!
WAAH WAAH
Wow! HE WAS SO HOT!! Especially when he smiled at the end!
EEP EEP
I know, right? I'VE GOT TO GO CHECK HIM OUT! ♡
I'LL GO WITH YOU! Right now!
• • • • • • • • • •
CHAK
There you are. ABOUT TIME.
Geez. TOOK YOU LONG ENOUGH.
I CALLED YOU HERE AN HOUR AGO.

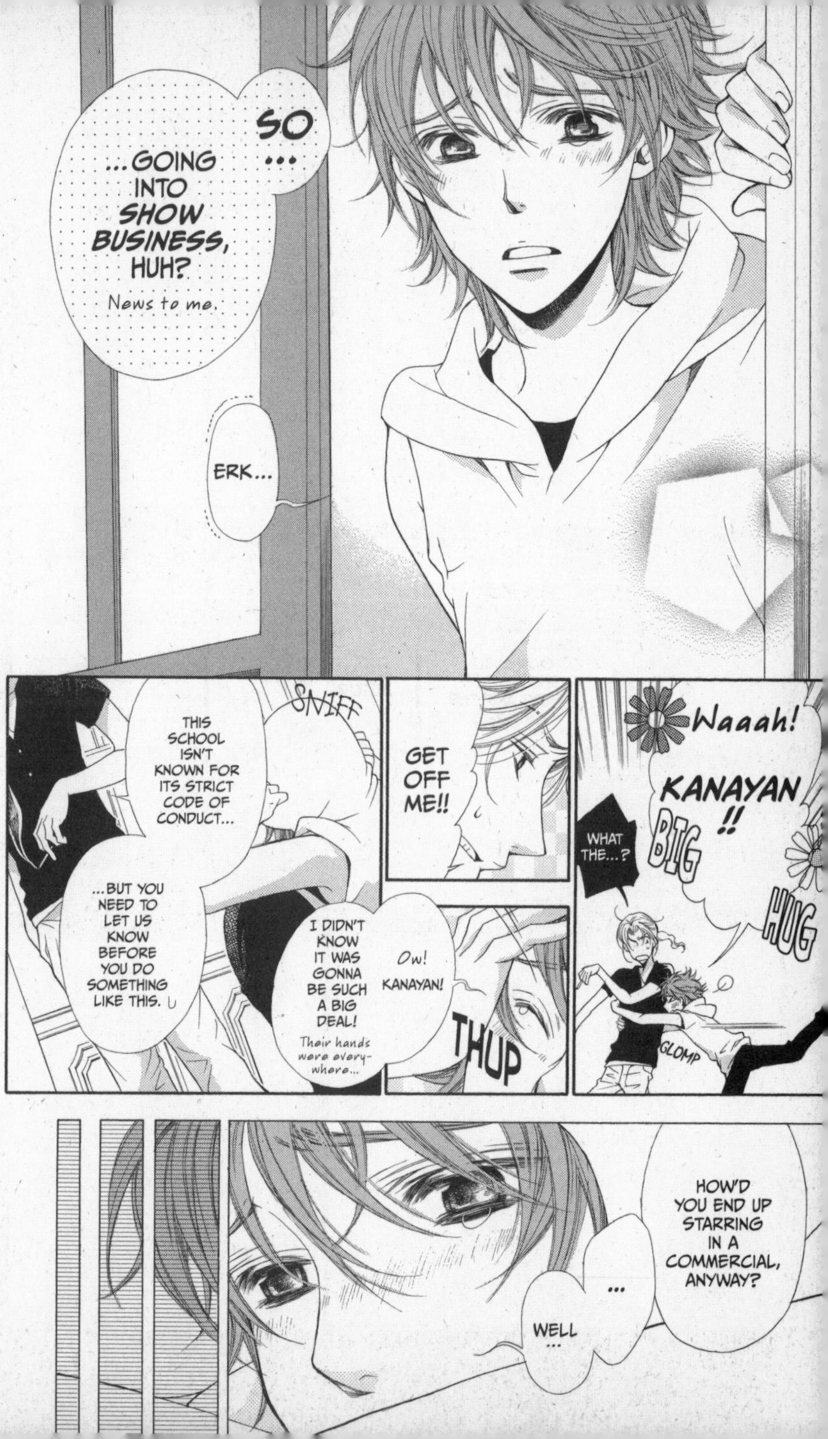
SO...
...GOING INTO SHOW BUSINESS, HUH?
News to me.
ERK...
Waaah!
KANAYAN!!
BIG
HUG
WHAT THE...?
GLOMP
GET OFF ME!!
Ow! KANAYAN!
THUP
SNIFF
THIS SCHOOL ISN'T KNOWN FOR ITS STRICT CODE OF CONDUCT...
...BUT YOU NEED TO LET US KNOW BEFORE YOU DO SOMETHING LIKE THIS.
I DIDN'T KNOW IT WAS GONNA BE SUCH A BIG DEAL!
Their hands were every-where...
HOW'D YOU END UP STARRING IN A COMMERCIAL, ANYWAY?
...
WELL...

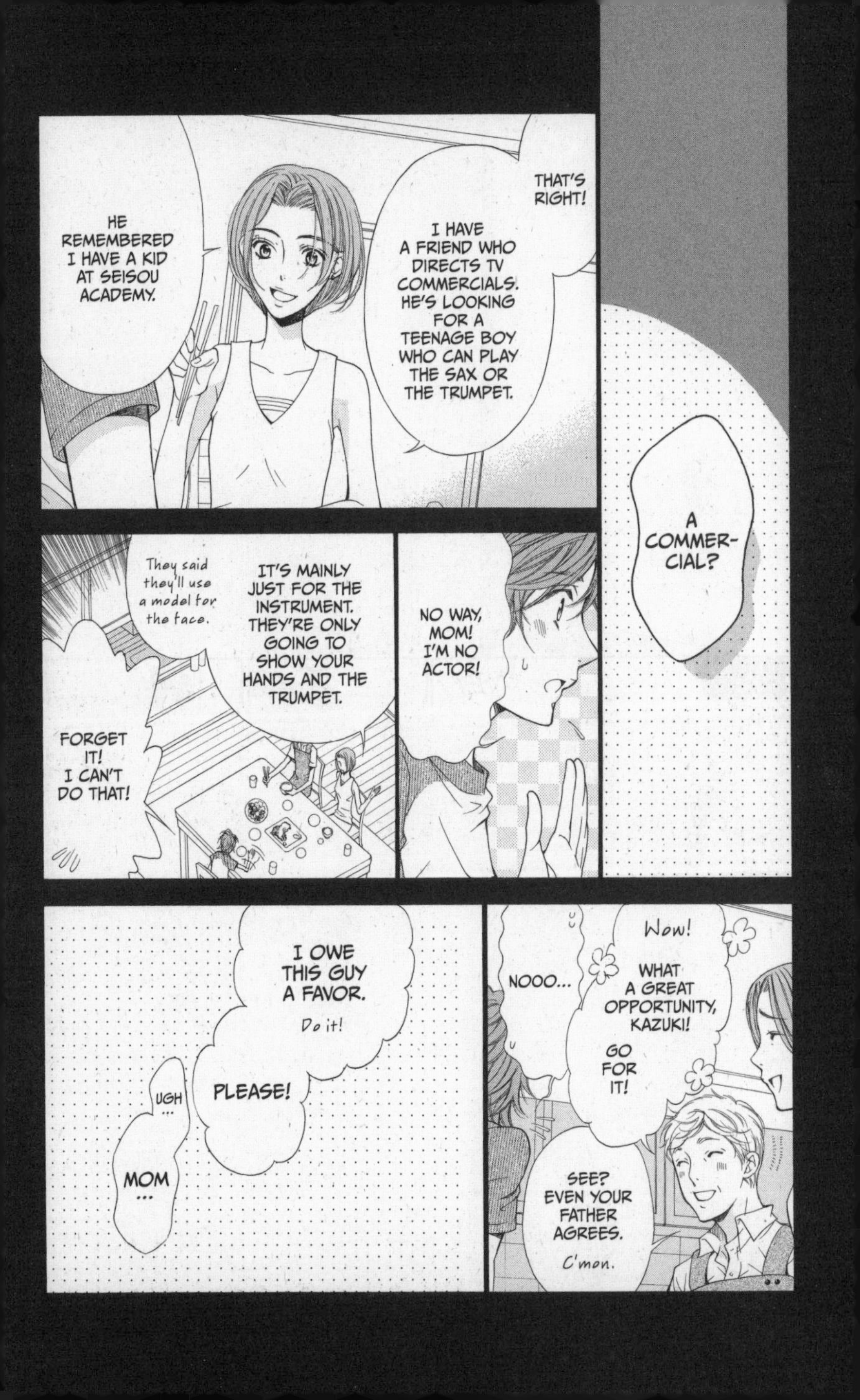
A COMMERCIAL?
THAT'S RIGHT!
I HAVE A FRIEND WHO DIRECTS TV COMMERCIALS. HE'S LOOKING FOR A TEENAGE BOY WHO CAN PLAY THE SAX OR THE TRUMPET.
HE REMEMBERED I HAVE A KID AT SEISOU ACADEMY.
NO WAY, MOM! I'M NO ACTOR!
IT'S MAINLY JUST FOR THE INSTRUMENT. THEY'RE ONLY GOING TO SHOW YOUR HANDS AND THE TRUMPET.
They said they'll use a model for the face.
FORGET IT! I CAN'T DO THAT!
Wow!
WHAT A GREAT OPPORTUNITY, KAZUKI!
GO FOR IT!
NOOO...
SEE? EVEN YOUR FATHER AGREES.
C'mon.
I OWE THIS GUY A FAVOR.
Do it!
PLEASE!
UGH...
MOM...

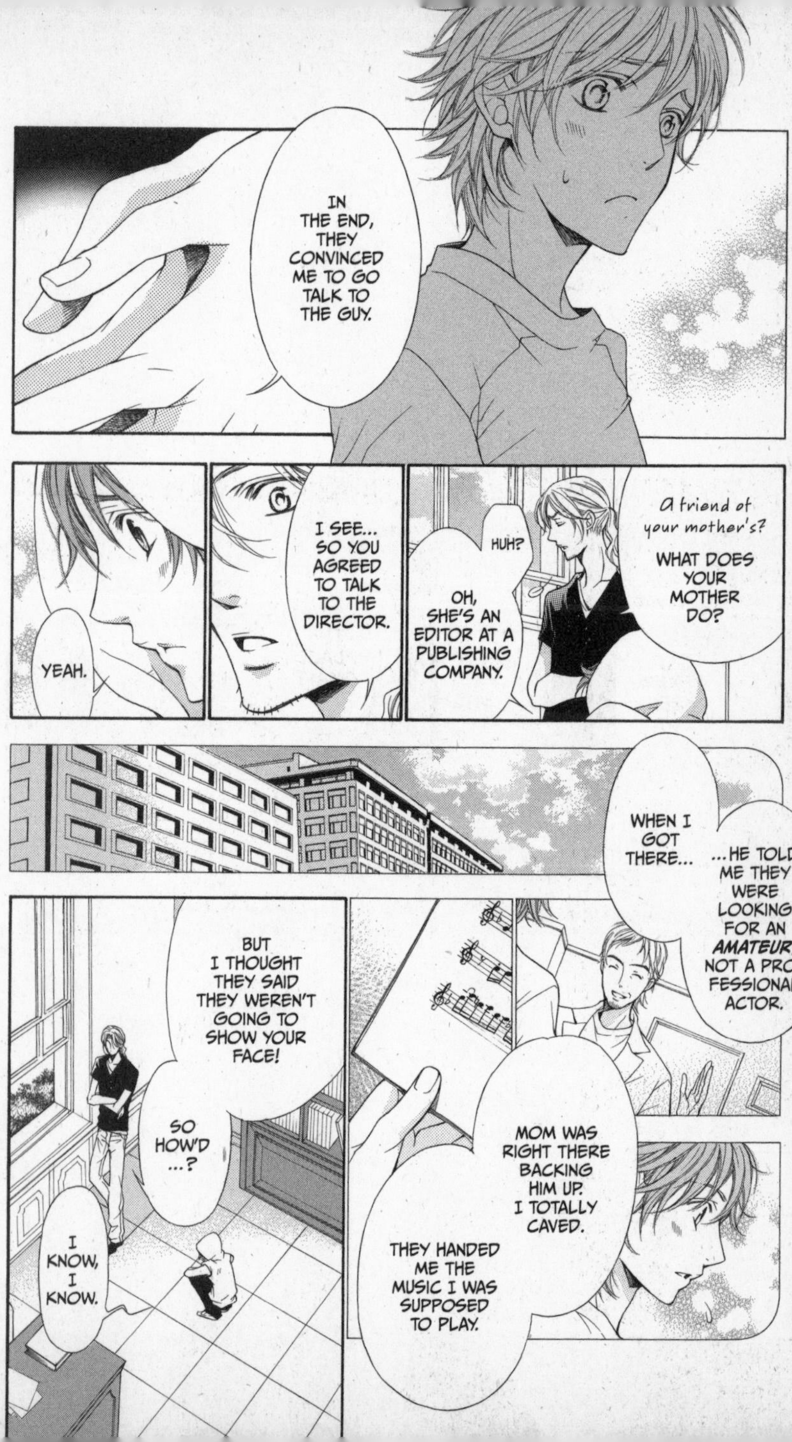
IN THE END, THEY CONVINCED ME TO GO TALK TO THE GUY.
A friend of your mother's?
WHAT DOES YOUR MOTHER DO?
HUH?
OH, SHE'S AN EDITOR AT A PUBLISHING COMPANY.
I SEE... SO YOU AGREED TO TALK TO THE DIRECTOR.
YEAH.
WHEN I GOT THERE...
...HE TOLD ME THEY WERE LOOKING FOR AN *AMATEUR*, NOT A PRO-FESSIONAL ACTOR.
MOM WAS RIGHT THERE BACKING HIM UP. I TOTALLY CAVED.
THEY HANDED ME THE MUSIC I WAS SUPPOSED TO PLAY.
BUT I THOUGHT THEY SAID THEY WEREN'T GOING TO SHOW YOUR FACE!
SO HOW'D ...?
I KNOW, I KNOW.

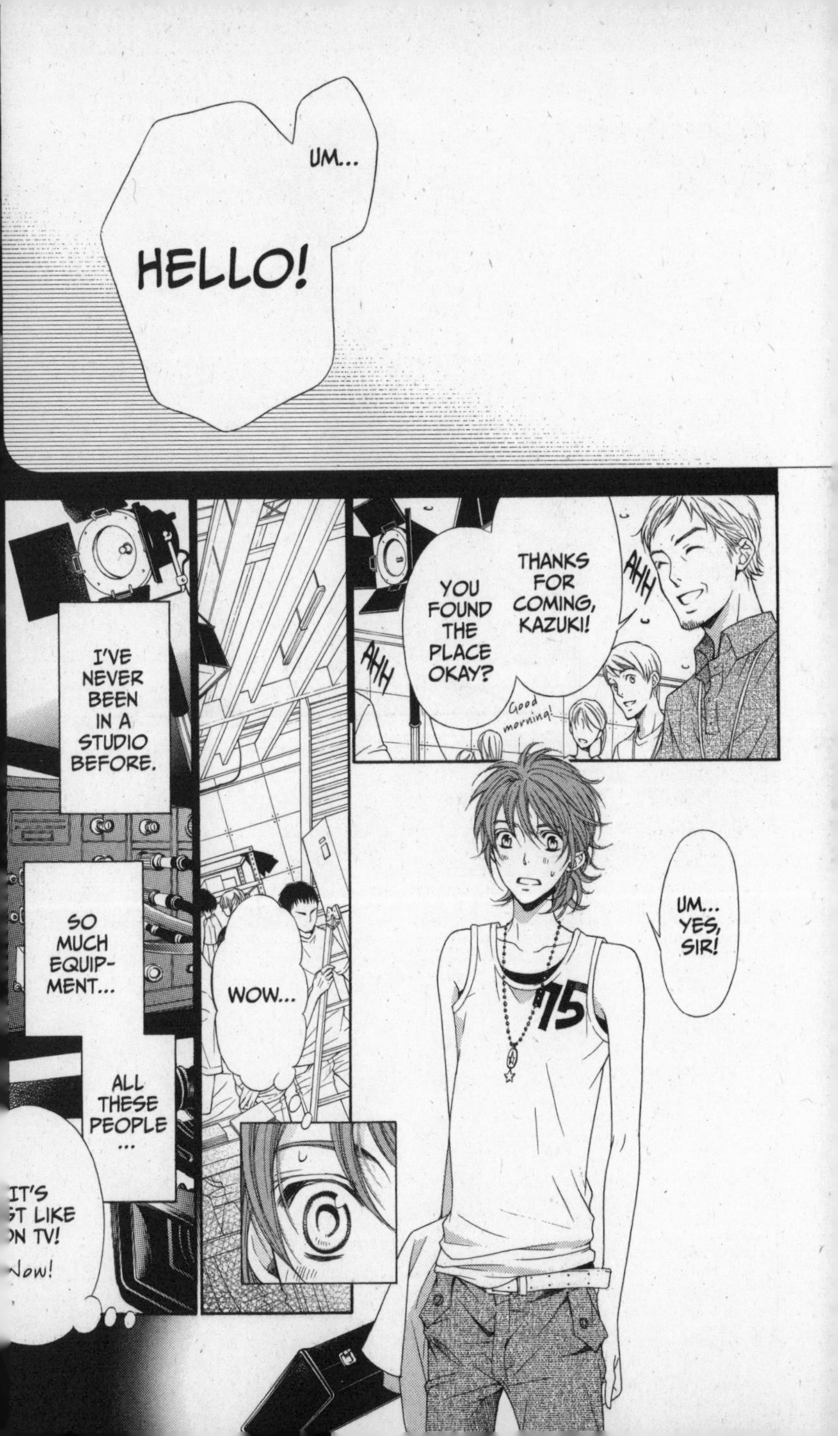
UM... HELLO!
AHH
THANKS FOR COMING, KAZUKI!
YOU FOUND THE PLACE OKAY?
AHH
Good morning!
UM... YES, SIR!
WOW...
I'VE NEVER BEEN IN A STUDIO BEFORE.
SO MUCH EQUIPMENT...
ALL THESE PEOPLE...
IT'S
LIKE
ON TV!
Wow!

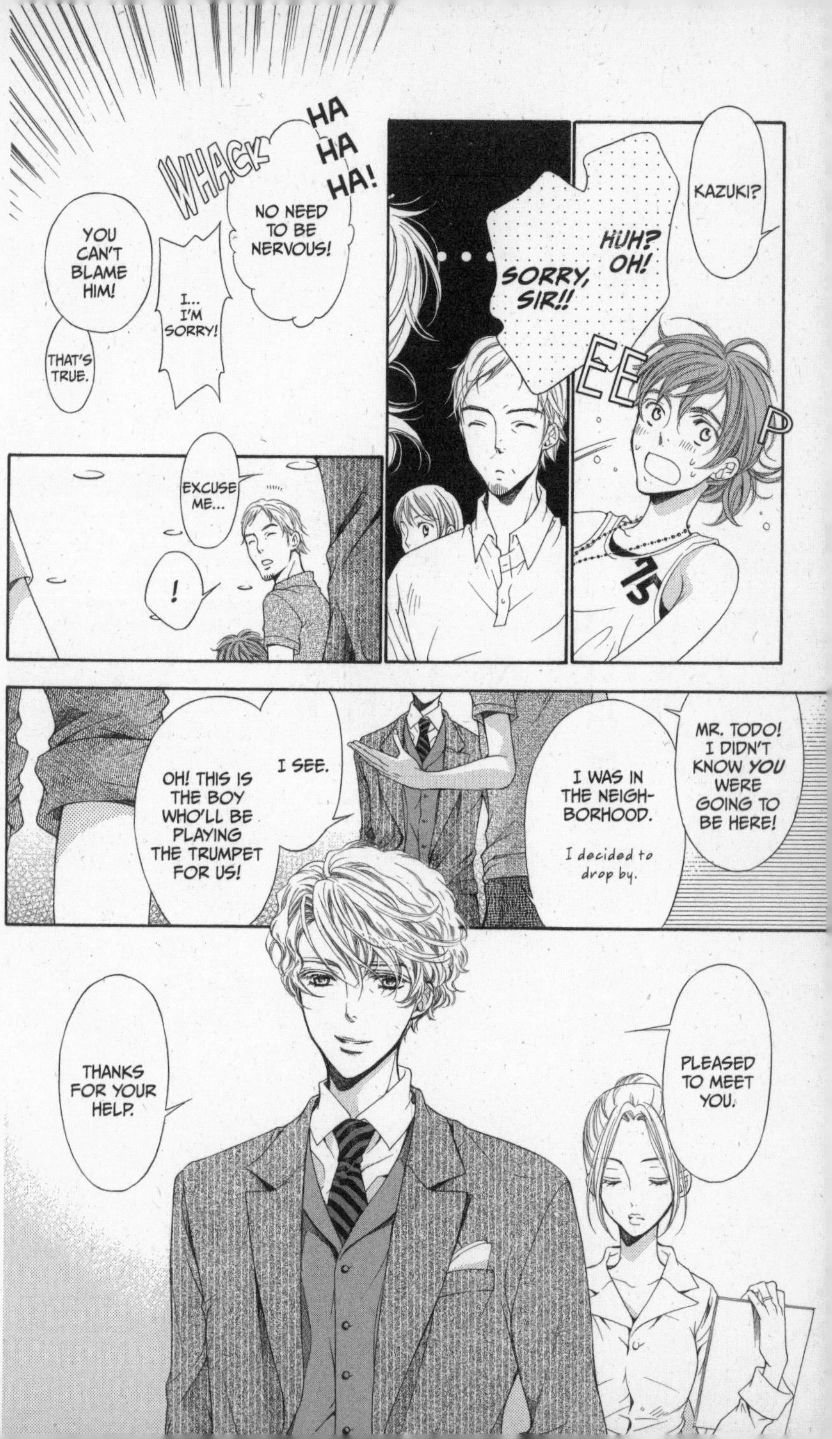

KAZUKI?
HUH? OH!
SORRY, SIR!!
EEP
...
HA HA HA!
WHACK
NO NEED TO BE NERVOUS!
I... I'M SORRY!
YOU CAN'T BLAME HIM!
THAT'S TRUE.
EXCUSE ME...
!
MR. TODO! I DIDN'T KNOW *YOU* WERE GOING TO BE HERE!
I WAS IN THE NEIGHBORHOOD.
I decided to drop by.
I SEE.
OH! THIS IS THE BOY WHO'LL BE PLAYING THE TRUMPET FOR US!
PLEASED TO MEET YOU.
THANKS FOR YOUR HELP.

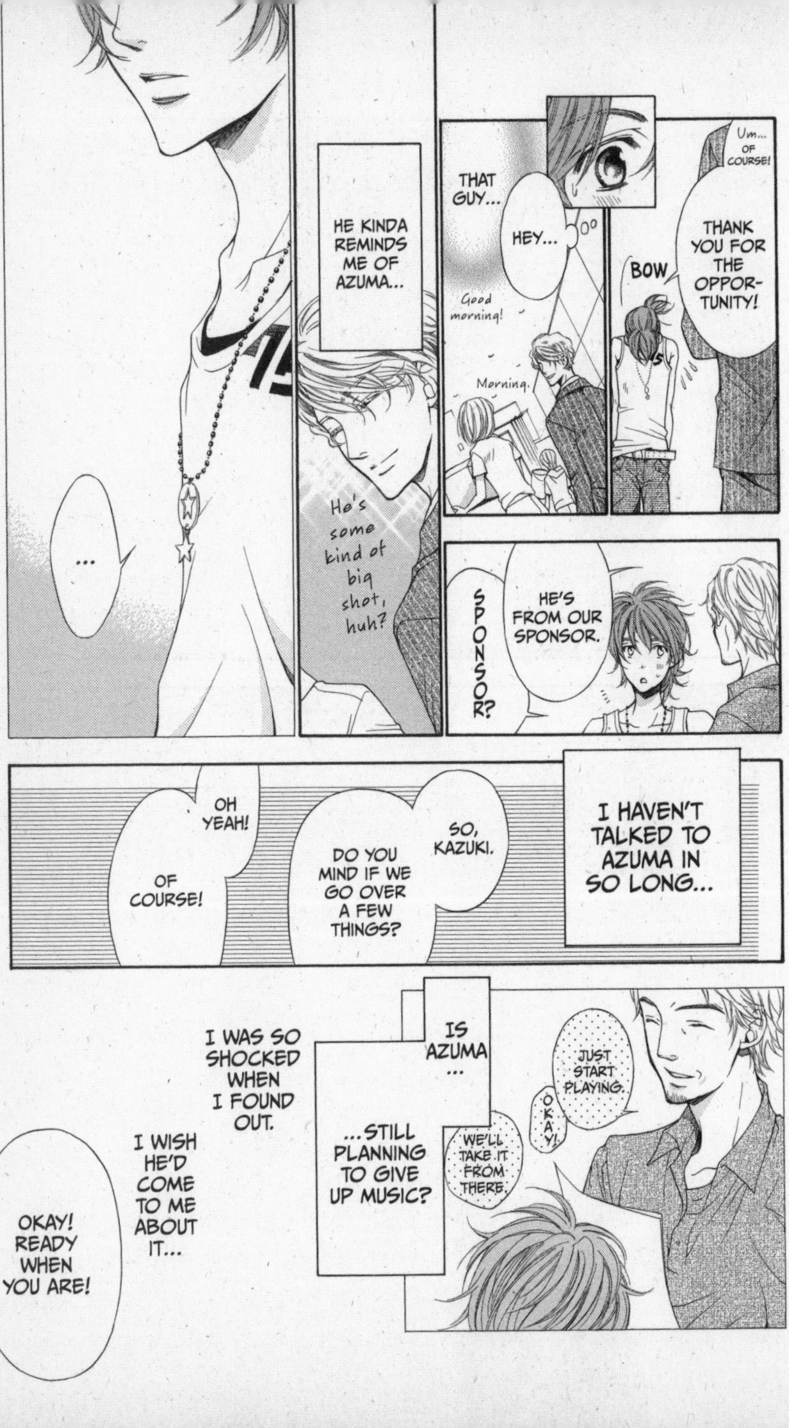
Um... OF COURSE!
THANK YOU FOR THE OPPORTUNITY!
BOW
THAT GUY...
HEY...
Good morning!
Morning.
HE'S FROM OUR SPONSOR.
SPONSOR?
HE KINDA REMINDS ME OF AZUMA...
He's some kind of big shot, huh?
...
I HAVEN'T TALKED TO AZUMA IN SO LONG...
SO, KAZUKI.
DO YOU MIND IF WE GO OVER A FEW THINGS?
OH YEAH!
OF COURSE!
JUST START PLAYING.
OKAY!
WE'LL TAKE IT FROM THERE.
IS AZUMA...
...STILL PLANNING TO GIVE UP MUSIC?
I WAS SO SHOCKED WHEN I FOUND OUT.
I WISH HE'D COME TO ME ABOUT IT...
OKAY! READY WHEN YOU ARE!

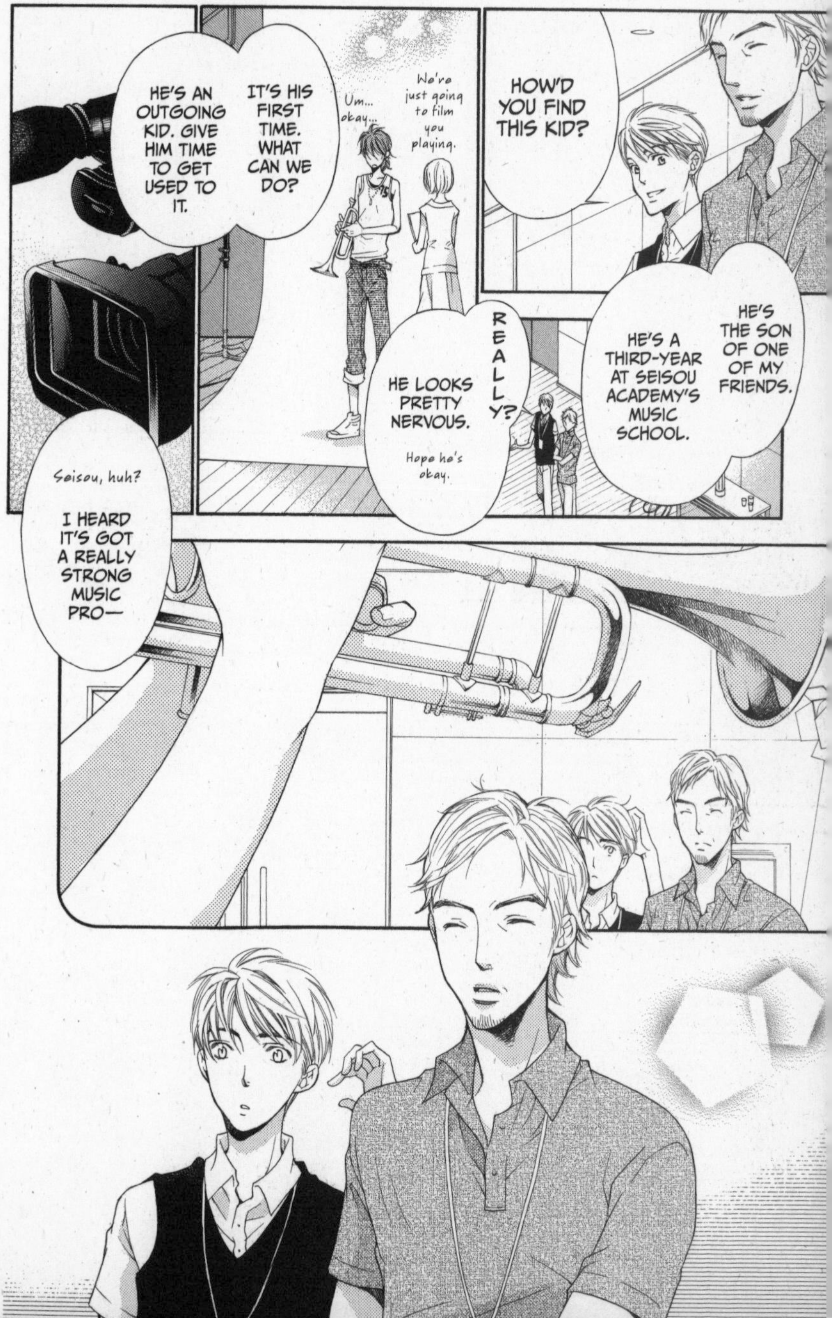
HOW'D YOU FIND THIS KID?
HE'S THE SON OF ONE OF MY FRIENDS.
HE'S A THIRD-YEAR AT SEISOU ACADEMY'S MUSIC SCHOOL.
REALLY?
HE LOOKS PRETTY NERVOUS.
Hope he's okay.
We're just going to film you playing.
Um... okay...
IT'S HIS FIRST TIME. WHAT CAN WE DO?
HE'S AN OUTGOING KID. GIVE HIM TIME TO GET USED TO IT.
Seisou, huh?
I HEARD IT'S GOT A REALLY STRONG MUSIC PRO—

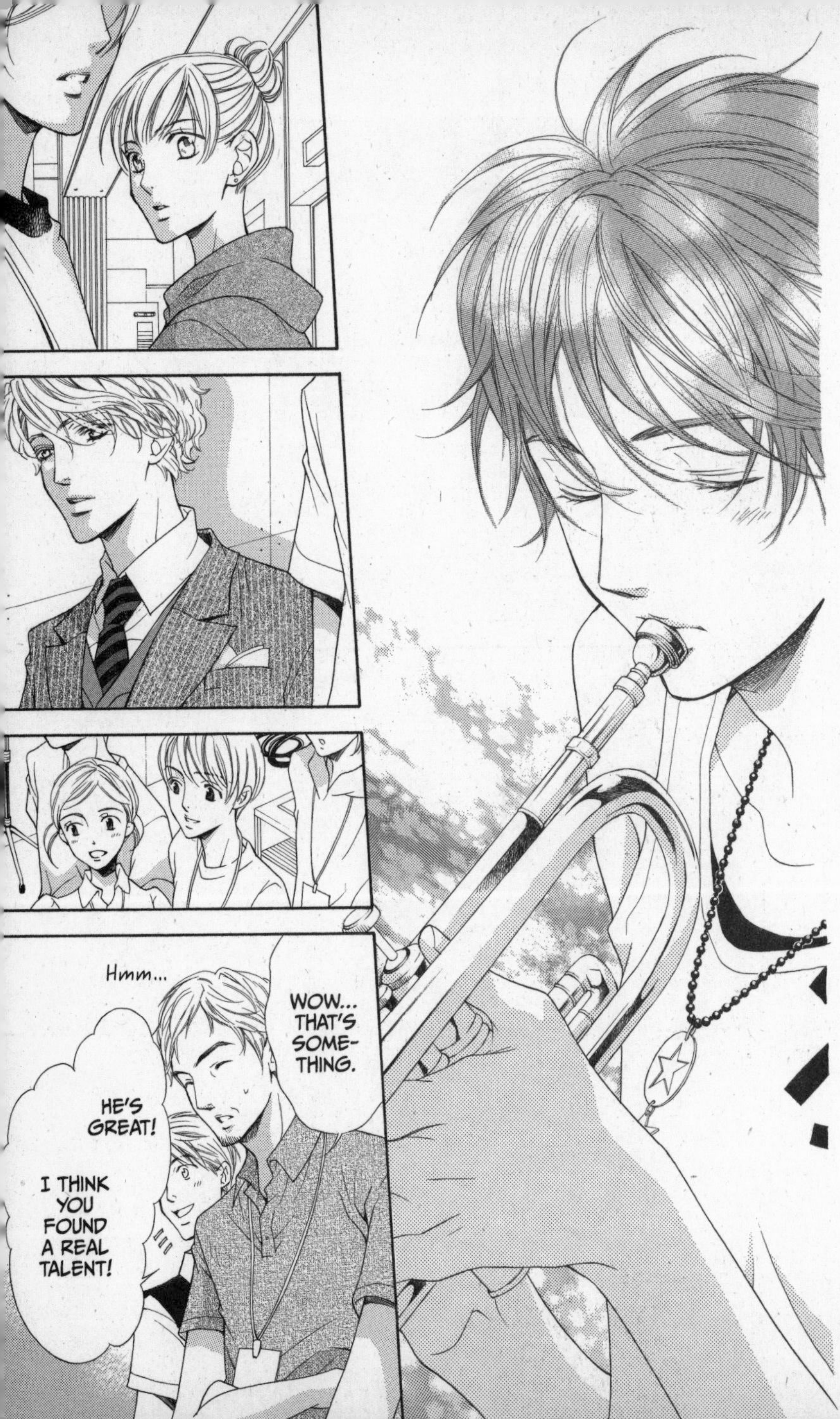
WOW... THAT'S SOME-THING.
Hmm...
HE'S GREAT!
I THINK YOU FOUND A REAL TALENT!

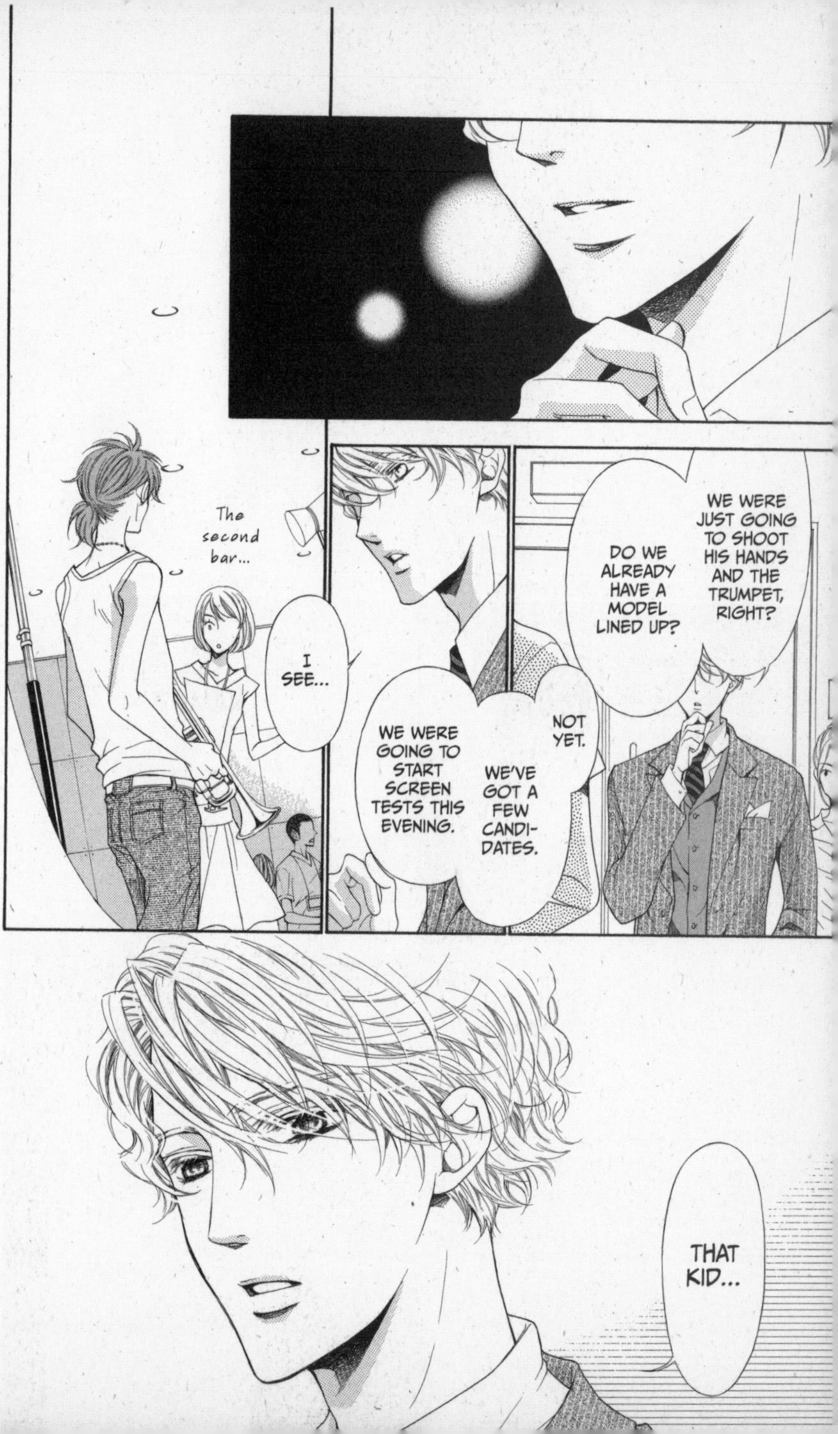
WE WERE JUST GOING TO SHOOT HIS HANDS AND THE TRUMPET, RIGHT?
DO WE ALREADY HAVE A MODEL LINED UP?
NOT YET.
WE'VE GOT A FEW CANDIDATES.
WE WERE GOING TO START SCREEN TESTS THIS EVENING.
The second bar...
I SEE...
THAT KID...

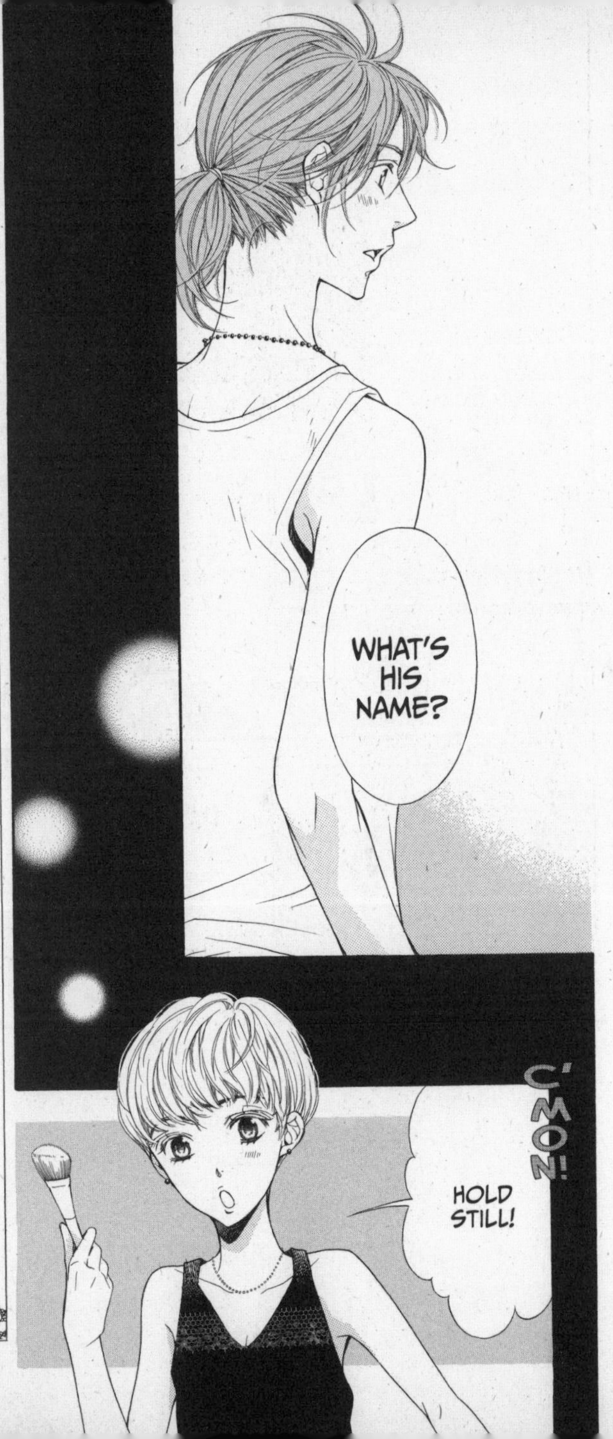
WHAT'S HIS NAME?
C'MON!
HOLD STILL!

Hello! Long time no see. Yuki Kure here. Thank you for purchasing *La Corda* volume 12.

I did a full-color illustration for the title page of Measure 50 (I realize it's black and white in the book) to celebrate reaching the 50th chapter. They're all dressed in costume designs readers submitted for a "*La Corda* Character Costume Contest" a while back.

Thank you so much for your designs. ♡

They were all lovely. It made me smile to see the characters in crazy costumes. I think I received the most illustratons of Len, Kazuki and Kahoko. There were a lot of pictures of Azuma in kimonos and Keiichi in capris. I always want to put Keiichi in flood pants too. Kazuki's costumes had the most variety, but there were quite a few of him in clown outfits...

I really enjoyed the contest.♡ I think I had more fun than anyone because I got to see all the illustrations!

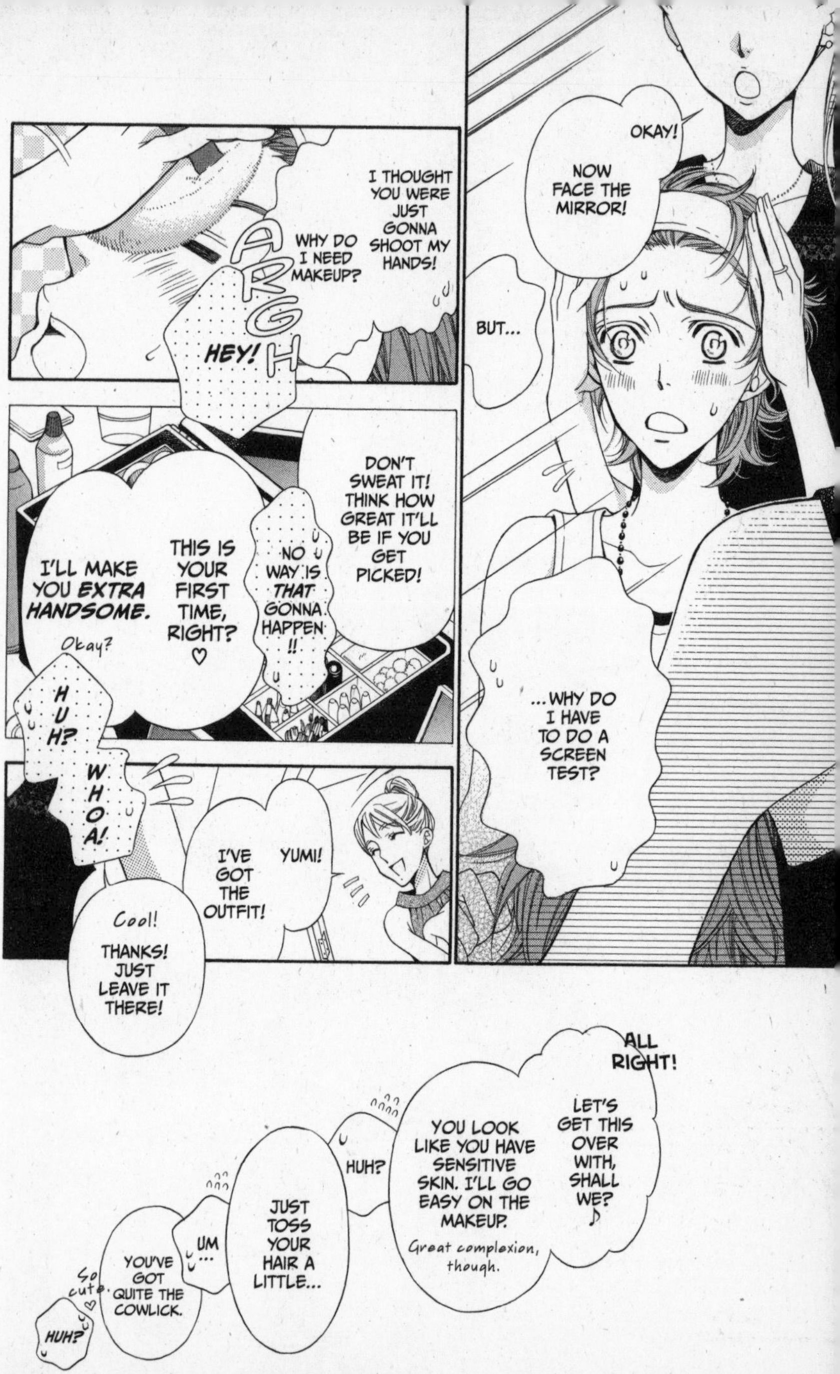
OKAY!
NOW FACE THE MIRROR!
BUT...
...WHY DO I HAVE TO DO A SCREEN TEST?
I THOUGHT YOU WERE JUST GONNA SHOOT MY HANDS!
WHY DO I NEED MAKEUP?
ARGH
HEY!
DON'T SWEAT IT! THINK HOW GREAT IT'LL BE IF YOU GET PICKED!
NO WAY IS *THAT* GONNA HAPPEN!!
THIS IS YOUR FIRST TIME, RIGHT? ♡
I'LL MAKE YOU **EXTRA HANDSOME.**
Okay?
HUH?
WHOA!
YUMI!
I'VE GOT THE OUTFIT!
Cool!
THANKS! JUST LEAVE IT THERE!
ALL RIGHT!
LET'S GET THIS OVER WITH, SHALL WE? ♪
YOU LOOK LIKE YOU HAVE SENSITIVE SKIN. I'LL GO EASY ON THE MAKEUP.
Great complexion, though.
HUH?
JUST TOSS YOUR HAIR A LITTLE...
UM...
YOU'VE GOT QUITE THE COWLICK.
So cute. ♡
HUH?

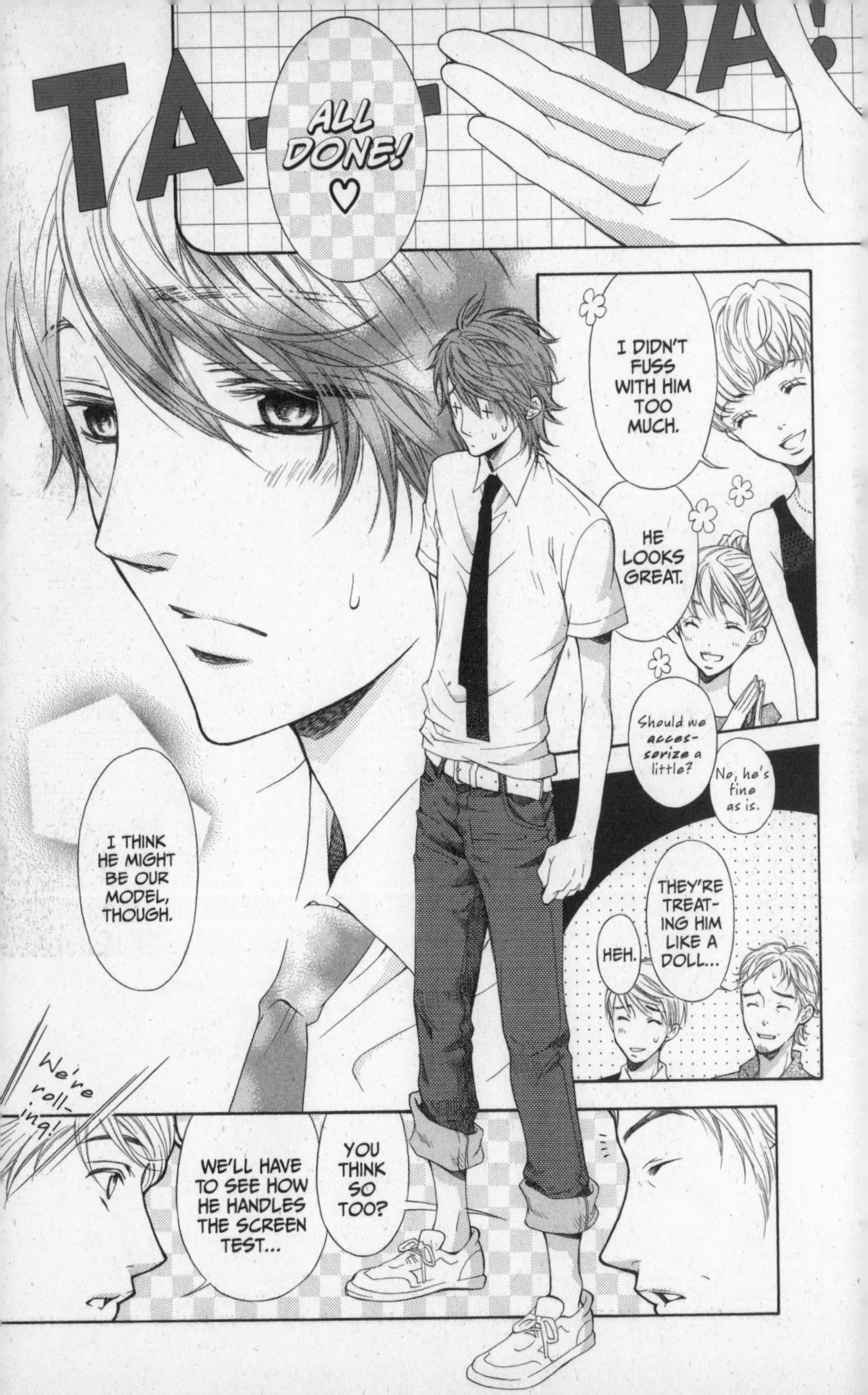
TA-DA!
ALL DONE! ♥
I DIDN'T FUSS WITH HIM TOO MUCH.
HE LOOKS GREAT.
Should we accessorize a little?
No, he's fine as is.
THEY'RE TREATING HIM LIKE A DOLL...
HEH.
I THINK HE MIGHT BE OUR MODEL, THOUGH.
YOU THINK SO TOO?
WE'LL HAVE TO SEE HOW HE HANDLES THE SCREEN TEST...
We're rolling!

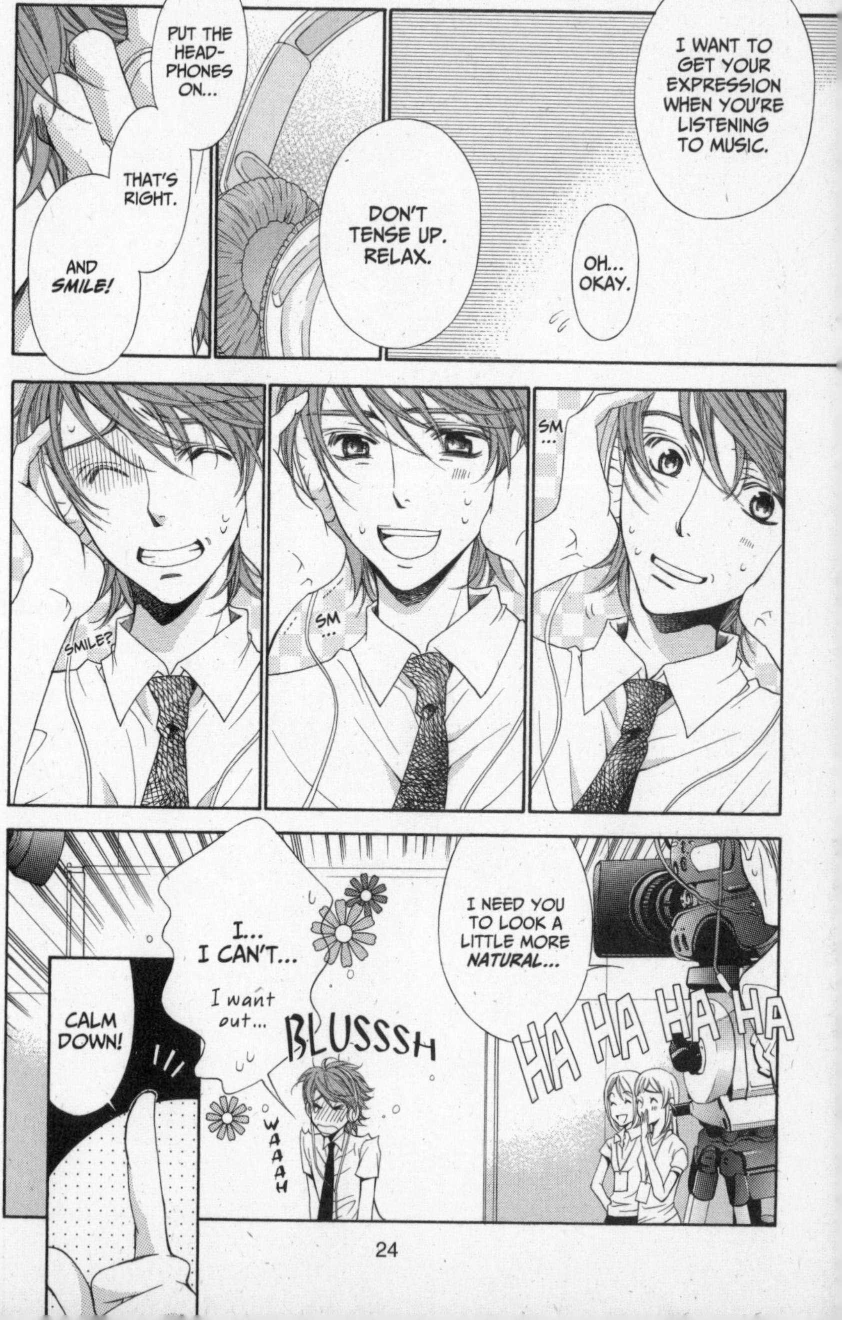
I WANT TO GET YOUR EXPRESSION WHEN YOU'RE LISTENING TO MUSIC.
OH... OKAY.
DON'T TENSE UP. RELAX.
PUT THE HEAD-PHONES ON...
THAT'S RIGHT.
AND SMILE!
SM...
SM...
SMILE?
I NEED YOU TO LOOK A LITTLE MORE NATURAL...
HA HA HA HA
I... I CAN'T...
I want out...
BLUSSSH
WAAAH
CALM DOWN!

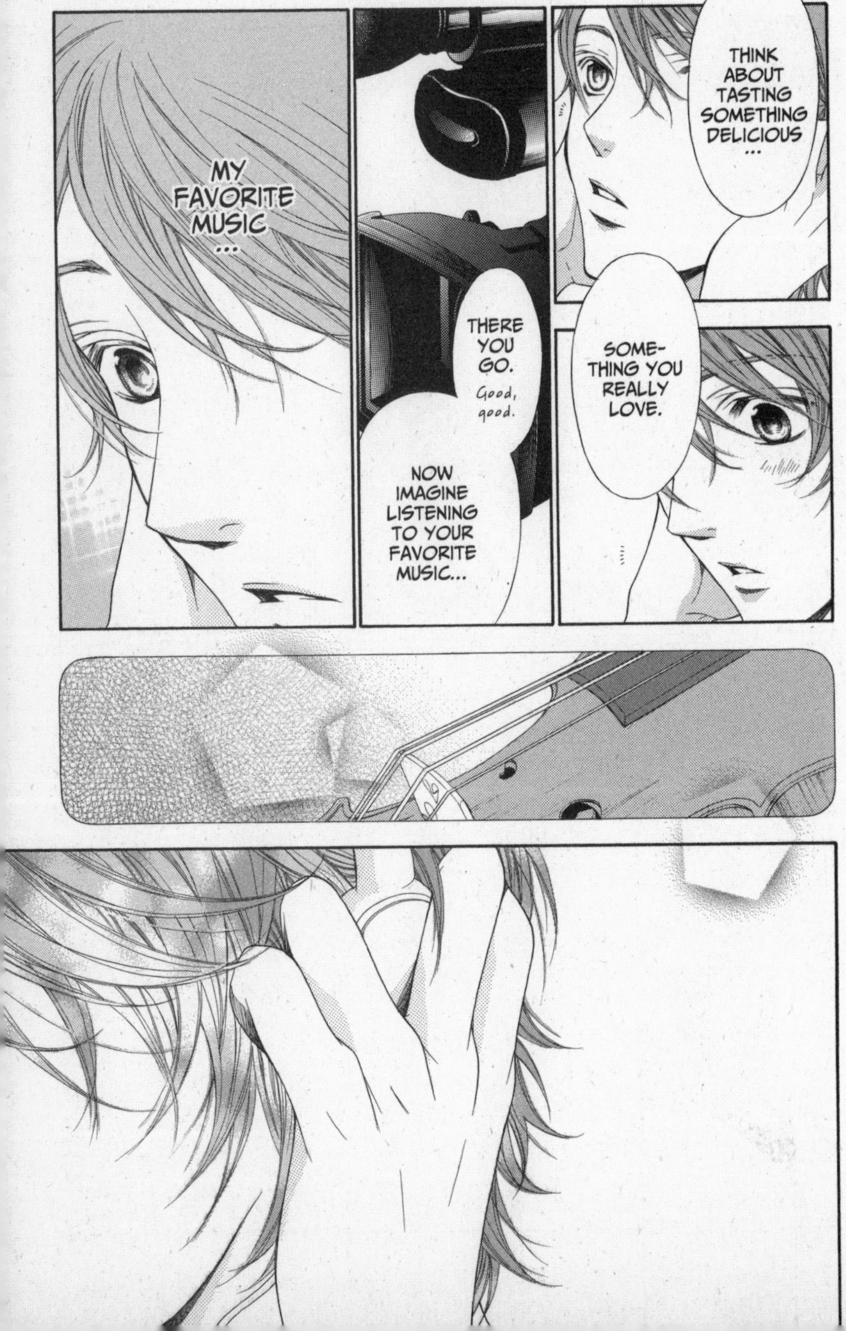
THINK ABOUT TASTING SOMETHING DELICIOUS...
SOME-THING YOU REALLY LOVE.
THERE YOU GO.
Good, good.
NOW IMAGINE LISTENING TO YOUR FAVORITE MUSIC...
MY FAVORITE MUSIC...

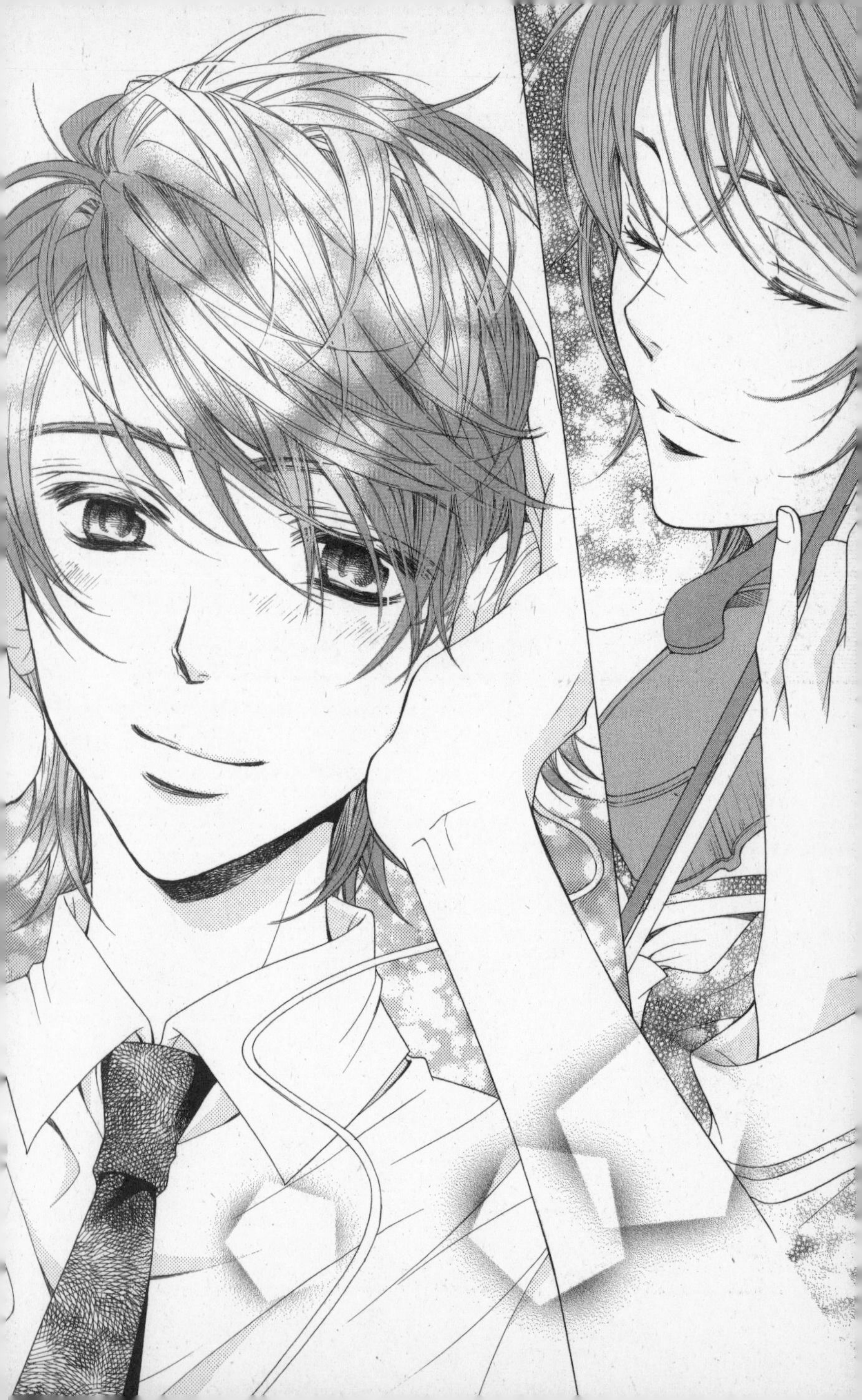

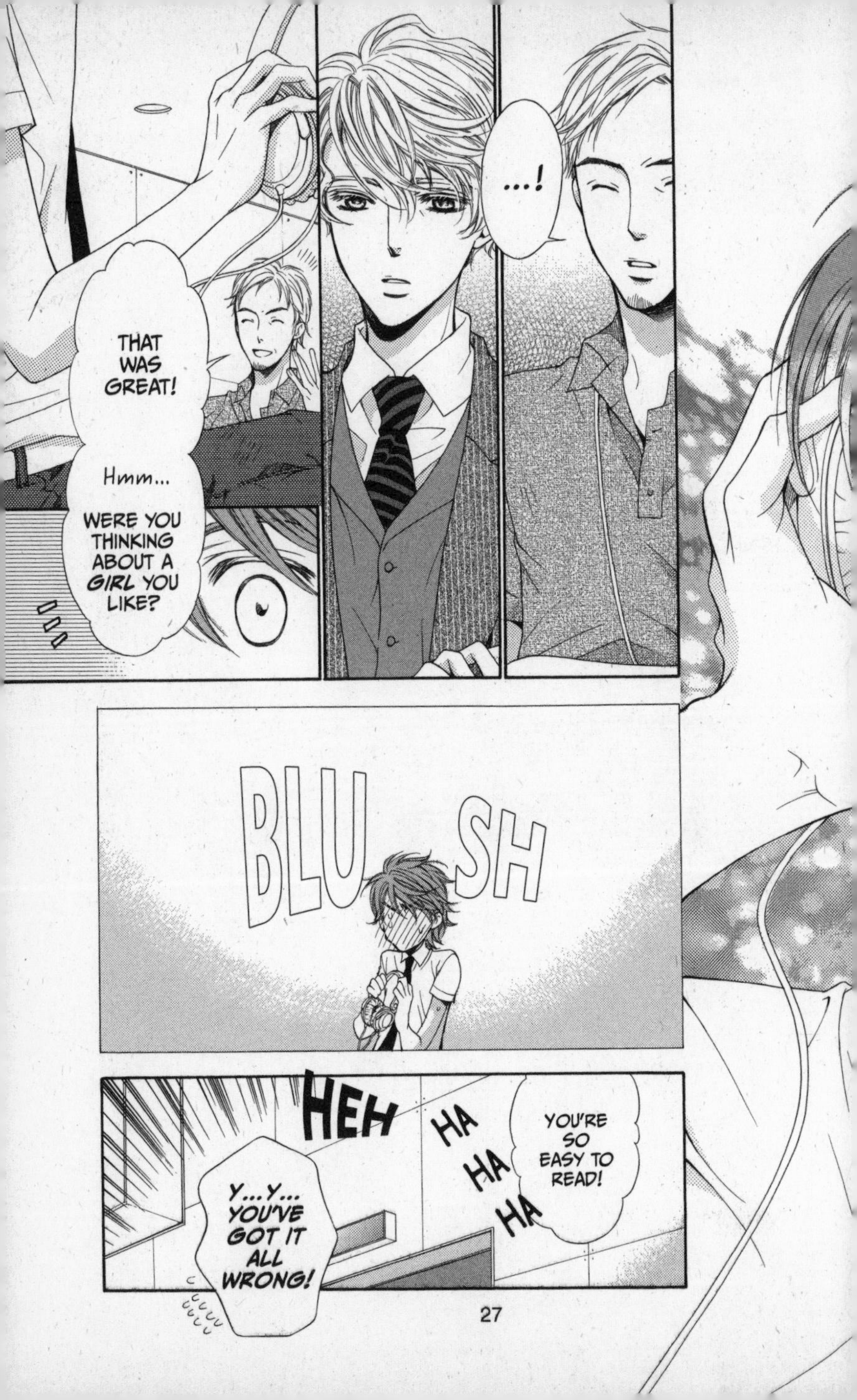
...!
THAT WAS GREAT!
Hmm... WERE YOU THINKING ABOUT A GIRL YOU LIKE?
BLUSH
YOU'RE SO EASY TO READ!
HEH HA HA HA
Y...Y... YOU'VE GOT IT ALL WRONG!

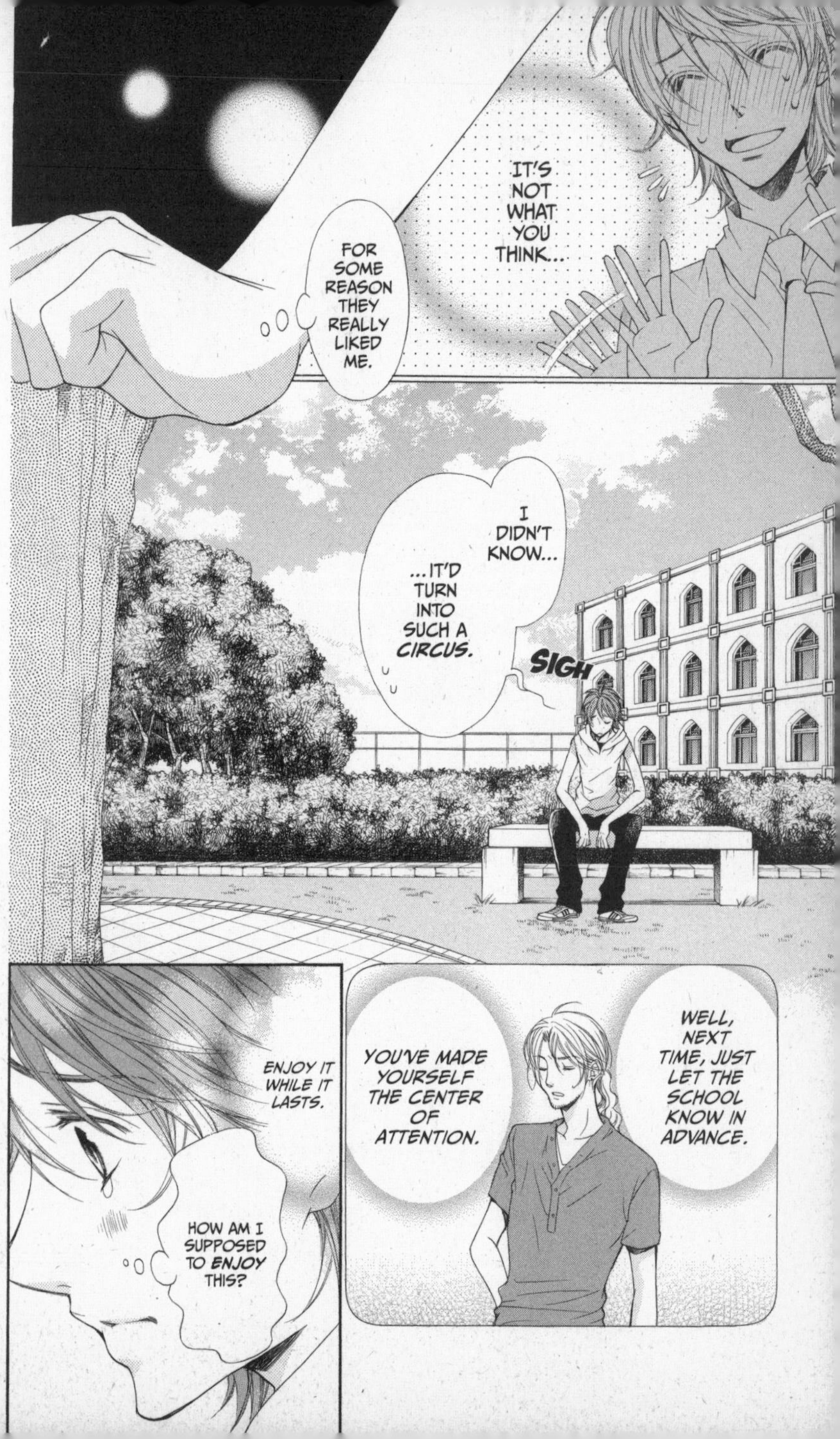
IT'S NOT WHAT YOU THINK...
FOR SOME REASON THEY REALLY LIKED ME.
I DIDN'T KNOW...
...IT'D TURN INTO SUCH A *CIRCUS.*
SIGH
WELL, NEXT TIME, JUST LET THE SCHOOL KNOW IN ADVANCE.
YOU'VE MADE YOURSELF THE CENTER OF ATTENTION.
ENJOY IT WHILE IT LASTS.
HOW AM I SUPPOSED TO *ENJOY* THIS?

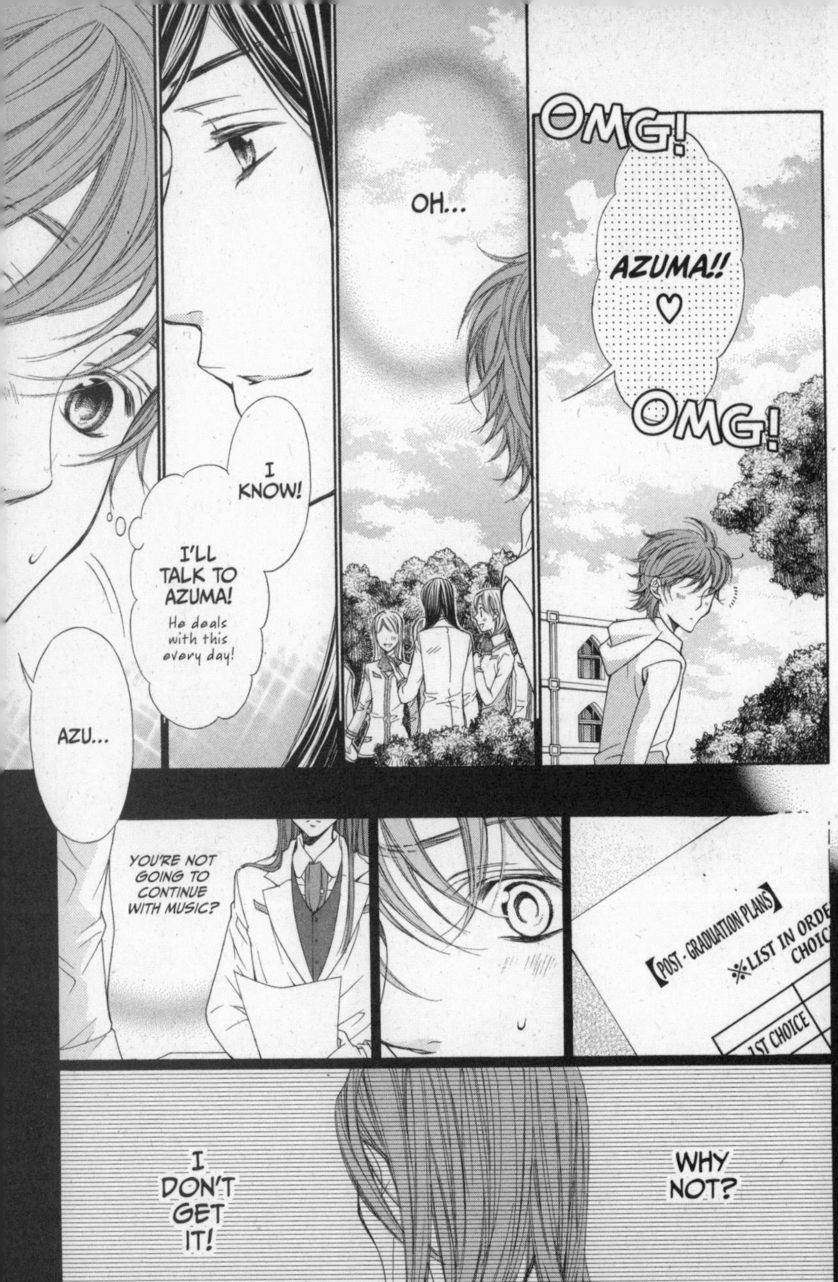
OMG!
AZUMA!! ♡
OMG!
OH...
I KNOW!
I'LL TALK TO AZUMA! He deals with this every day!
AZU...
【POST - GRADUATION PLANS】
※LIST IN ORDE CHOIC
1ST CHOICE
YOU'RE NOT GOING TO CONTINUE WITH MUSIC?
WHY NOT?
I DON'T GET IT!

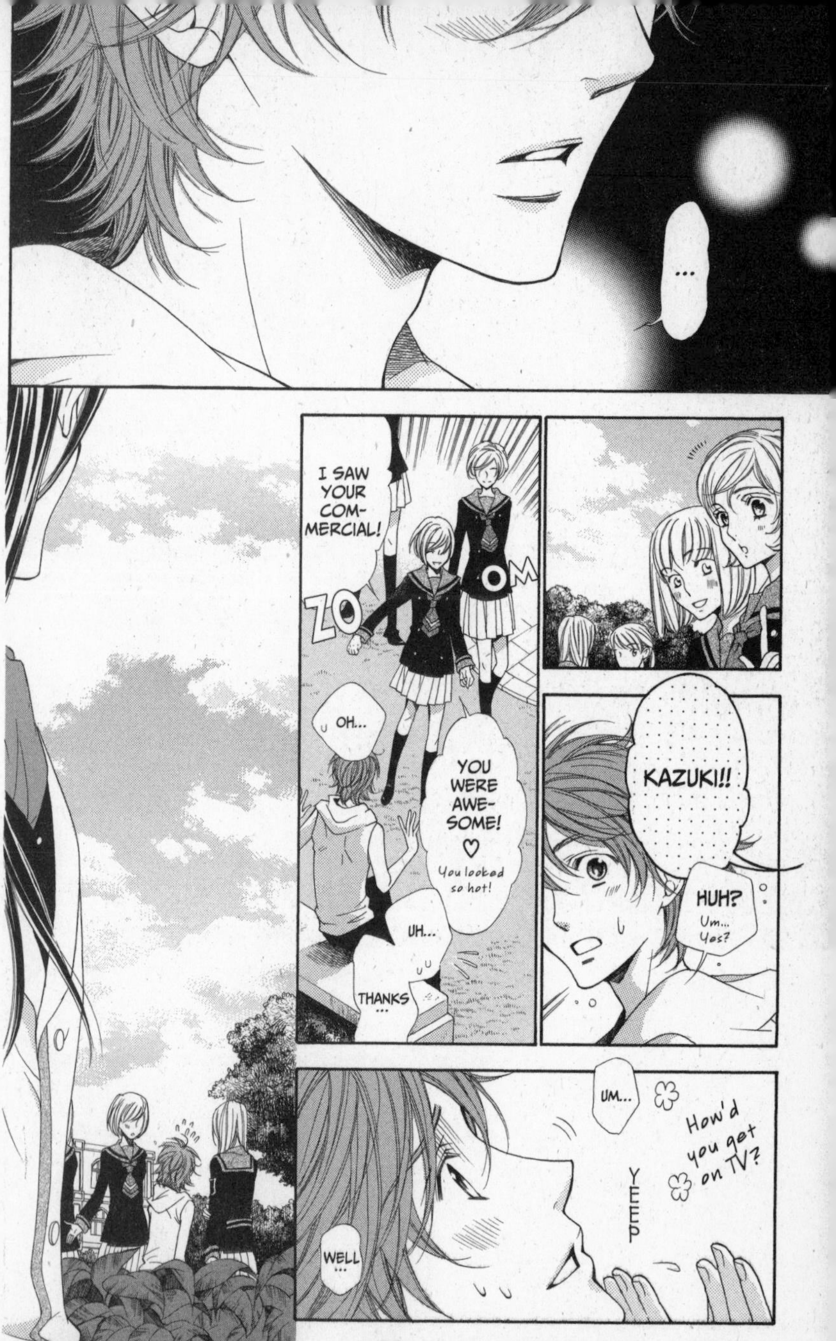
...
KAZUKI!!
HUH?
Um... Yes?
I SAW YOUR COM-MERCIAL!
ZOOM
OH...
YOU WERE AWE-SOME! ♡
You looked so hot!
UH...
THANKS...
UM...
How'd you get on TV?
YEEP
WELL...

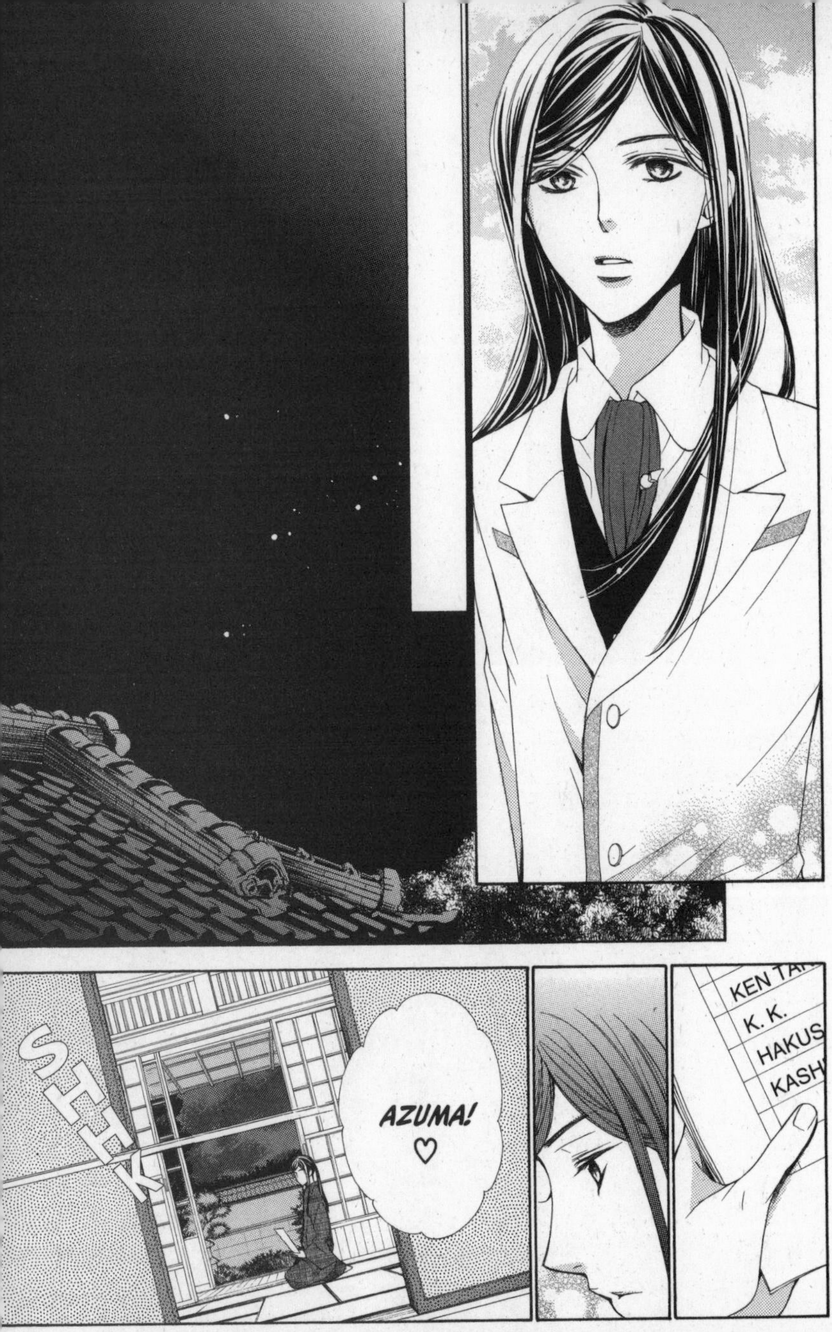
KEN TA
K. K.
HAKUS
KASH
AZUMA! ♡
SHHK

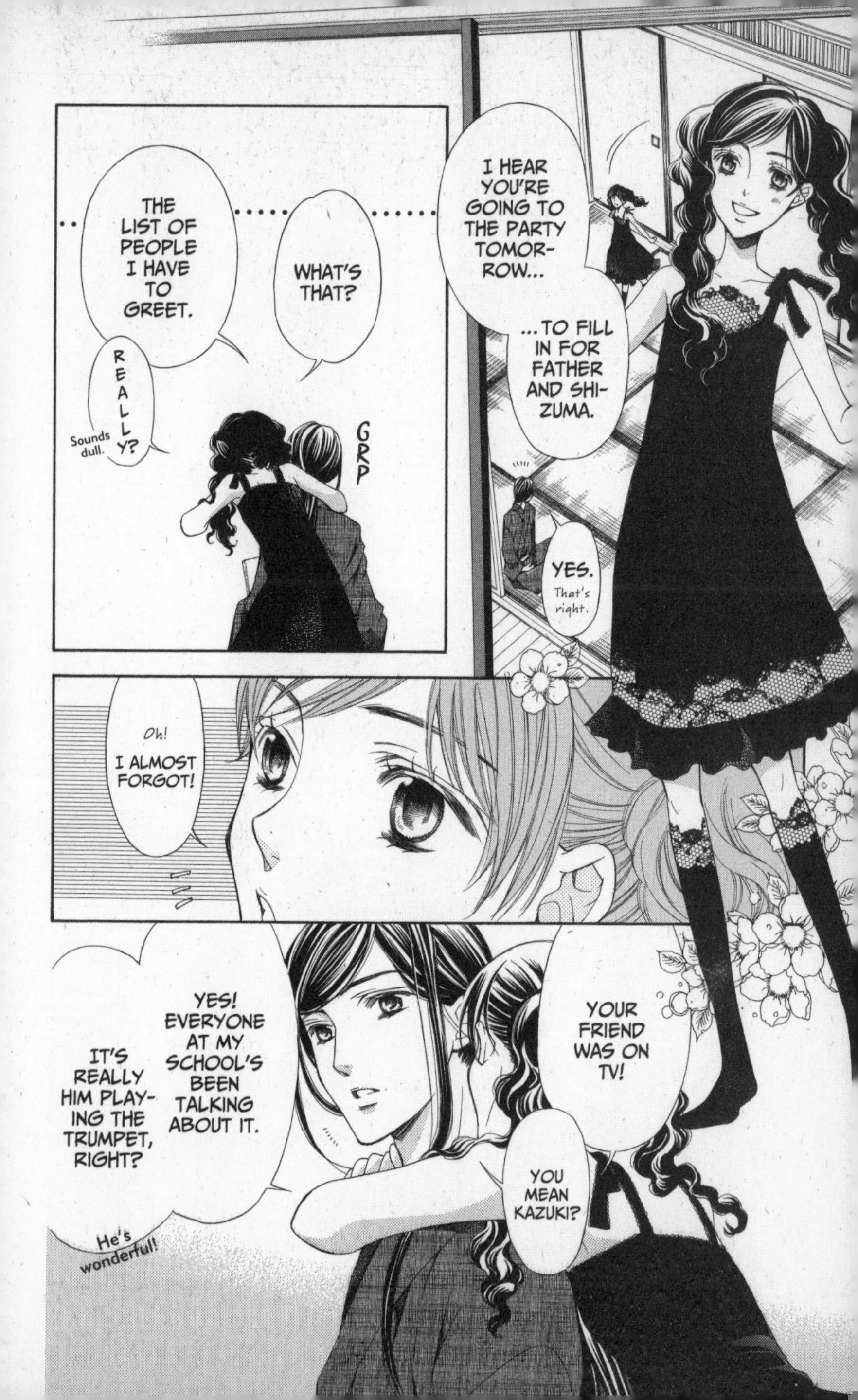
I HEAR YOU'RE GOING TO THE PARTY TOMORROW...
...TO FILL IN FOR FATHER AND SHIZUMA.
YES.
That's right.
WHAT'S THAT?
THE LIST OF PEOPLE I HAVE TO GREET.
GRP
REALLY?
Sounds dull.
Oh!
I ALMOST FORGOT!
YOUR FRIEND WAS ON TV!
YOU MEAN KAZUKI?
YES! EVERYONE AT MY SCHOOL'S BEEN TALKING ABOUT IT.
IT'S REALLY HIM PLAYING THE TRUMPET, RIGHT?
He's wonderful!

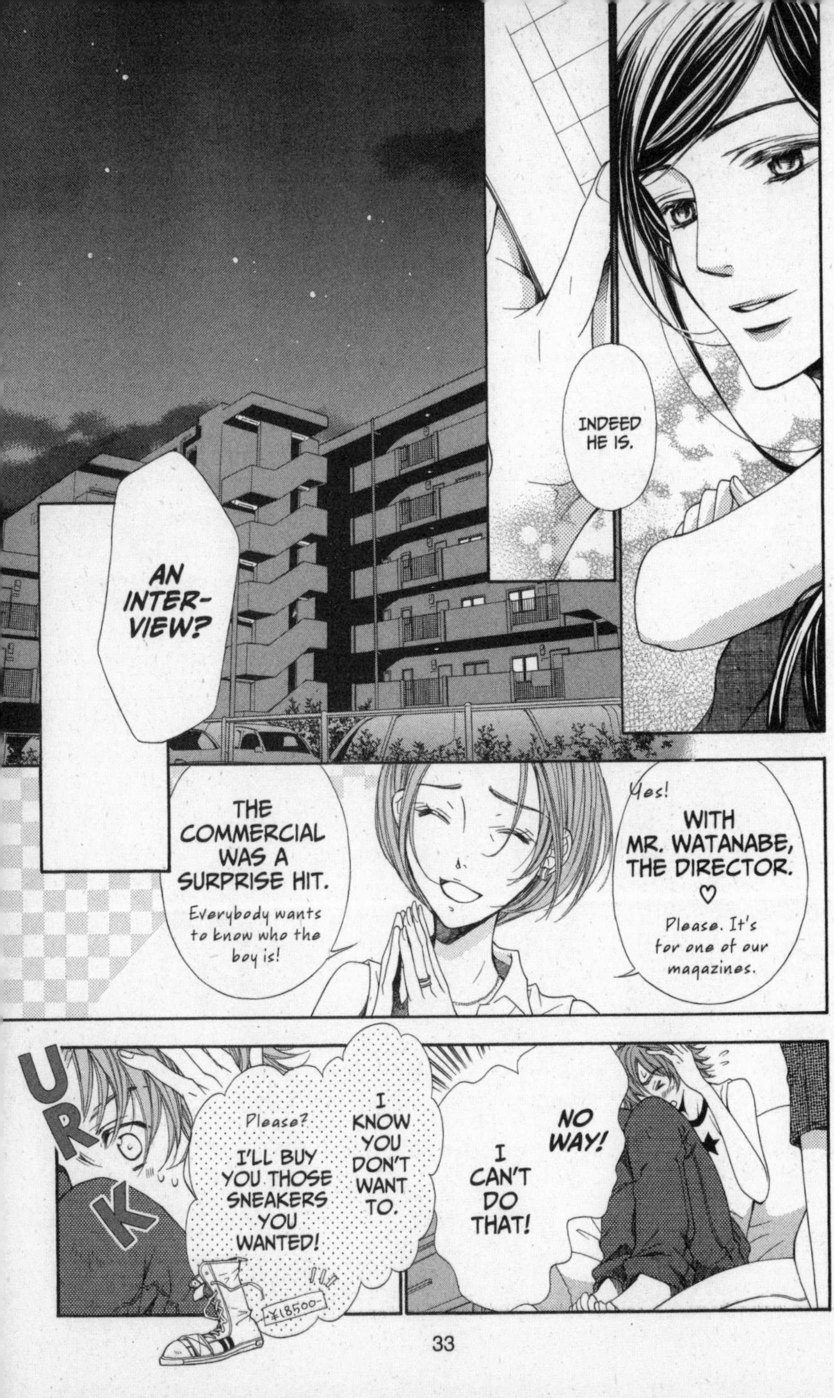
INDEED HE IS.
AN INTER-VIEW?
Yes! WITH MR. WATANABE, THE DIRECTOR. ♡
Please. It's for one of our magazines.
THE COMMERCIAL WAS A SURPRISE HIT.
Everybody wants to know who the boy is!
NO WAY!
I CAN'T DO THAT!
I KNOW YOU DON'T WANT TO.
Please?
I'LL BUY YOU THOSE SNEAKERS YOU WANTED!
URK
¥18500-

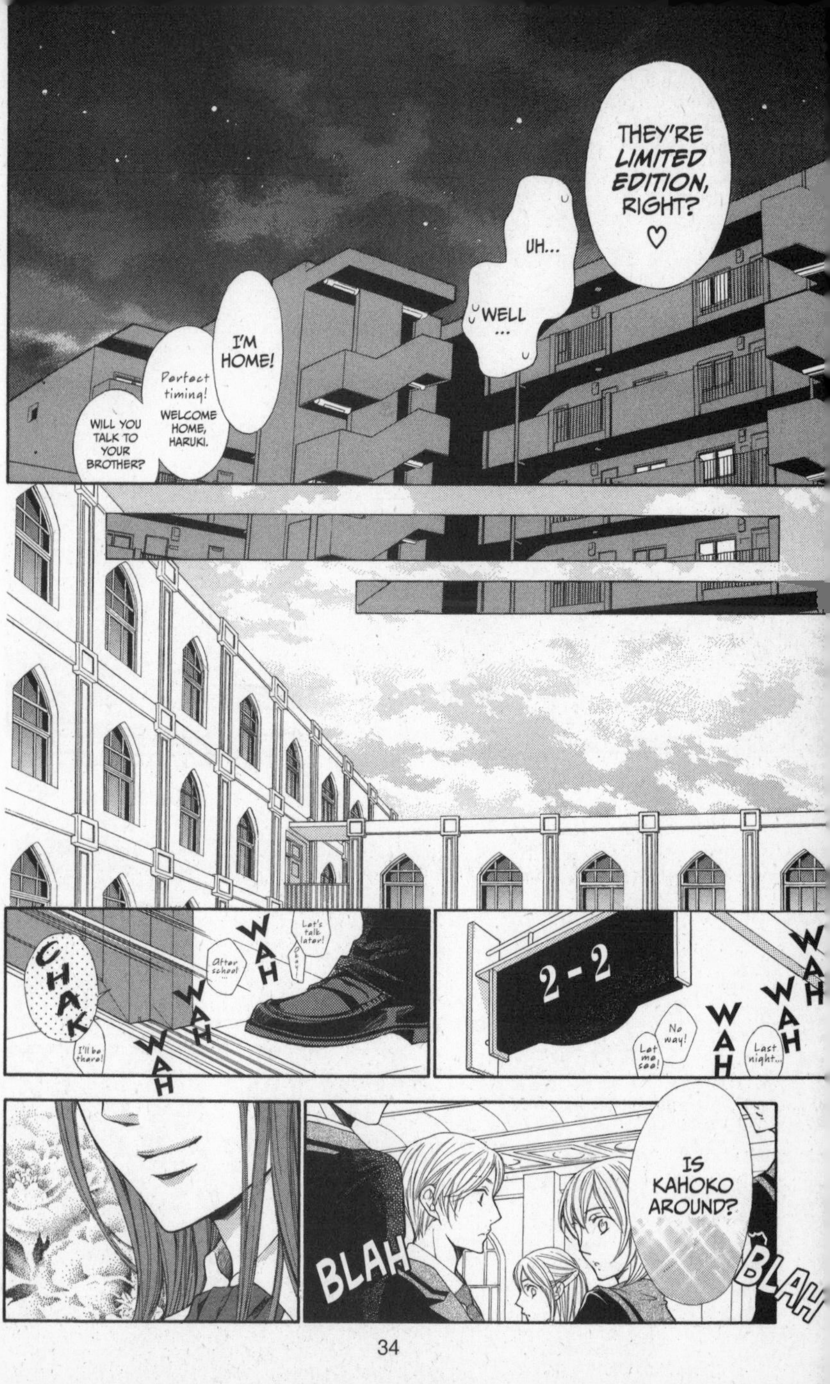
THEY'RE LIMITED EDITION, RIGHT? ♡
UH...
WELL ...
I'M HOME!
Perfect timing!
WELCOME HOME, HARUKI.
WILL YOU TALK TO YOUR BROTHER?
2-2
WAH WAH WAH
Last night...
No way!
Let me see!
Let's talk later!
Okay!
WAH
After school...
WAH
CHAK
I'll be there!
WAH
IS KAHOKO AROUND?
BLAH
BLAH

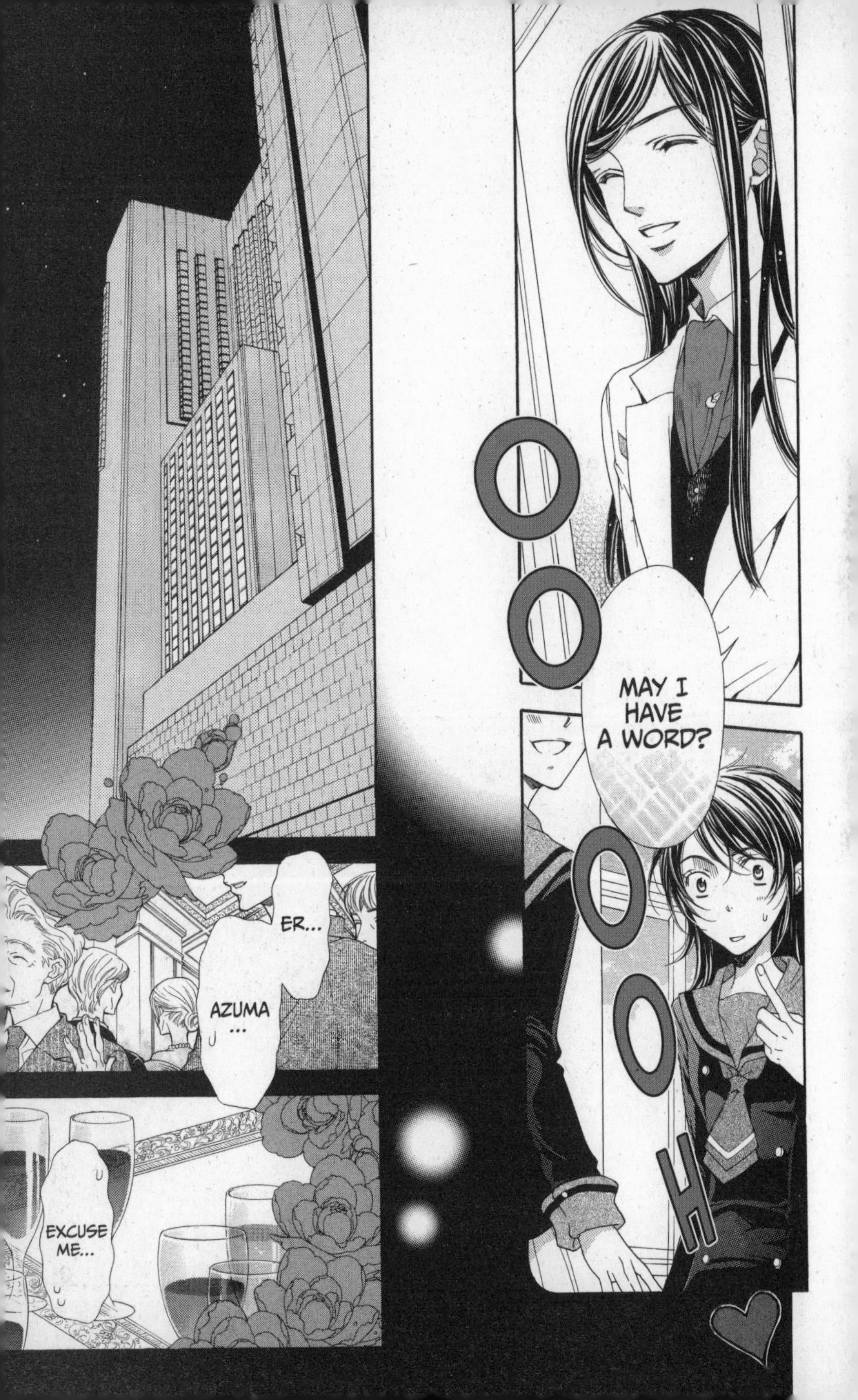
MAY I HAVE A WORD?
ER...
AZUMA...
EXCUSE ME...

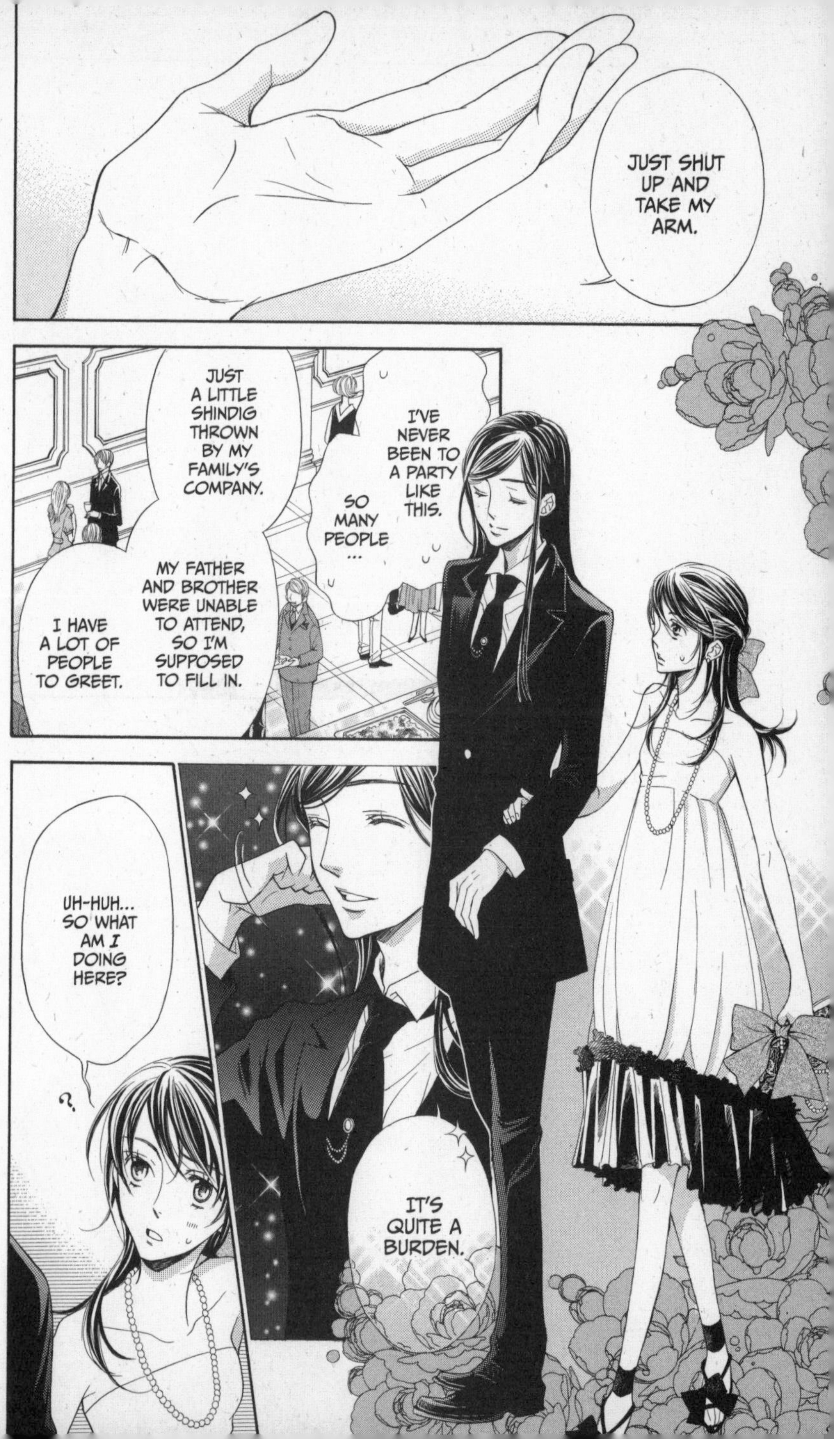
JUST SHUT UP AND TAKE MY ARM.
I'VE NEVER BEEN TO A PARTY LIKE THIS.
SO MANY PEOPLE...
JUST A LITTLE SHINDIG THROWN BY MY FAMILY'S COMPANY.
MY FATHER AND BROTHER WERE UNABLE TO ATTEND, SO I'M SUPPOSED TO FILL IN.
I HAVE A LOT OF PEOPLE TO GREET.
IT'S QUITE A BURDEN.
UH-HUH... SO WHAT AM I DOING HERE?
?

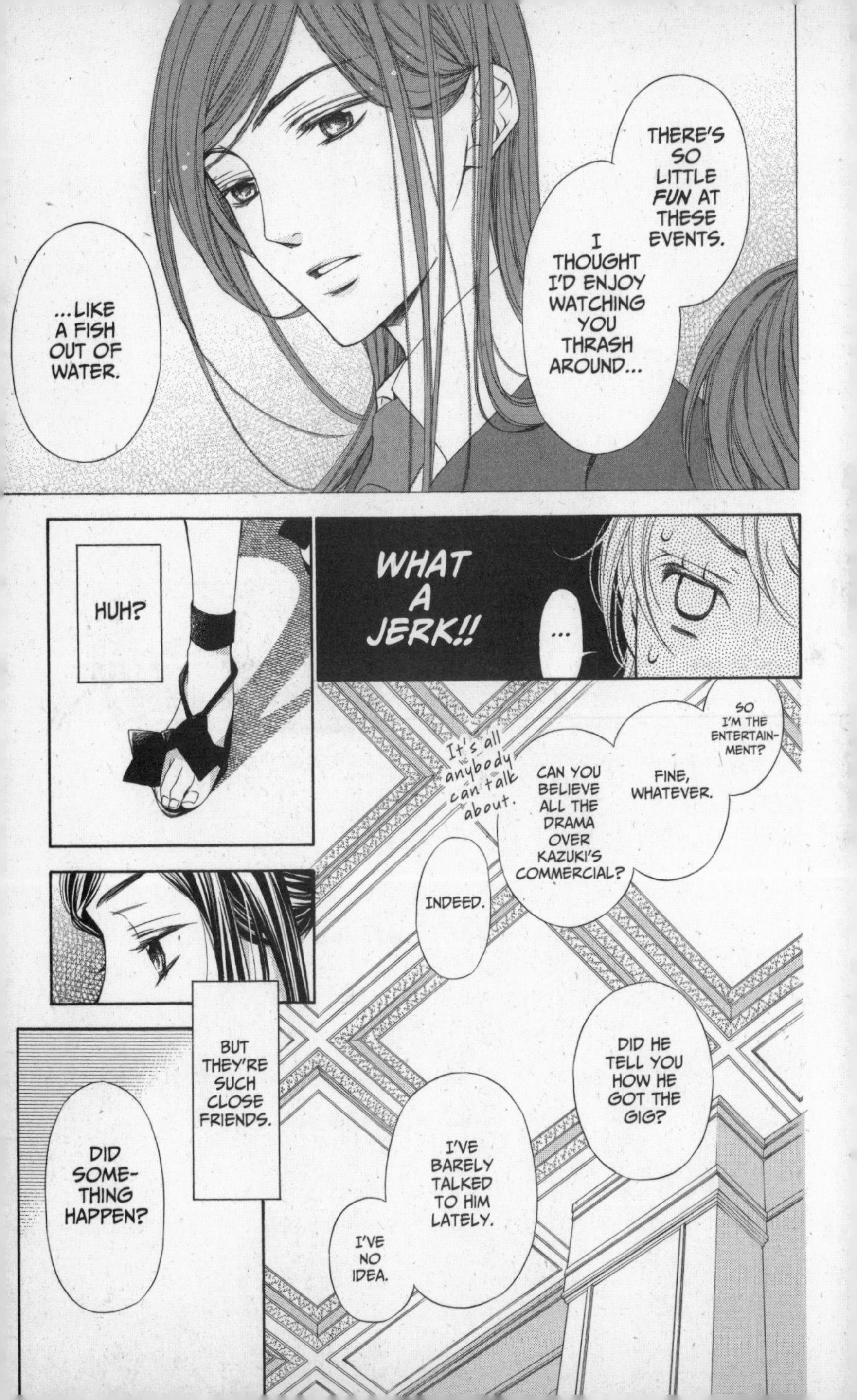
THERE'S SO LITTLE FUN AT THESE EVENTS.
I THOUGHT I'D ENJOY WATCHING YOU THRASH AROUND...
...LIKE A FISH OUT OF WATER.
...
WHAT A JERK!!
HUH?
SO I'M THE ENTERTAINMENT?
FINE, WHATEVER.
It's all anybody can talk about.
CAN YOU BELIEVE ALL THE DRAMA OVER KAZUKI'S COMMERCIAL?
INDEED.
DID HE TELL YOU HOW HE GOT THE GIG?
I'VE BARELY TALKED TO HIM LATELY.
I'VE NO IDEA.
BUT THEY'RE SUCH CLOSE FRIENDS.
DID SOMETHING HAPPEN?

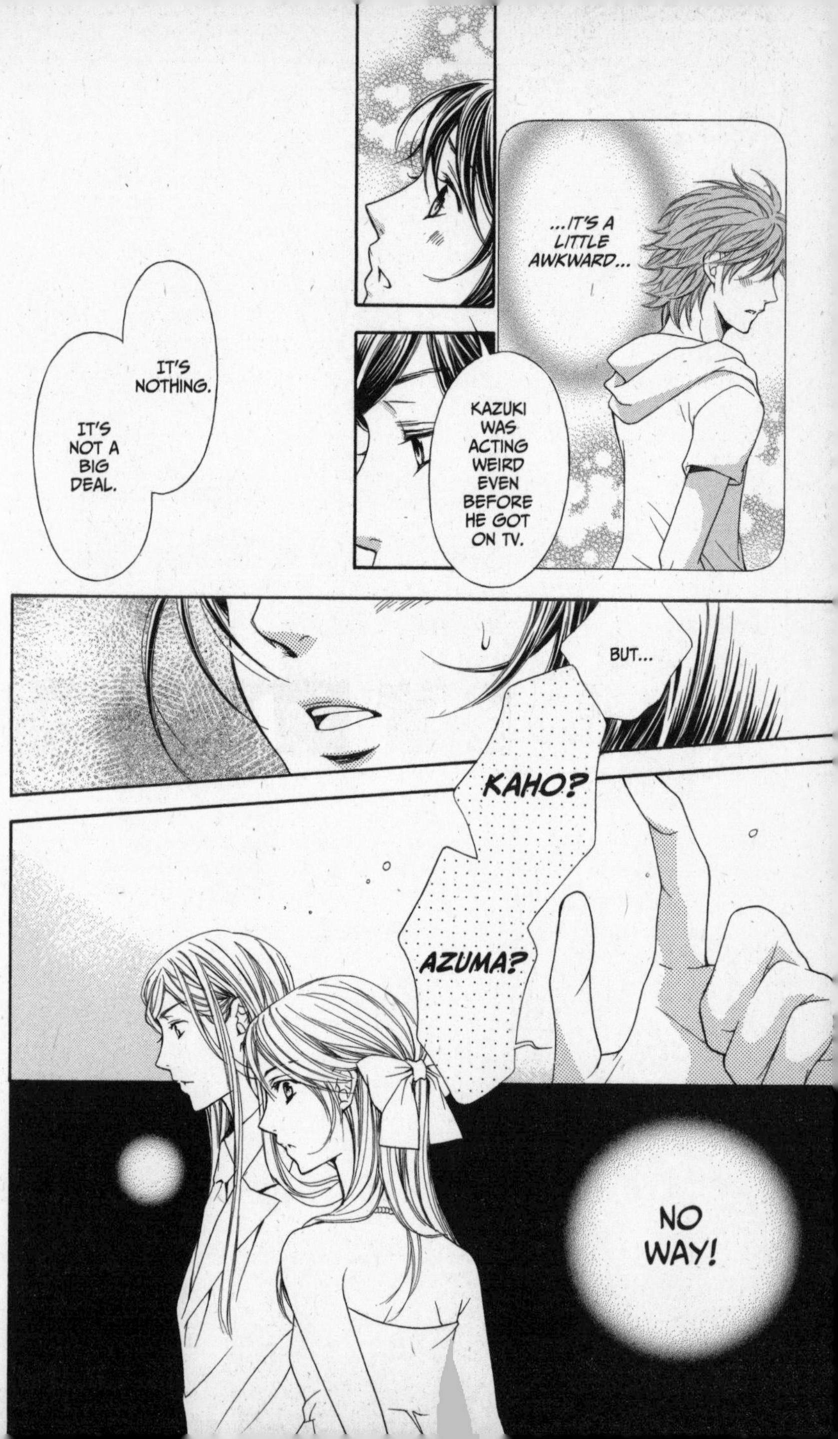
...IT'S A LITTLE AWKWARD...
KAZUKI WAS ACTING WEIRD EVEN BEFORE HE GOT ON TV.
IT'S NOTHING.
IT'S NOT A BIG DEAL.
BUT...
KAHO?
AZUMA?
NO WAY!

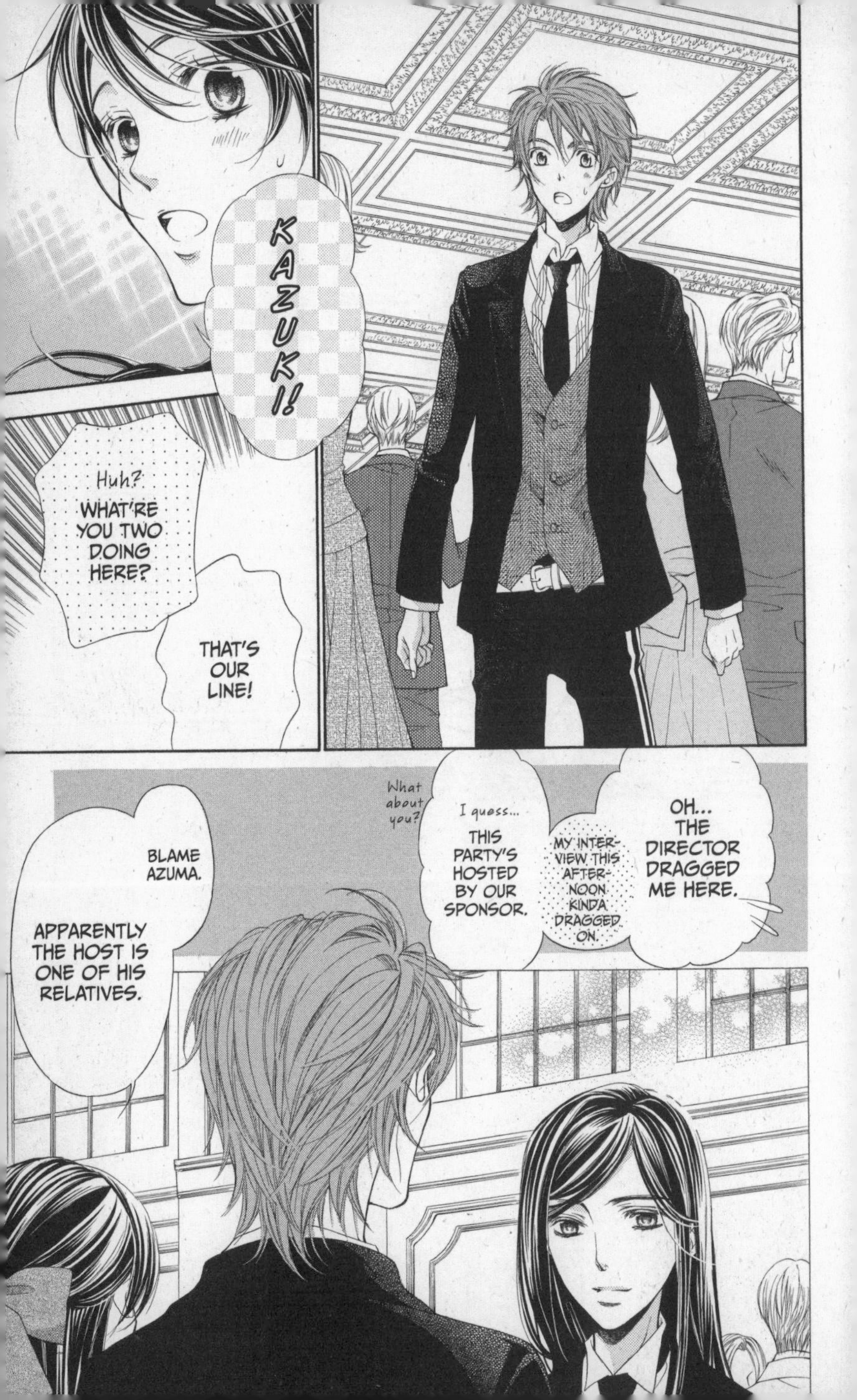
KAZUKI!
Huh?
WHAT'RE YOU TWO DOING HERE?
THAT'S OUR LINE!
OH... THE DIRECTOR DRAGGED ME HERE.
MY INTER-VIEW THIS AFTER-NOON KINDA DRAGGED ON.
I guess...
THIS PARTY'S HOSTED BY OUR SPONSOR.
What about you?
BLAME AZUMA.
APPARENTLY THE HOST IS ONE OF HIS RELATIVES.

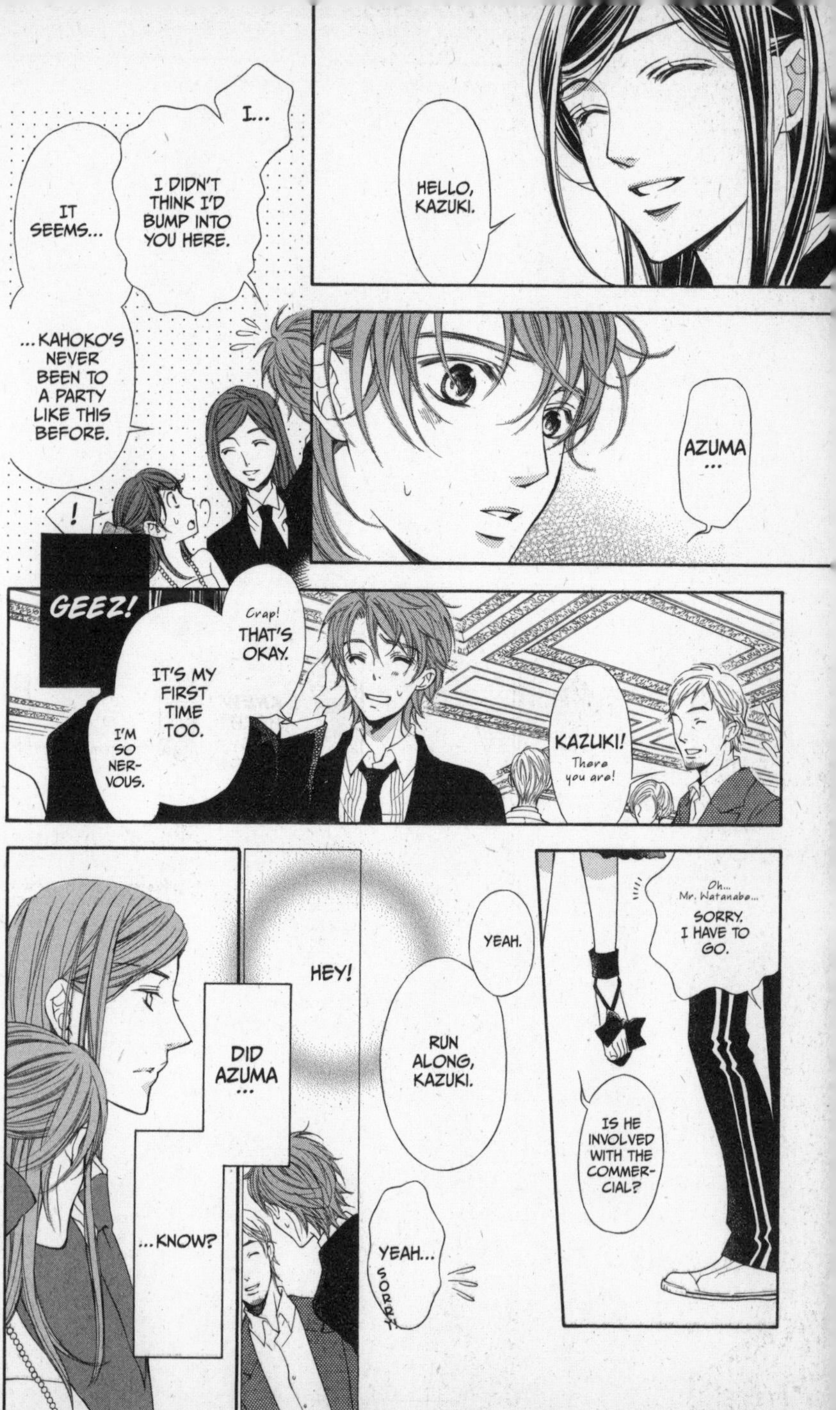
HELLO, KAZUKI.
AZUMA...
I...
I DIDN'T THINK I'D BUMP INTO YOU HERE.
IT SEEMS...
...KAHOKO'S NEVER BEEN TO A PARTY LIKE THIS BEFORE.
!
KAZUKI! There you are!
Crap! THAT'S OKAY.
IT'S MY FIRST TIME TOO.
I'M SO NERVOUS.
GEEZ!
Oh... Mr. Watanabe...
SORRY. I HAVE TO GO.
IS HE INVOLVED WITH THE COMMERCIAL?
YEAH.
RUN ALONG, KAZUKI.
HEY!
YEAH...
SORRY
DID AZUMA...
...KNOW?

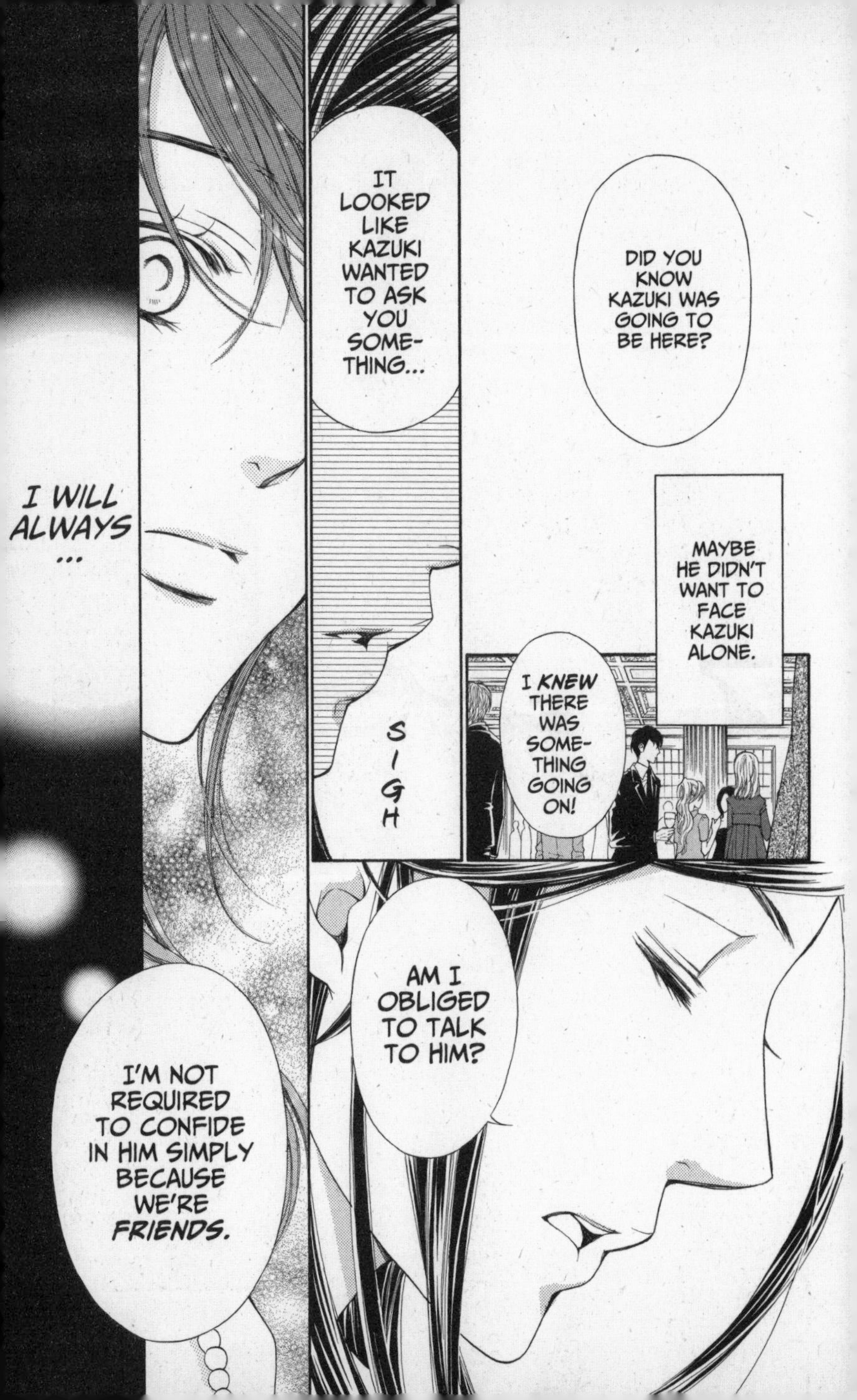
DID YOU KNOW KAZUKI WAS GOING TO BE HERE?
MAYBE HE DIDN'T WANT TO FACE KAZUKI ALONE.
I *KNEW* THERE WAS SOME-THING GOING ON!
IT LOOKED LIKE KAZUKI WANTED TO ASK YOU SOME-THING...
SIGH
AM I OBLIGED TO TALK TO HIM?
I WILL ALWAYS...
I'M NOT REQUIRED TO CONFIDE IN HIM SIMPLY BECAUSE WE'RE *FRIENDS*.

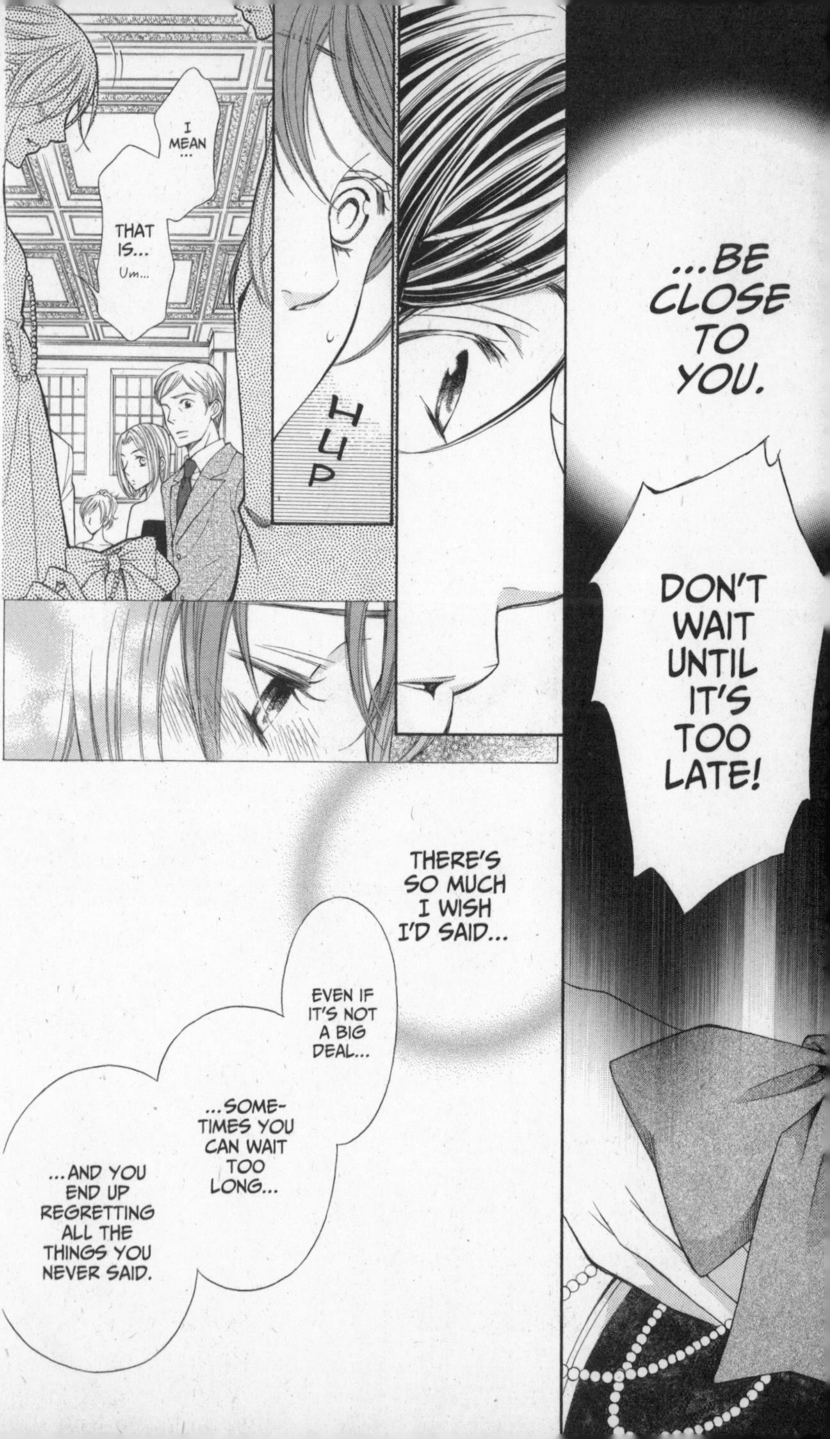
...BE CLOSE TO YOU.
DON'T WAIT UNTIL IT'S TOO LATE!
HUP
I MEAN...
THAT IS...
Um...
THERE'S SO MUCH I WISH I'D SAID...
EVEN IF IT'S NOT A BIG DEAL...
...SOMETIMES YOU CAN WAIT TOO LONG...
...AND YOU END UP REGRETTING ALL THE THINGS YOU NEVER SAID.

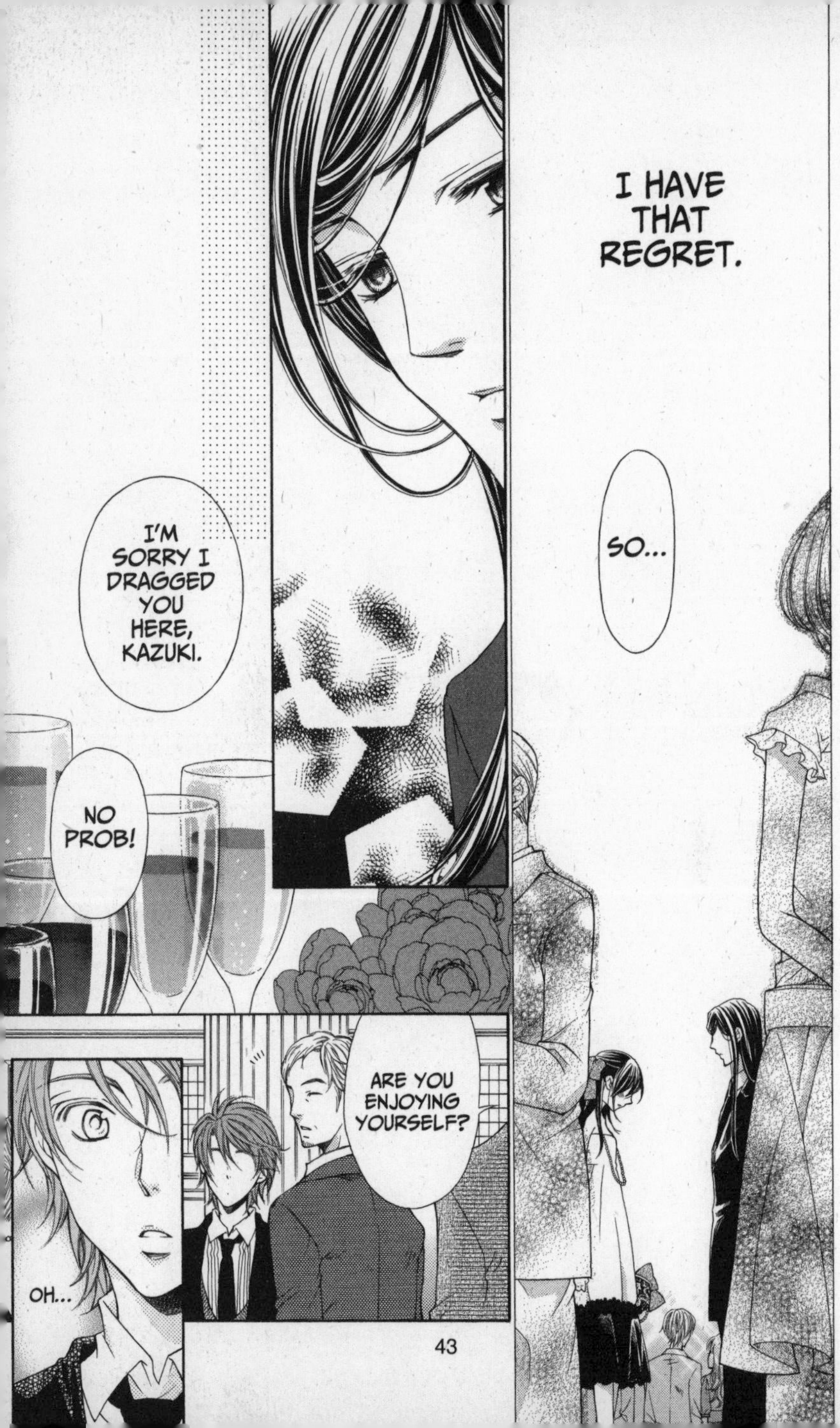
I HAVE THAT REGRET.
SO...
I'M SORRY I DRAGGED YOU HERE, KAZUKI.
NO PROB!
ARE YOU ENJOYING YOURSELF?
OH...

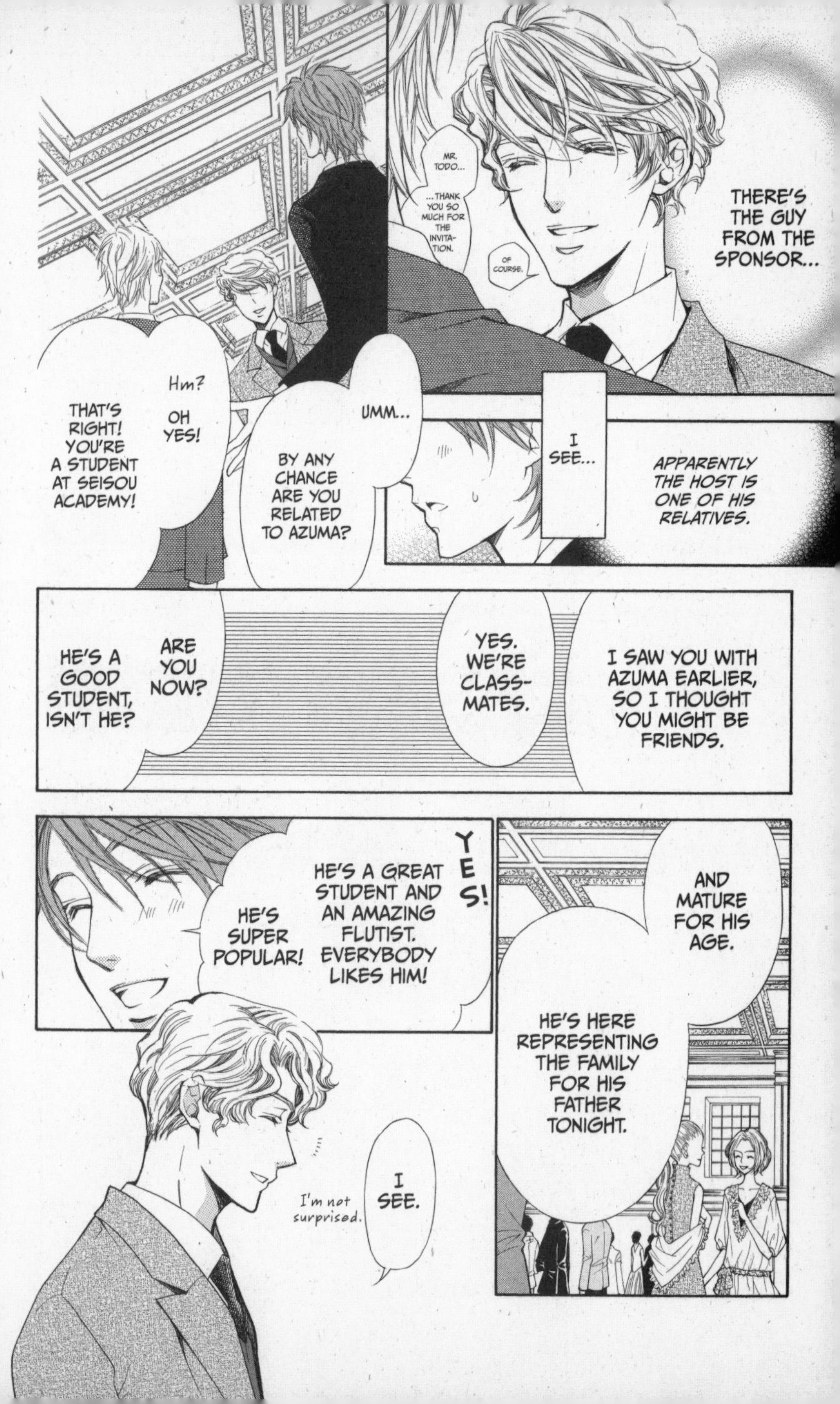
THERE'S THE GUY FROM THE SPONSOR...
MR. TODO...
...THANK YOU SO MUCH FOR THE INVITATION.
OF COURSE.
APPARENTLY THE HOST IS ONE OF HIS RELATIVES.
I SEE...
UMM...
BY ANY CHANCE ARE YOU RELATED TO AZUMA?
Hm?
OH YES!
THAT'S RIGHT! YOU'RE A STUDENT AT SEISOU ACADEMY!
I SAW YOU WITH AZUMA EARLIER, SO I THOUGHT YOU MIGHT BE FRIENDS.
YES. WE'RE CLASSMATES.
ARE YOU NOW?
HE'S A GOOD STUDENT, ISN'T HE?
AND MATURE FOR HIS AGE.
HE'S HERE REPRESENTING THE FAMILY FOR HIS FATHER TONIGHT.
YES!
HE'S A GREAT STUDENT AND AN AMAZING FLUTIST. EVERYBODY LIKES HIM!
HE'S SUPER POPULAR!
I SEE.
I'm not surprised.

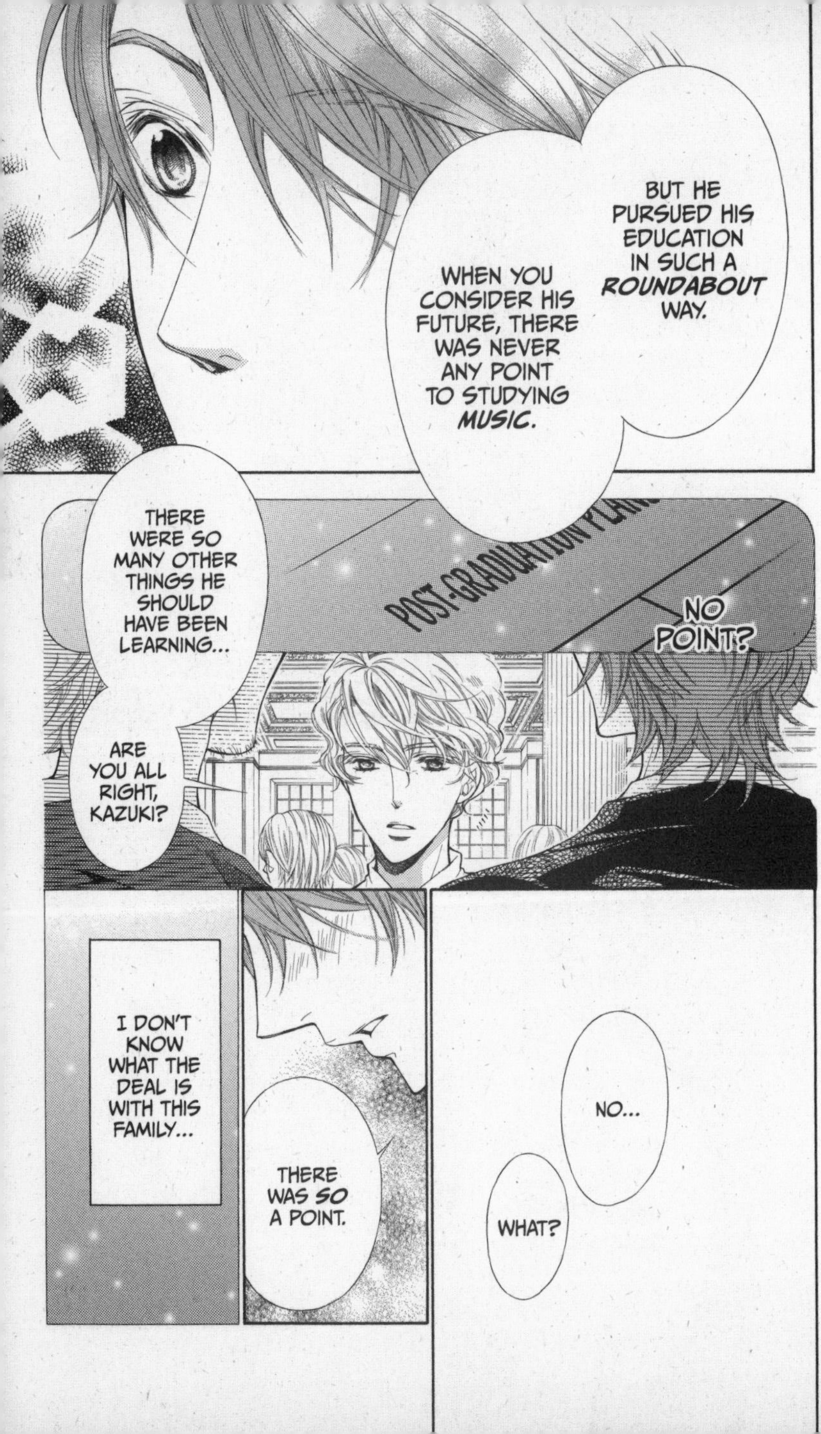
BUT HE PURSUED HIS EDUCATION IN SUCH A *ROUNDABOUT* WAY.
WHEN YOU CONSIDER HIS FUTURE, THERE WAS NEVER ANY POINT TO STUDYING *MUSIC*.
THERE WERE SO MANY OTHER THINGS HE SHOULD HAVE BEEN LEARNING...
POST-GRADUATION
NO POINT?
ARE YOU ALL RIGHT, KAZUKI?
NO...
WHAT?
THERE WAS *SO* A POINT.
I DON'T KNOW WHAT THE DEAL IS WITH THIS FAMILY...

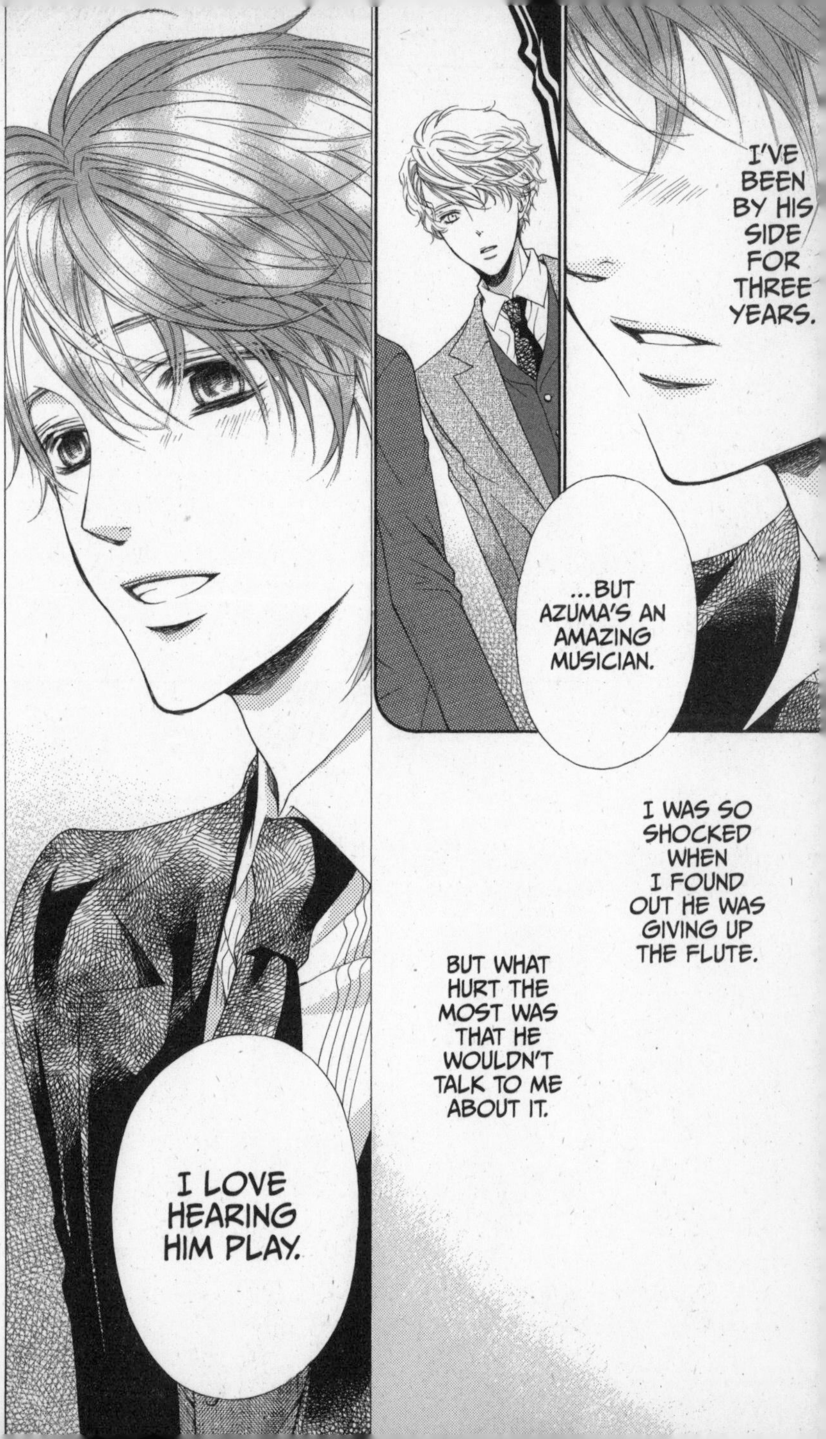
I'VE BEEN BY HIS SIDE FOR THREE YEARS.
...BUT AZUMA'S AN AMAZING MUSICIAN.
I WAS SO SHOCKED WHEN I FOUND OUT HE WAS GIVING UP THE FLUTE.
BUT WHAT HURT THE MOST WAS THAT HE WOULDN'T TALK TO ME ABOUT IT.
I LOVE HEARING HIM PLAY.

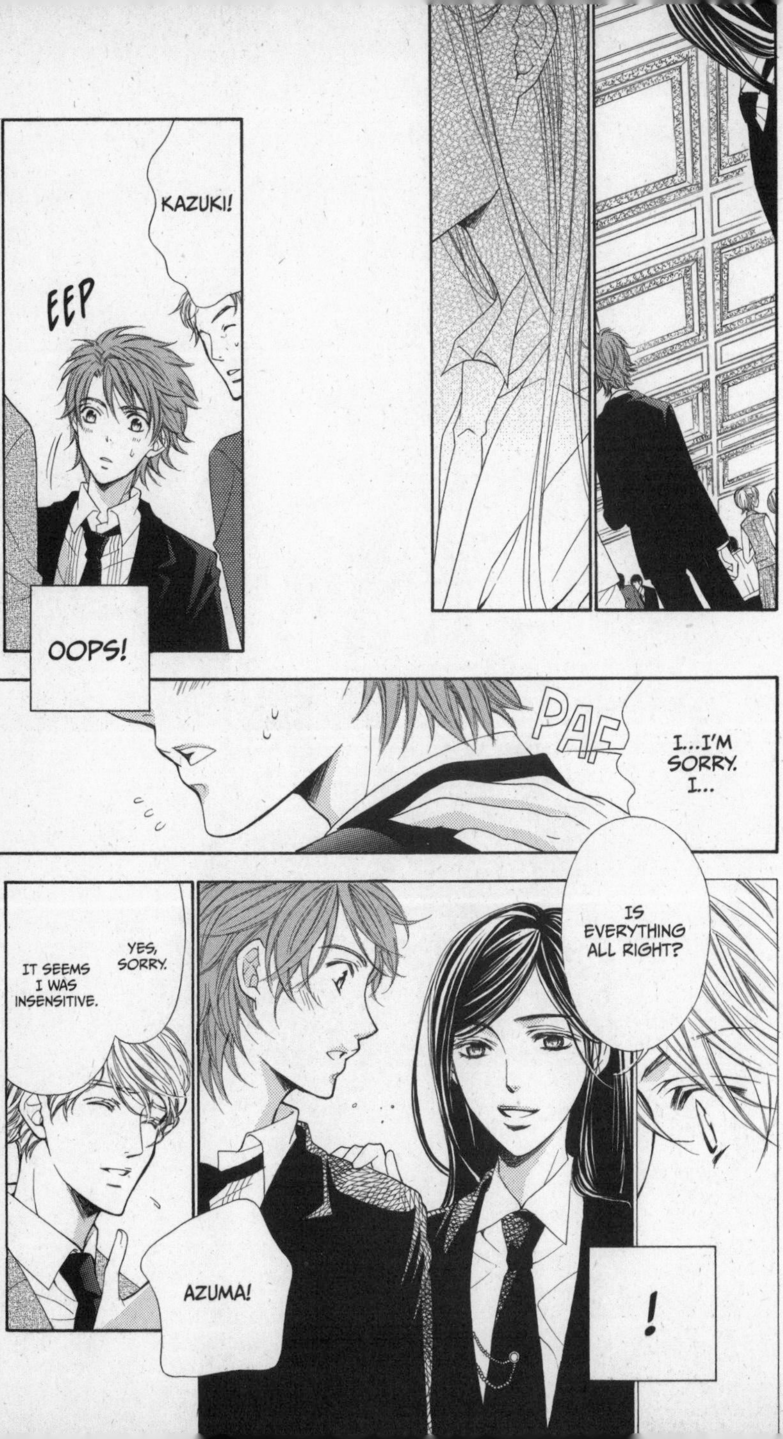
KAZUKI!
EEP
OOPS!
PAF
I...I'M SORRY. I...
IS EVERYTHING ALL RIGHT?
!
AZUMA!
YES, SORRY.
IT SEEMS I WAS INSENSITIVE.

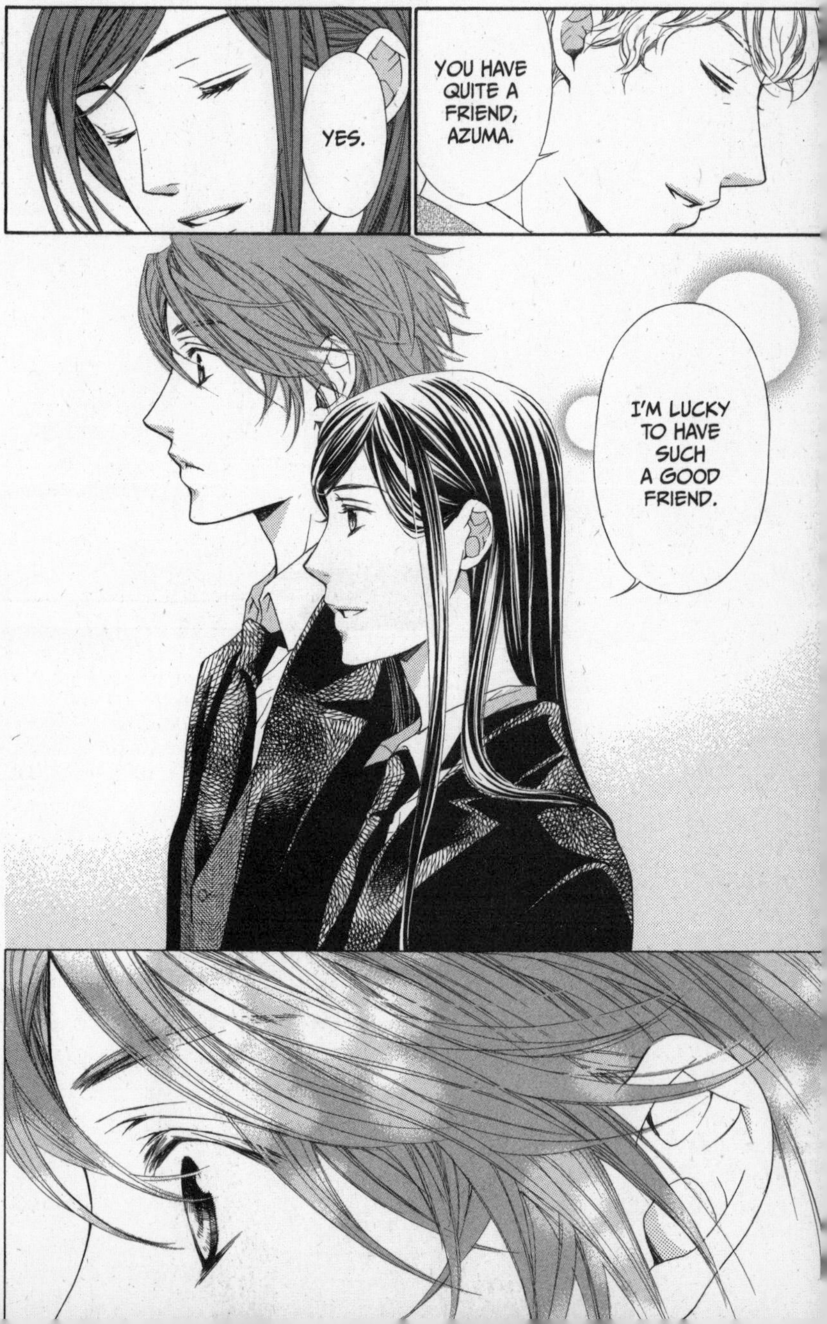
YOU HAVE QUITE A FRIEND, AZUMA.
YES.
I'M LUCKY TO HAVE SUCH A GOOD FRIEND.

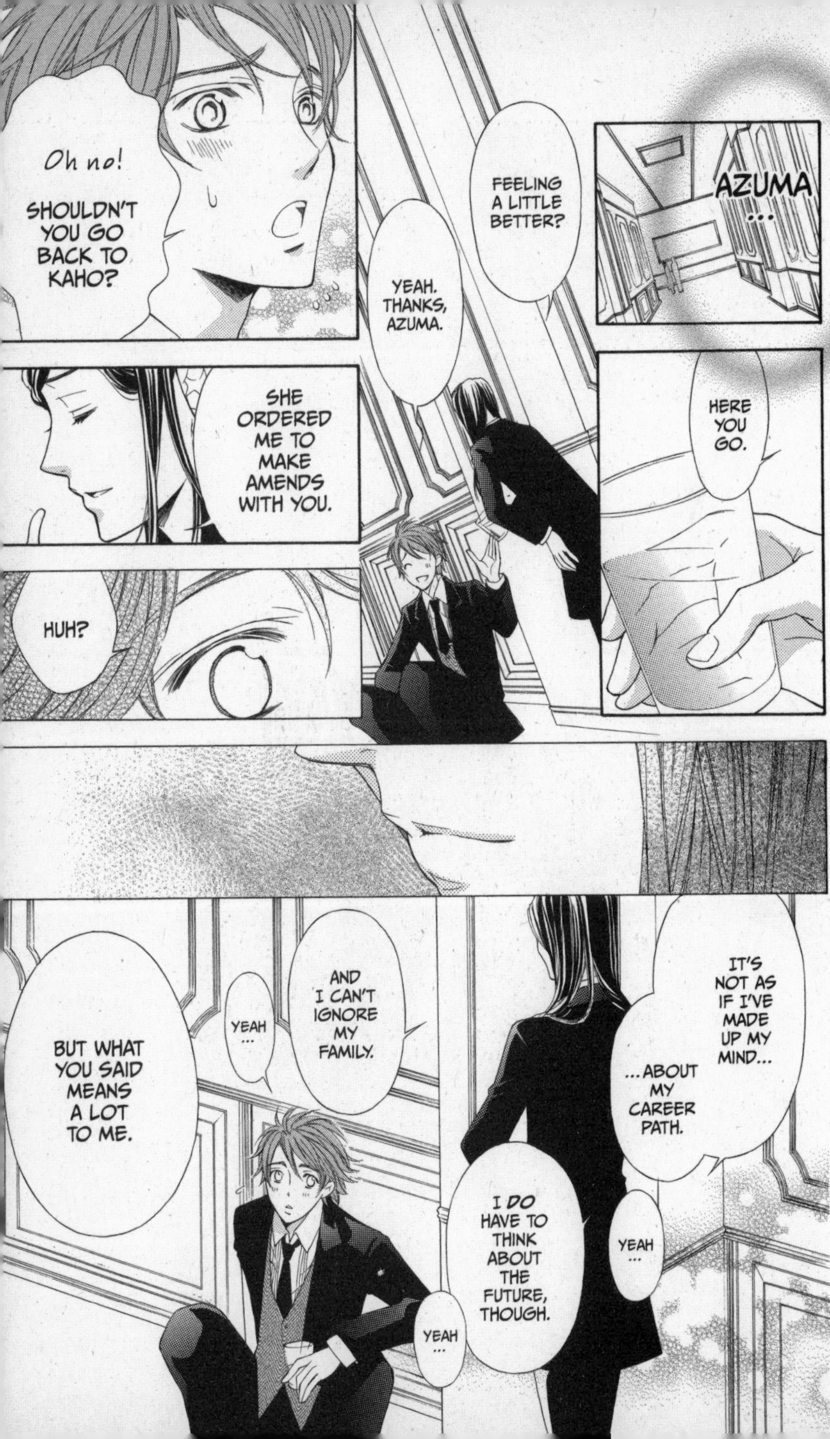
AZUMA...
HERE YOU GO.
FEELING A LITTLE BETTER?
YEAH. THANKS, AZUMA.
Oh no!
SHOULDN'T YOU GO BACK TO KAHO?
SHE ORDERED ME TO MAKE AMENDS WITH YOU.
HUH?
IT'S NOT AS IF I'VE MADE UP MY MIND...
...ABOUT MY CAREER PATH.
YEAH...
I DO HAVE TO THINK ABOUT THE FUTURE, THOUGH.
YEAH...
AND I CAN'T IGNORE MY FAMILY.
YEAH...
BUT WHAT YOU SAID MEANS A LOT TO ME.

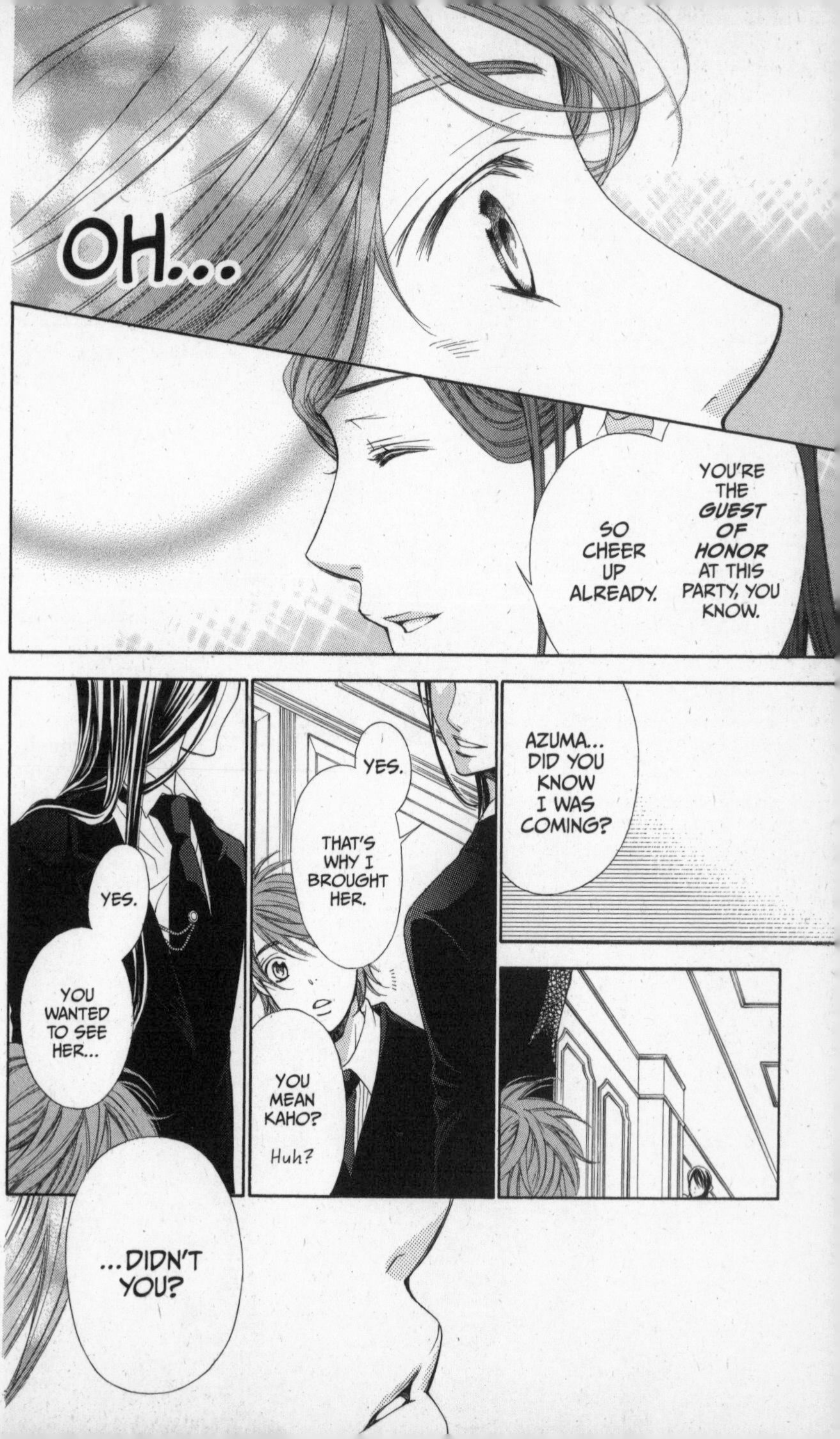
OH...
YOU'RE THE *GUEST OF HONOR* AT THIS PARTY, YOU KNOW.
SO CHEER UP ALREADY.
AZUMA... DID YOU KNOW I WAS COMING?
YES.
THAT'S WHY I BROUGHT HER.
YOU MEAN KAHO?
Huh?
YES.
YOU WANTED TO SEE HER...
...DIDN'T YOU?

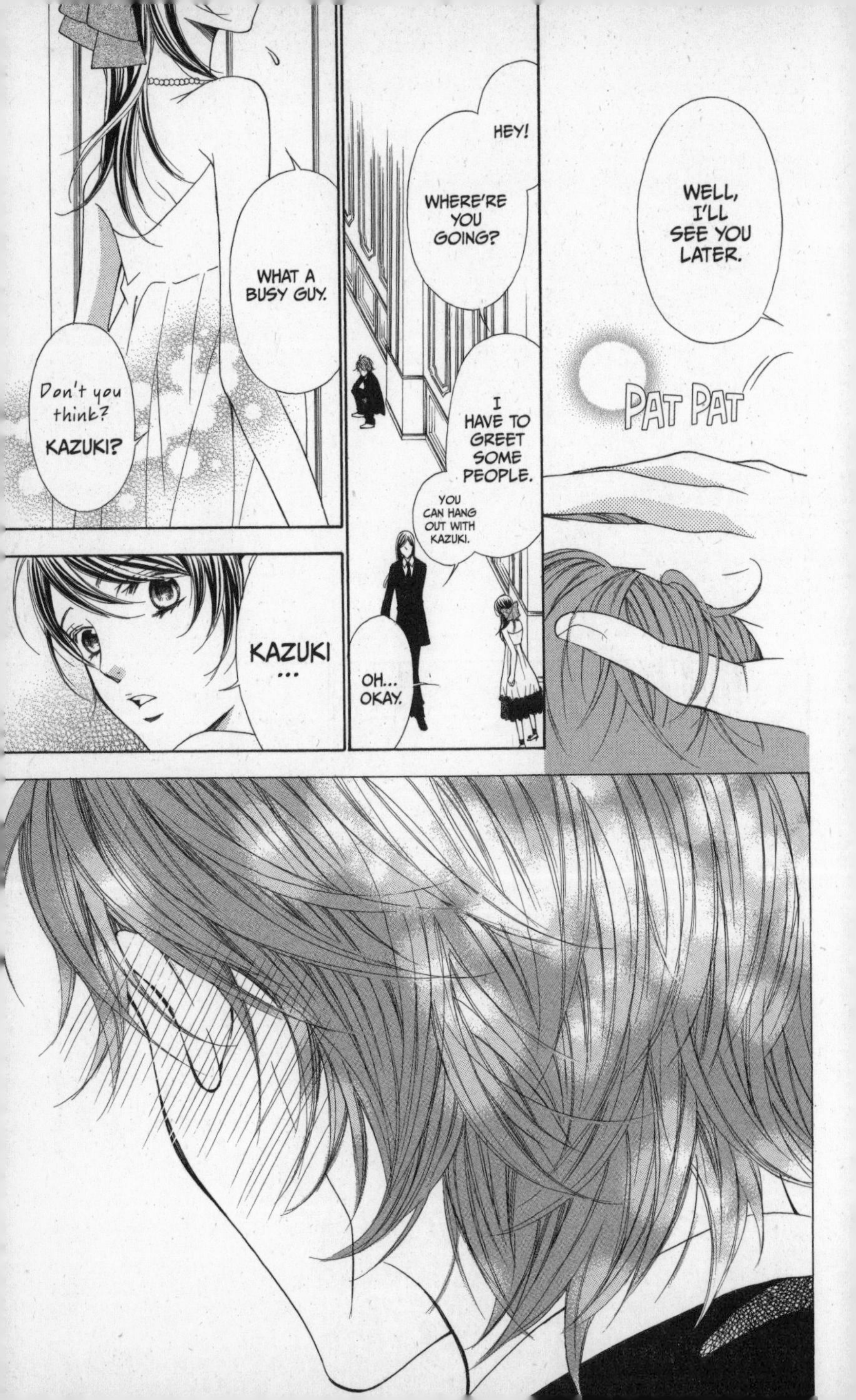
WELL, I'LL SEE YOU LATER.
PAT PAT
HEY!
WHERE'RE YOU GOING?
I HAVE TO GREET SOME PEOPLE.
YOU CAN HANG OUT WITH KAZUKI.
OH... OKAY.
WHAT A BUSY GUY.
Don't you think?
KAZUKI?
KAZUKI ...

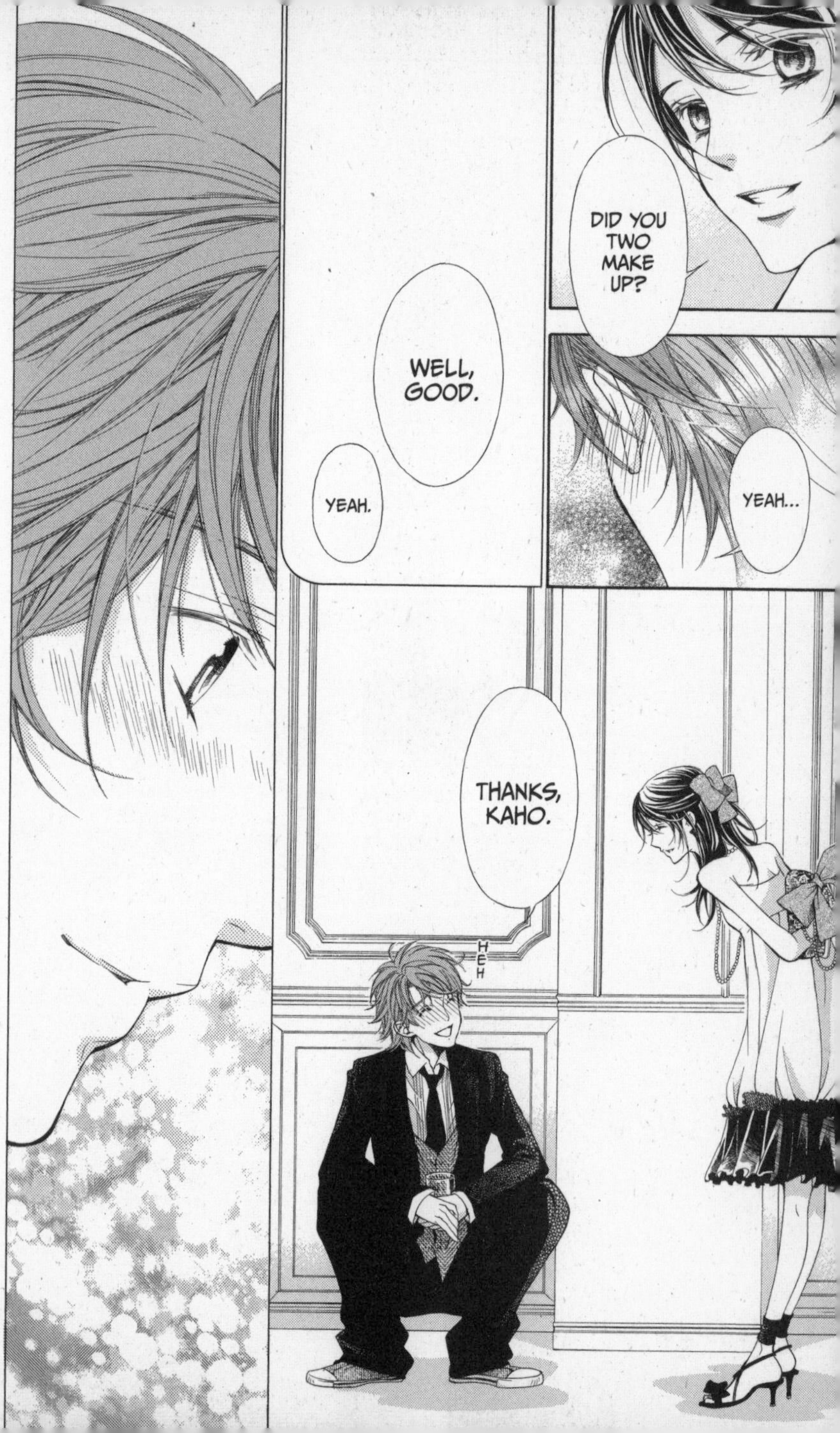
DID YOU TWO MAKE UP?
YEAH...
WELL, GOOD.
YEAH.
THANKS, KAHO.
HEH

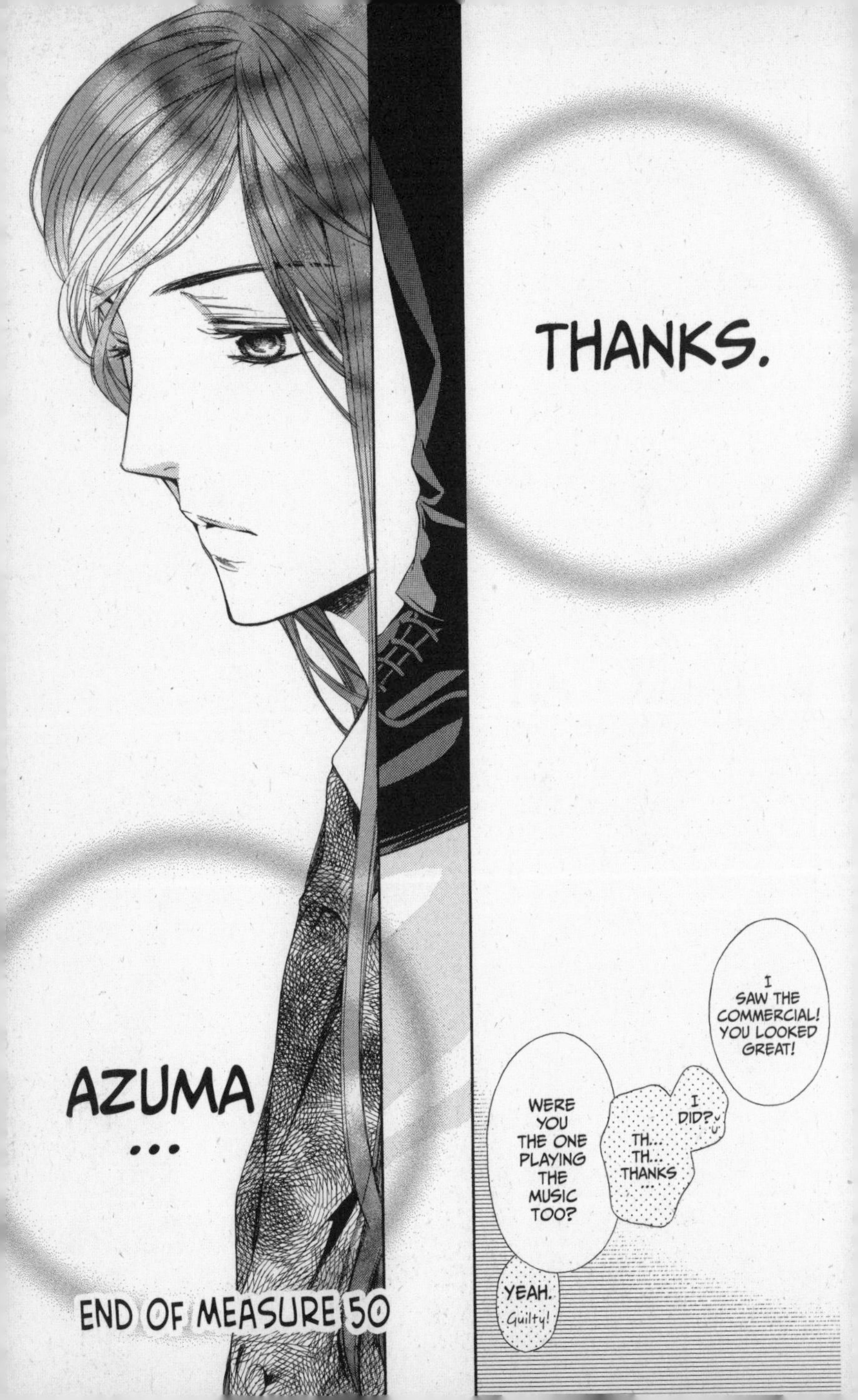
THANKS.
I SAW THE COMMERCIAL! YOU LOOKED GREAT!
I DID?
TH... TH... THANKS...
WERE YOU THE ONE PLAYING THE MUSIC TOO?
YEAH.
Guilty!
AZUMA ...
END OF MEASURE 50

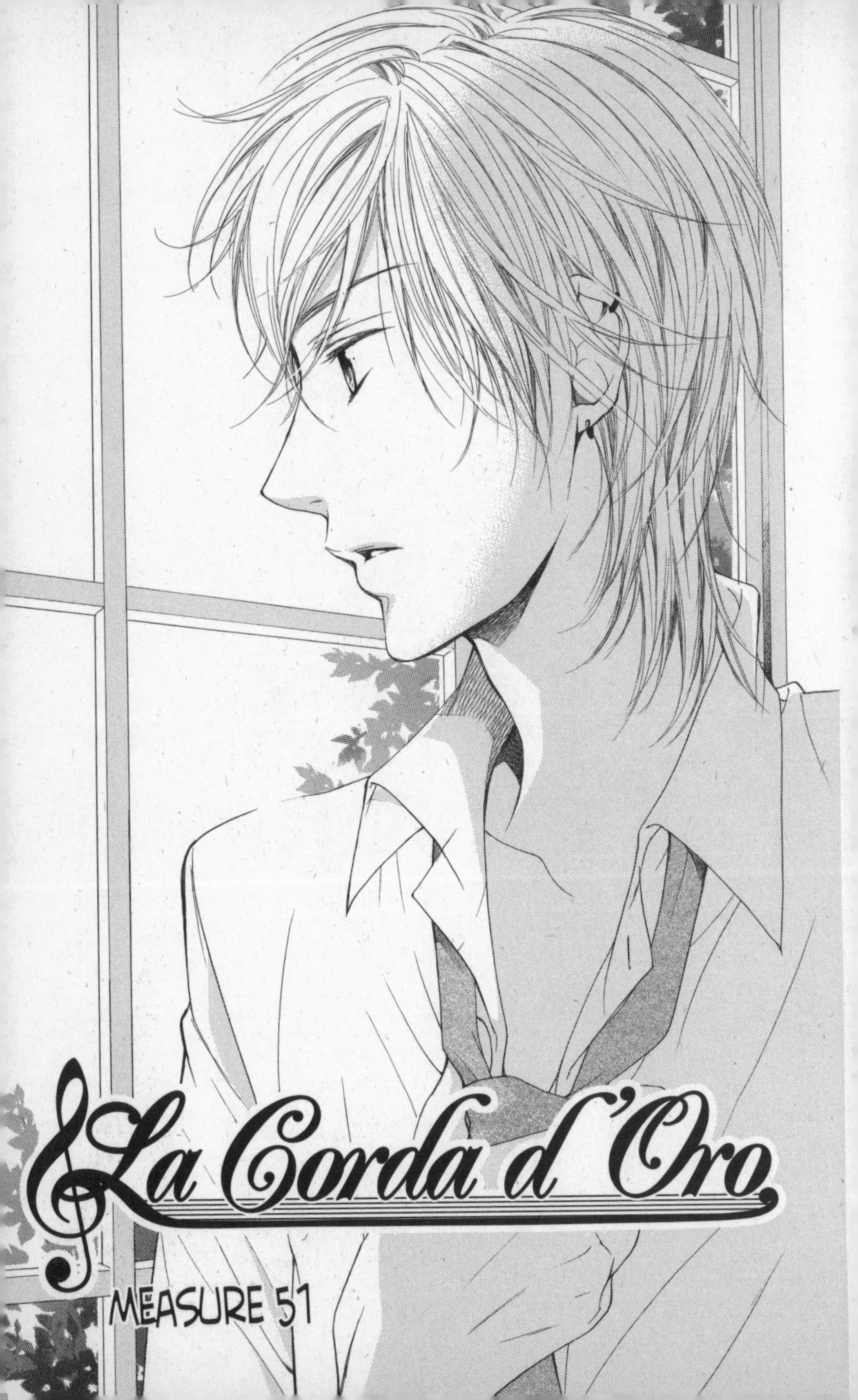
La Corda d'Oro
MEASURE 51

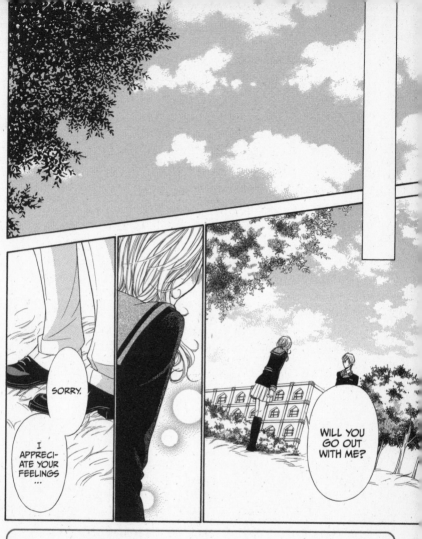

WILL YOU GO OUT WITH ME?
SORRY.
I APPRECI- ATE YOUR FEELINGS ...

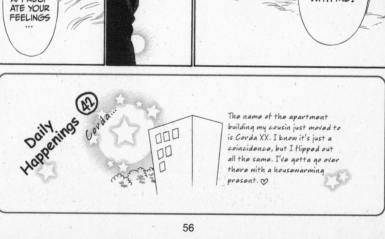

Daily Happenings 42
Corda...

The name of the apartment building my cousin just moved to is Corda XX. I know it's just a coincidence, but I flipped out all the same. I've gotta go over there with a housewarming present. ♡

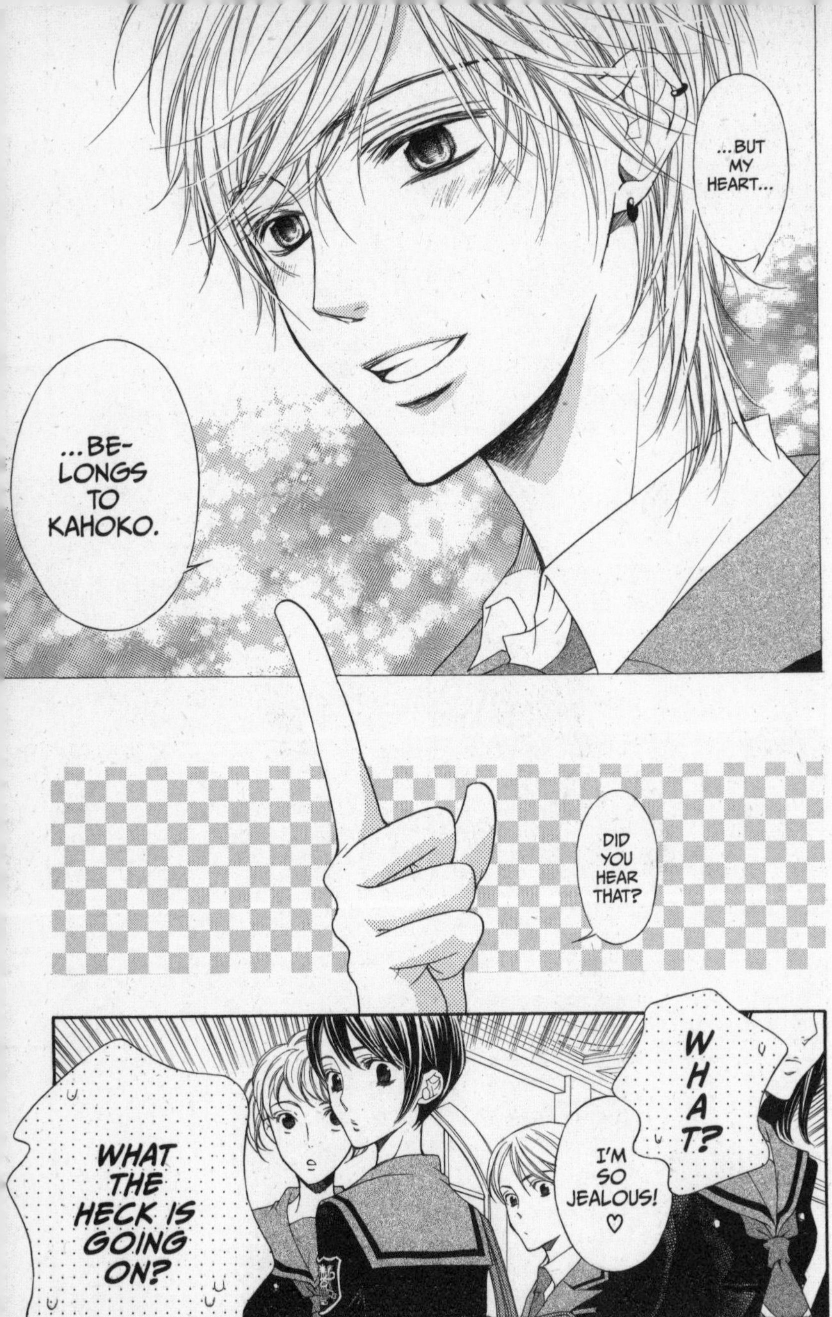
...BUT MY HEART...
...BE-LONGS TO KAHOKO.
DID YOU HEAR THAT?
WHAT?
I'M SO JEALOUS! ♡
WHAT THE HECK IS GOING ON?

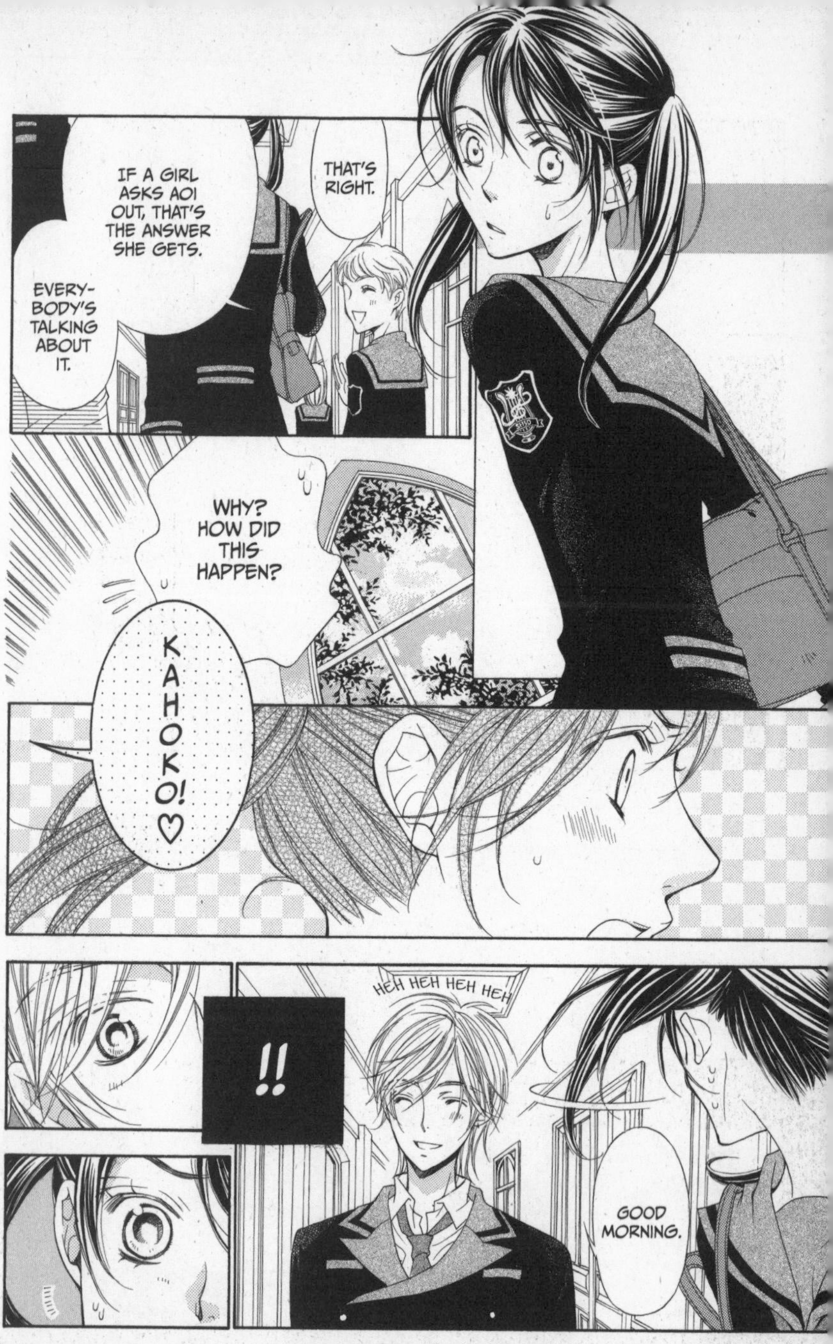
THAT'S RIGHT.
IF A GIRL ASKS AOI OUT, THAT'S THE ANSWER SHE GETS.
EVERY-BODY'S TALKING ABOUT IT.
WHY? HOW DID THIS HAPPEN?
KAHOKO!♡
HEH HEH HEH HEH
GOOD MORNING.
!!

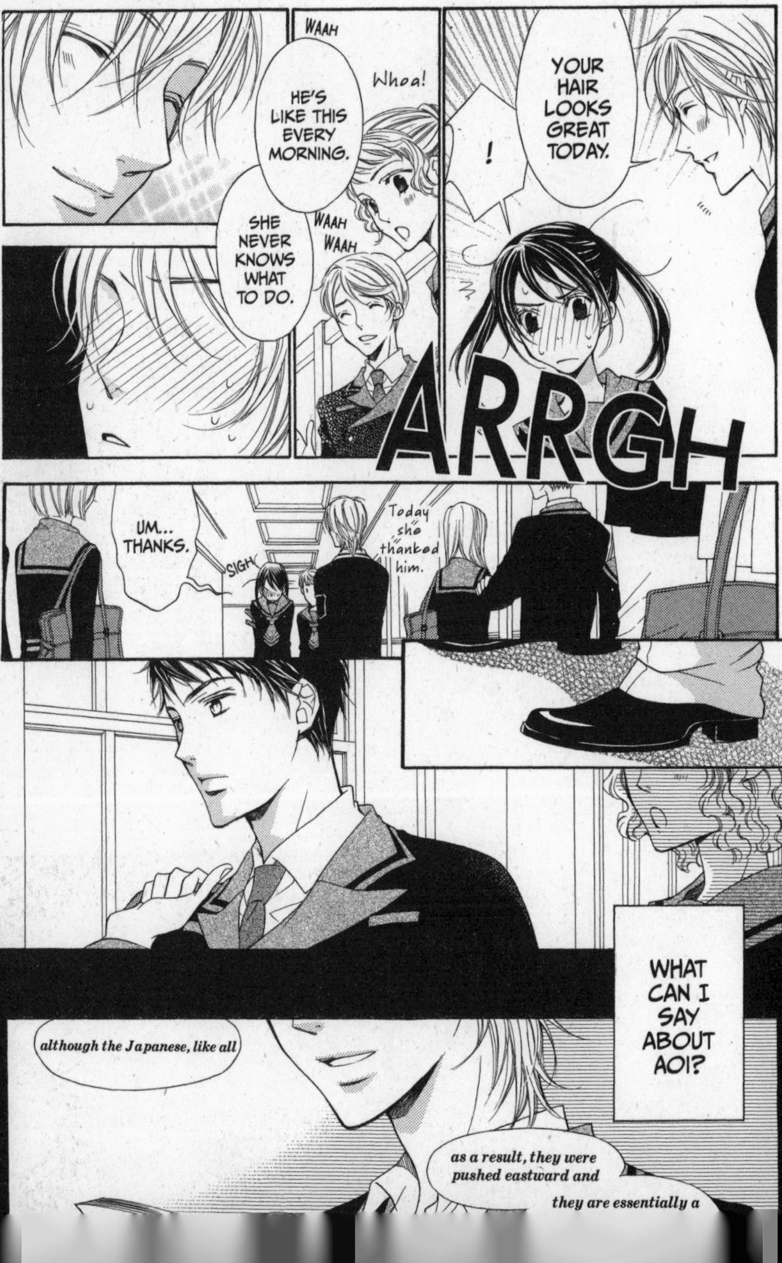
YOUR HAIR LOOKS GREAT TODAY.
!
WAAH
Whoa!
HE'S LIKE THIS EVERY MORNING.
WAAH WAAH
SHE NEVER KNOWS WHAT TO DO.
ARRGH
Today she thanked him.
SIGH
UM... THANKS.
WHAT CAN I SAY ABOUT AOI?
although the Japanese, like all
as a result, they were pushed eastward and
they are essentially a

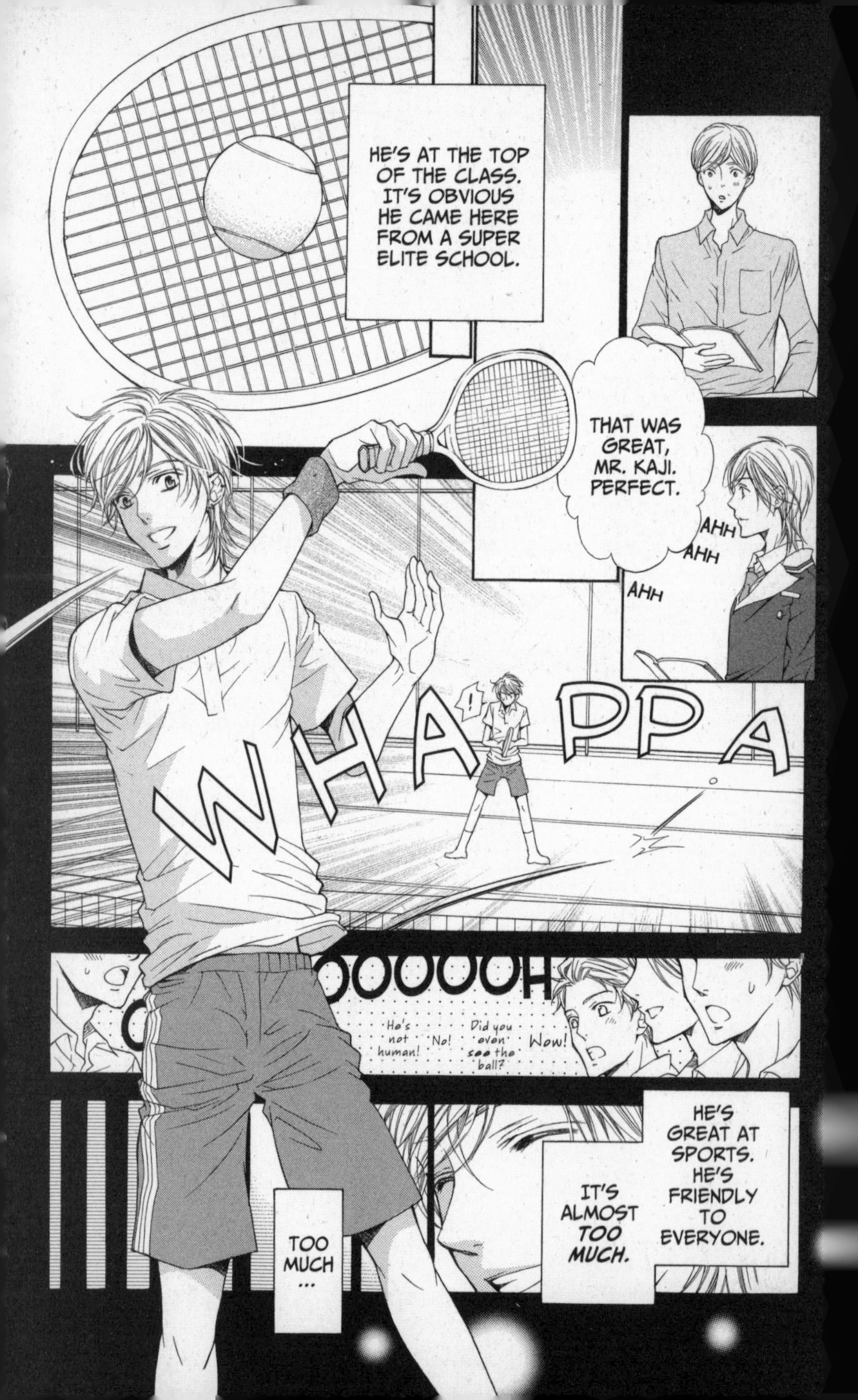
HE'S AT THE TOP OF THE CLASS. IT'S OBVIOUS HE CAME HERE FROM A SUPER ELITE SCHOOL.
THAT WAS GREAT, MR. KAJI. PERFECT.
AHH
AHH
AHH
WHAPPA
!
OOOOOOH
Wow!
Did you even see the ball?
No!
He's not human!
HE'S GREAT AT SPORTS. HE'S FRIENDLY TO EVERYONE.
IT'S ALMOST TOO MUCH.
TOO MUCH...

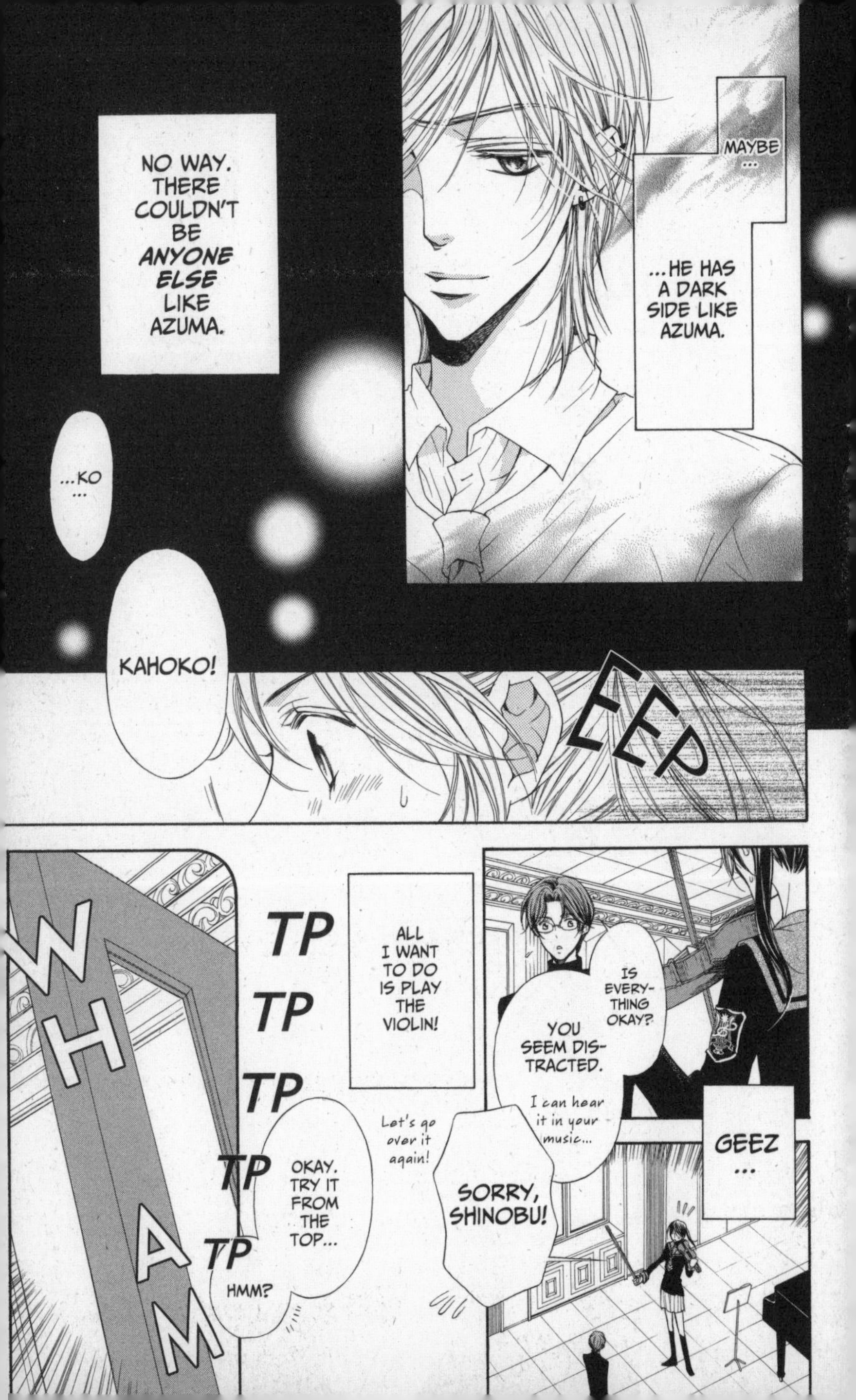
MAYBE...
...HE HAS A DARK SIDE LIKE AZUMA.
NO WAY. THERE COULDN'T BE ANYONE ELSE LIKE AZUMA.
...KO...
KAHOKO!
EEP
IS EVERY-THING OKAY?
YOU SEEM DIS-TRACTED.
I can hear it in your music...
GEEZ...
SORRY, SHINOBU!
Let's go over it again!
ALL I WANT TO DO IS PLAY THE VIOLIN!
TP
TP
TP
TP
TP
OKAY. TRY IT FROM THE TOP...
HMM?
WHAM

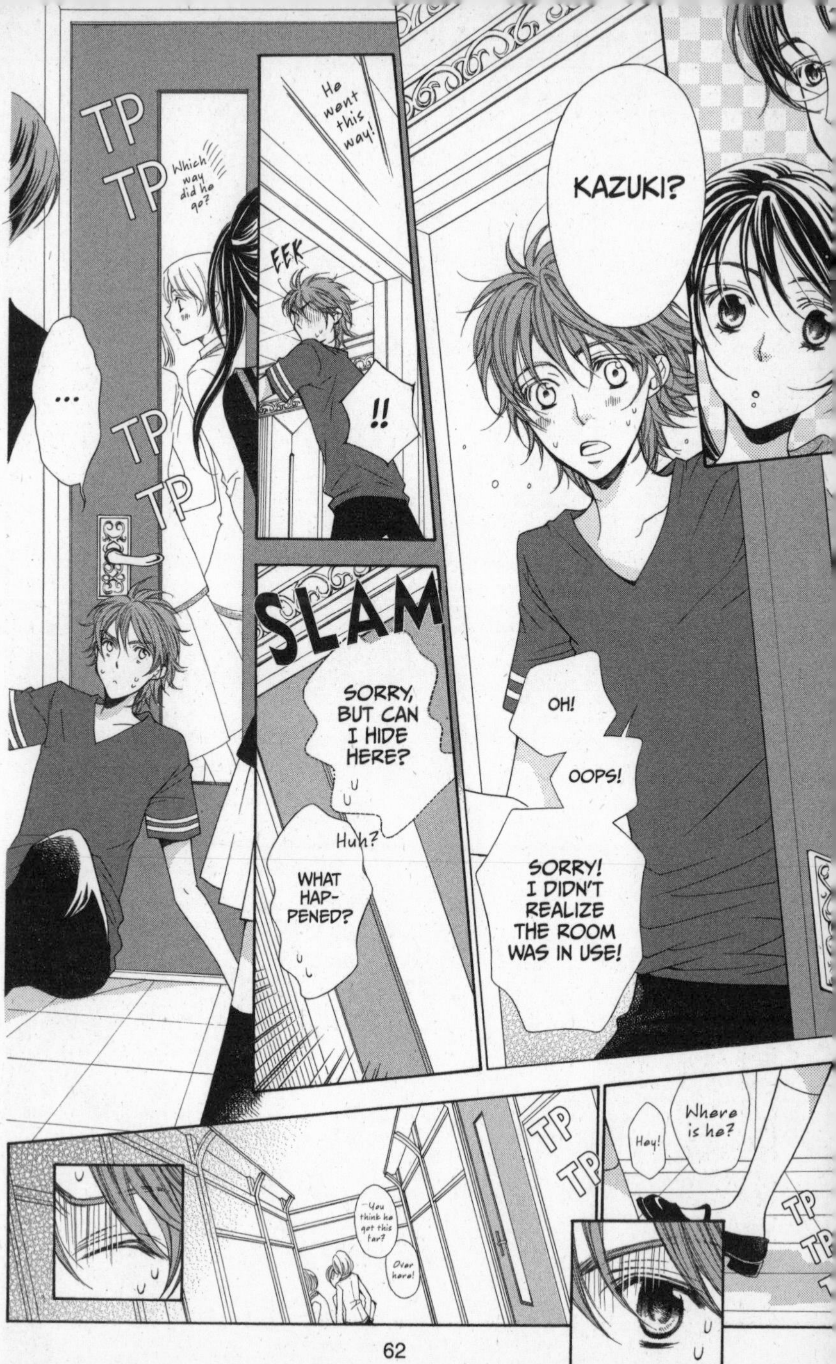
KAZUKI?
OH!
OOPS!
SORRY! I DIDN'T REALIZE THE ROOM WAS IN USE!
He went this way!
EEK
!!
SLAM
SORRY, BUT CAN I HIDE HERE?
Huh?
WHAT HAP-PENED?
TP TP
Which way did he go?
...
TP TP
Where is he?
Hey!
TP TP
TP TP
—You think he got this far?
Over here!

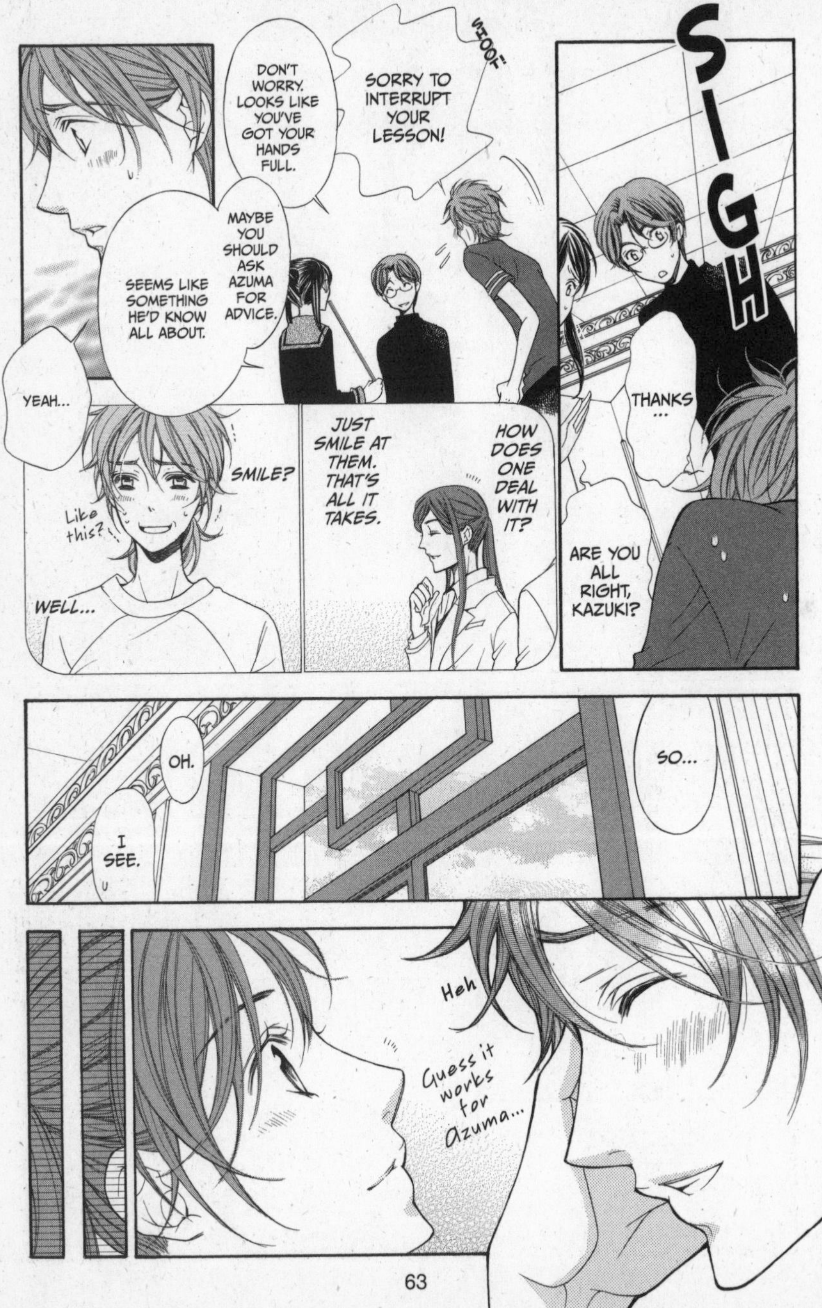
SIGH
THANKS...
ARE YOU ALL RIGHT, KAZUKI?
SHOOT!
SORRY TO INTERRUPT YOUR LESSON!
DON'T WORRY. LOOKS LIKE YOU'VE GOT YOUR HANDS FULL.
MAYBE YOU SHOULD ASK AZUMA FOR ADVICE.
SEEMS LIKE SOMETHING HE'D KNOW ALL ABOUT.
YEAH...
HOW DOES ONE DEAL WITH IT?
JUST SMILE AT THEM. THAT'S ALL IT TAKES.
SMILE?
WELL...
Like this?
SO...
OH.
I SEE.
Heh
Guess it works for Azuma...

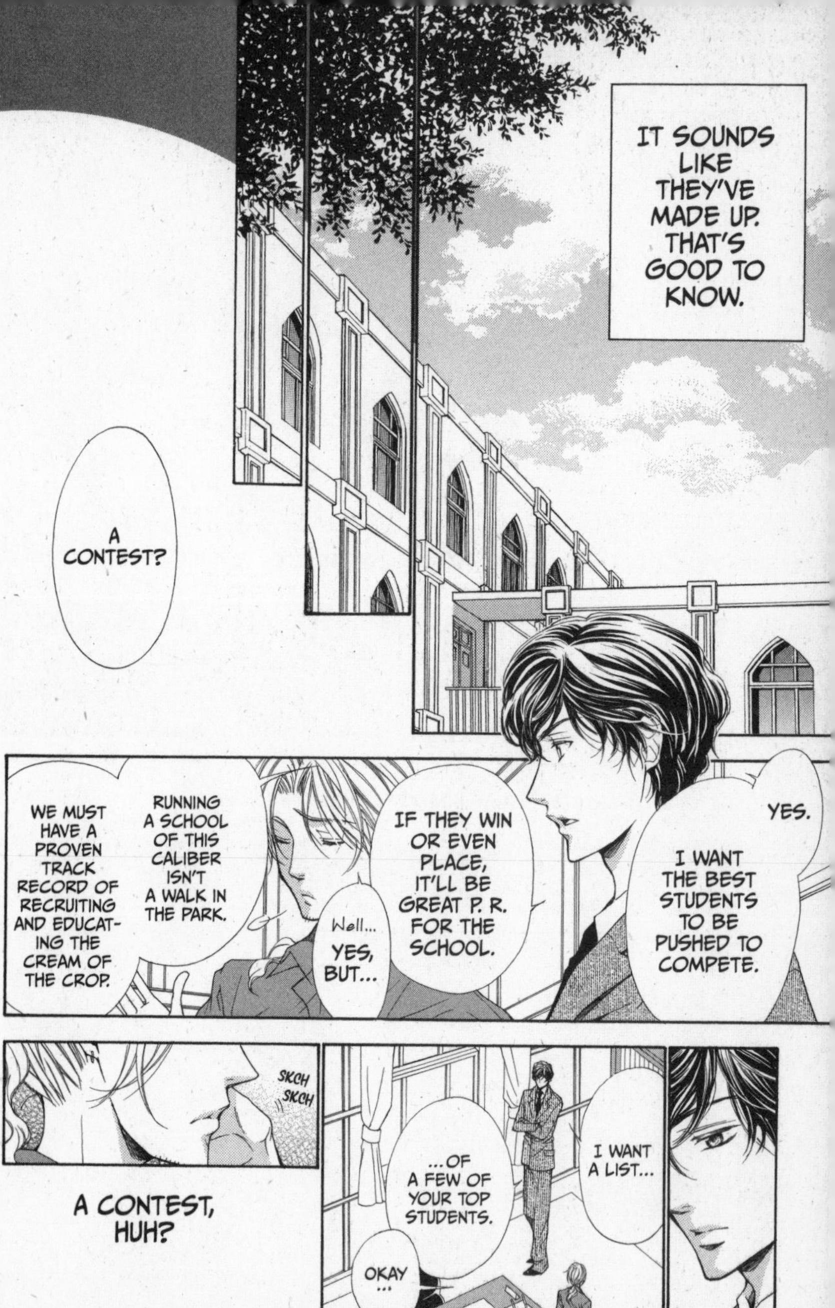
IT SOUNDS LIKE THEY'VE MADE UP. THAT'S GOOD TO KNOW.
A CONTEST?
YES.
I WANT THE BEST STUDENTS TO BE PUSHED TO COMPETE.
IF THEY WIN OR EVEN PLACE, IT'LL BE GREAT P. R. FOR THE SCHOOL.
Well... YES, BUT...
RUNNING A SCHOOL OF THIS CALIBER ISN'T A WALK IN THE PARK.
WE MUST HAVE A PROVEN TRACK RECORD OF RECRUITING AND EDUCATING THE CREAM OF THE CROP.
I WANT A LIST...
...OF A FEW OF YOUR TOP STUDENTS.
OKAY...
SKCH SKCH
A CONTEST, HUH?

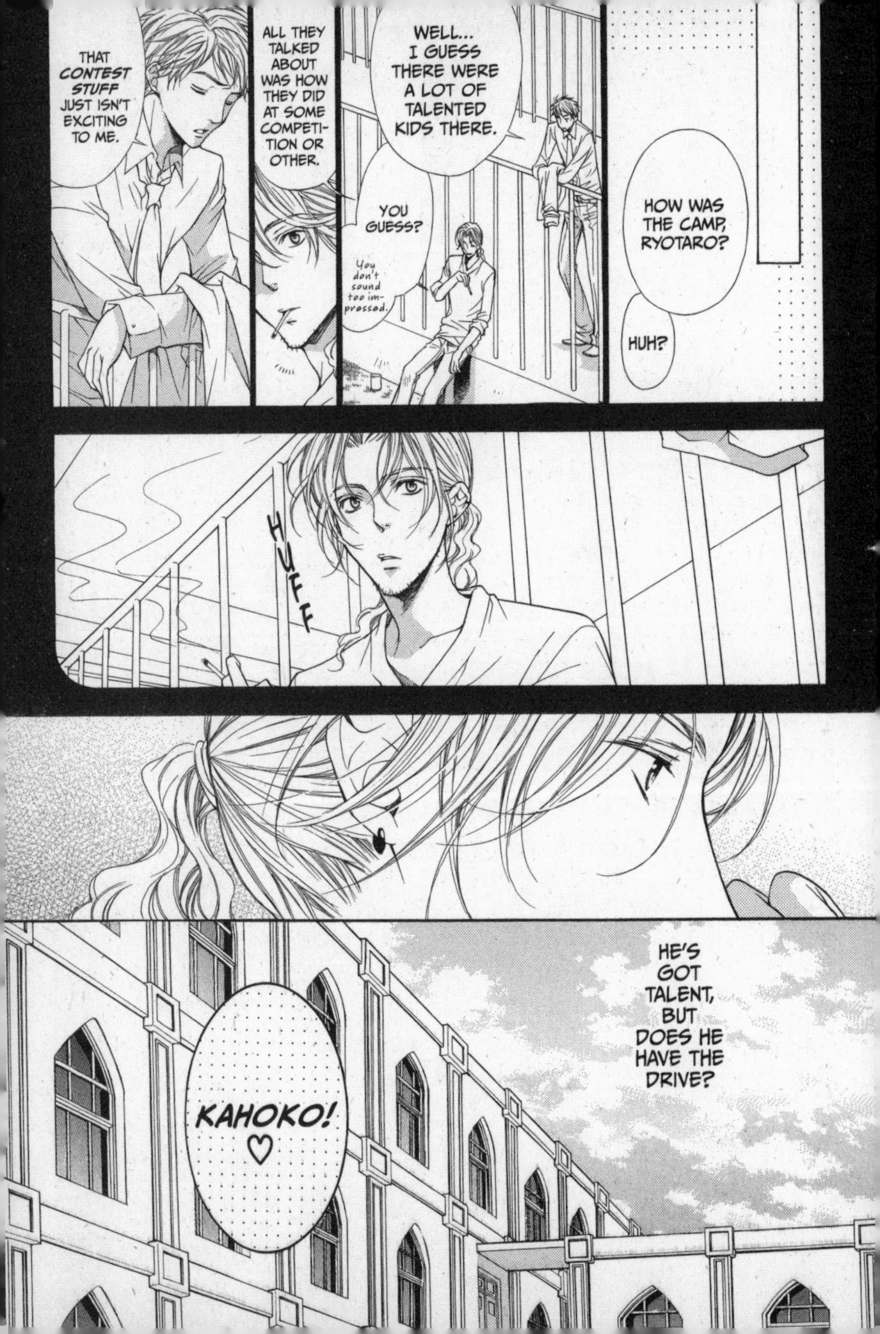
HOW WAS THE CAMP, RYOTARO?
HUH?
WELL... I GUESS THERE WERE A LOT OF TALENTED KIDS THERE.
YOU GUESS?
You don't sound too impressed.
ALL THEY TALKED ABOUT WAS HOW THEY DID AT SOME COMPETITION OR OTHER.
THAT CONTEST STUFF JUST ISN'T EXCITING TO ME.
HUFF
HE'S GOT TALENT, BUT DOES HE HAVE THE DRIVE?
KAHOKO! ♡

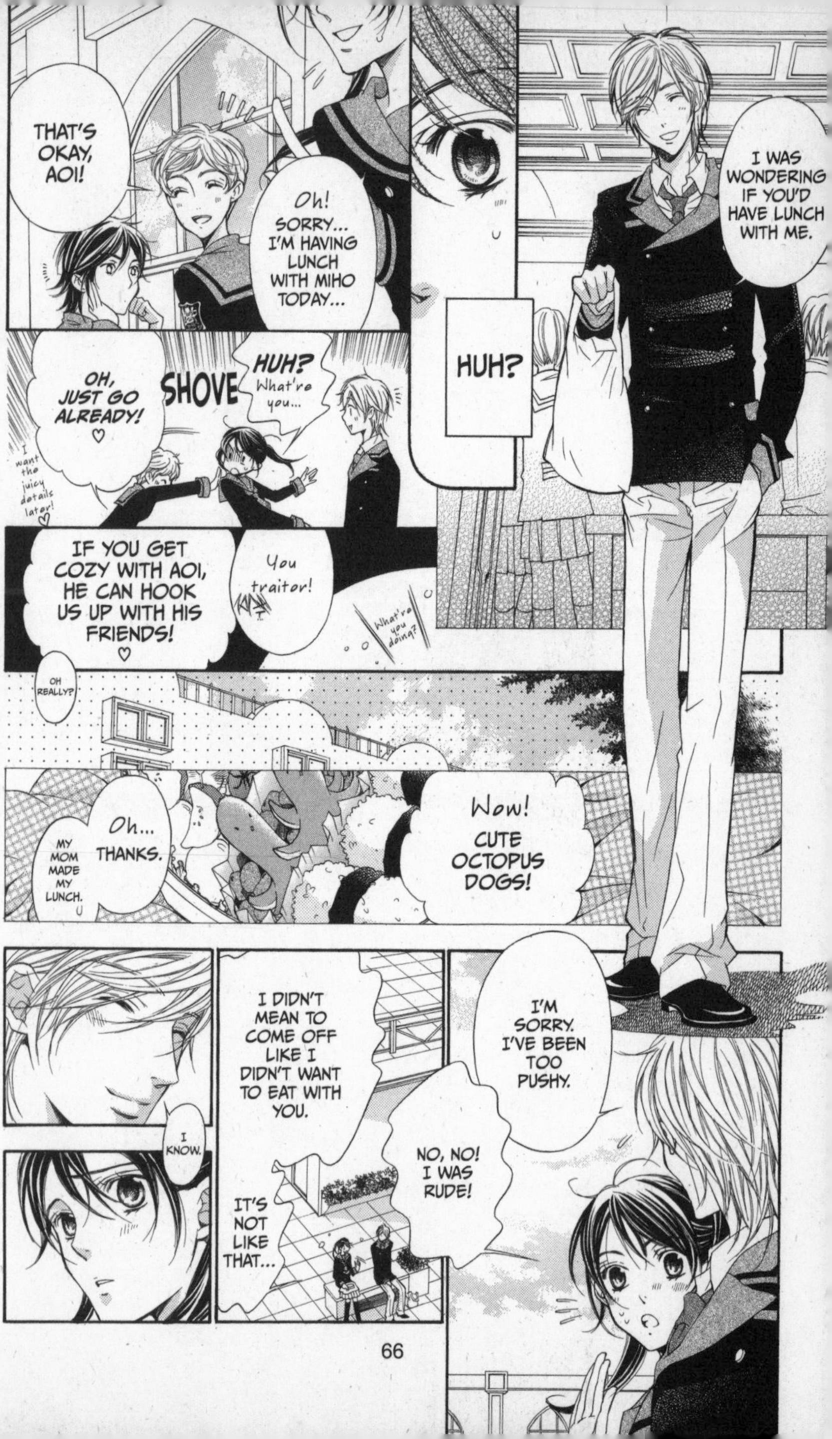
I WAS WONDERING IF YOU'D HAVE LUNCH WITH ME.
HUH?
Oh! SORRY... I'M HAVING LUNCH WITH MIHO TODAY...
THAT'S OKAY, AOI!
HUH? What're you...
SHOVE
OH, JUST GO ALREADY! ♡
I want the juicy details later! ♡
What're you doing?
You traitor!
IF YOU GET COZY WITH AOI, HE CAN HOOK US UP WITH HIS FRIENDS! ♡
OH REALLY?
Wow! CUTE OCTOPUS DOGS!
Oh... THANKS.
MY MOM MADE MY LUNCH.
I'M SORRY. I'VE BEEN TOO PUSHY.
NO, NO! I WAS RUDE!
I DIDN'T MEAN TO COME OFF LIKE I DIDN'T WANT TO EAT WITH YOU.
IT'S NOT LIKE THAT...
I KNOW.

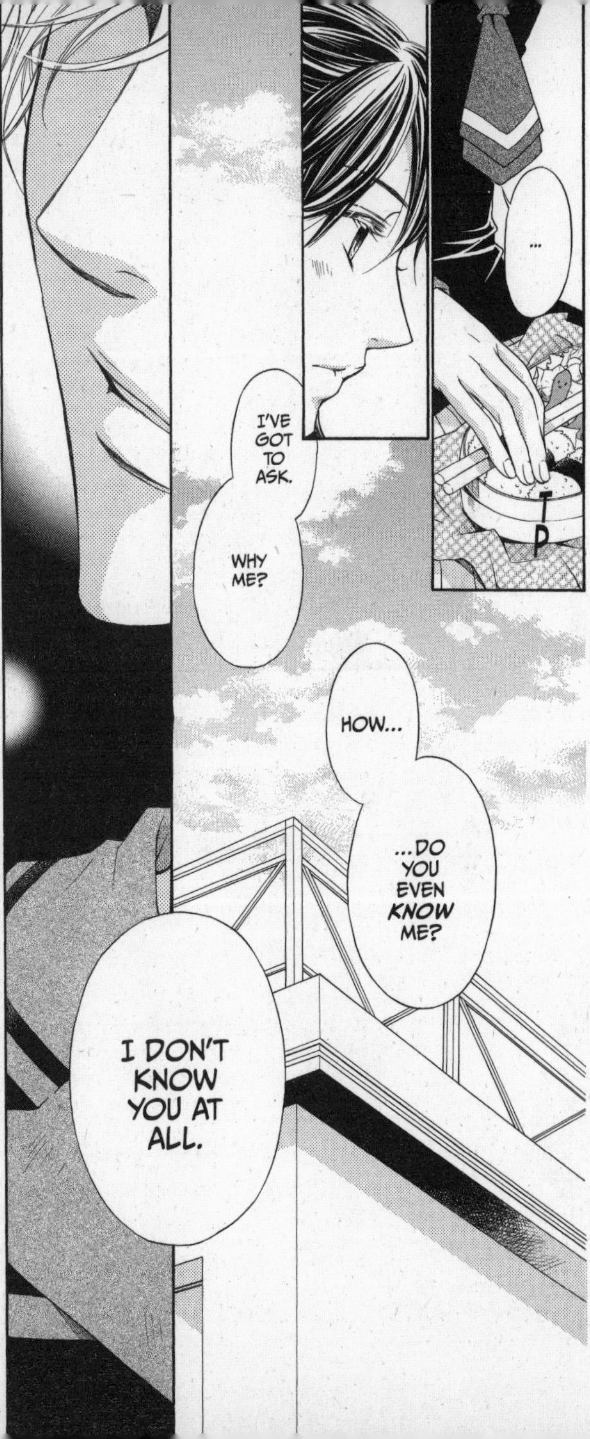
...
TP
I'VE GOT TO ASK.
WHY ME?
HOW...
...DO YOU EVEN *KNOW* ME?
I DON'T KNOW YOU AT ALL.

For this set of sketches, instead of dressing the characters up, I'm going to put them in glasses. I'll play with the youngest and oldest characters. First up is Kanayan.

Measure 50 turned out kind of like a side story. With Kazuki breaking into the entertainment industry, the third-years are on fire!

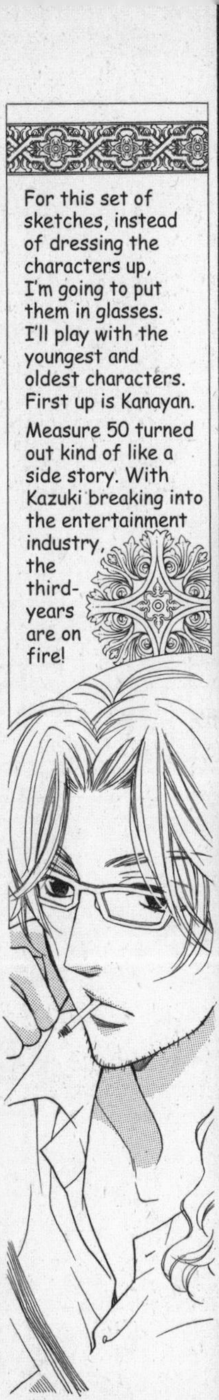

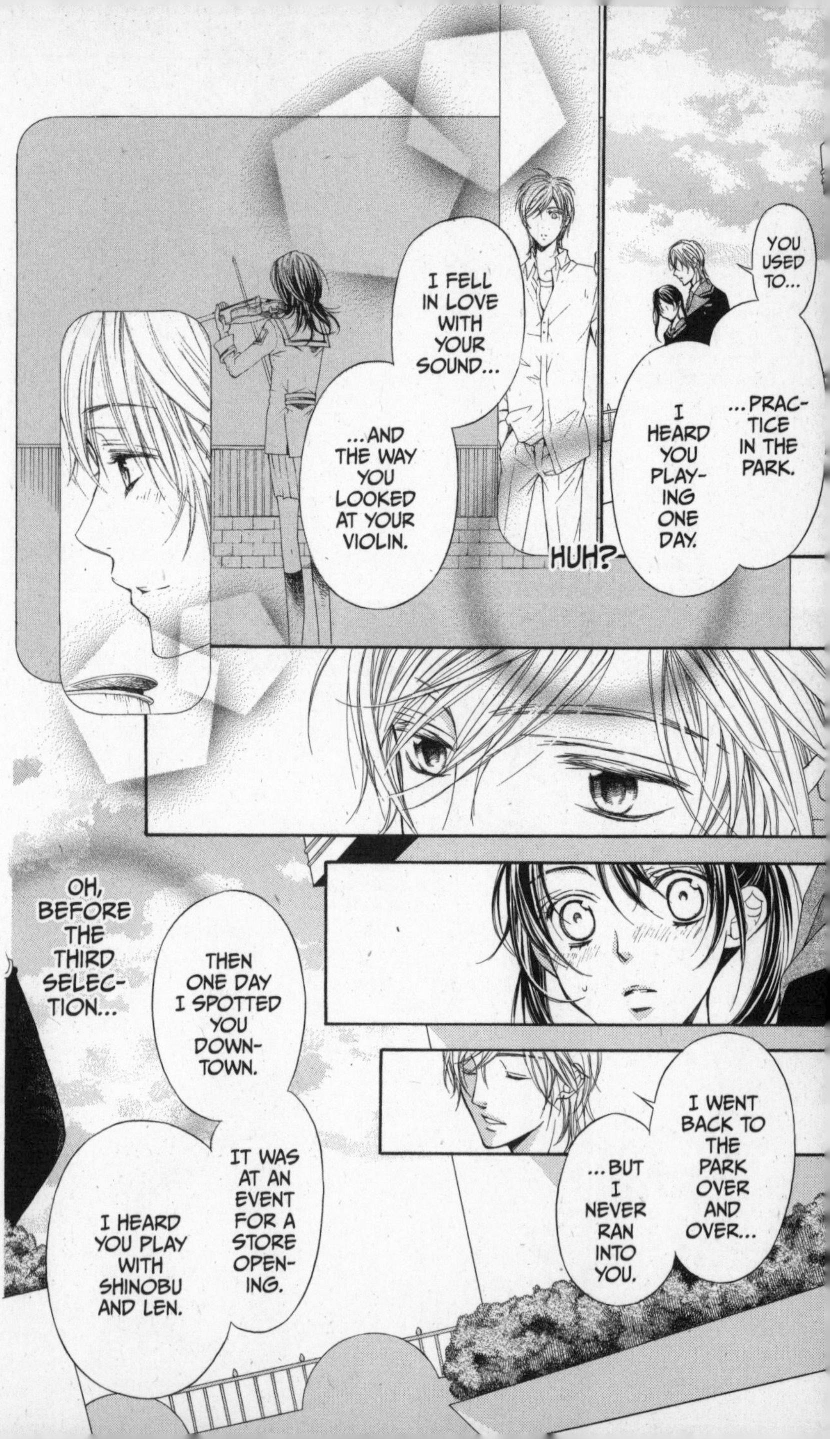
YOU USED TO...
...PRACTICE IN THE PARK.
I HEARD YOU PLAYING ONE DAY.
HUH?
I FELL IN LOVE WITH YOUR SOUND...
...AND THE WAY YOU LOOKED AT YOUR VIOLIN.
I WENT BACK TO THE PARK OVER AND OVER...
...BUT I NEVER RAN INTO YOU.
THEN ONE DAY I SPOTTED YOU DOWNTOWN.
OH, BEFORE THE THIRD SELECTION...
IT WAS AT AN EVENT FOR A STORE OPENING.
I HEARD YOU PLAY WITH SHINOBU AND LEN.

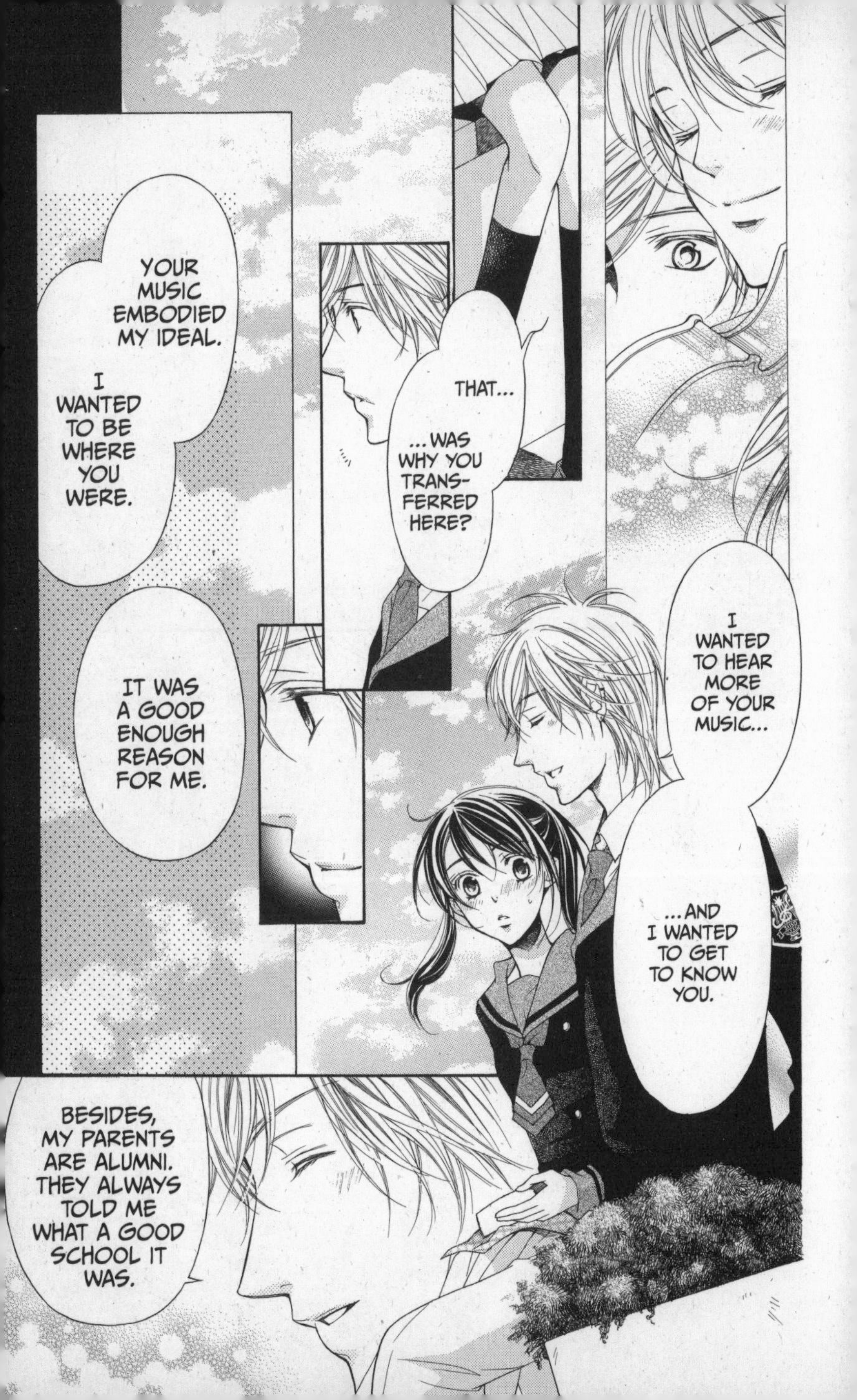
THAT...
...WAS WHY YOU TRANS-FERRED HERE?
YOUR MUSIC EMBODIED MY IDEAL.
I WANTED TO BE WHERE YOU WERE.
IT WAS A GOOD ENOUGH REASON FOR ME.
I WANTED TO HEAR MORE OF YOUR MUSIC...
...AND I WANTED TO GET TO KNOW YOU.
BESIDES, MY PARENTS ARE ALUMNI. THEY ALWAYS TOLD ME WHAT A GOOD SCHOOL IT WAS.

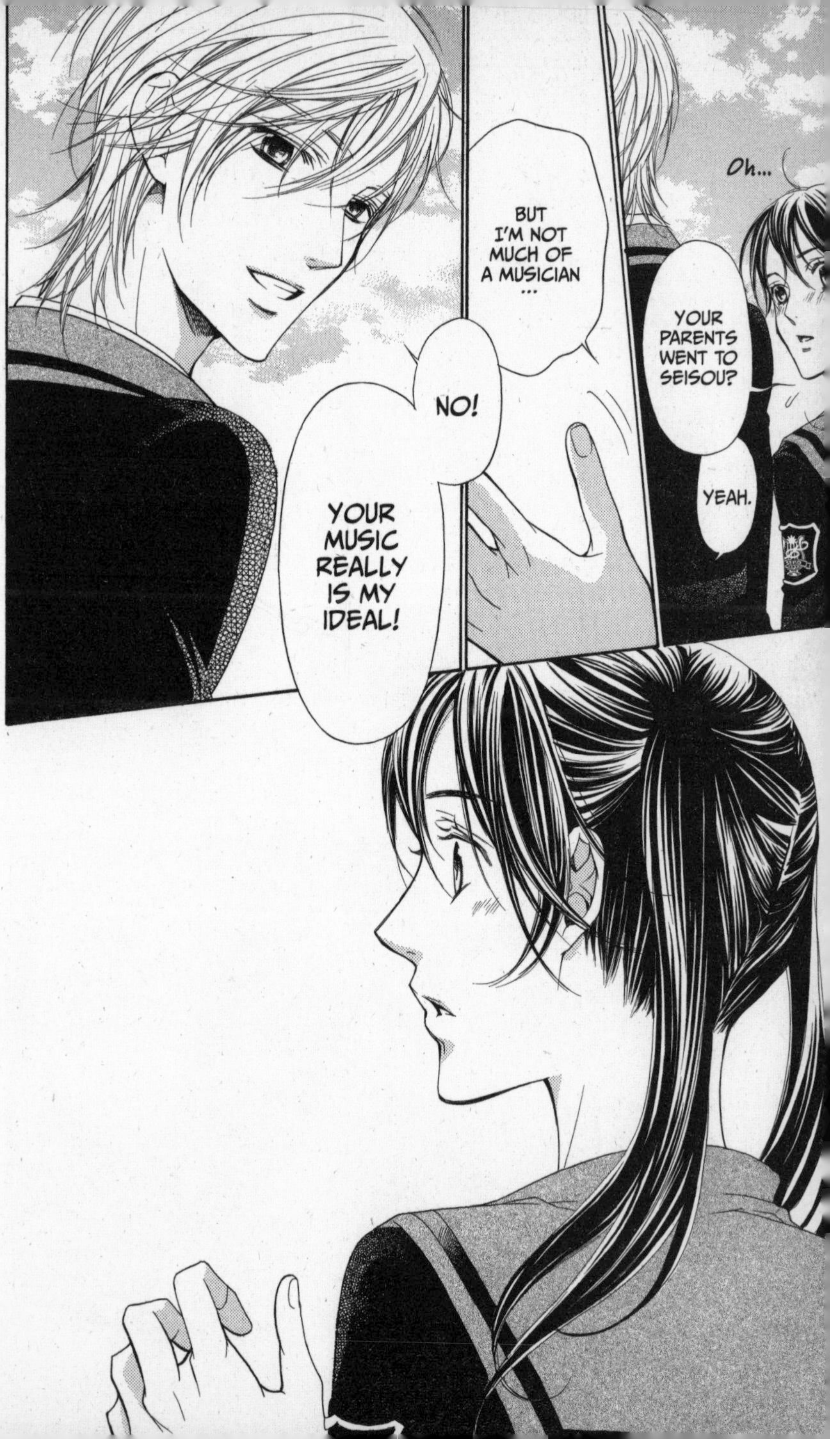
Oh...
YOUR PARENTS WENT TO SEISOU?
YEAH.
BUT I'M NOT MUCH OF A MUSICIAN ...
NO!
YOUR MUSIC REALLY IS MY IDEAL!

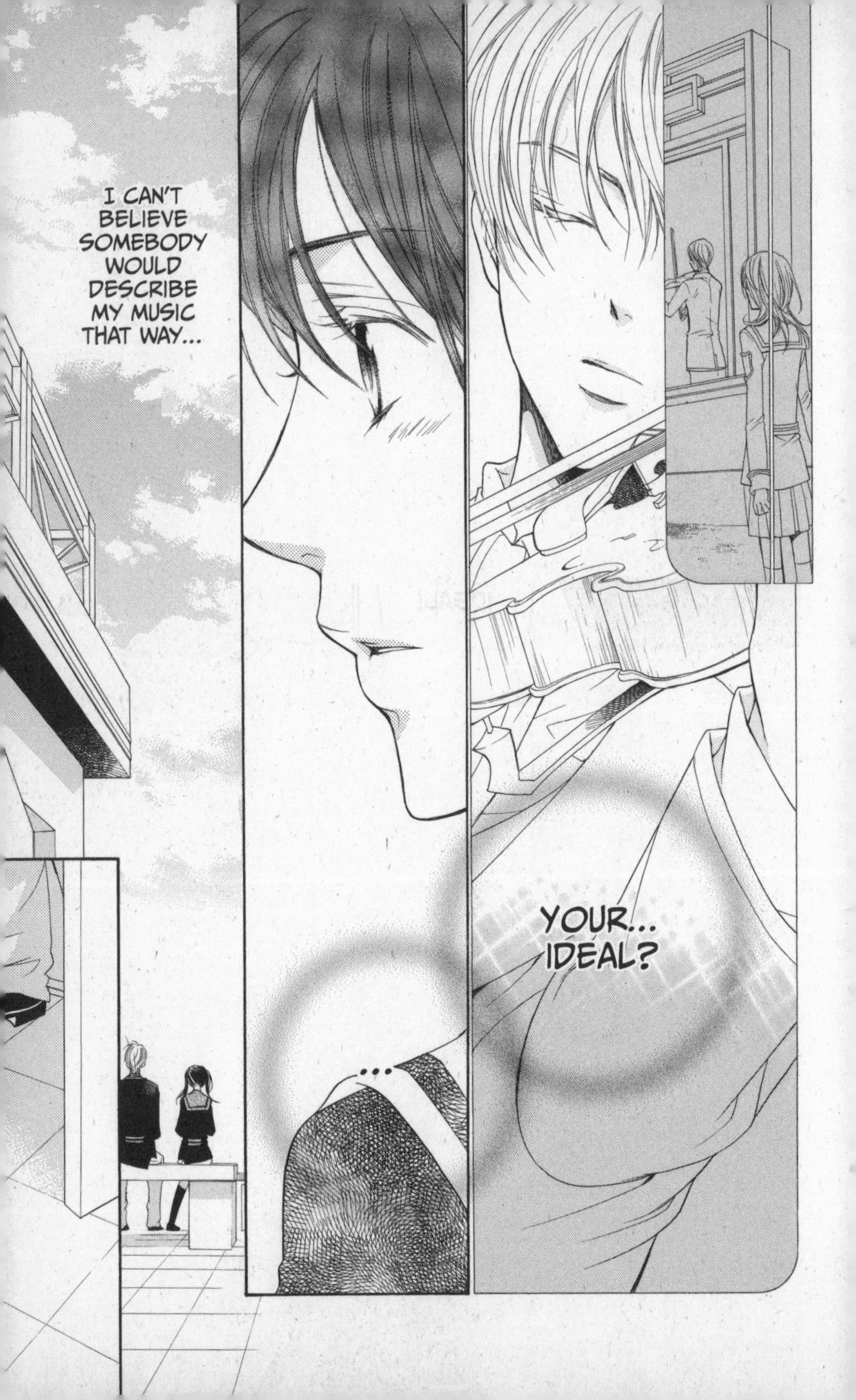
YOUR... IDEAL?
...
I CAN'T BELIEVE SOMEBODY WOULD DESCRIBE MY MUSIC THAT WAY...

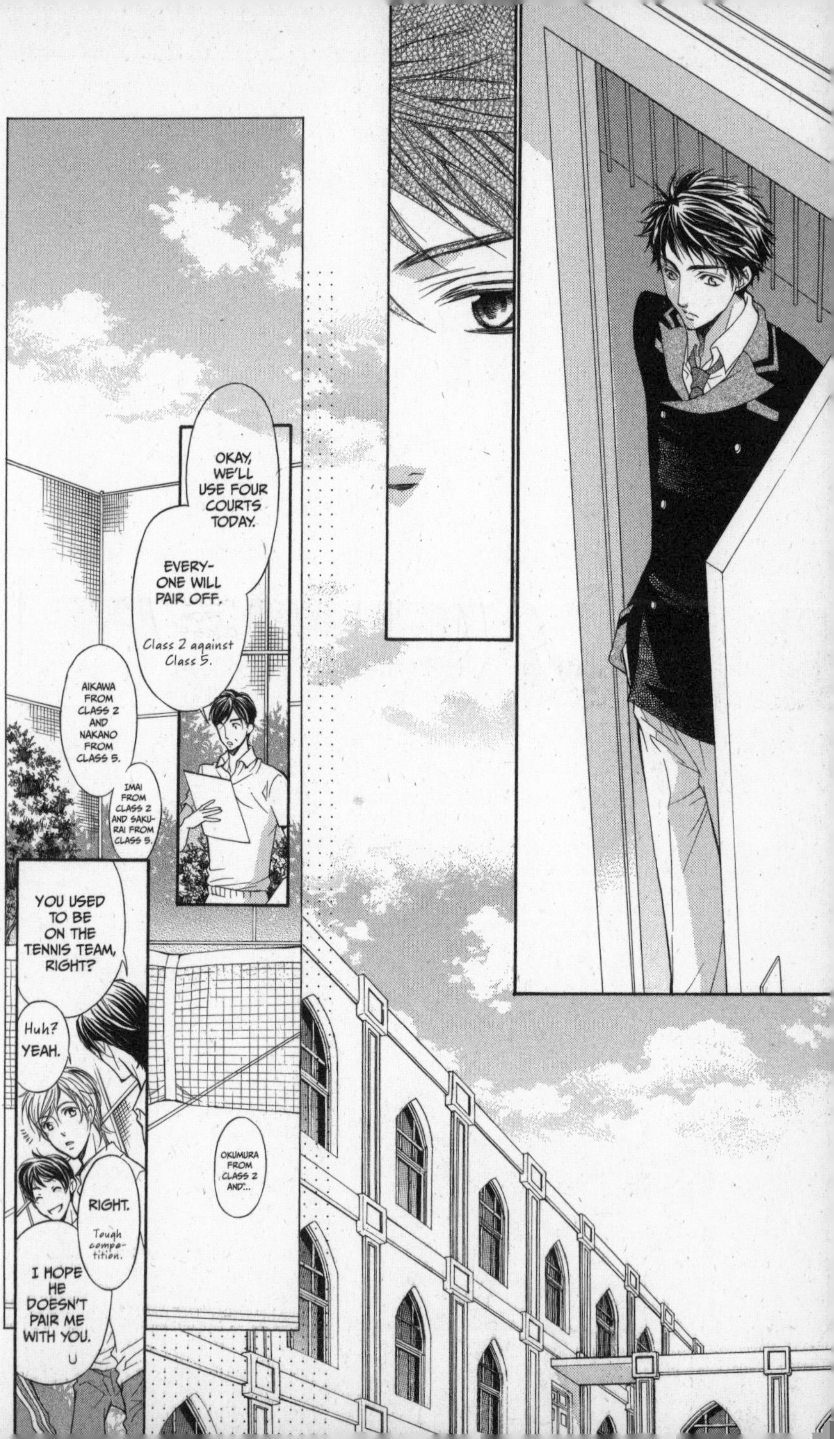
OKAY, WE'LL USE FOUR COURTS TODAY.
EVERY-ONE WILL PAIR OFF.
Class 2 against Class 5.
AIKAWA FROM CLASS 2 AND NAKANO FROM CLASS 5.
IMAI FROM CLASS 2 AND SAKU-RAI FROM CLASS 5.
OKUMURA FROM CLASS 2 AND...
YOU USED TO BE ON THE TENNIS TEAM, RIGHT?
Huh? YEAH.
RIGHT.
Tough compe-tition.
I HOPE HE DOESN'T PAIR ME WITH YOU.

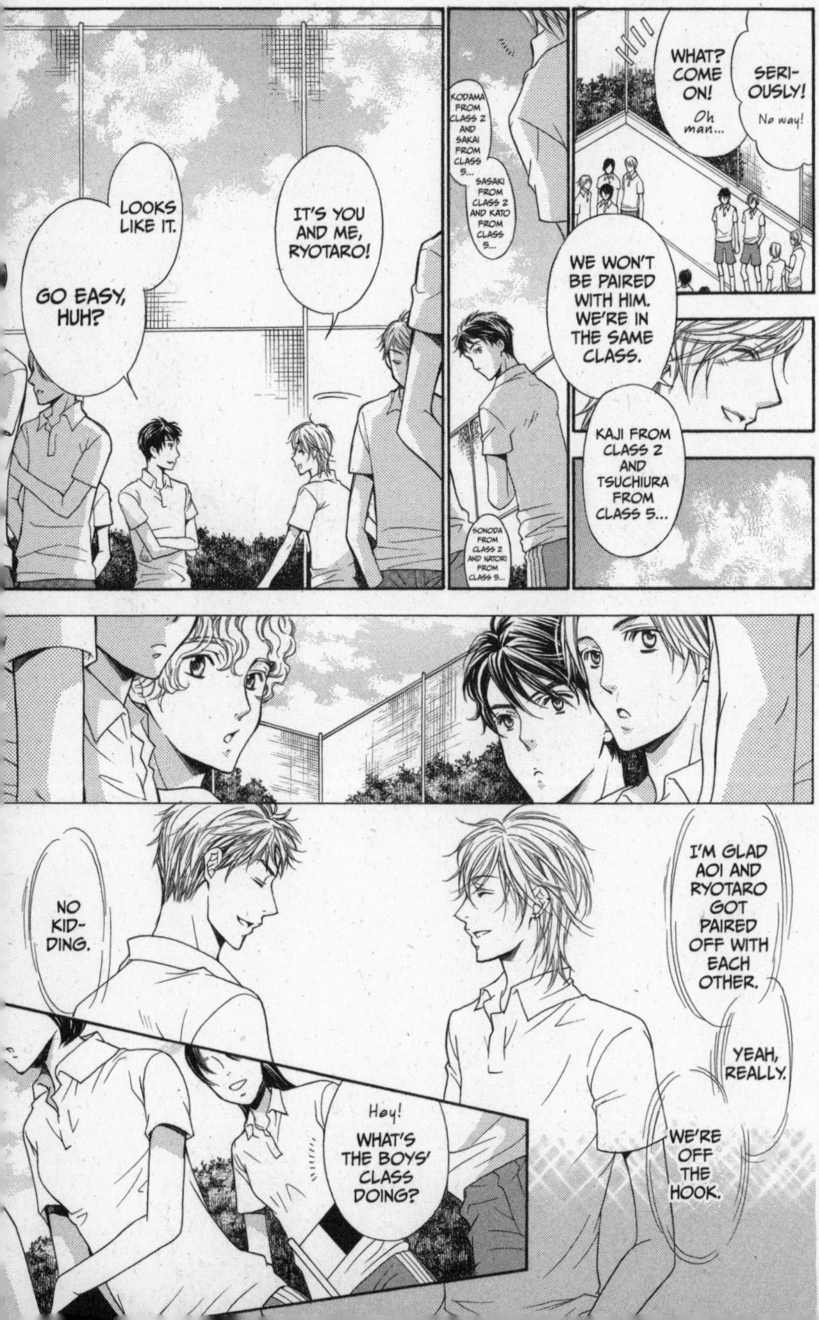
SERI-OUSLY!
No way!
WHAT? COME ON!
Oh man...
KAJI FROM CLASS 2 AND TSUCHIURA FROM CLASS 5...
KODAMA FROM CLASS 2 AND SAKAI FROM CLASS 5...
SASAKI FROM CLASS 2 AND KATO FROM CLASS 5...
WE WON'T BE PAIRED WITH HIM. WE'RE IN THE SAME CLASS.
SONODA FROM CLASS 2 AND NATORI FROM CLASS 5...
IT'S YOU AND ME, RYOTARO!
LOOKS LIKE IT.
GO EASY, HUH?
I'M GLAD AOI AND RYOTARO GOT PAIRED OFF WITH EACH OTHER.
NO KID-DING.
YEAH, REALLY.
WE'RE OFF THE HOOK.
Hey!
WHAT'S THE BOYS' CLASS DOING?

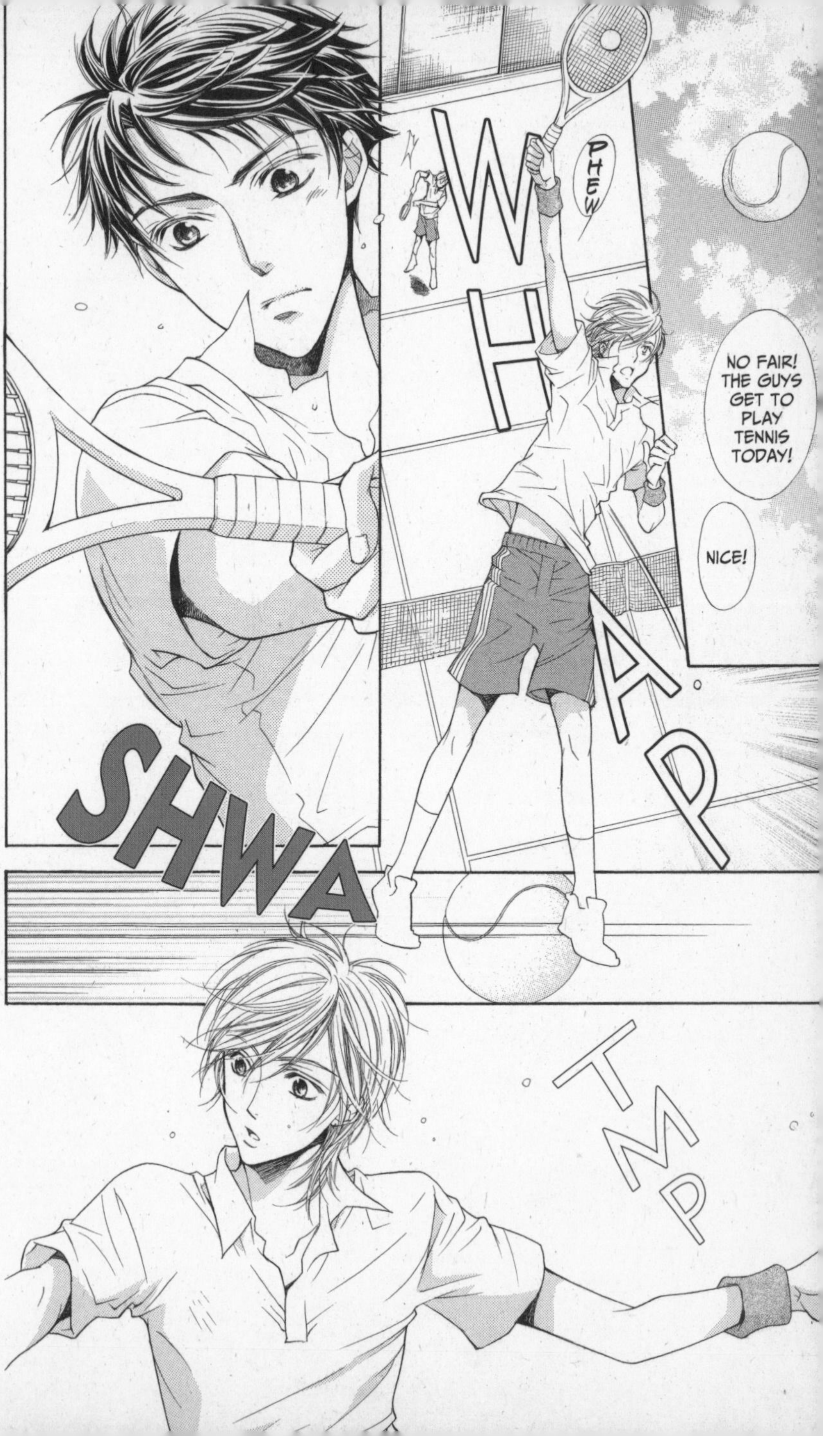
NO FAIR! THE GUYS GET TO PLAY TENNIS TODAY!
NICE!
PHEW
WHAP
SHWA
TMP

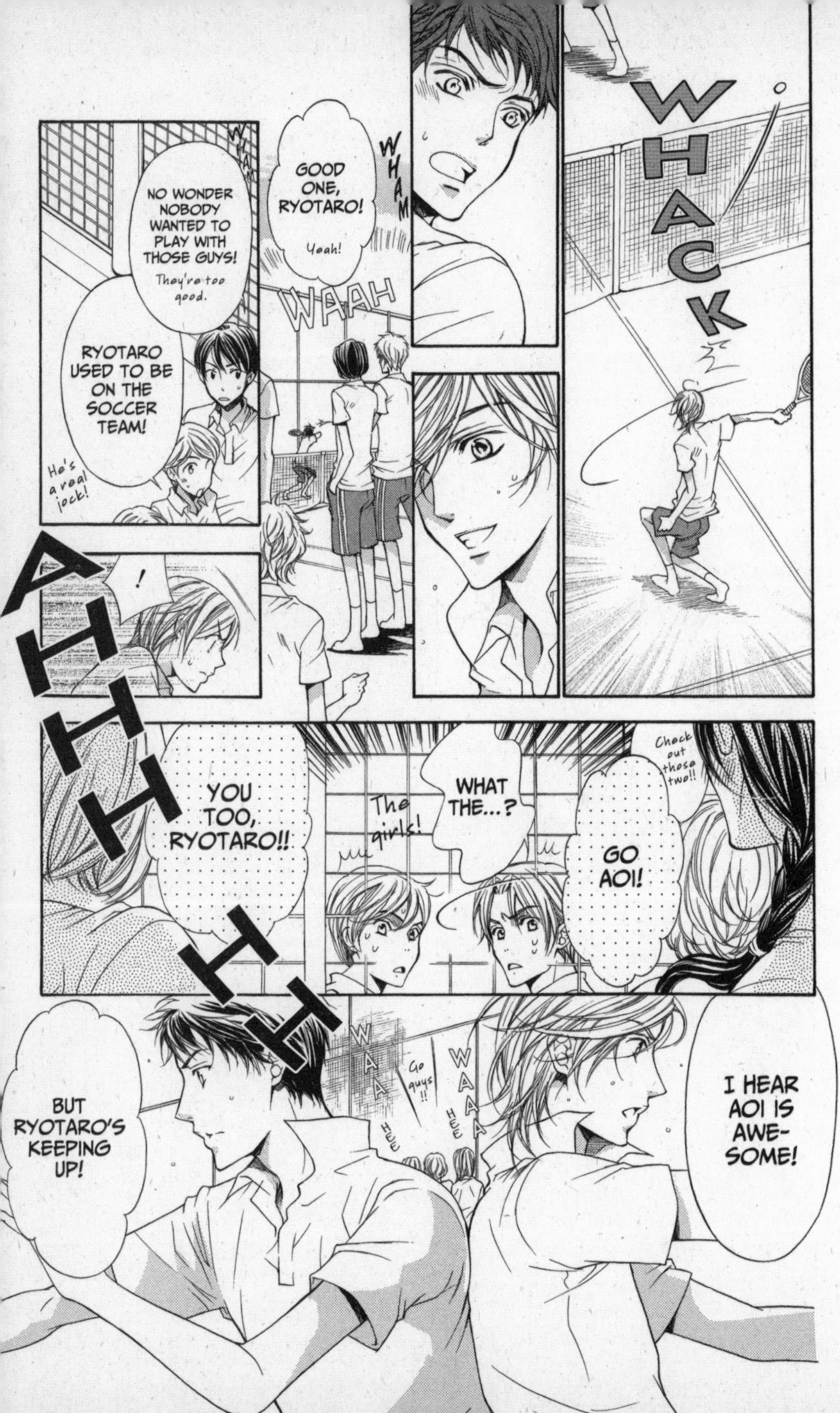
WHACK
WHAM
GOOD ONE, RYOTARO!
Yeah!
WHAM
NO WONDER NOBODY WANTED TO PLAY WITH THOSE GUYS!
They're too good.
RYOTARO USED TO BE ON THE SOCCER TEAM!
He's a real jock!
WAAH
AHHHH
!
Check out those two!!
GO AOI!
WHAT THE...?
The girls!
YOU TOO, RYOTARO!!
I HEAR AOI IS AWE-SOME!
WAAA
HEE
Go guys!!
WAAA
HEE
BUT RYOTARO'S KEEPING UP!

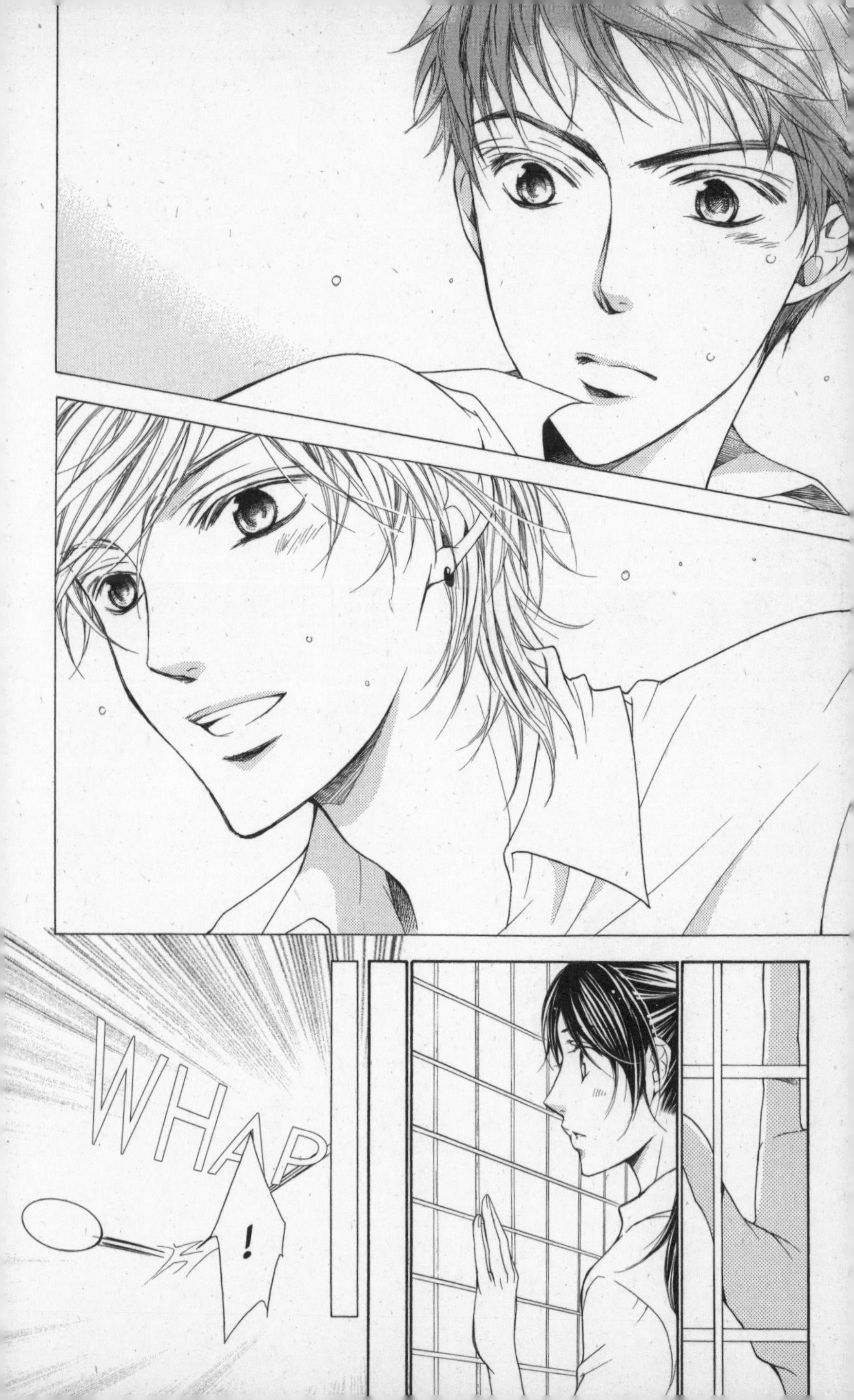
WHAP
!

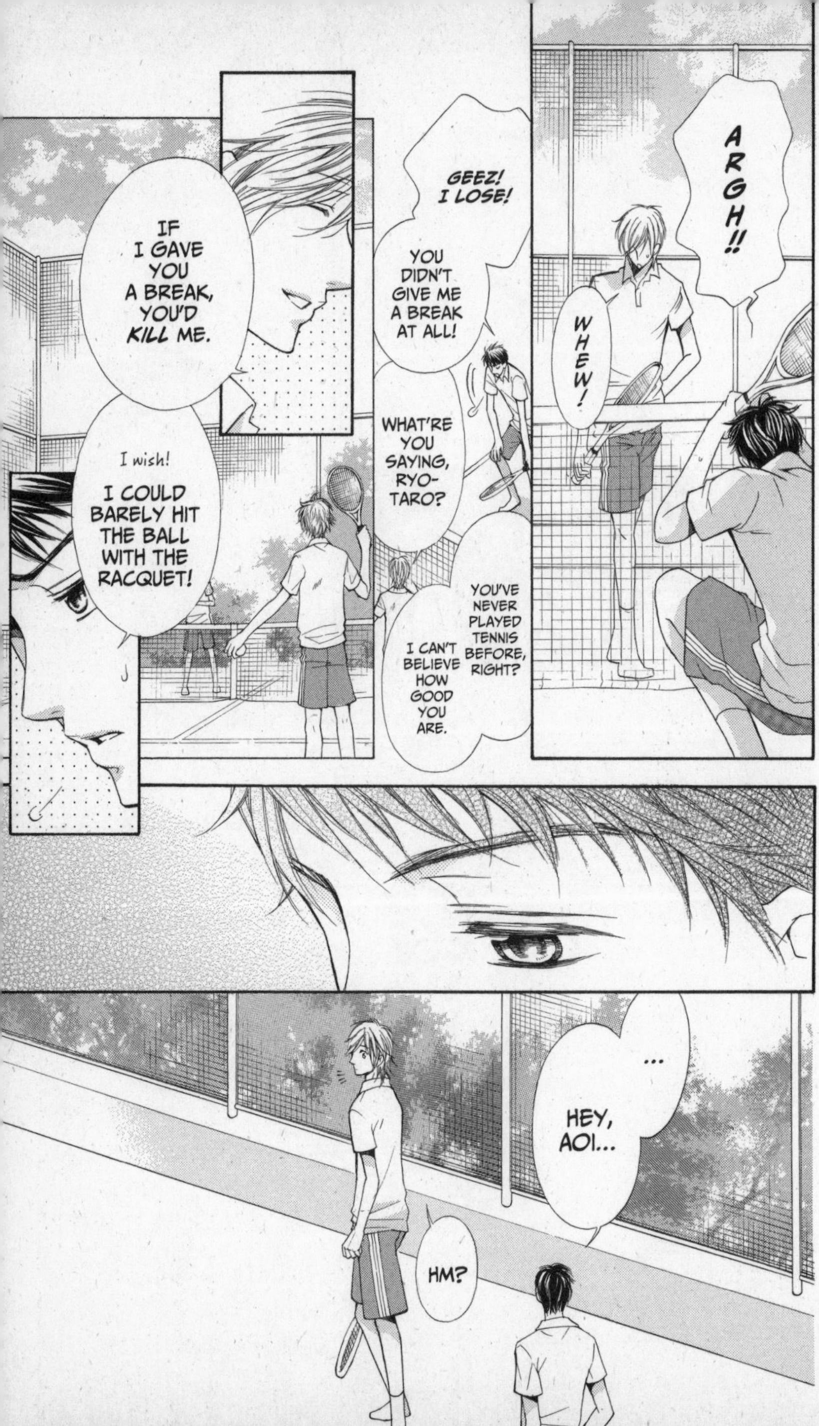
ARGH!!
WHEW!
GEEZ! I LOSE!
YOU DIDN'T GIVE ME A BREAK AT ALL!
WHAT'RE YOU SAYING, RYO-TARO?
YOU'VE NEVER PLAYED TENNIS BEFORE, RIGHT?
I CAN'T BELIEVE HOW GOOD YOU ARE.
IF I GAVE YOU A BREAK, YOU'D *KILL* ME.
I wish!
I COULD BARELY HIT THE BALL WITH THE RACQUET!
...
HEY, AOI...
HM?

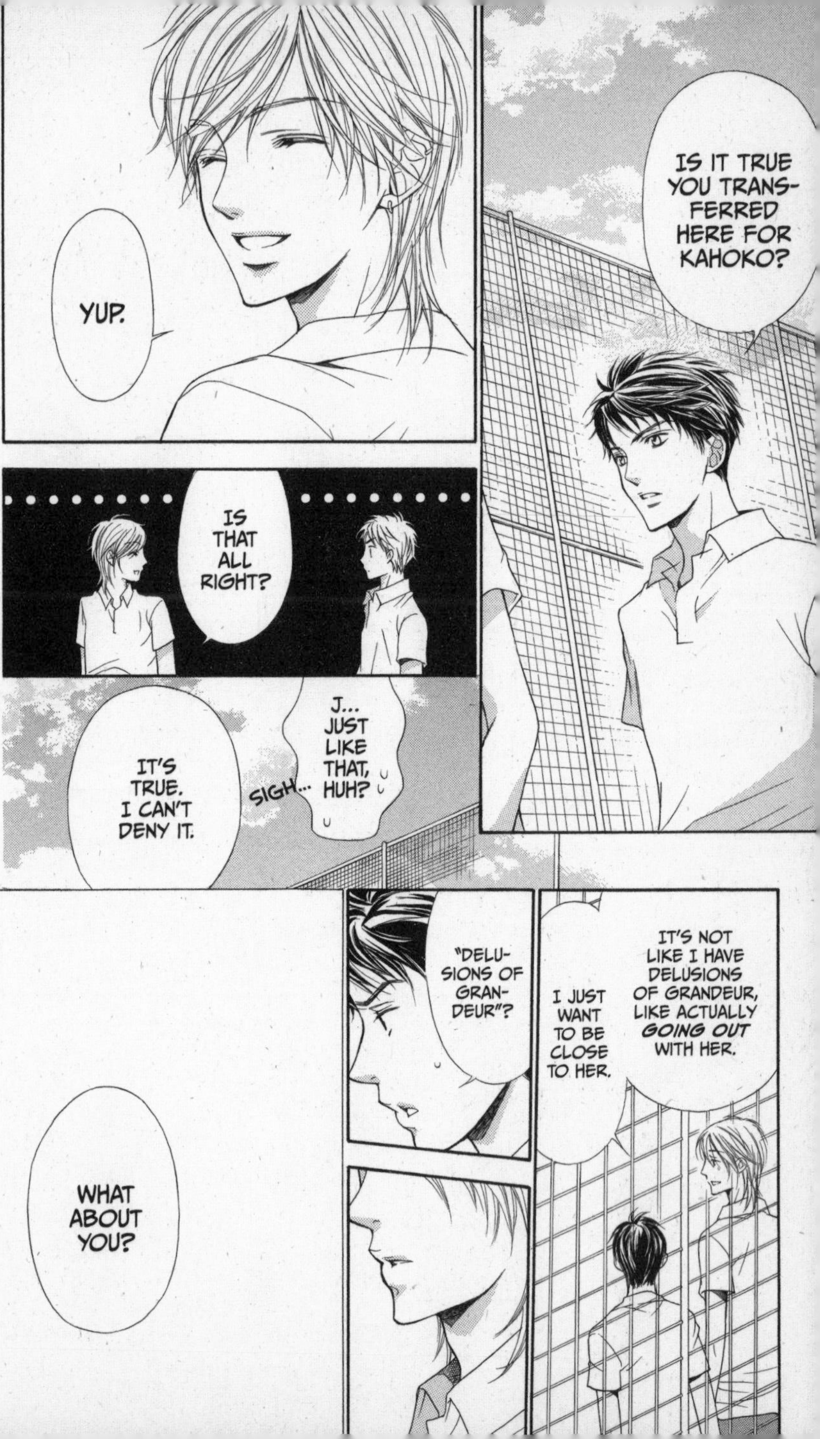
IS IT TRUE YOU TRANSFERRED HERE FOR KAHOKO?
YUP.
IS THAT ALL RIGHT?
J... JUST LIKE THAT, HUH?
SIGH...
IT'S TRUE. I CAN'T DENY IT.
IT'S NOT LIKE I HAVE DELUSIONS OF GRANDEUR, LIKE ACTUALLY *GOING OUT* WITH HER.
I JUST WANT TO BE CLOSE TO HER.
"DELUSIONS OF GRANDEUR"?
WHAT ABOUT YOU?

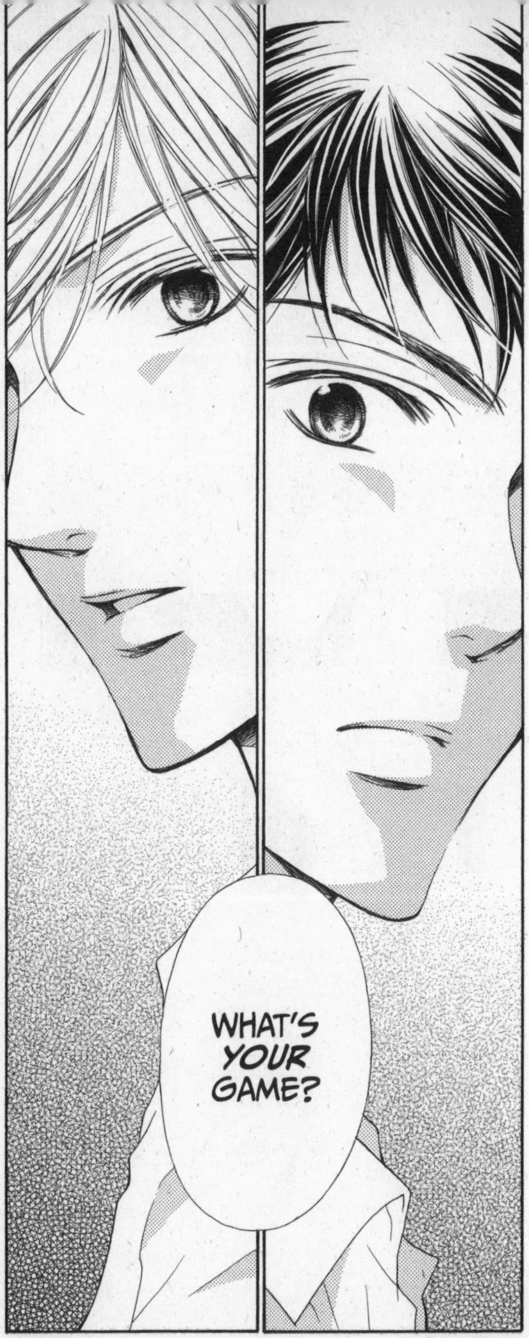
WHAT'S YOUR GAME?
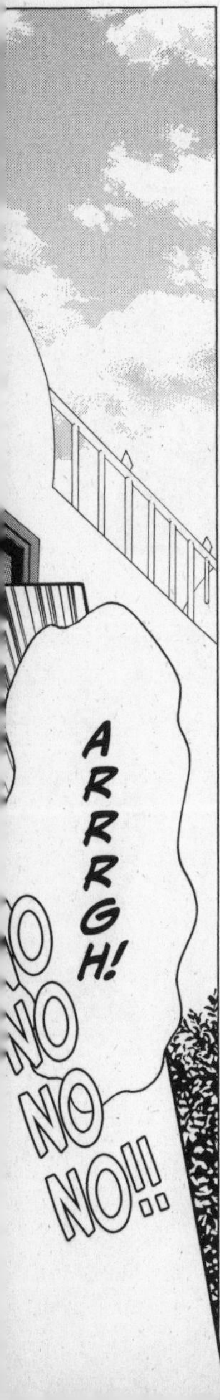
ARRRGH!
NO NO NO NO!!

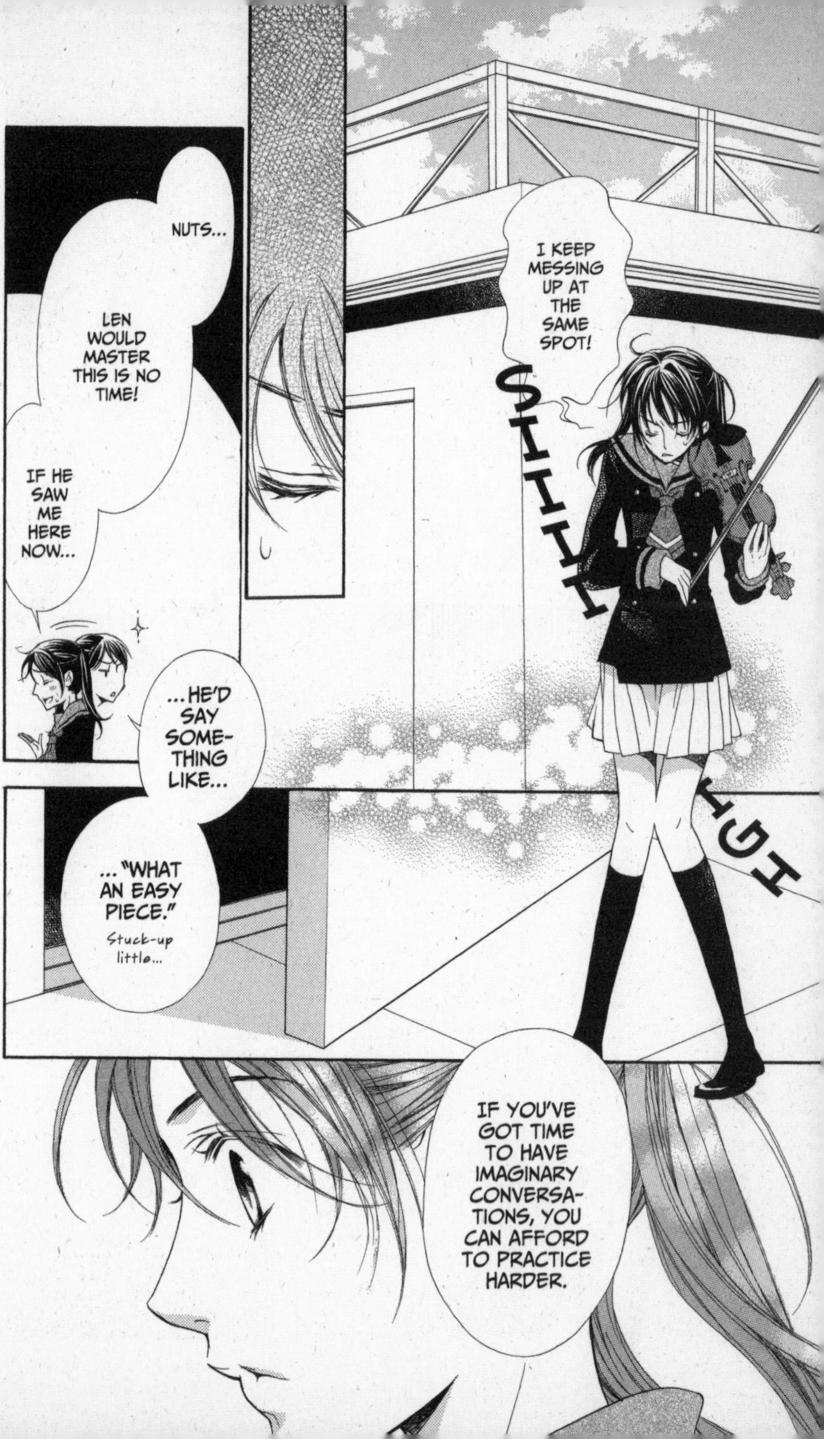
I KEEP MESSING UP AT THE SAME SPOT!
SIIIIIGH
NUTS...
LEN WOULD MASTER THIS IS NO TIME!
IF HE SAW ME HERE NOW...
...HE'D SAY SOME-THING LIKE...
..."WHAT AN EASY PIECE."
Stuck-up little...
IF YOU'VE GOT TIME TO HAVE IMAGINARY CONVERSA-TIONS, YOU CAN AFFORD TO PRACTICE HARDER.

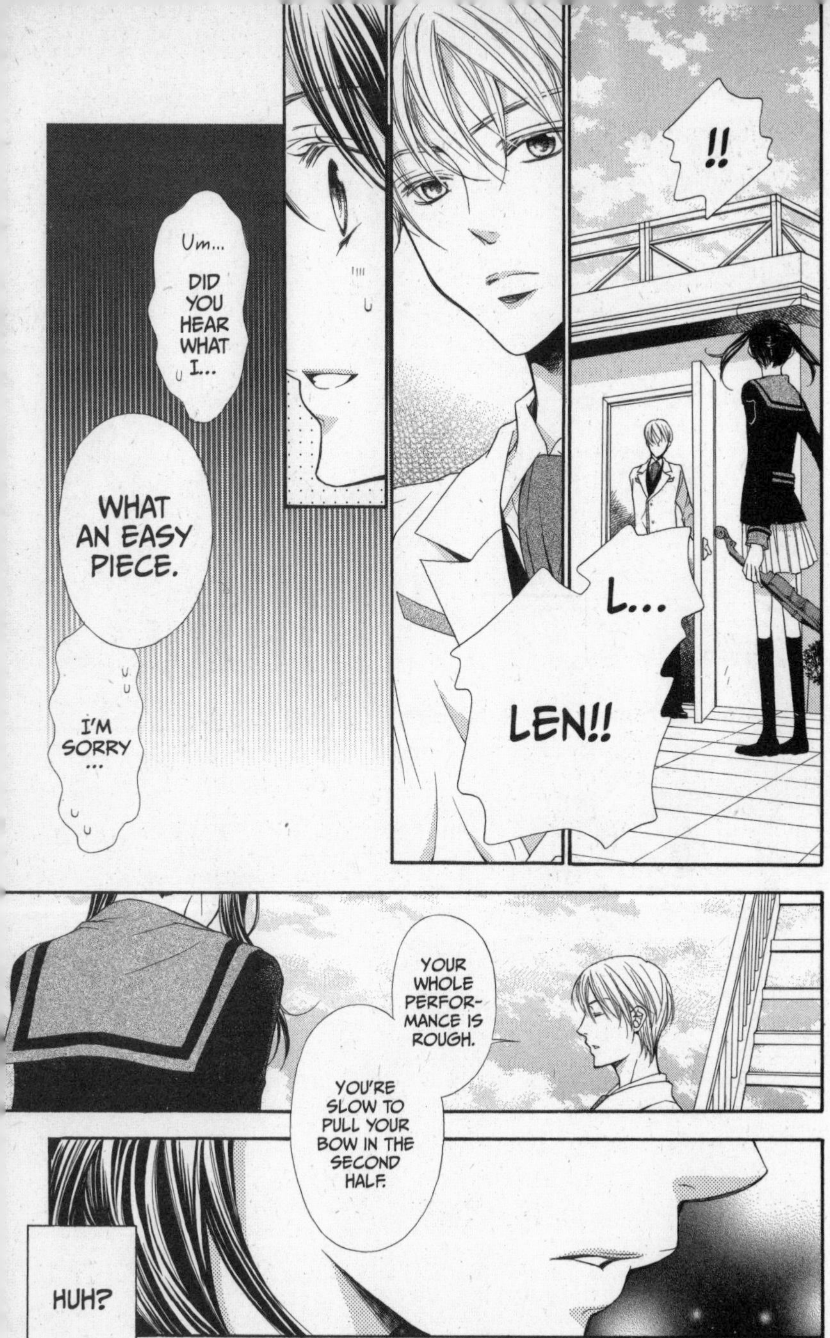
!!
L...
LEN!!
Um... DID YOU HEAR WHAT I...
WHAT AN EASY PIECE.
I'M SORRY...
YOUR WHOLE PERFORMANCE IS ROUGH.
YOU'RE SLOW TO PULL YOUR BOW IN THE SECOND HALF.
HUH?

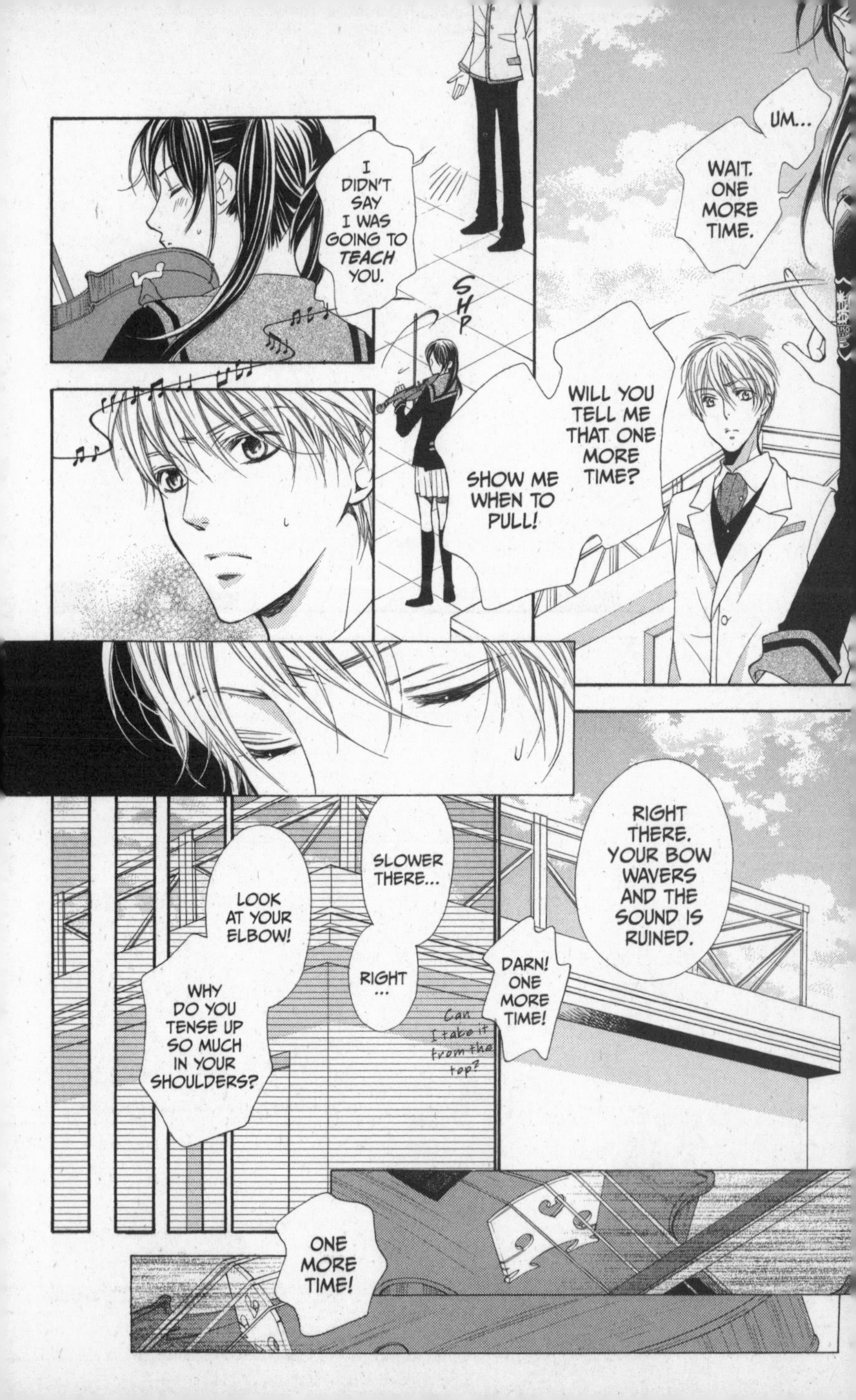
UM...
WAIT. ONE MORE TIME.
WILL YOU TELL ME THAT ONE MORE TIME?
I DIDN'T SAY I WAS GOING TO *TEACH* YOU.
SHP
SHOW ME WHEN TO PULL!
RIGHT THERE. YOUR BOW WAVERS AND THE SOUND IS RUINED.
SLOWER THERE...
LOOK AT YOUR ELBOW!
DARN! ONE MORE TIME!
Can I take it from the top?
RIGHT...
WHY DO YOU TENSE UP SO MUCH IN YOUR SHOULDERS?
ONE MORE TIME!

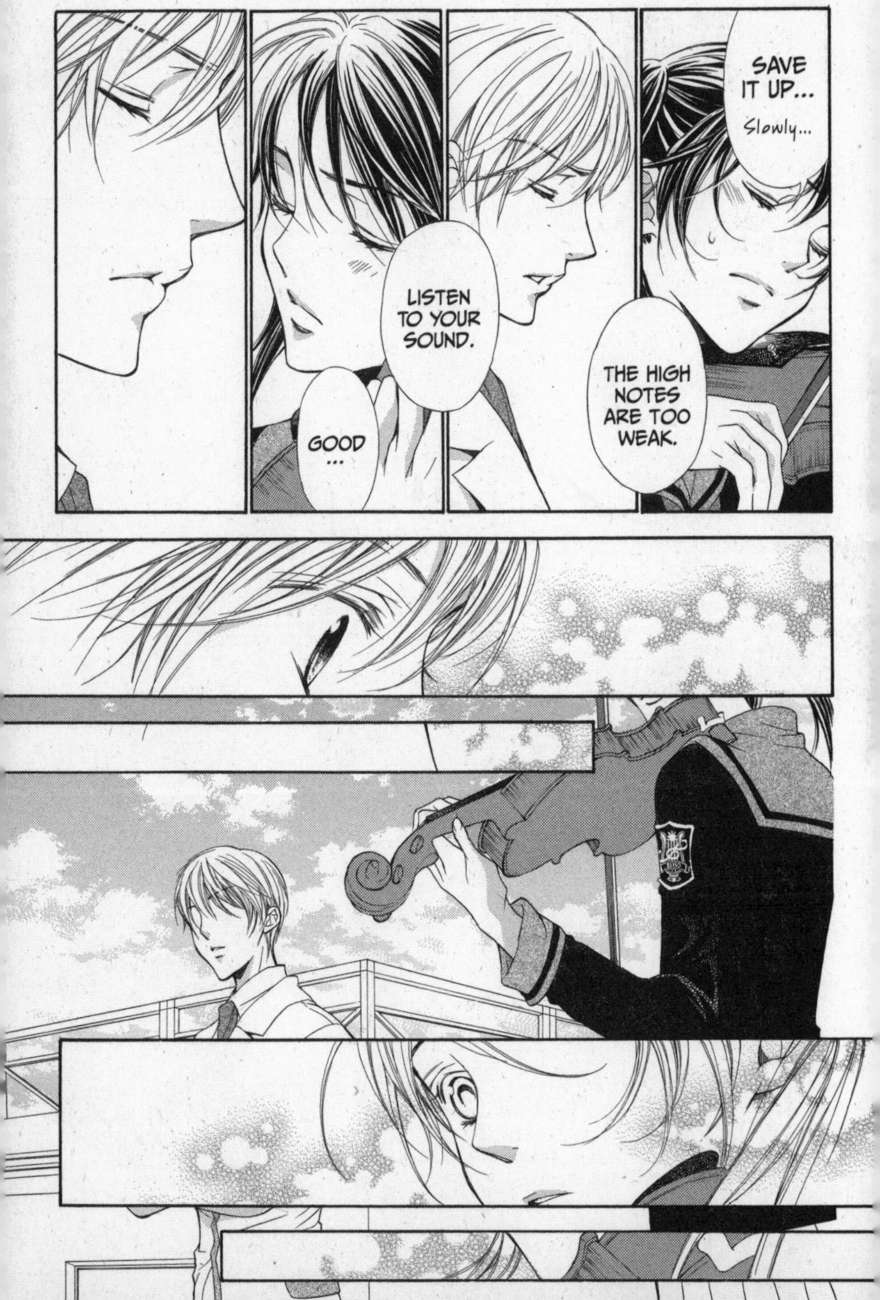
SAVE IT UP...
Slowly...
THE HIGH NOTES ARE TOO WEAK.
LISTEN TO YOUR SOUND.
GOOD ...

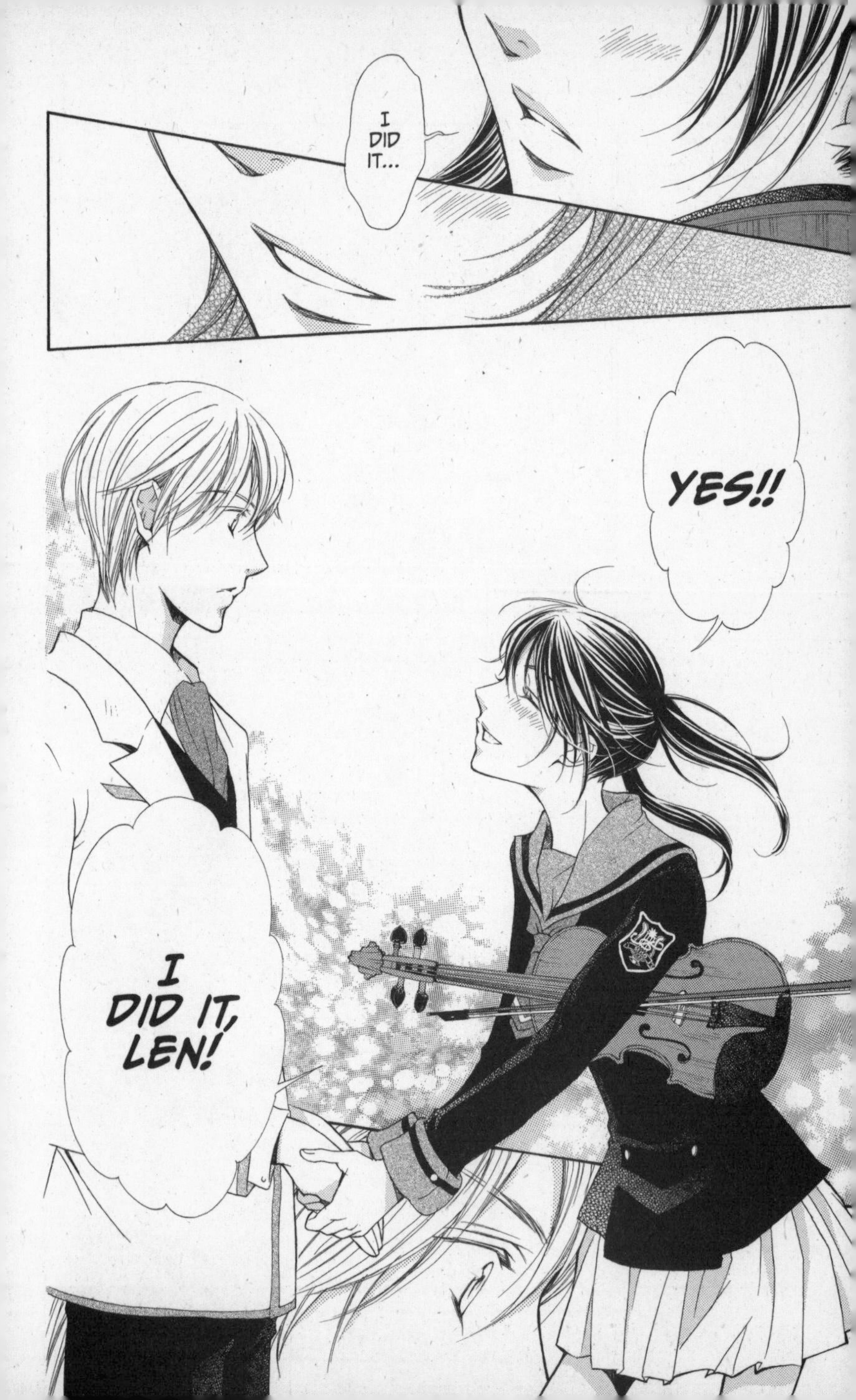
I DID IT...
YES!!
I DID IT, LEN!

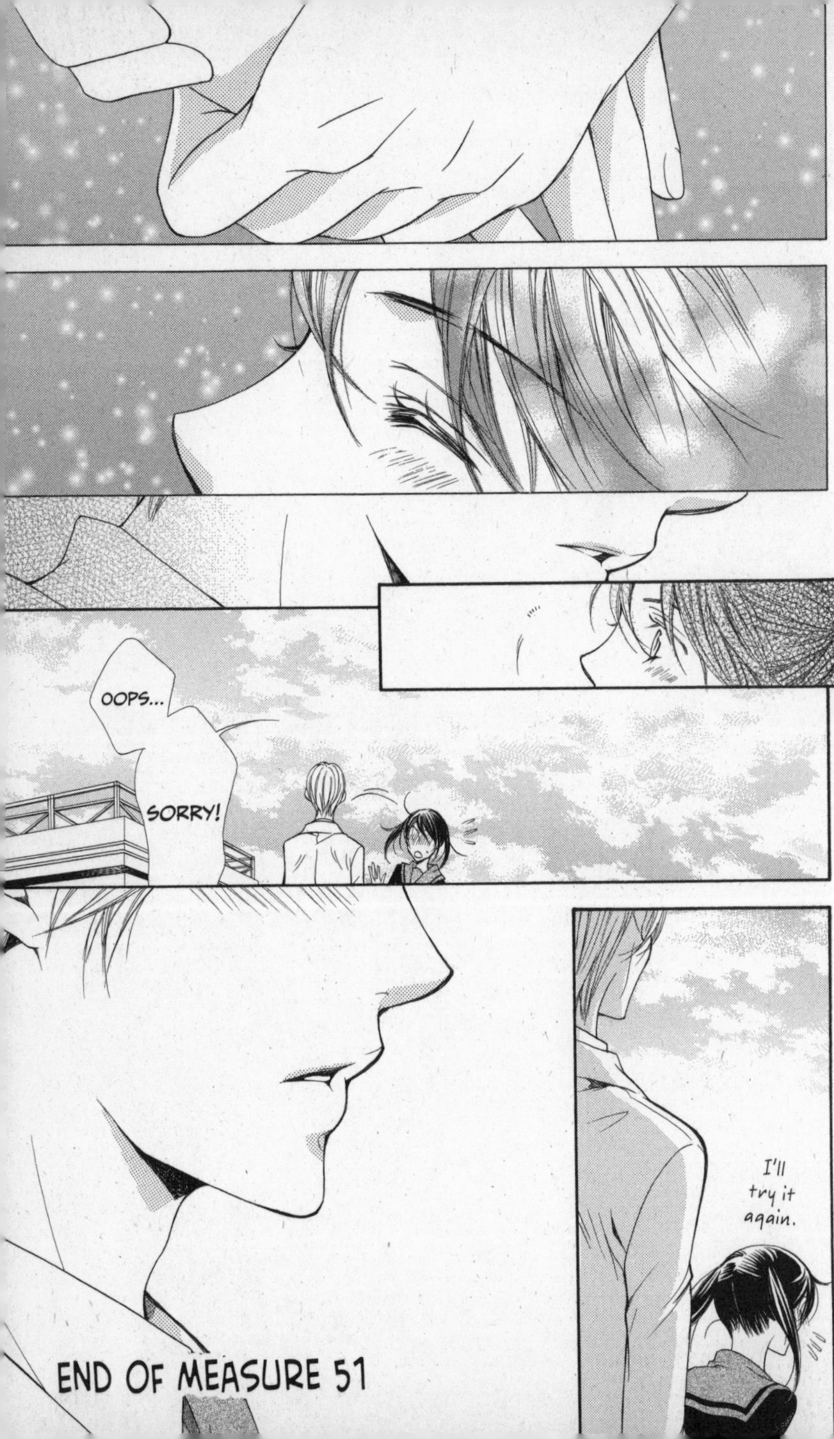
OOPS...
SORRY!
I'll try it again.
END OF MEASURE 51

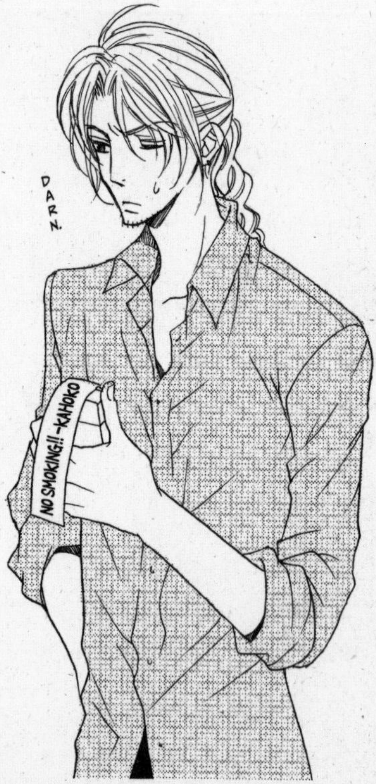
DARN.
NO SMOKING!! -KAHOKO

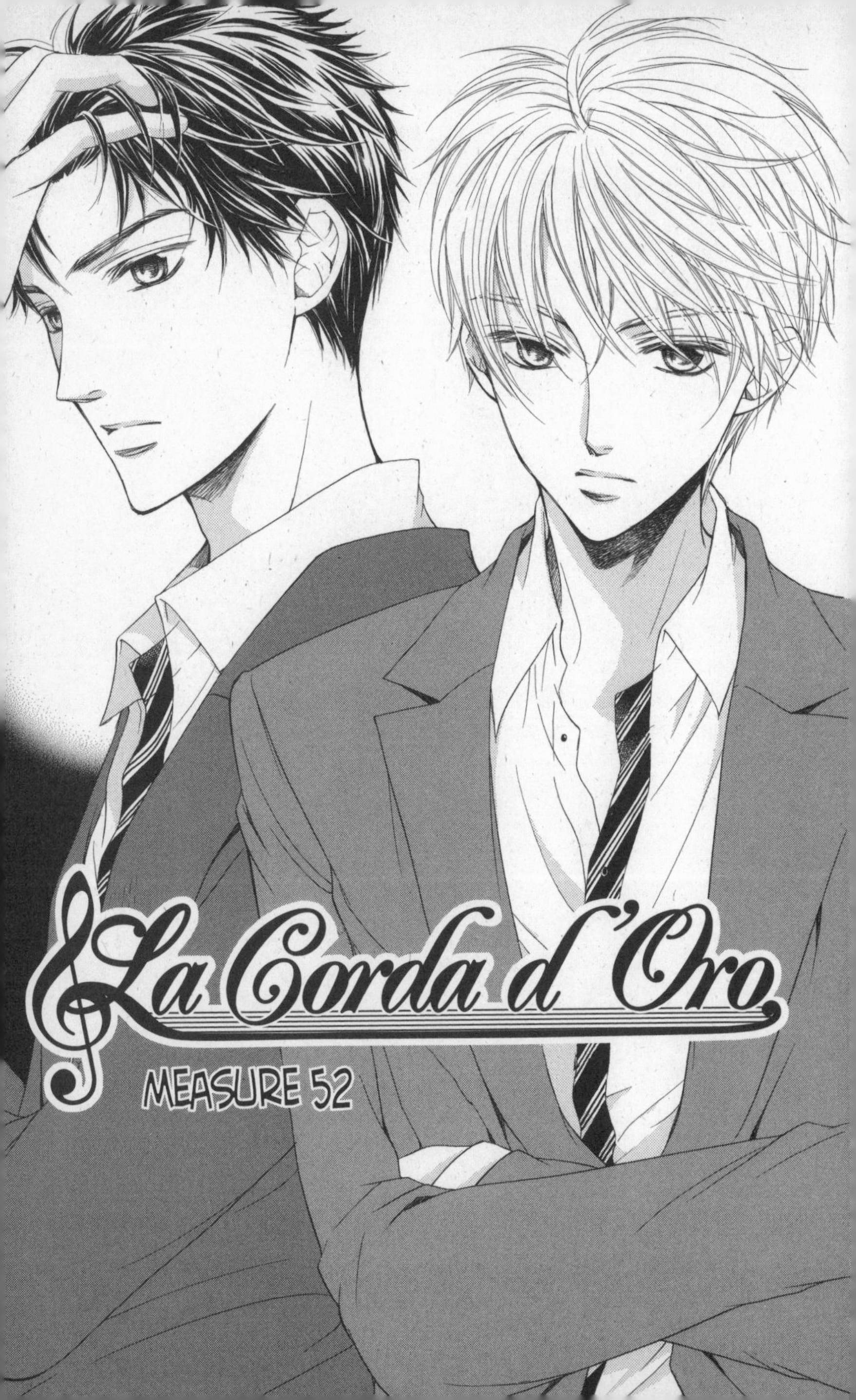
La Corda d'Oro
MEASURE 52

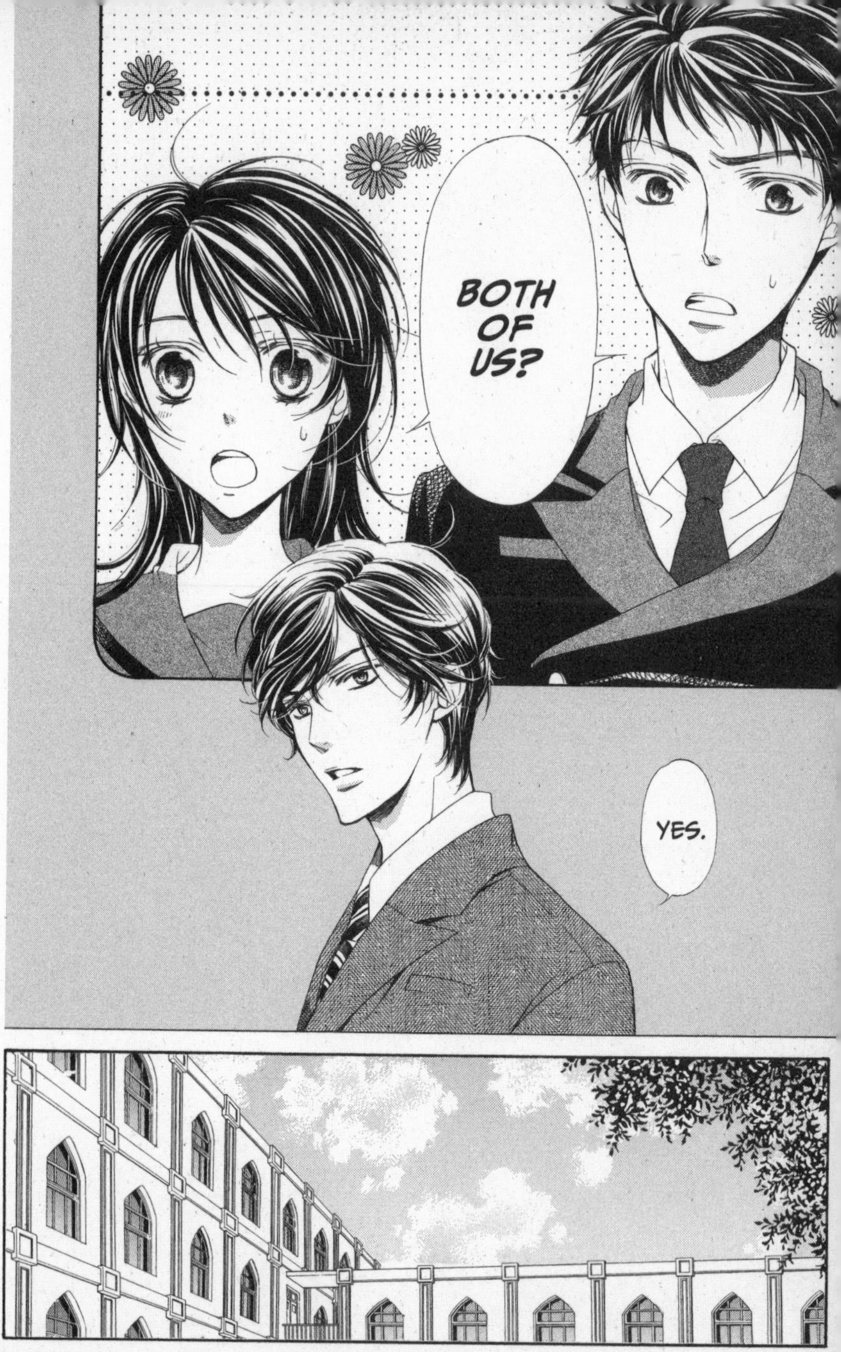
BOTH OF US?
YES.

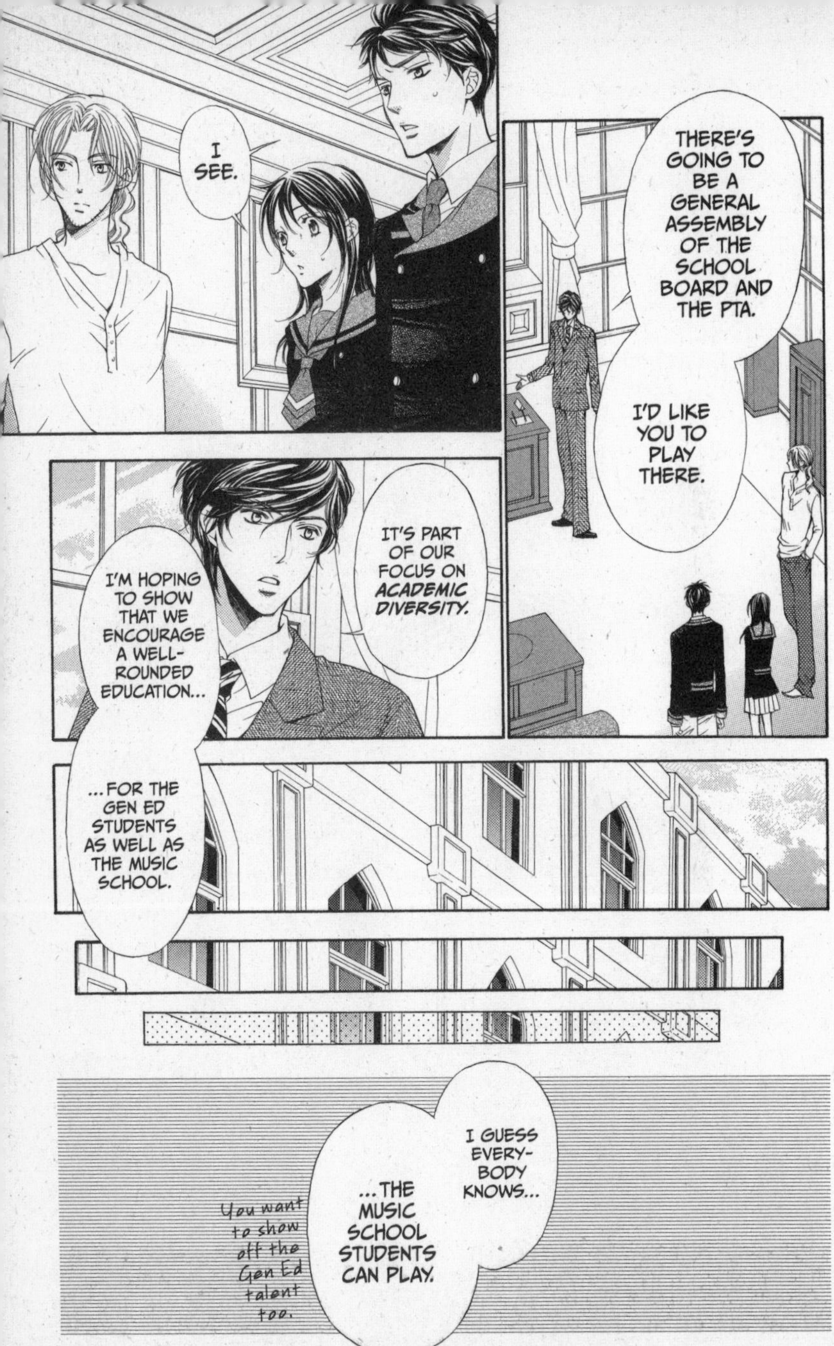
THERE'S GOING TO BE A GENERAL ASSEMBLY OF THE SCHOOL BOARD AND THE PTA.
I'D LIKE YOU TO PLAY THERE.
I SEE.
IT'S PART OF OUR FOCUS ON *ACADEMIC DIVERSITY.*
I'M HOPING TO SHOW THAT WE ENCOURAGE A WELL-ROUNDED EDUCATION...
...FOR THE GEN ED STUDENTS AS WELL AS THE MUSIC SCHOOL.
I GUESS EVERY-BODY KNOWS...
...THE MUSIC SCHOOL STUDENTS CAN PLAY.
You want to show off the Gen Ed talent too.

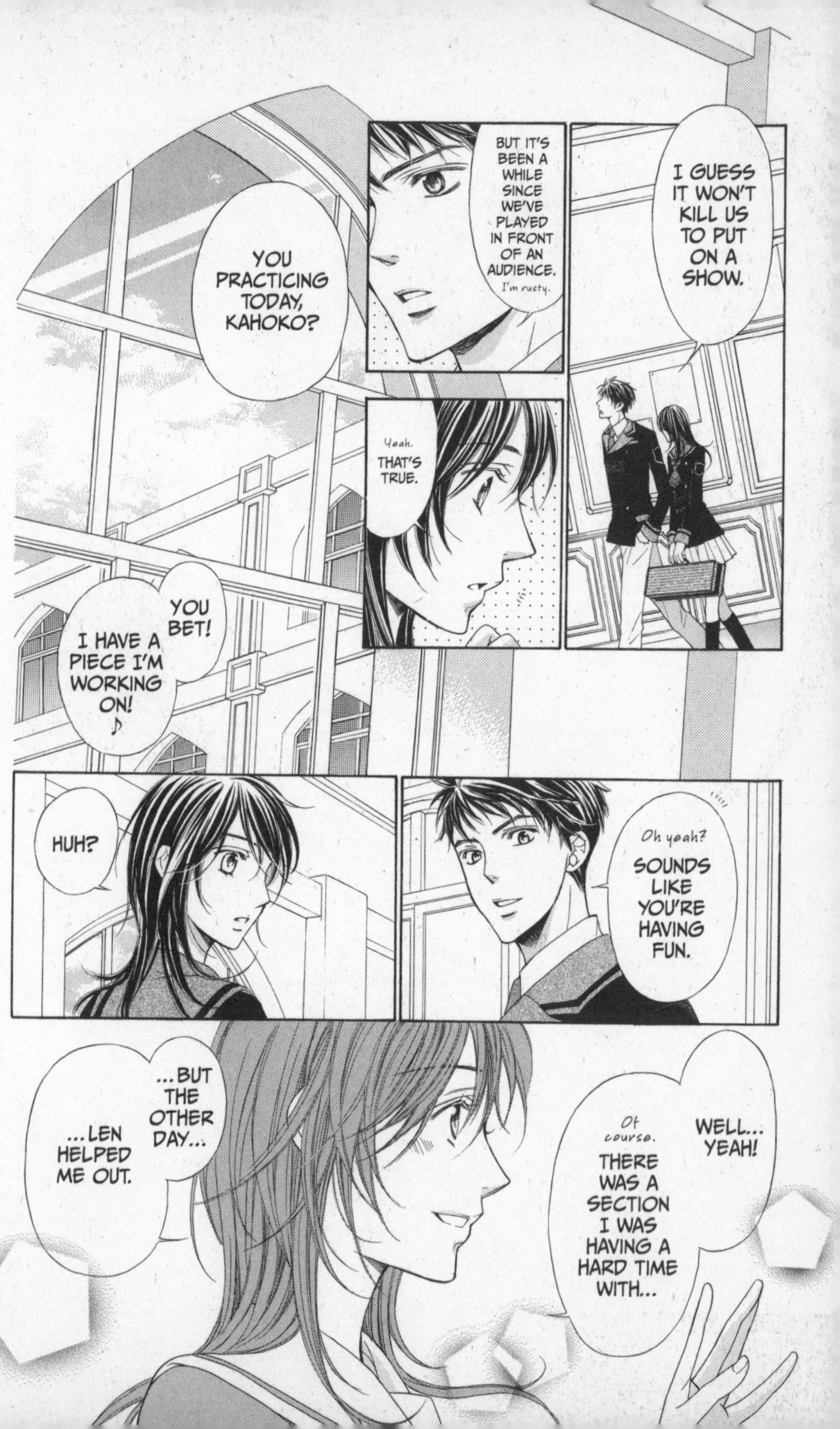
I GUESS IT WON'T KILL US TO PUT ON A SHOW.
BUT IT'S BEEN A WHILE SINCE WE'VE PLAYED IN FRONT OF AN AUDIENCE. I'm rusty.
Yeah. THAT'S TRUE.
YOU PRACTICING TODAY, KAHOKO?
YOU BET! I HAVE A PIECE I'M WORKING ON! ♪
Oh yeah? SOUNDS LIKE YOU'RE HAVING FUN.
HUH?
WELL... YEAH!
Of course. THERE WAS A SECTION I WAS HAVING A HARD TIME WITH...
...BUT THE OTHER DAY...
...LEN HELPED ME OUT.

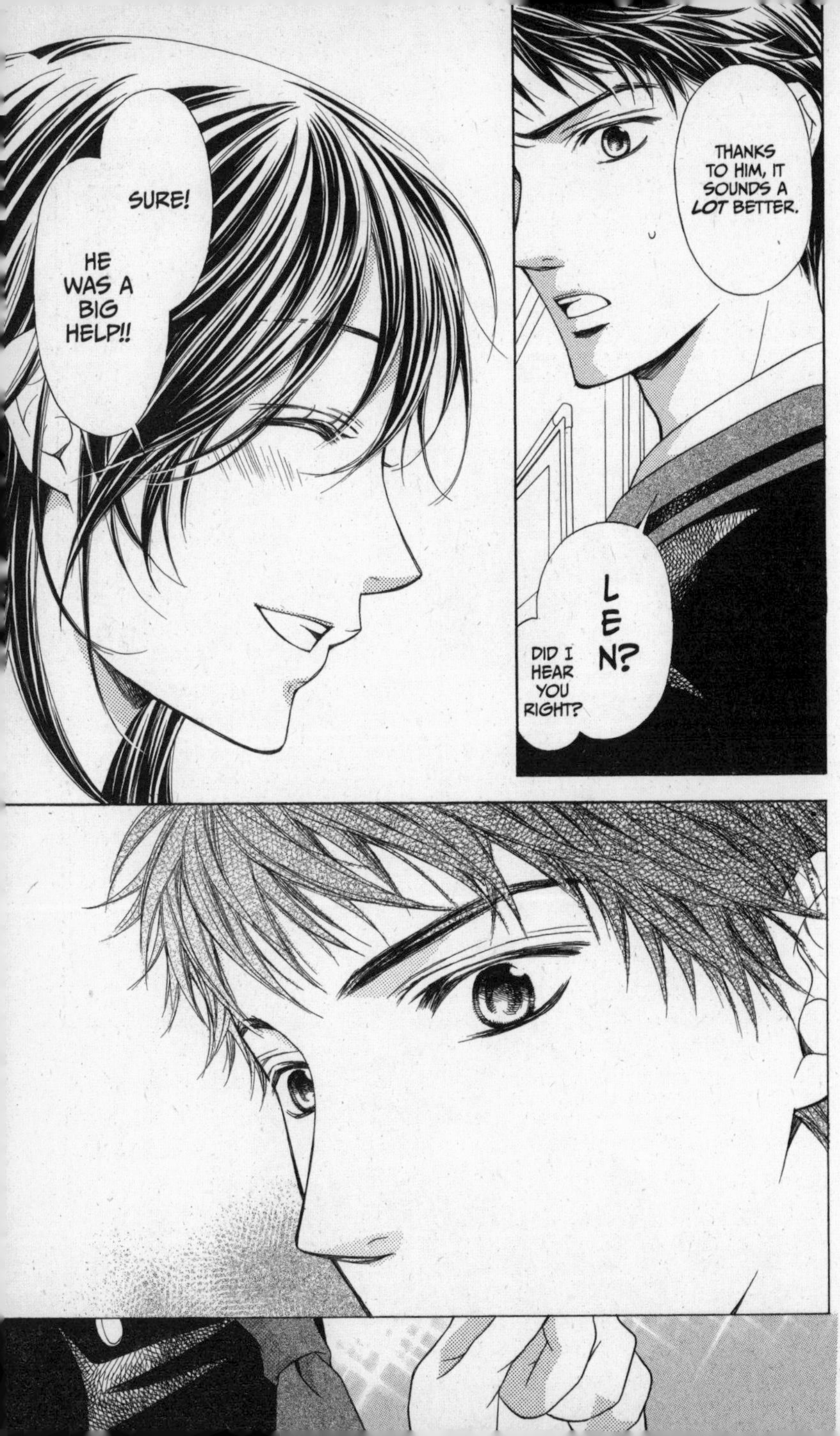
THANKS TO HIM, IT SOUNDS A *LOT* BETTER.
LEN?
DID I HEAR YOU RIGHT?
SURE!
HE WAS A BIG HELP!!

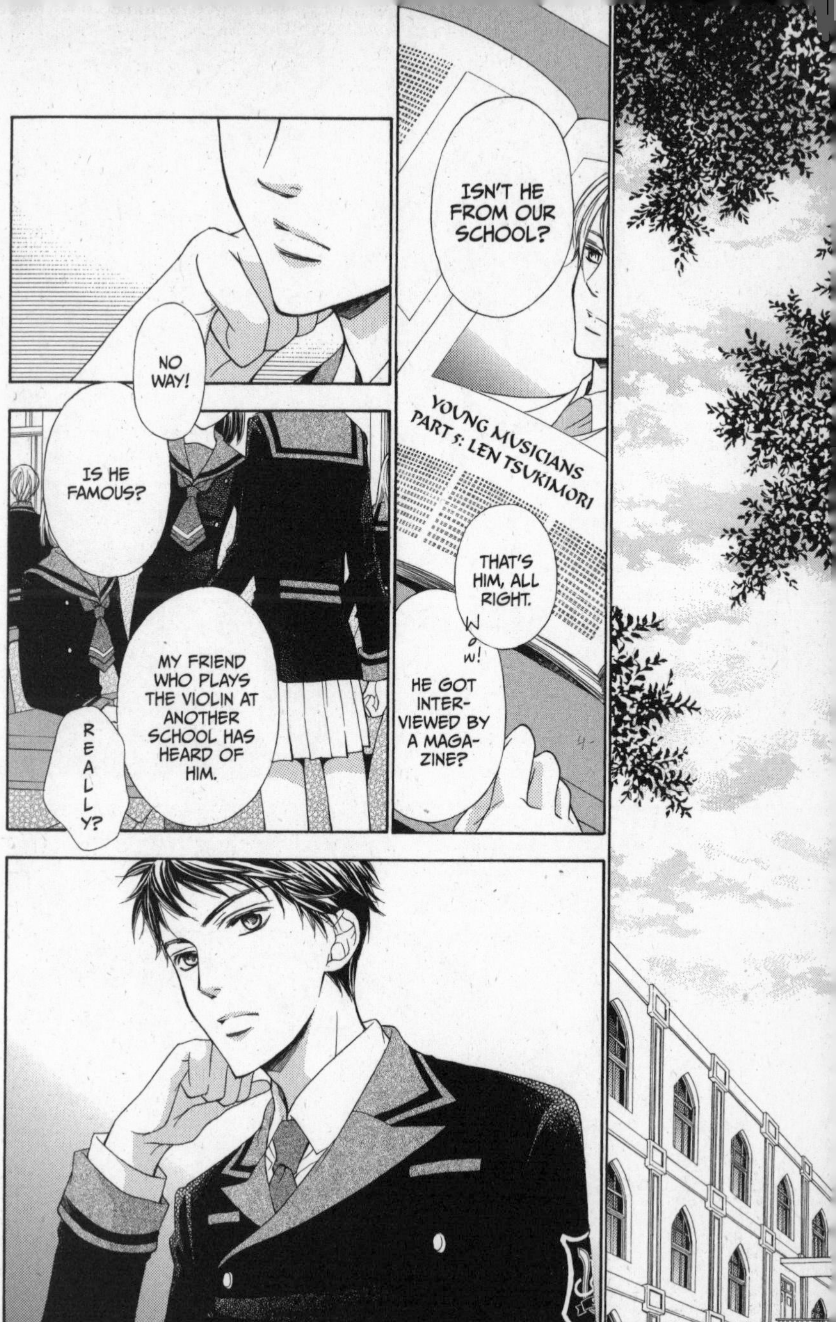
ISN'T HE FROM OUR SCHOOL?
YOUNG MUSICIANS PART 5: LEN TSUKIMORI
THAT'S HIM, ALL RIGHT.
WOW!
HE GOT INTERVIEWED BY A MAGAZINE?
NO WAY!
IS HE FAMOUS?
MY FRIEND WHO PLAYS THE VIOLIN AT ANOTHER SCHOOL HAS HEARD OF HIM.
REALLY?

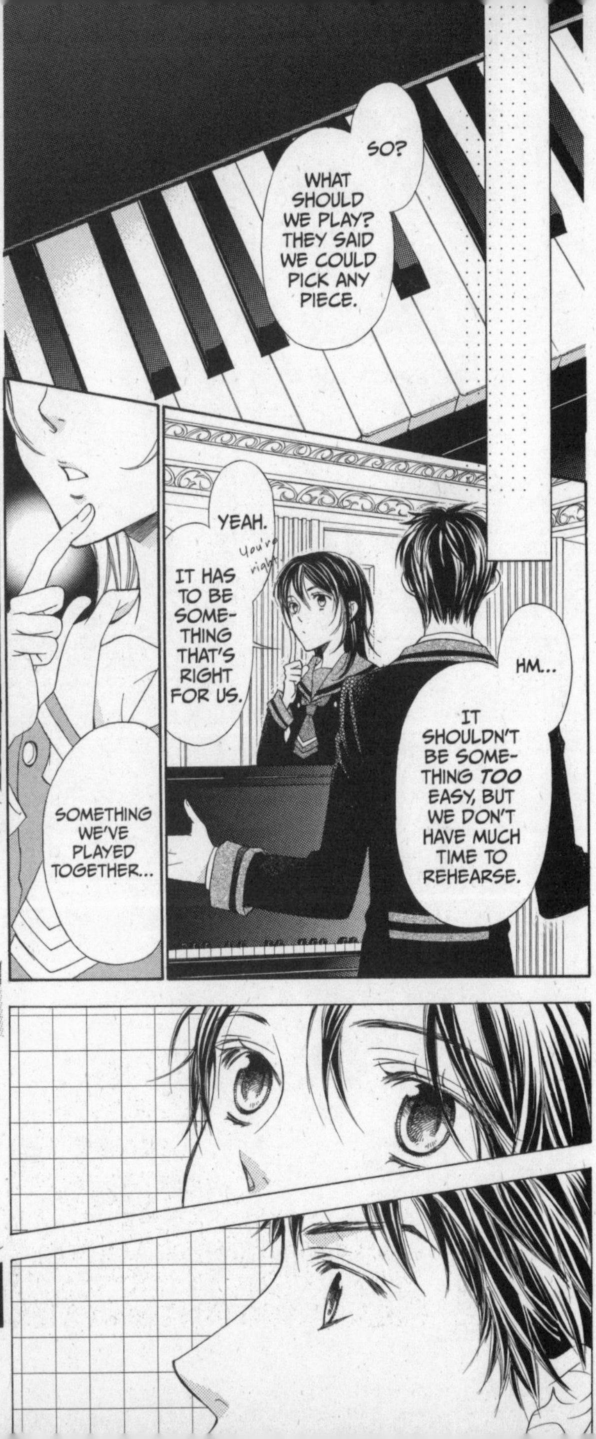
SO?
WHAT SHOULD WE PLAY? THEY SAID WE COULD PICK ANY PIECE.
HM...
IT SHOULDN'T BE SOMETHING *TOO* EASY, BUT WE DON'T HAVE MUCH TIME TO REHEARSE.
YEAH.
You're right
IT HAS TO BE SOMETHING THAT'S RIGHT FOR US.
SOMETHING WE'VE PLAYED TOGETHER...

Continuing from the last note...

The storyline about Kazuki getting into the entertainment business was in the video game (although it was a little different, I know), and I wanted to do it here. Kazuki can't say no to his family, especially his mother. He seems like the type who'll never go through a rebellious phase.

↓Here's Chairman Kira...

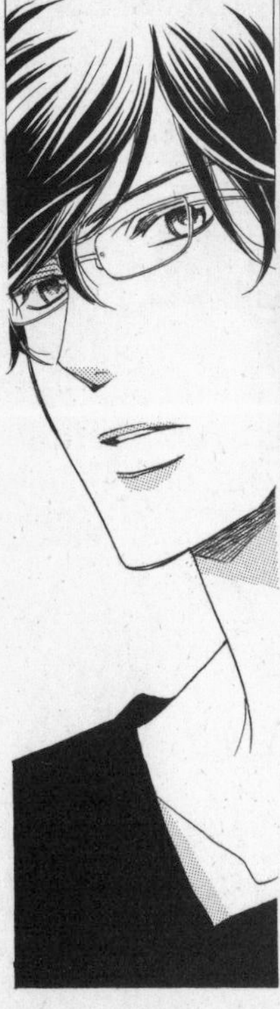

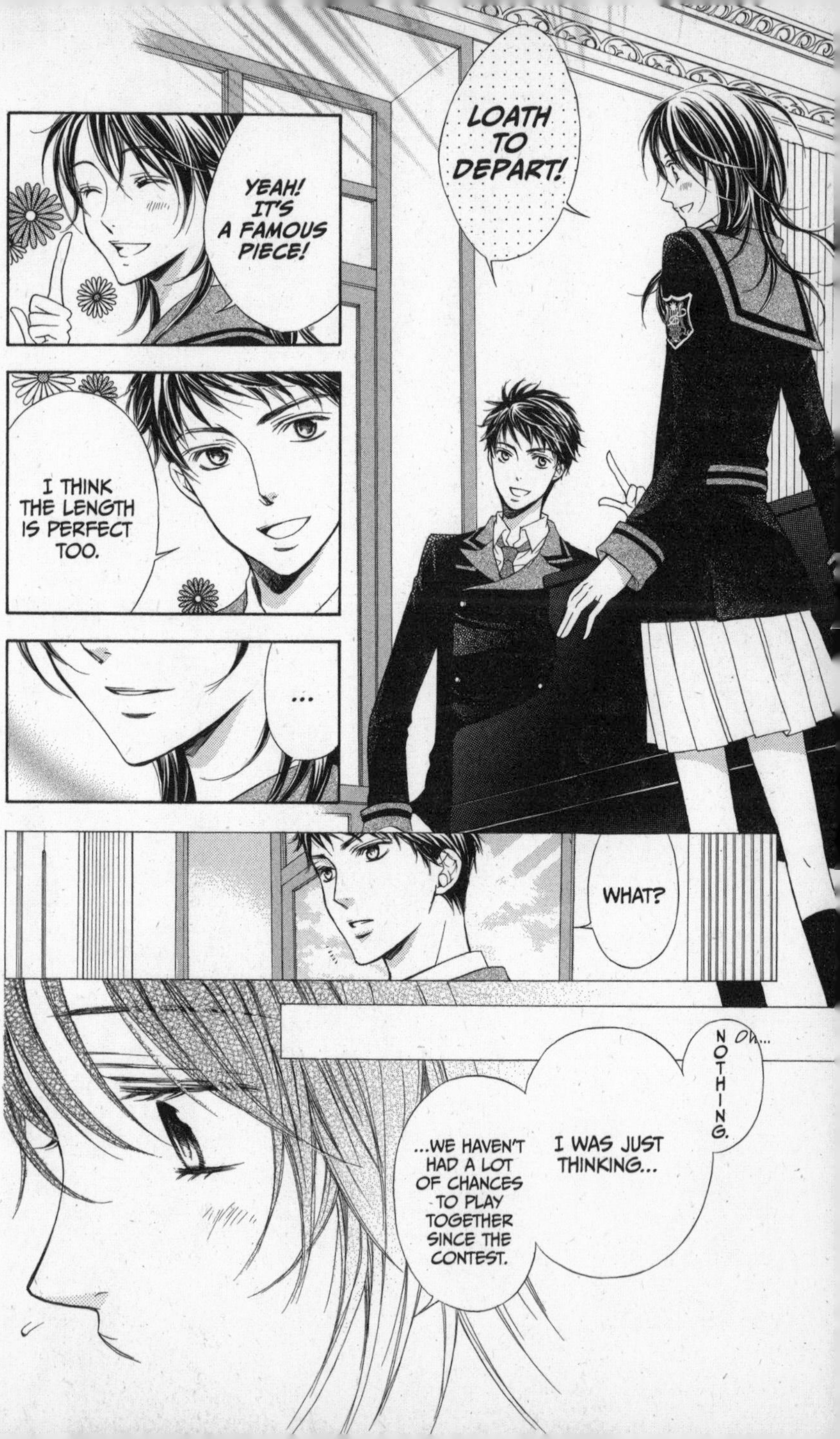
LOATH TO DEPART!
YEAH! IT'S A FAMOUS PIECE!
I THINK THE LENGTH IS PERFECT TOO.
...
WHAT?
Oh...
NOTHING.
I WAS JUST THINKING...
...WE HAVEN'T HAD A LOT OF CHANCES TO PLAY TOGETHER SINCE THE CONTEST.

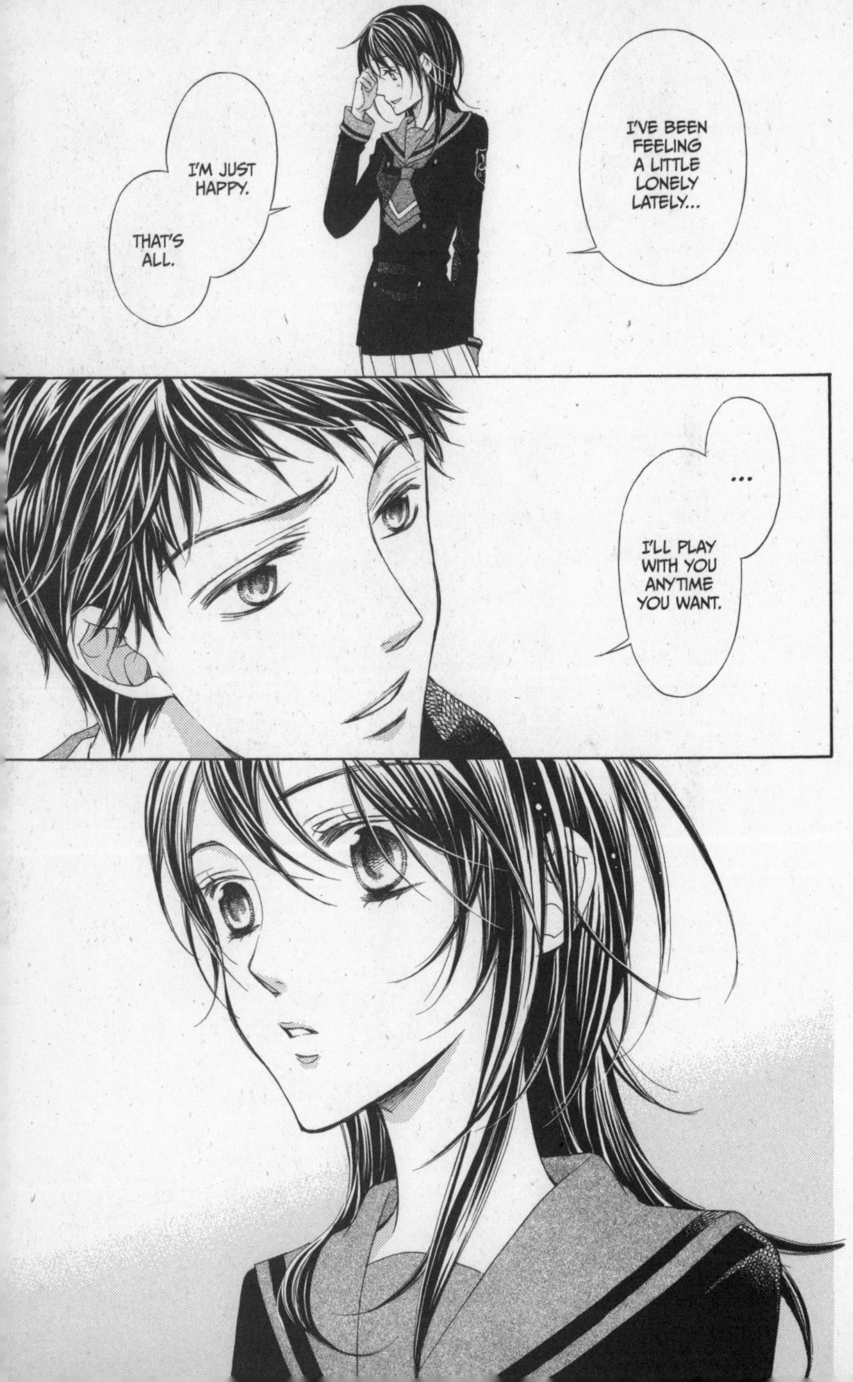
I'VE BEEN FEELING A LITTLE LONELY LATELY...
I'M JUST HAPPY.
THAT'S ALL.
...
I'LL PLAY WITH YOU ANYTIME YOU WANT.

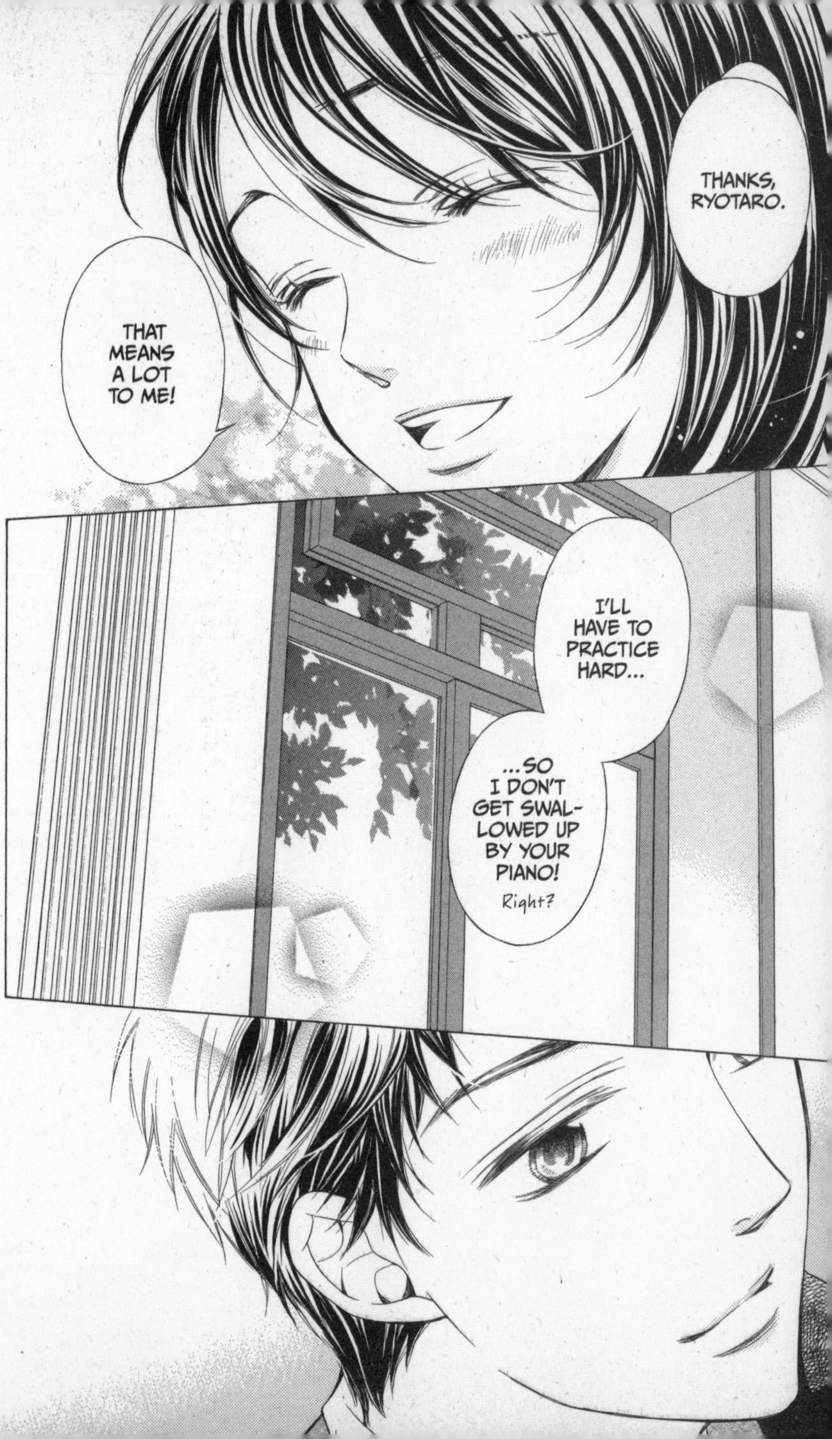
THANKS, RYOTARO.
THAT MEANS A LOT TO ME!
I'LL HAVE TO PRACTICE HARD...
...SO I DON'T GET SWAL-LOWED UP BY YOUR PIANO!
Right?

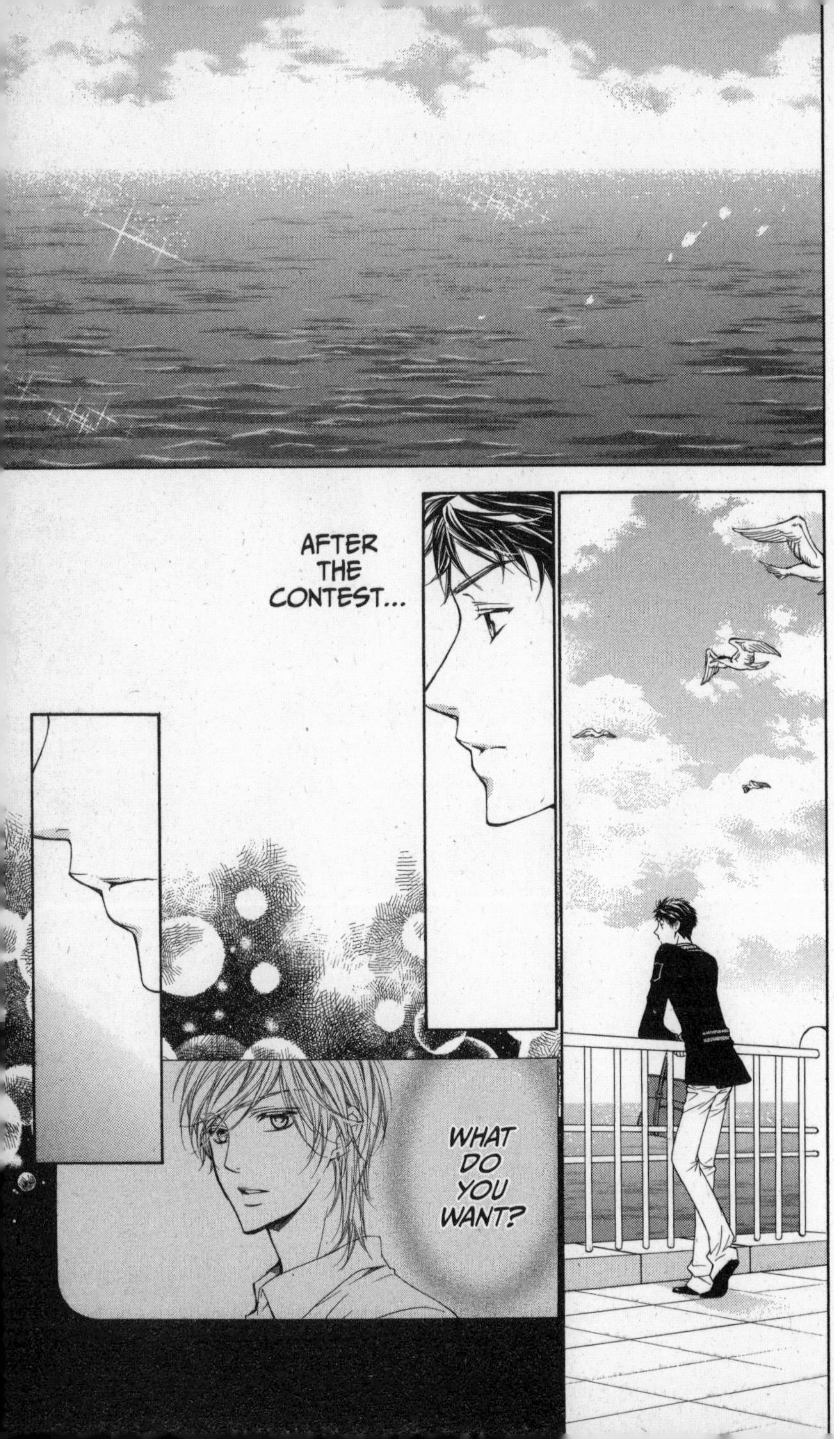
AFTER THE CONTEST...
WHAT DO YOU WANT?

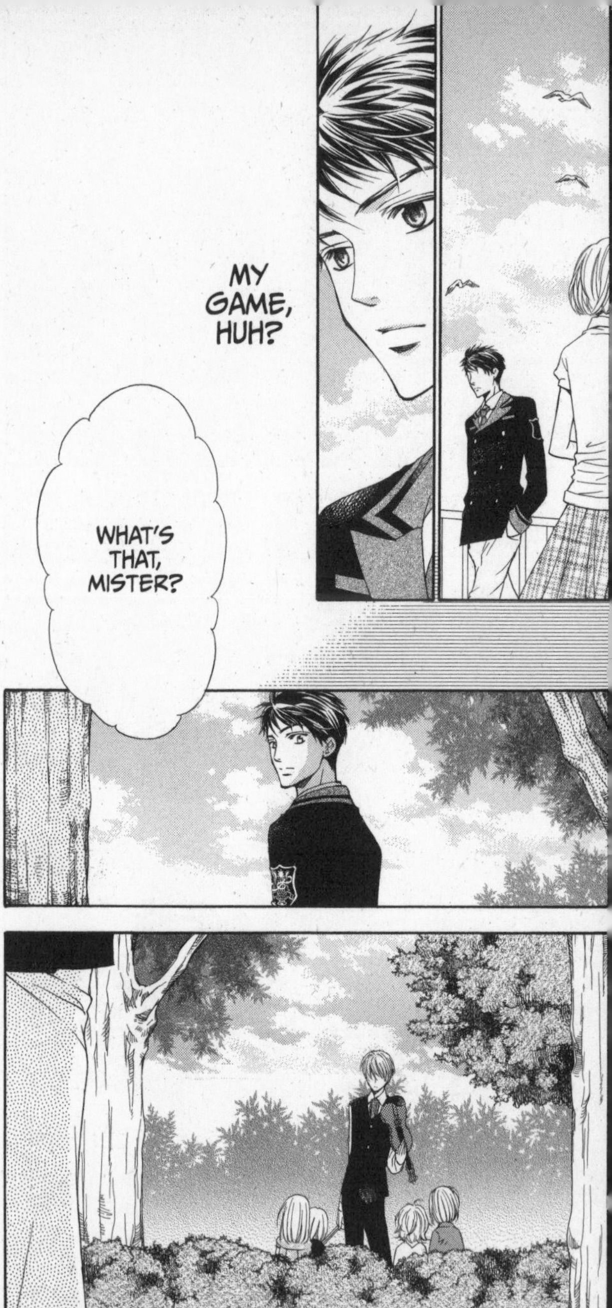
MY GAME, HUH?
WHAT'S THAT, MISTER?

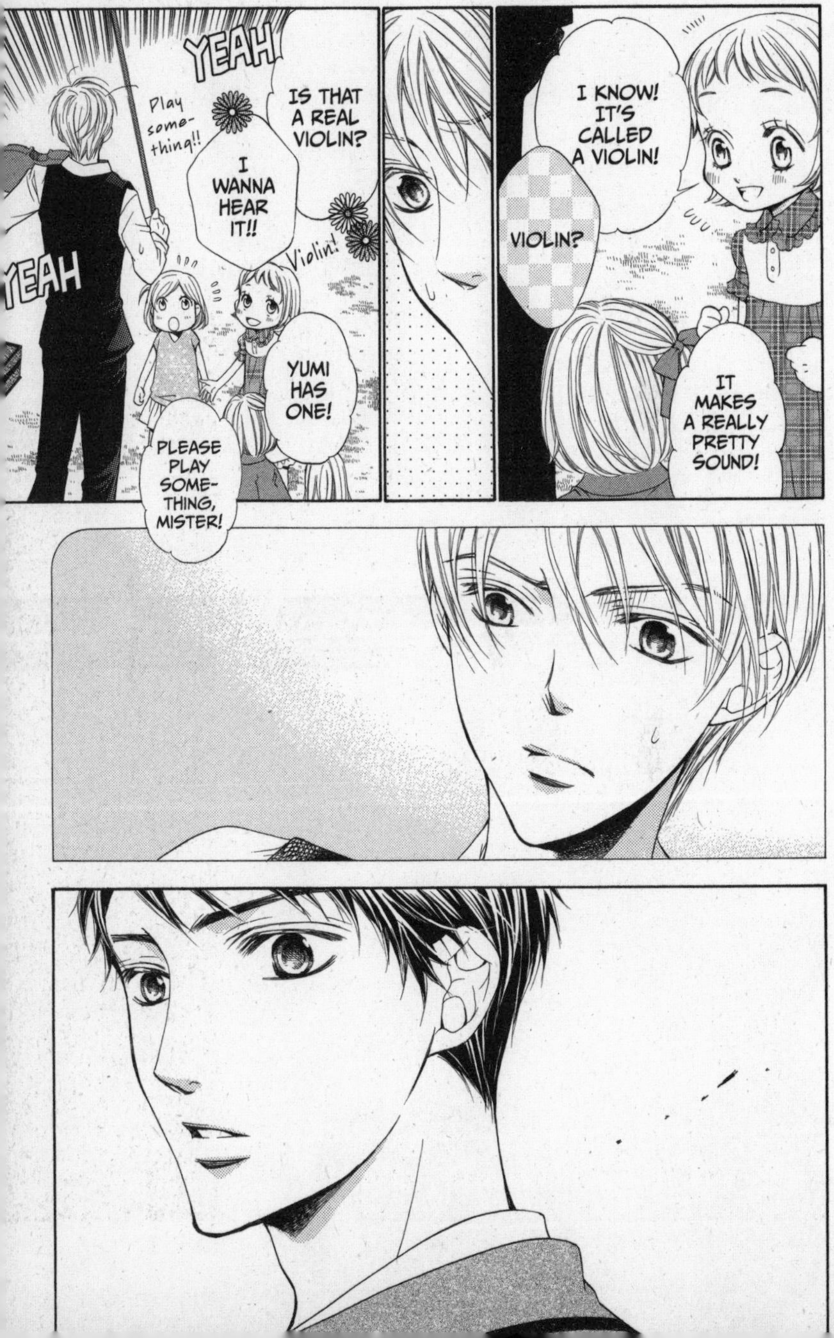
I KNOW! IT'S CALLED A VIOLIN!
VIOLIN?
IT MAKES A REALLY PRETTY SOUND!
YEAH
IS THAT A REAL VIOLIN?
Play some-thing!!
I WANNA HEAR IT!!
Violin!
YEAH
YUMI HAS ONE!
PLEASE PLAY SOME-THING, MISTER!

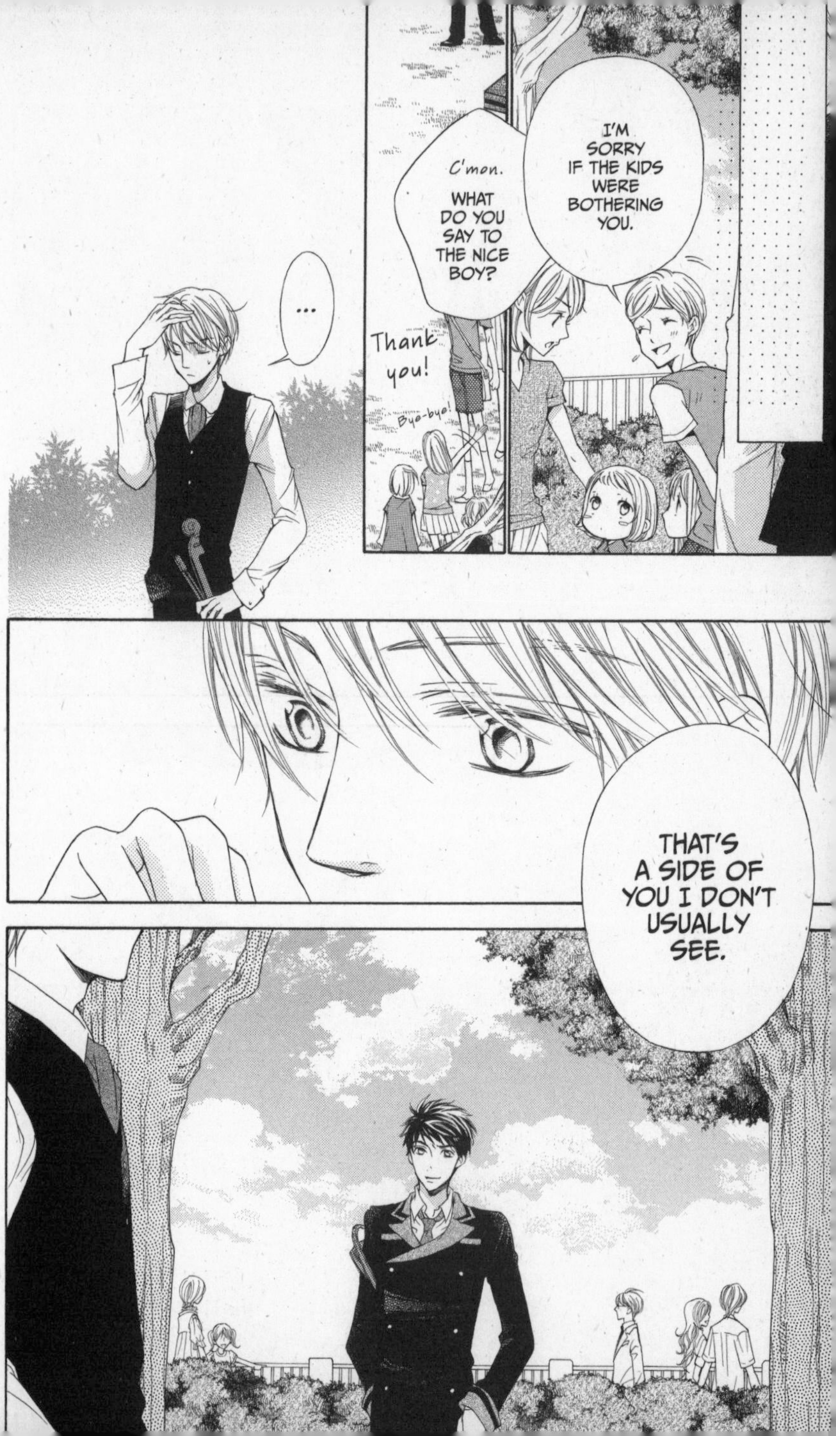
I'M SORRY IF THE KIDS WERE BOTHERING YOU.
C'mon.
WHAT DO YOU SAY TO THE NICE BOY?
Thank you!
Bye-bye!
...
THAT'S A SIDE OF YOU I DON'T USUALLY SEE.

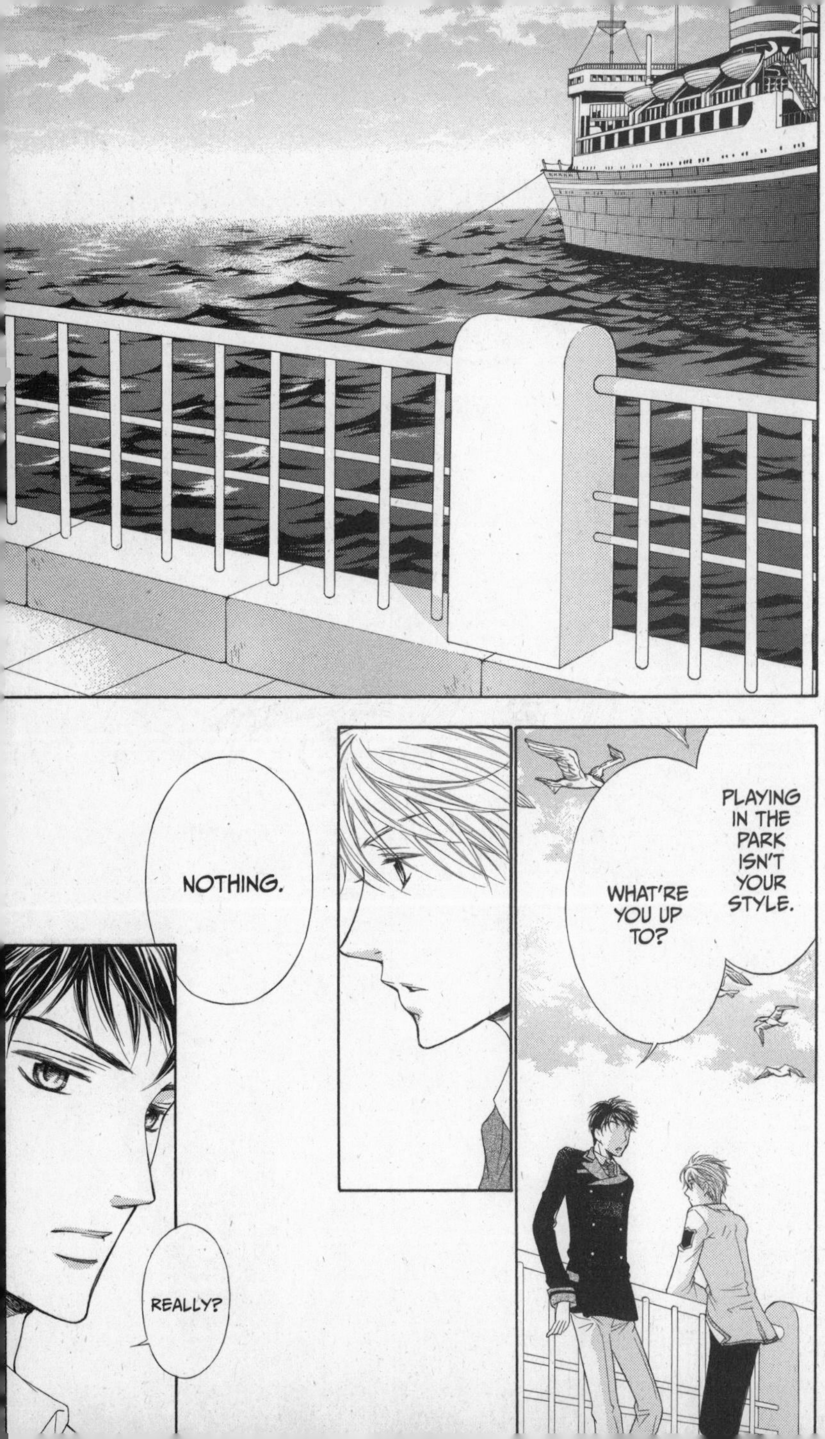
PLAYING IN THE PARK ISN'T YOUR STYLE.
WHAT'RE YOU UP TO?
NOTHING.
REALLY?

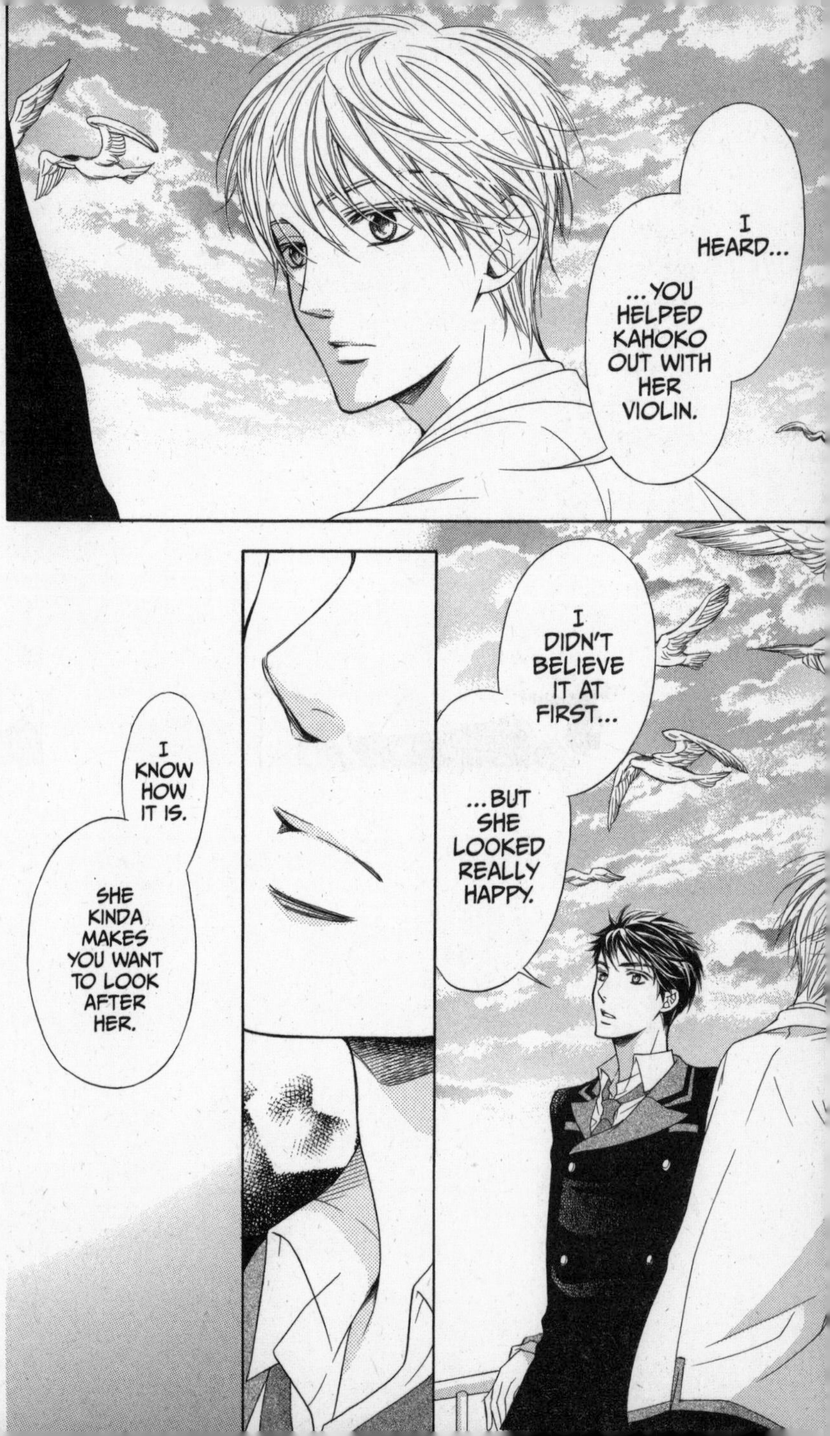
I HEARD...
...YOU HELPED KAHOKO OUT WITH HER VIOLIN.
I DIDN'T BELIEVE IT AT FIRST...
...BUT SHE LOOKED REALLY HAPPY.
I KNOW HOW IT IS.
SHE KINDA MAKES YOU WANT TO LOOK AFTER HER.

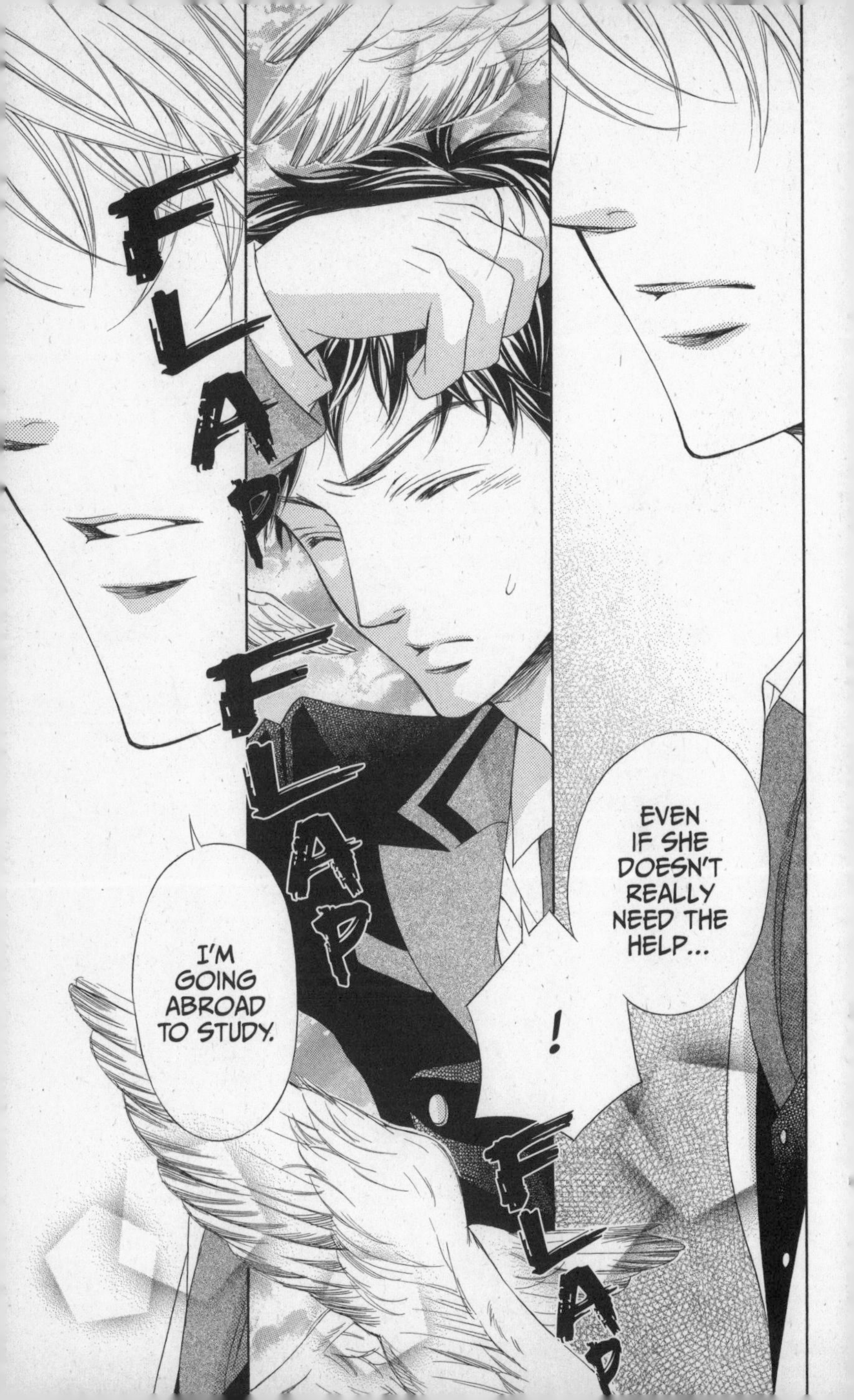
EVEN IF SHE DOESN'T REALLY NEED THE HELP...
!
FLAP
FLAP
FLAP
I'M GOING ABROAD TO STUDY.

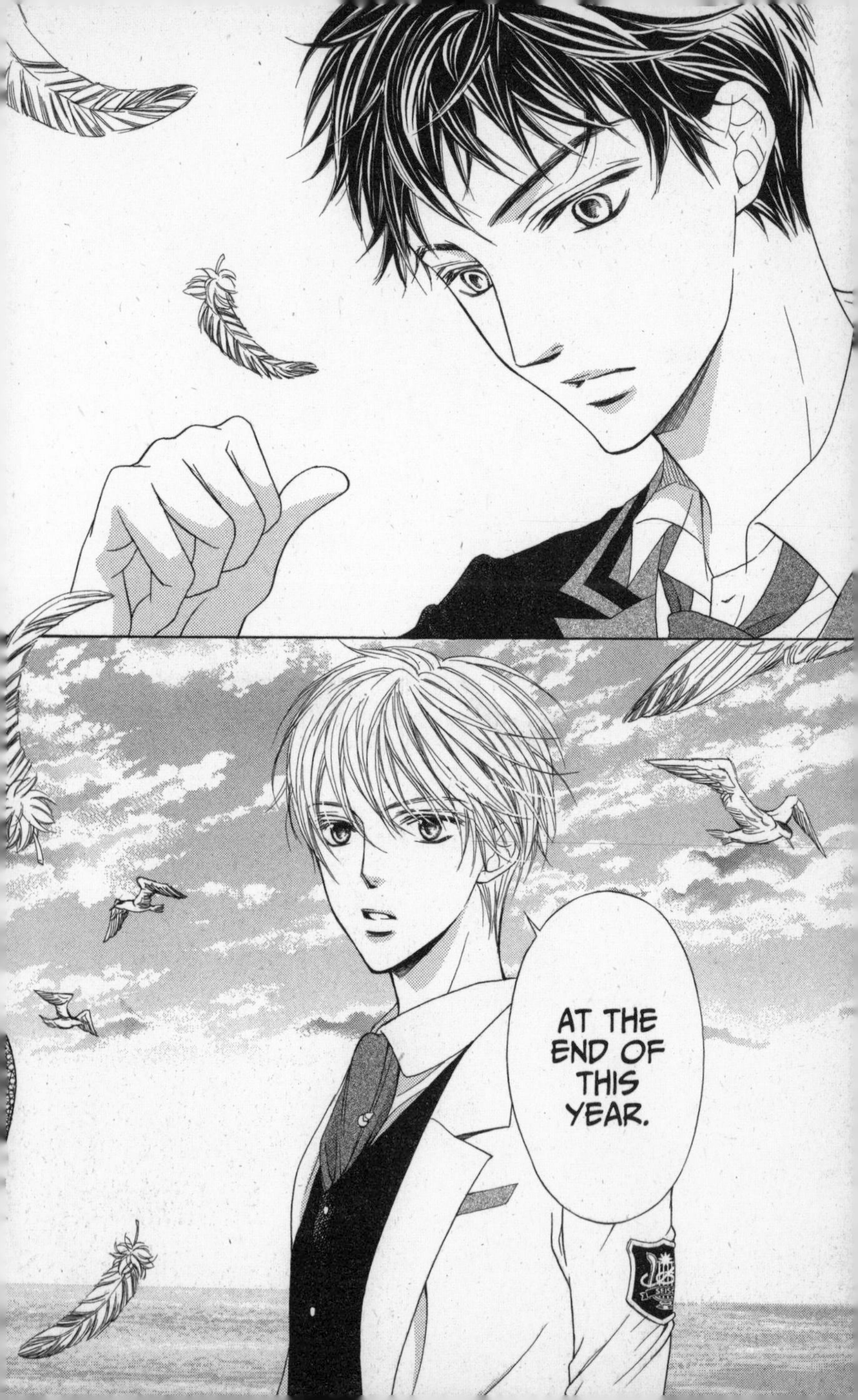
AT THE END OF THIS YEAR.

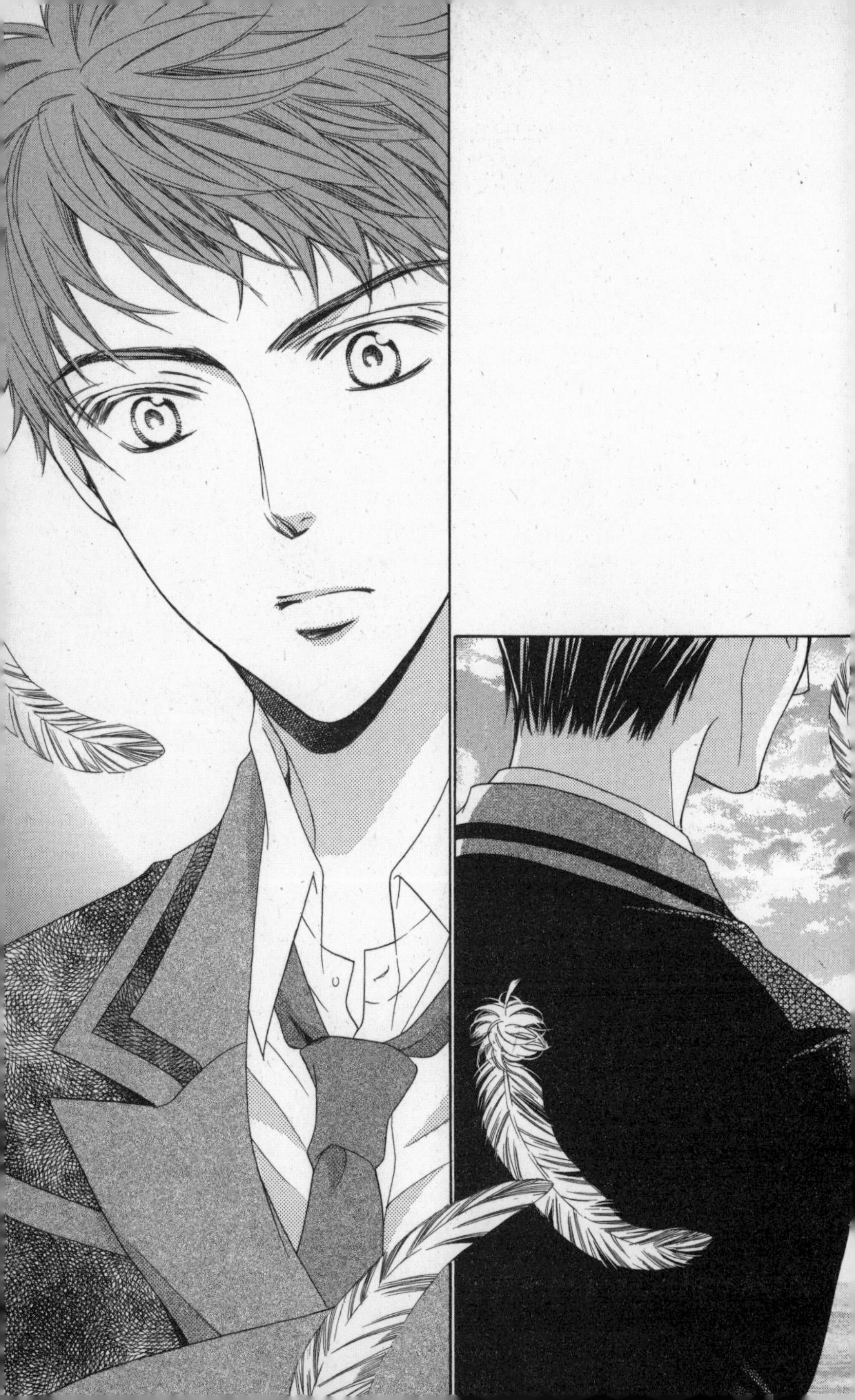

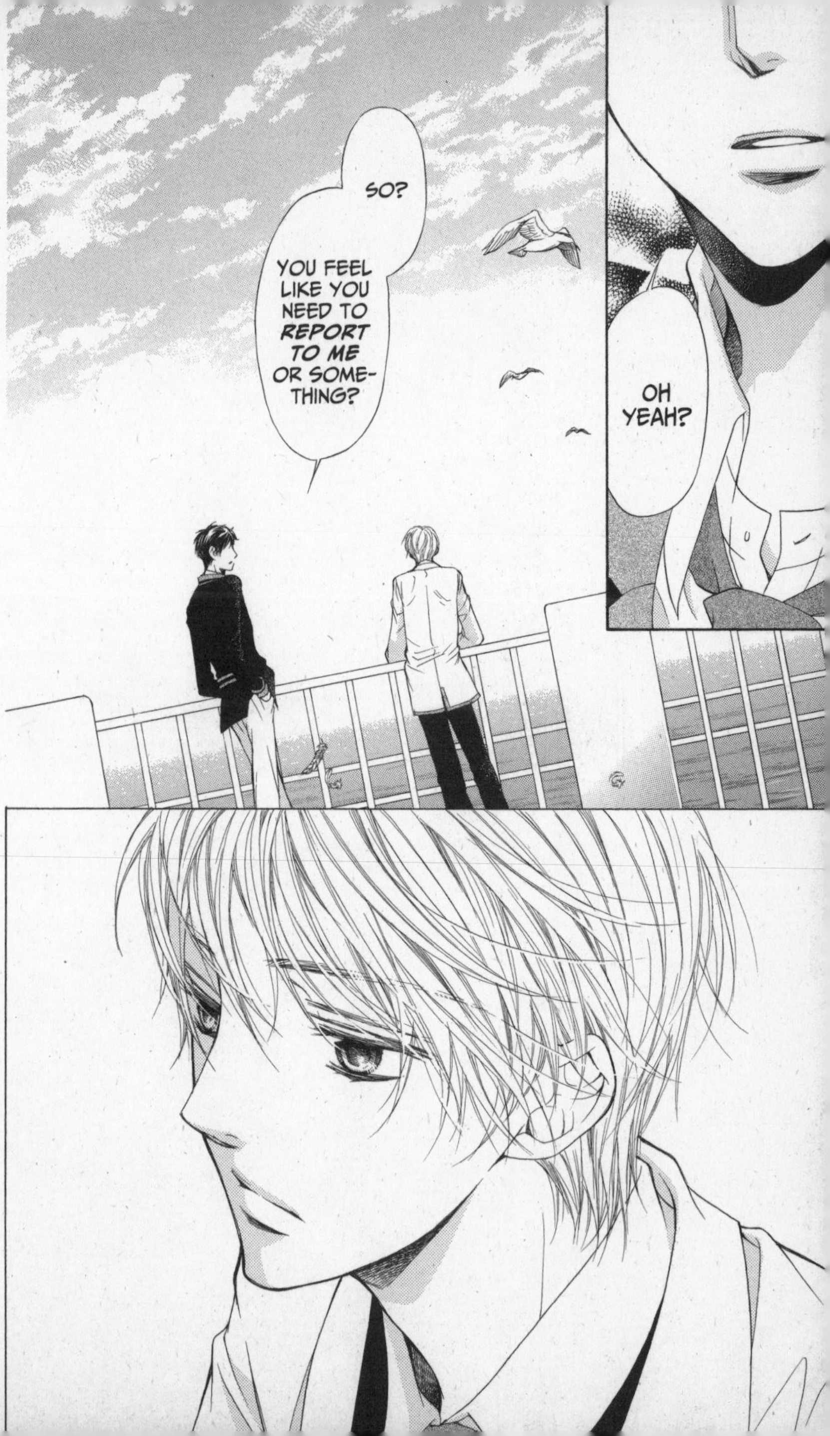
OH YEAH?
SO?
YOU FEEL LIKE YOU NEED TO *REPORT TO ME* OR SOME-THING?

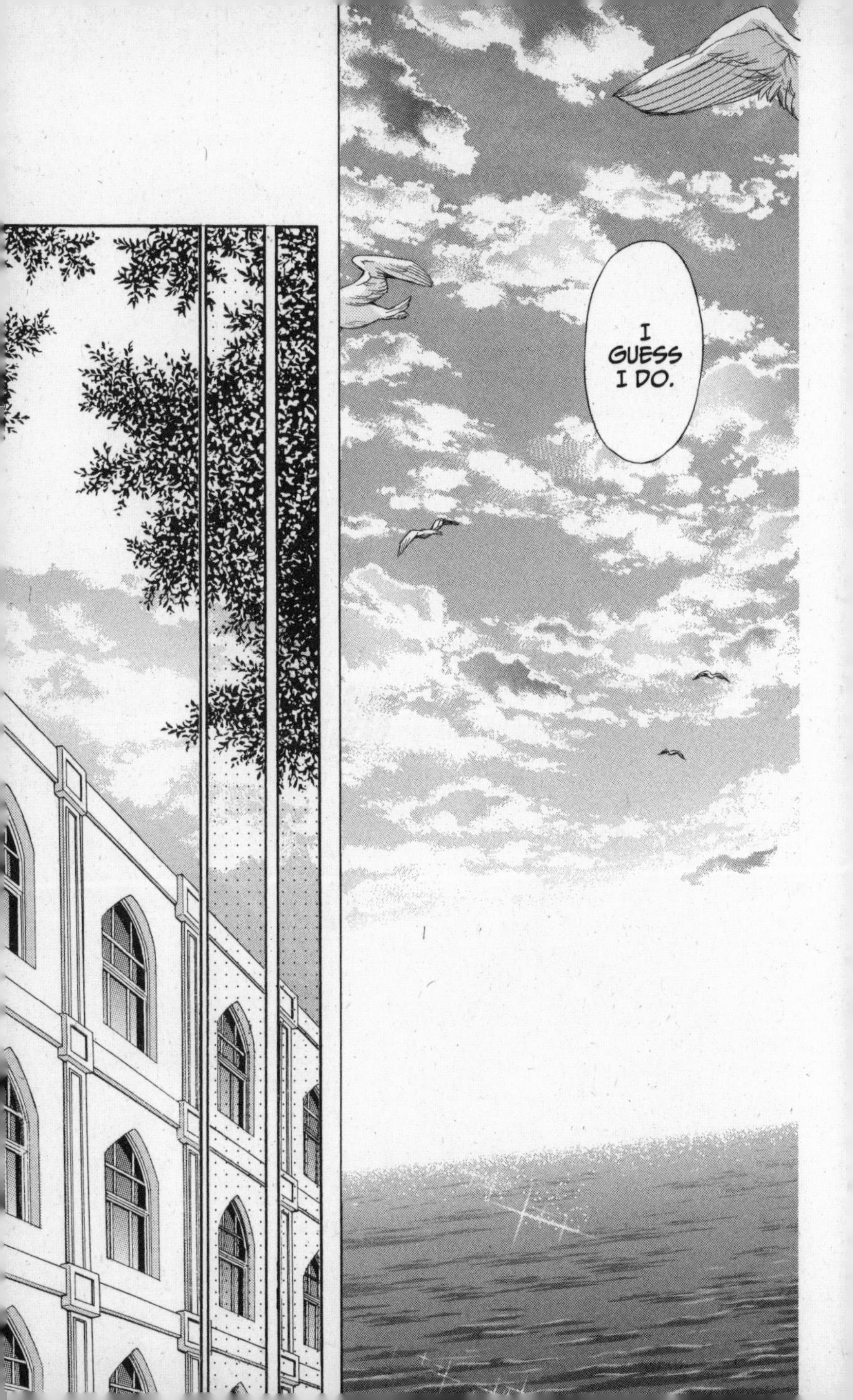
I GUESS I DO.

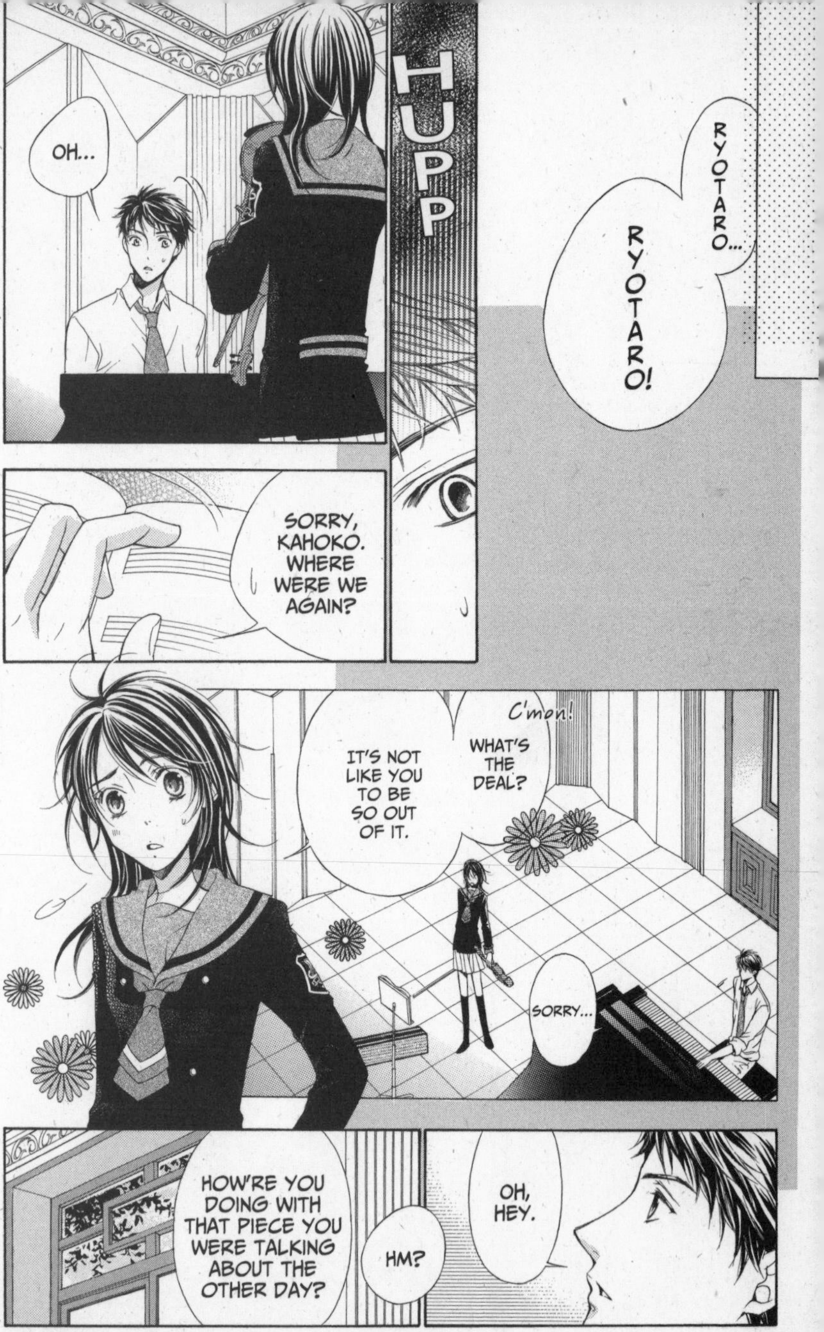
RYOTARO...
RYOTARO...
RYOTARO!
HUPP
OH...
SORRY, KAHOKO. WHERE WERE WE AGAIN?
C'mon!
WHAT'S THE DEAL?
IT'S NOT LIKE YOU TO BE SO OUT OF IT.
SORRY...
OH, HEY.
HM?
HOW'RE YOU DOING WITH THAT PIECE YOU WERE TALKING ABOUT THE OTHER DAY?

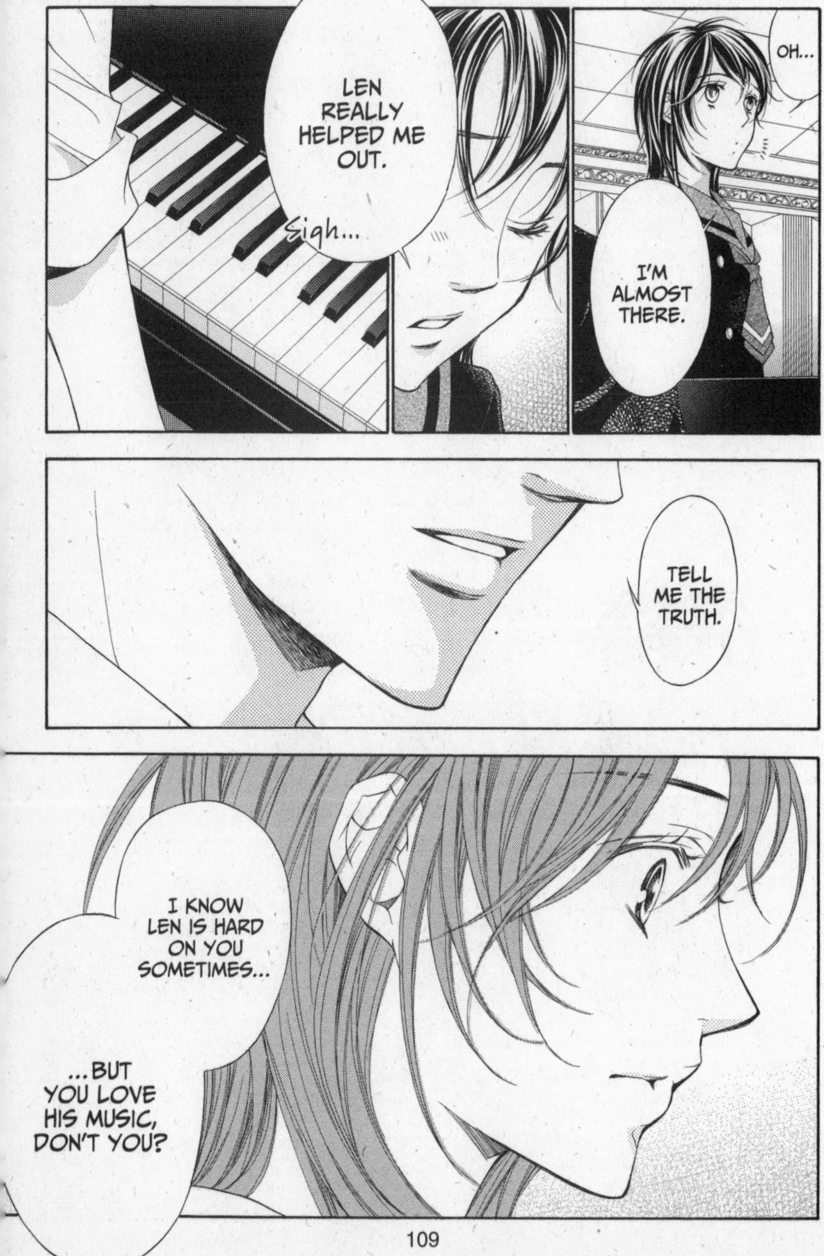
OH...
I'M ALMOST THERE.
LEN REALLY HELPED ME OUT.
Sigh...
TELL ME THE TRUTH.
I KNOW LEN IS HARD ON YOU SOMETIMES...
...BUT YOU LOVE HIS MUSIC, DON'T YOU?

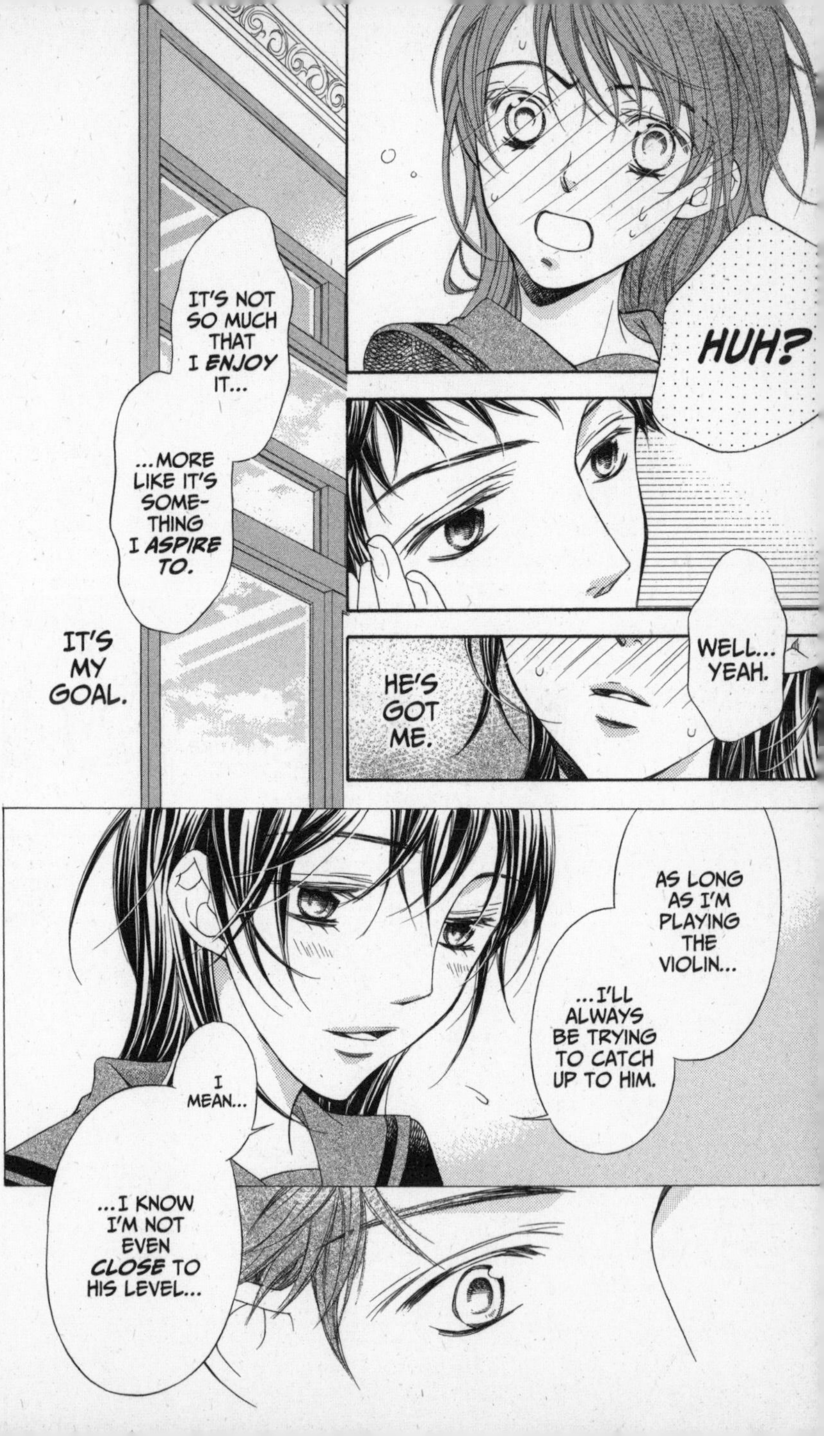
HUH?
WELL... YEAH.
HE'S GOT ME.
IT'S NOT SO MUCH THAT I *ENJOY* IT...
...MORE LIKE IT'S SOME-THING I *ASPIRE TO.*
IT'S MY GOAL.
AS LONG AS I'M PLAYING THE VIOLIN...
...I'LL ALWAYS BE TRYING TO CATCH UP TO HIM.
I MEAN...
...I KNOW I'M NOT EVEN ***CLOSE*** TO HIS LEVEL...

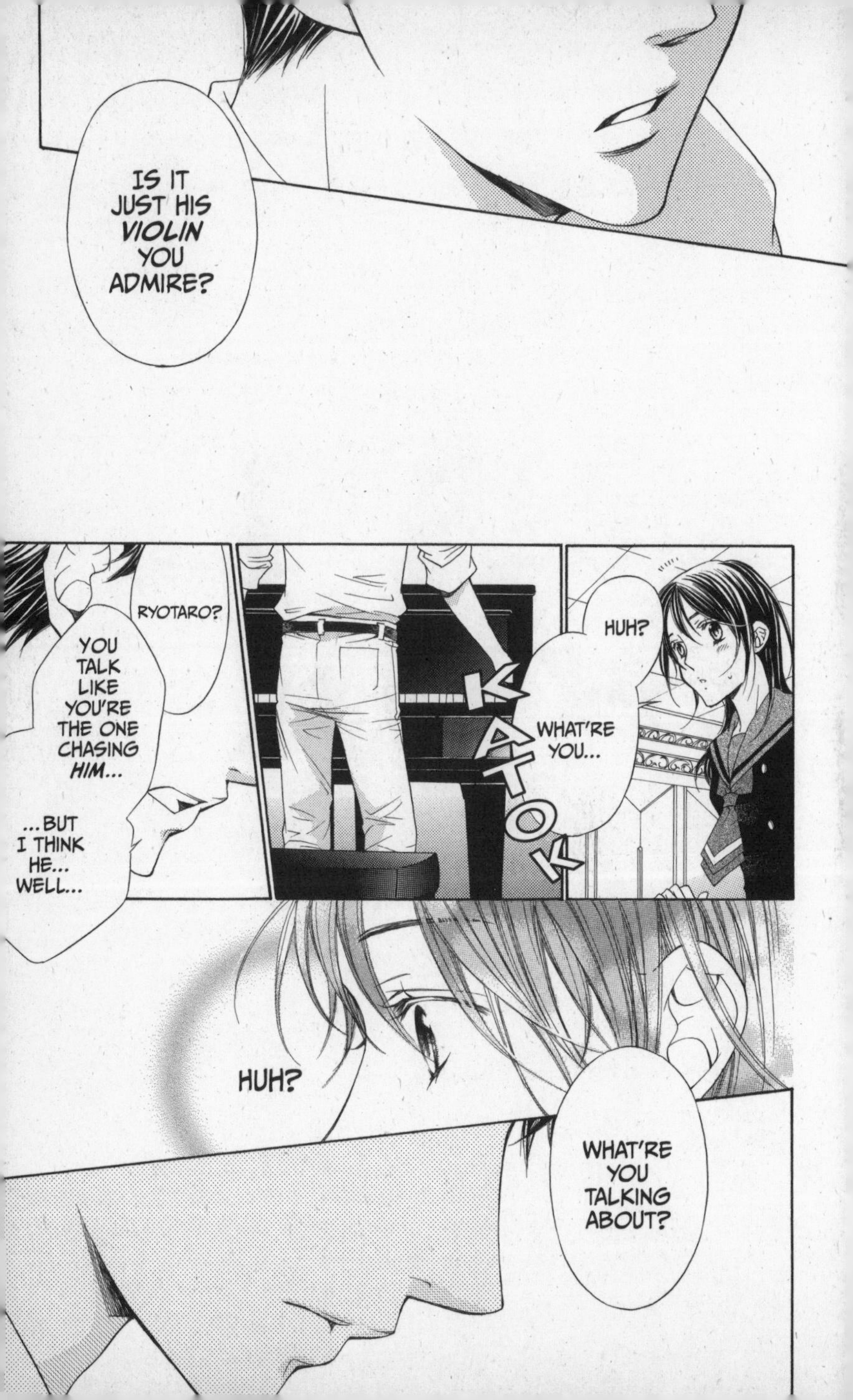
IS IT JUST HIS *VIOLIN* YOU ADMIRE?
HUH?
WHAT'RE YOU...
KATOK
RYOTARO?
YOU TALK LIKE YOU'RE THE ONE CHASING *HIM*...
...BUT I THINK HE... WELL...
WHAT'RE YOU TALKING ABOUT?
HUH?

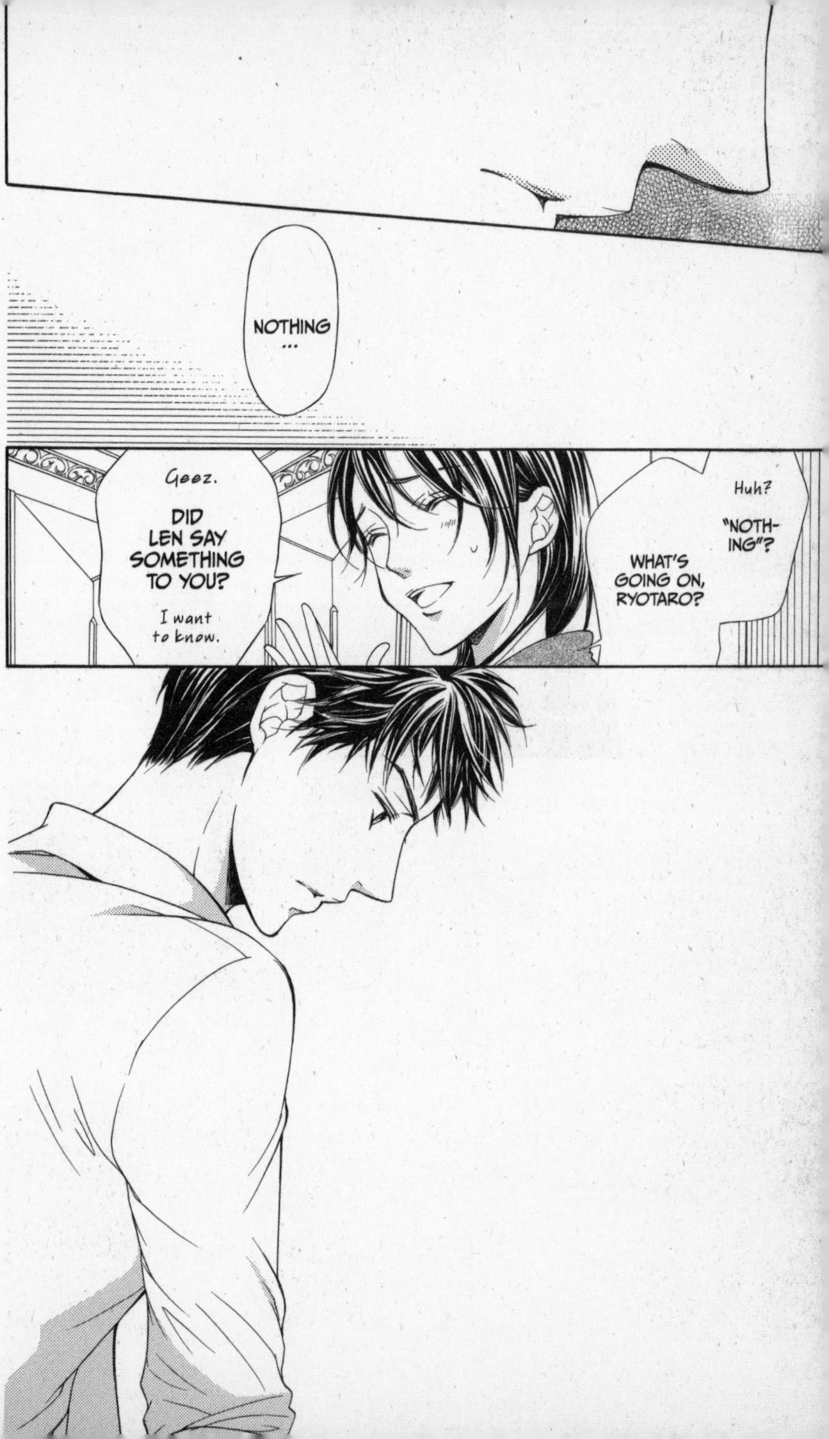
NOTHING ...
Huh?
"NOTHING"?
WHAT'S GOING ON, RYOTARO?
Geez.
DID LEN SAY SOMETHING TO YOU?
I want to know.

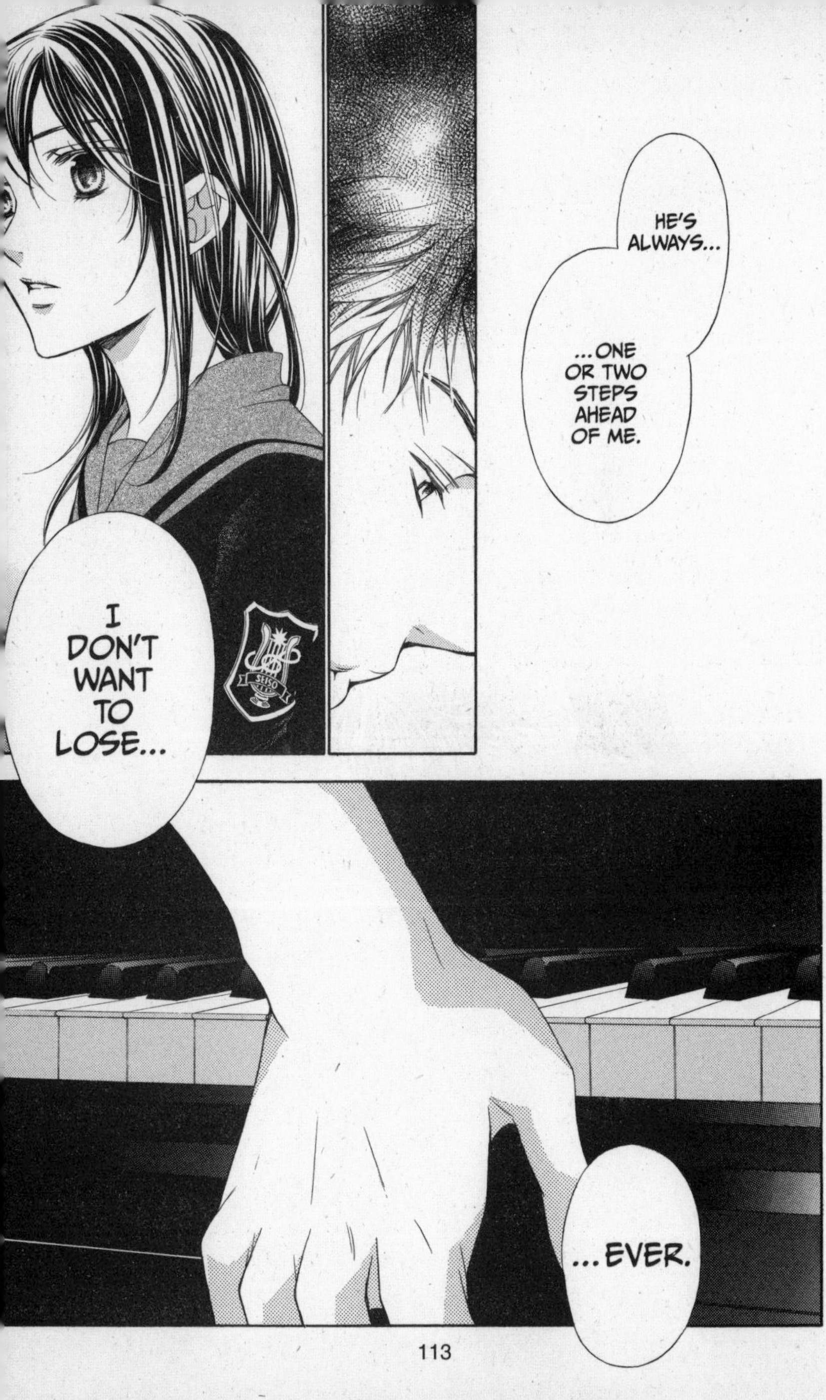
HE'S ALWAYS...
...ONE OR TWO STEPS AHEAD OF ME.
I DON'T WANT TO LOSE...
...EVER.

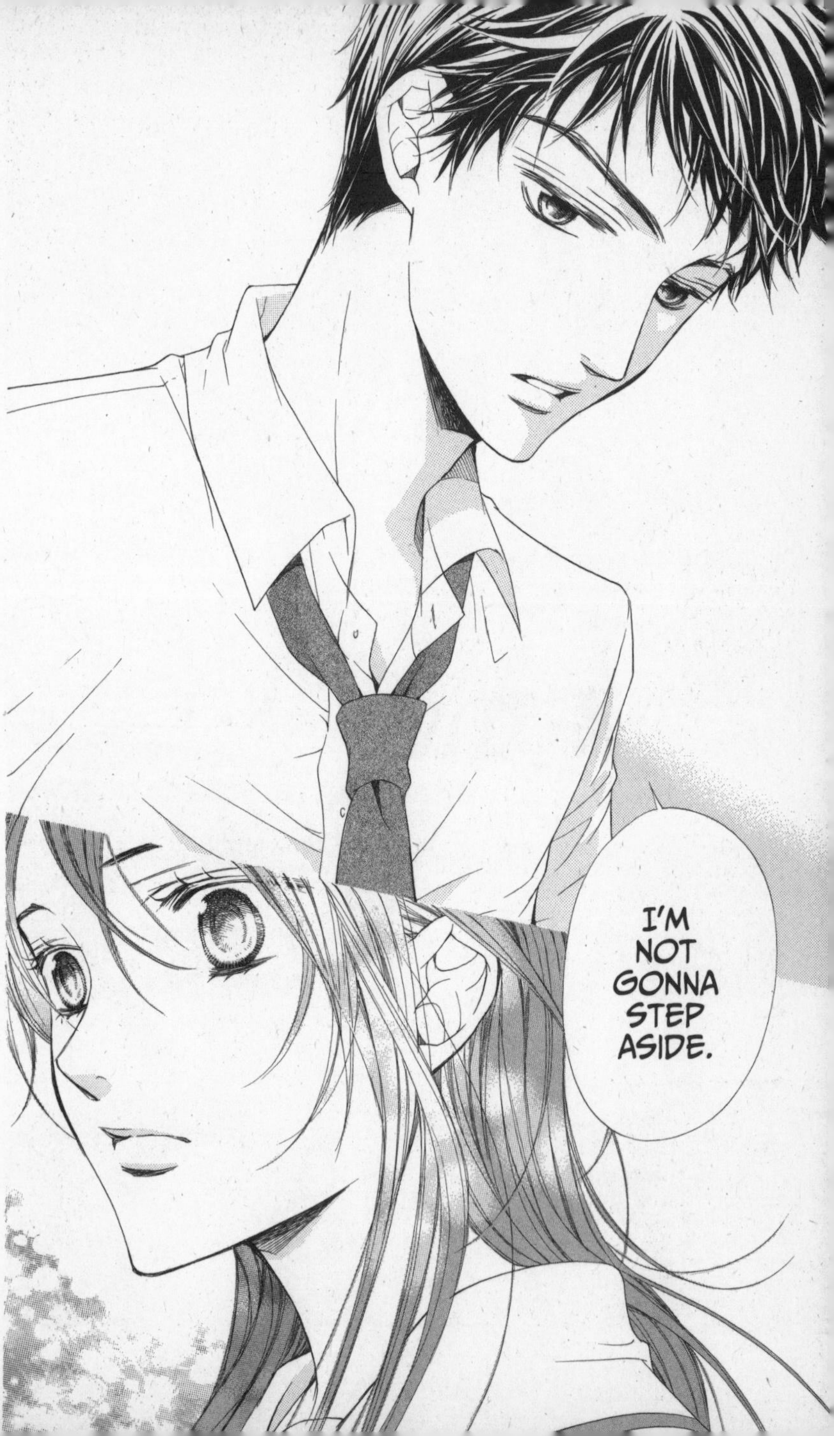
I'M NOT GONNA STEP ASIDE.

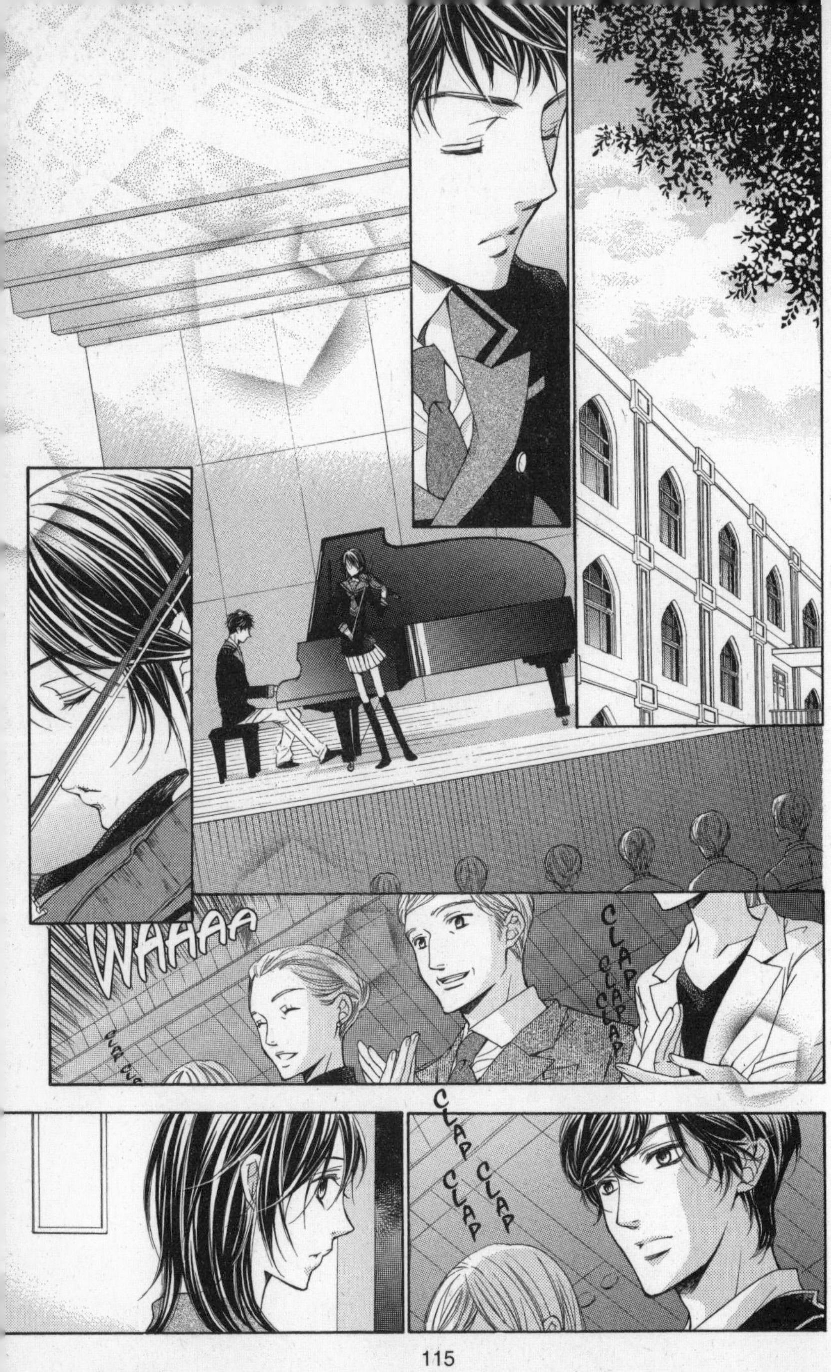
CLAP CLAP CLAP CLAP
WAAAA
CLAP CLAP CLAP CLAP

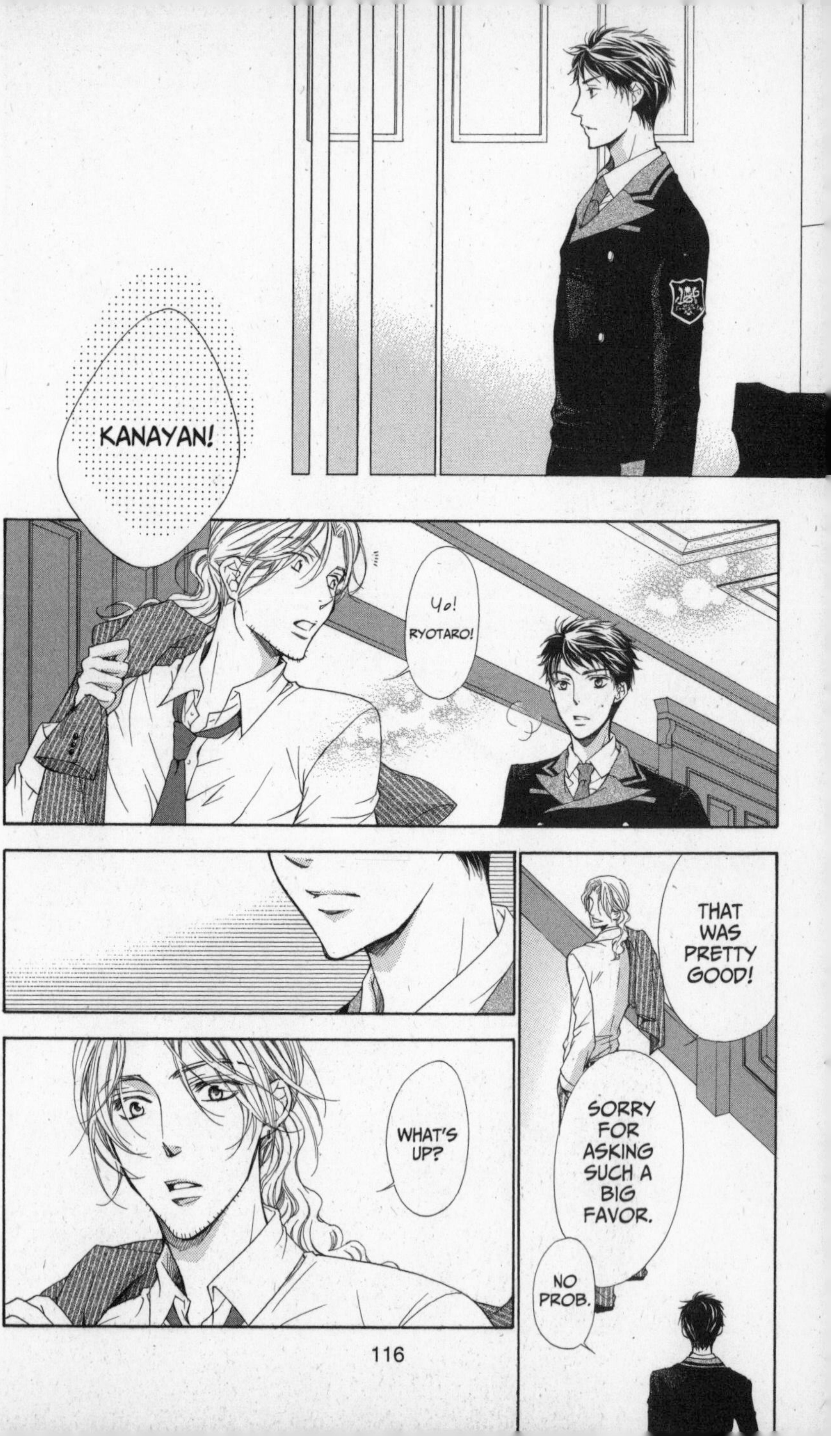
KANAYAN!
Yo! RYOTARO!
THAT WAS PRETTY GOOD!
SORRY FOR ASKING SUCH A BIG FAVOR.
NO PROB.
WHAT'S UP?

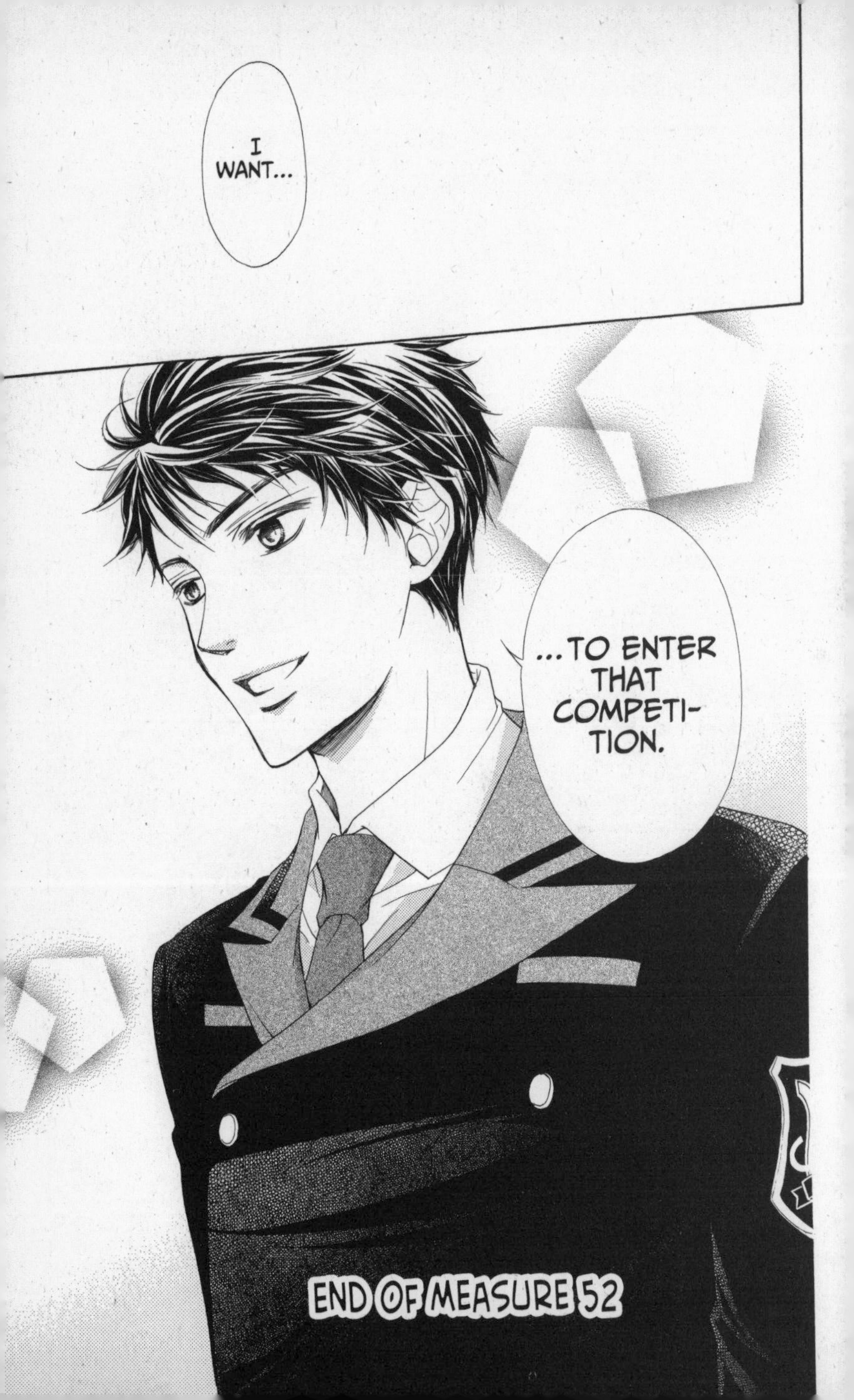
I WANT...
...TO ENTER THAT COMPETITION.
END OF MEASURE 52

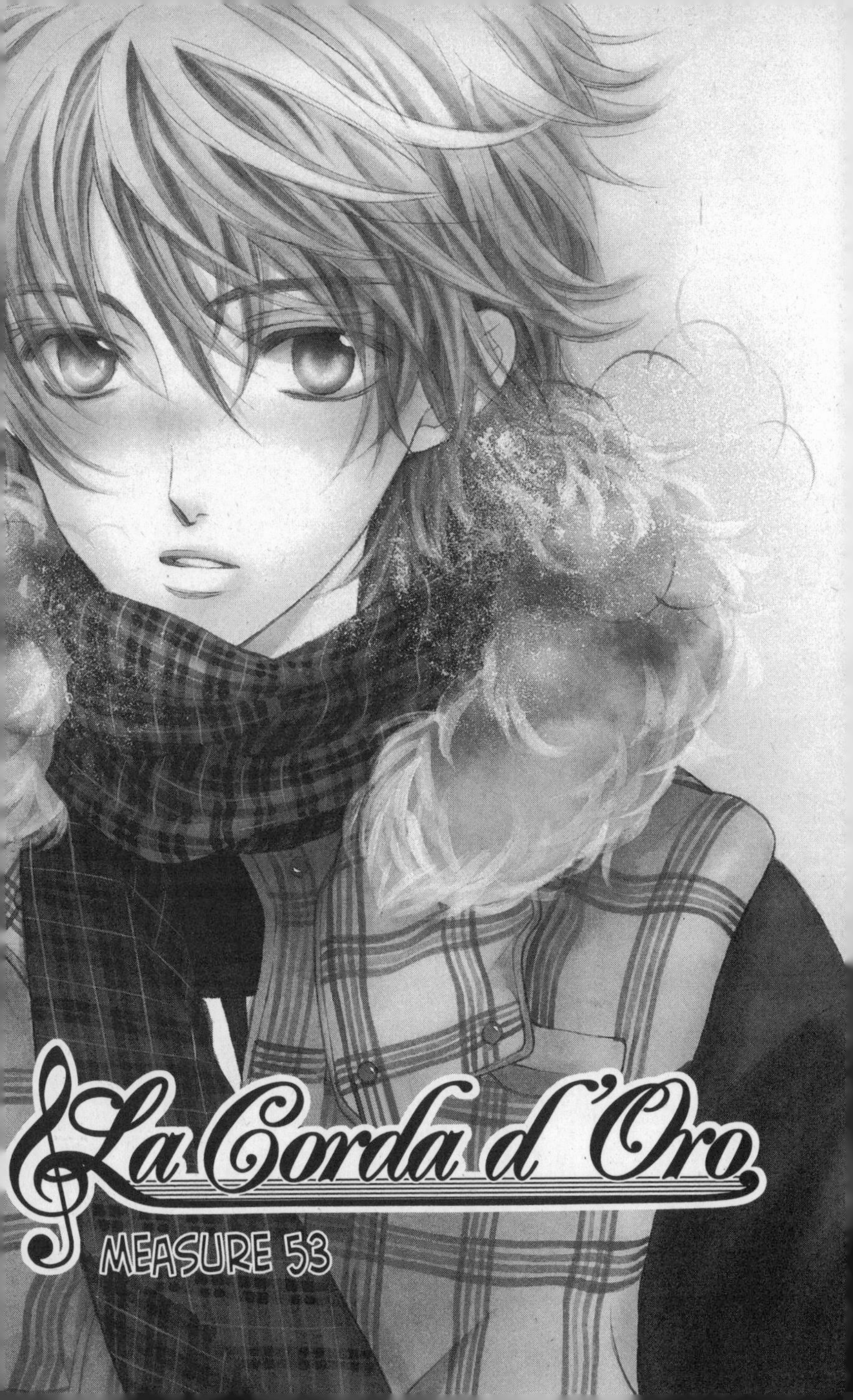
La Corda d'Oro
MEASURE 53

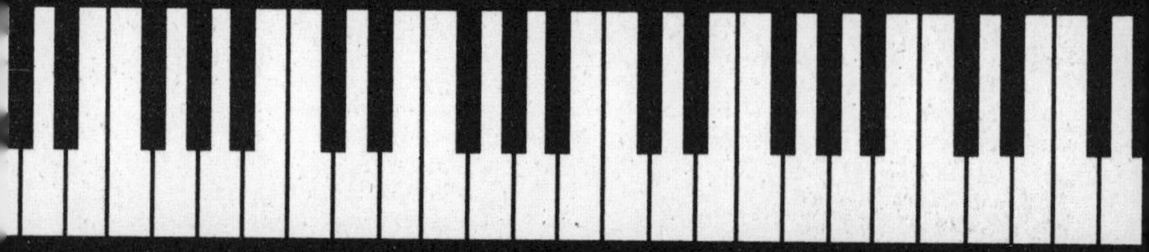

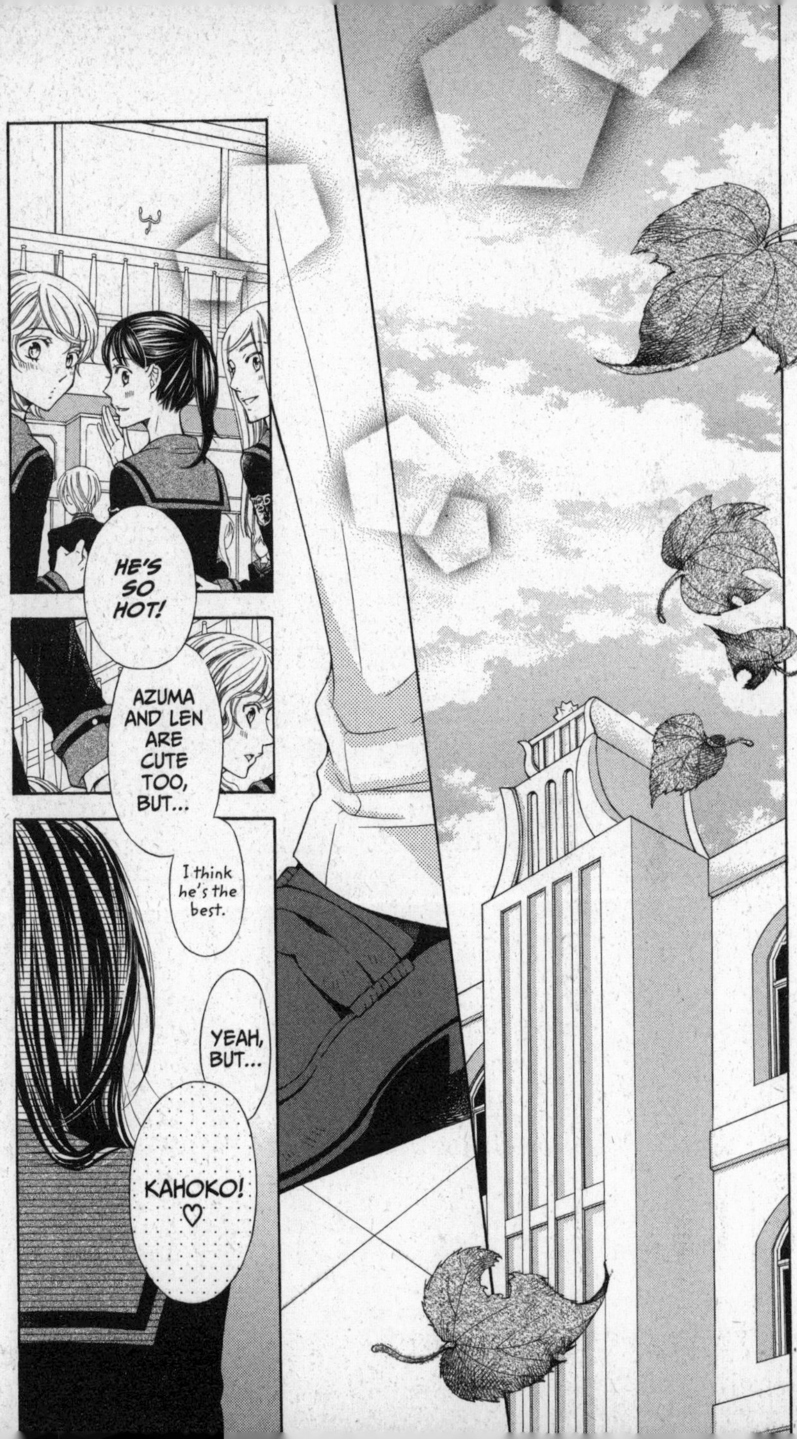
HE'S SO HOT!
AZUMA AND LEN ARE CUTE TOO, BUT...
I think he's the best.
YEAH, BUT...
KAHOKO! ♡

OH GOOD! I'M GLAD YOU'RE HERE!

MAY I JOIN YOU FOR LUNCH?

WHY *HER*?

PSSST

SHE'S SO PLAIN.

HE OUGHTA BE WITH A *HOT* GIRL.

PSSST

I KNOW, RIGHT?

I ALREADY MADE PLANS WITH MY FRIENDS.

KAHOKO?

EEP

Huh?

SORRY.

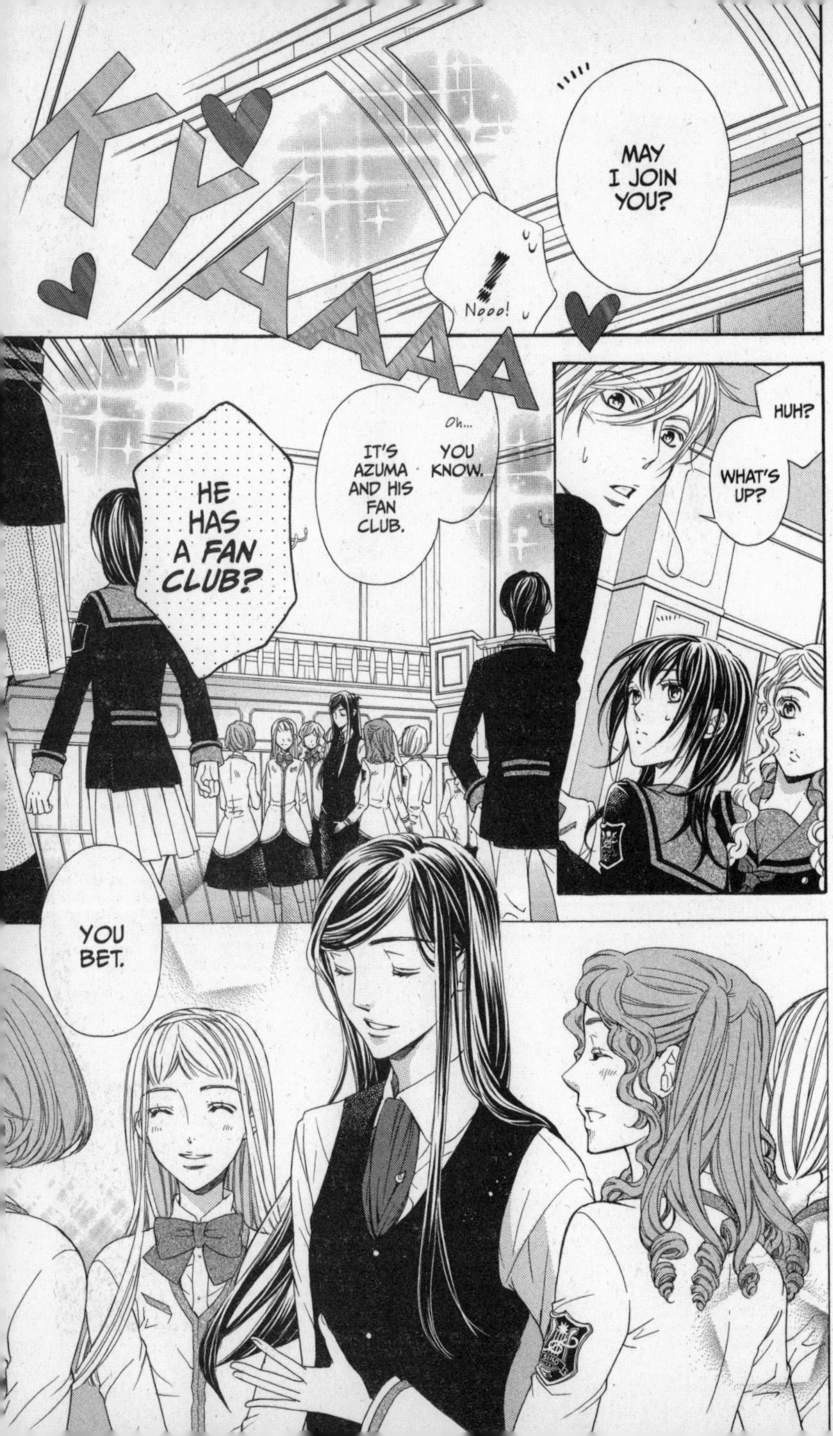
MAY I JOIN YOU?
!
Nooo!
KYAAAAAA
HUH?
WHAT'S UP?
Oh...
YOU KNOW.
IT'S AZUMA AND HIS FAN CLUB.
HE HAS A *FAN CLUB?*
YOU BET.

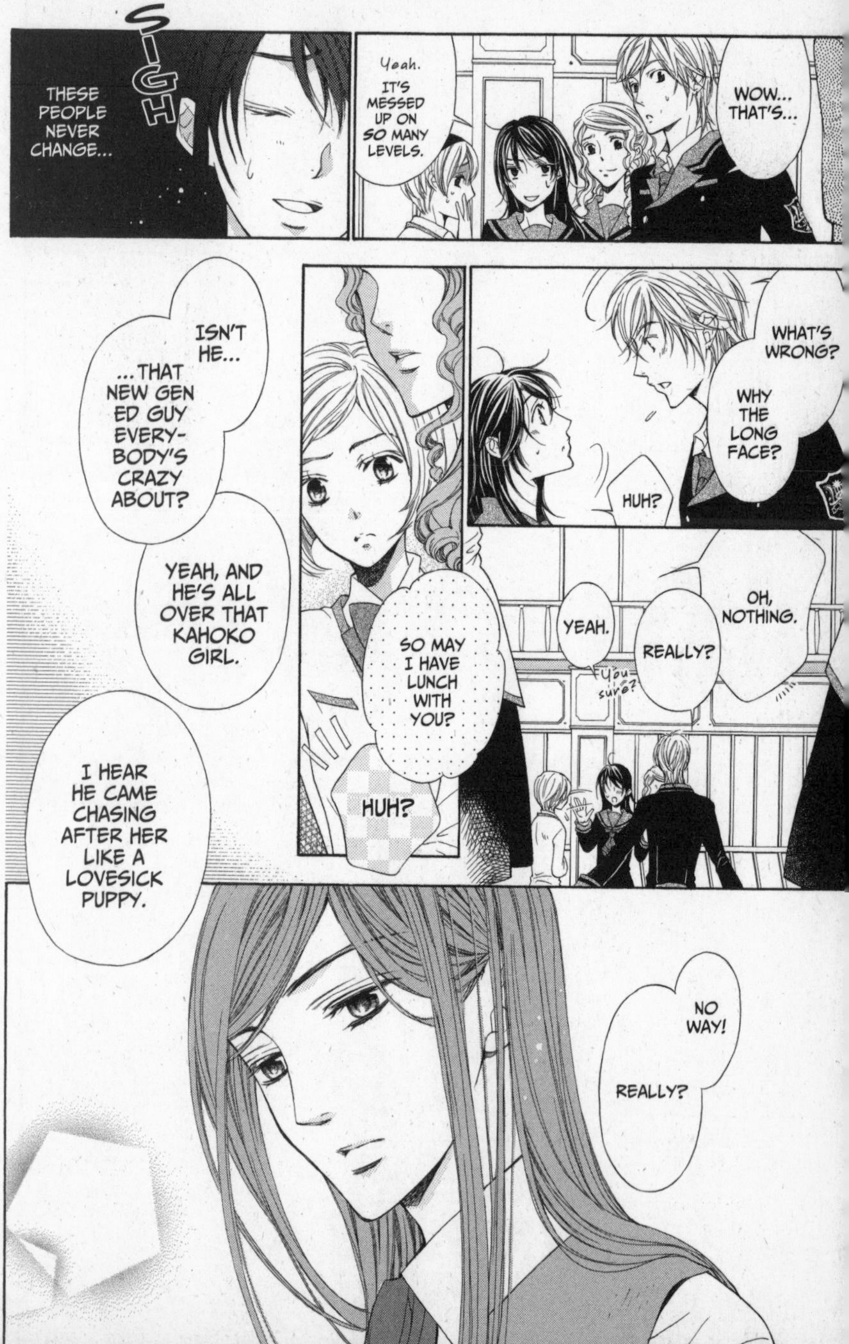
WOW... THAT'S...
Yeah.
IT'S MESSED UP ON SO MANY LEVELS.
SIGH
THESE PEOPLE NEVER CHANGE...
WHAT'S WRONG? WHY THE LONG FACE?
HUH?
OH, NOTHING.
REALLY?
You sure?
YEAH.
SO MAY I HAVE LUNCH WITH YOU?
HUH?
ISN'T HE... ...THAT NEW GEN ED GUY EVERYBODY'S CRAZY ABOUT?
YEAH, AND HE'S ALL OVER THAT KAHOKO GIRL.
I HEAR HE CAME CHASING AFTER HER LIKE A LOVESICK PUPPY.
NO WAY! REALLY?

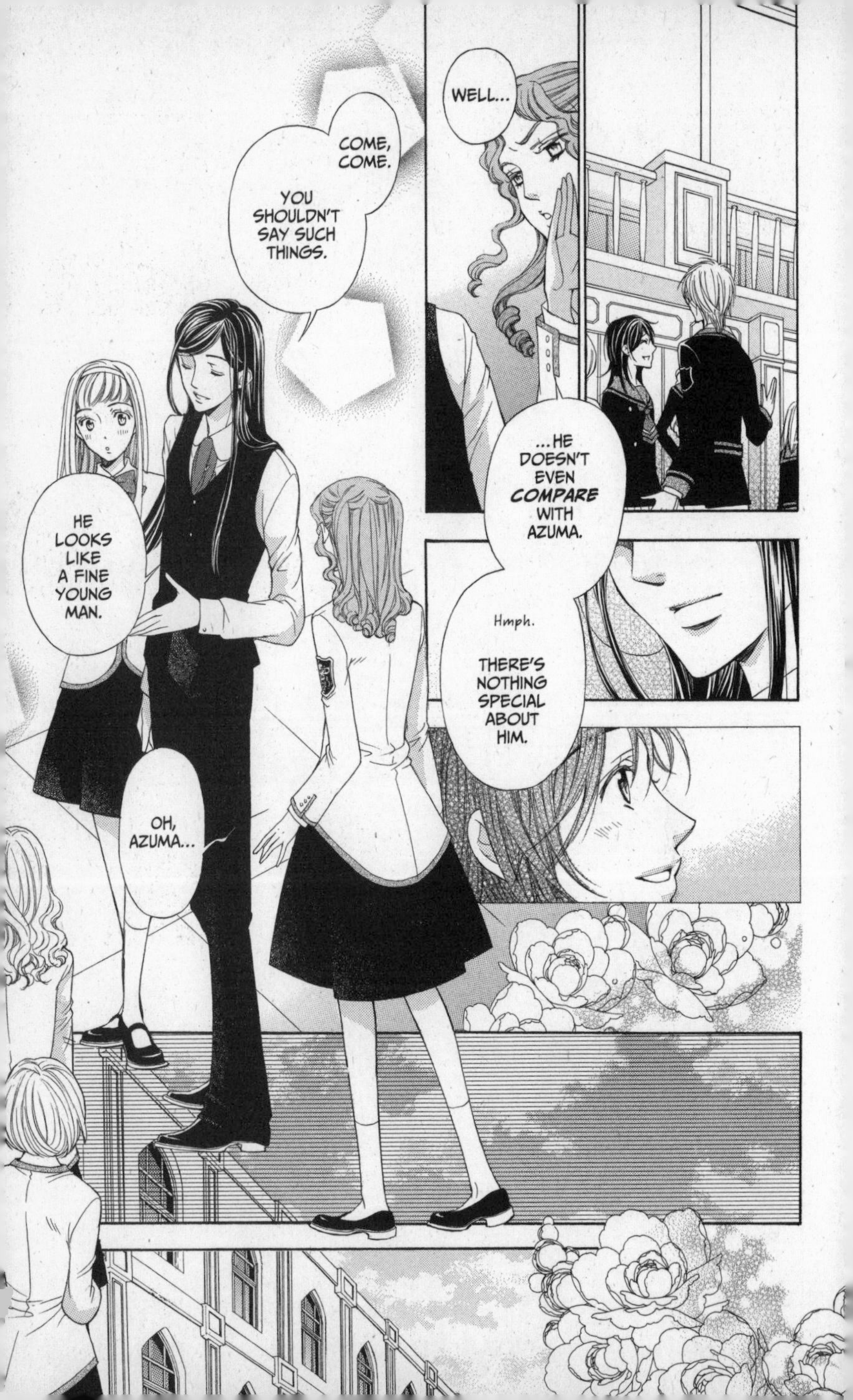
WELL...
...HE DOESN'T EVEN ***COMPARE*** WITH AZUMA.
Hmph.
THERE'S NOTHING SPECIAL ABOUT HIM.
COME, COME.
YOU SHOULDN'T SAY SUCH THINGS.
HE LOOKS LIKE A FINE YOUNG MAN.
OH, AZUMA...

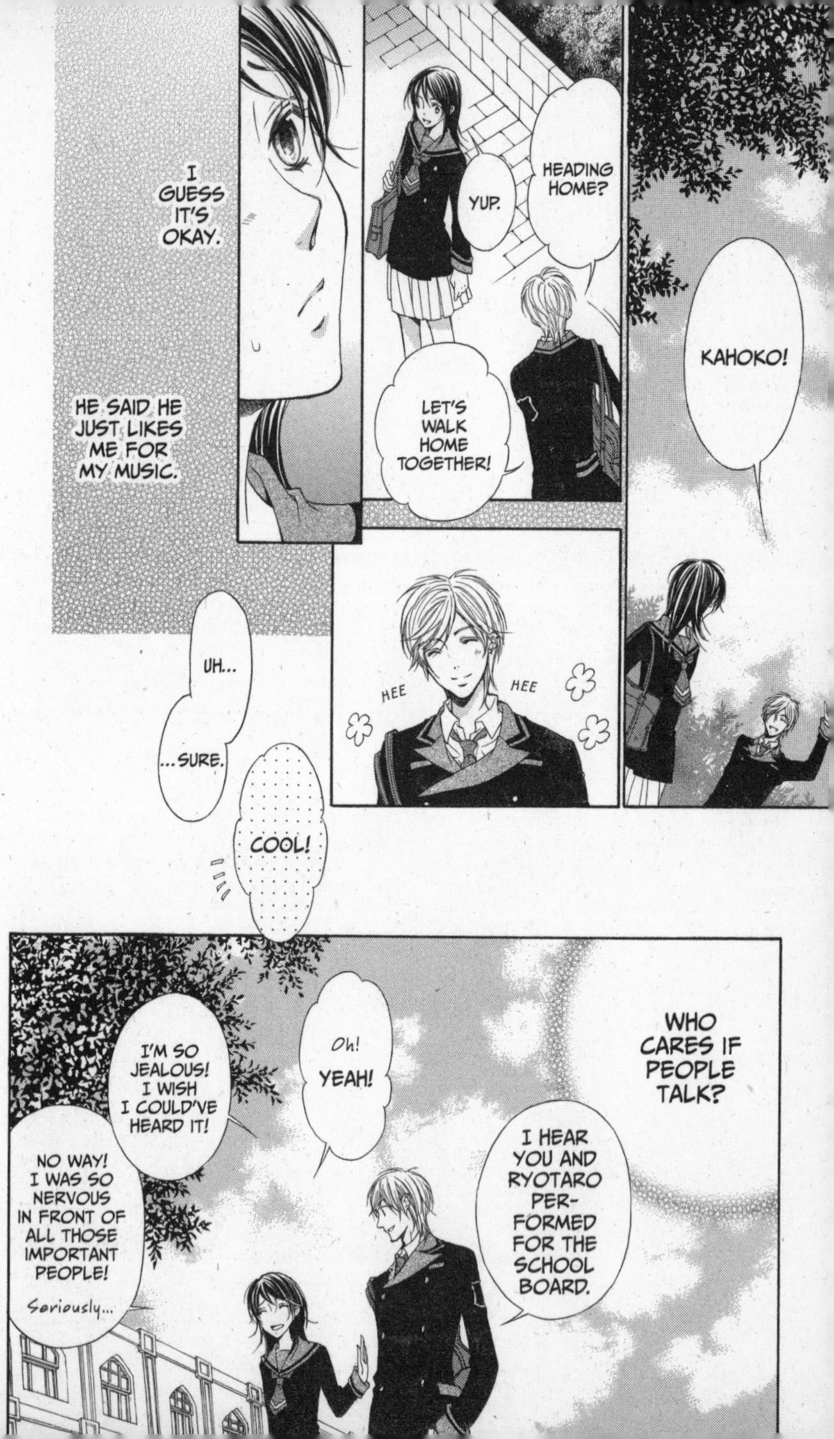
KAHOKO!
HEADING HOME?
YUP.
LET'S WALK HOME TOGETHER!
I GUESS IT'S OKAY.
HE SAID HE JUST LIKES ME FOR MY MUSIC.
HEE HEE
UH...
...SURE.
COOL!
WHO CARES IF PEOPLE TALK?
I HEAR YOU AND RYOTARO PER-FORMED FOR THE SCHOOL BOARD.
Oh! YEAH!
I'M SO JEALOUS! I WISH I COULD'VE HEARD IT!
NO WAY! I WAS SO NERVOUS IN FRONT OF ALL THOSE IMPORTANT PEOPLE!
Seriously...

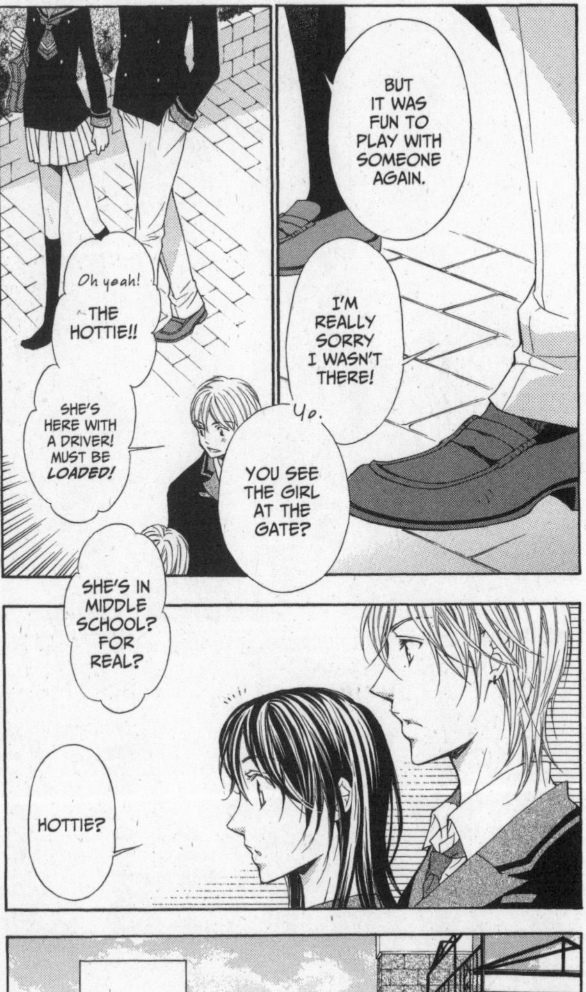
BUT IT WAS FUN TO PLAY WITH SOMEONE AGAIN.
I'M REALLY SORRY I WASN'T THERE!
Yo.
YOU SEE THE GIRL AT THE GATE?
Oh yeah!
THE HOTTIE!!
SHE'S HERE WITH A DRIVER! MUST BE LOADED!
SHE'S IN MIDDLE SCHOOL? FOR REAL?
HOTTIE?
OH!

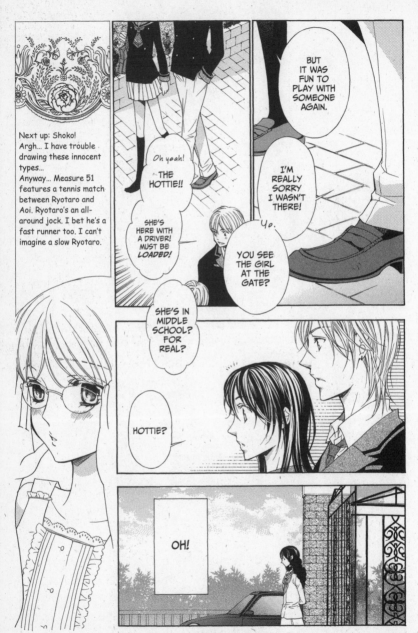

Next up: Shoko!
Argh... I have trouble drawing these innocent types...
Anyway... Measure 51 features a tennis match between Ryotaro and Aoi. Ryotaro's an all-around jock. I bet he's a fast runner too. I can't imagine a slow Ryotaro.

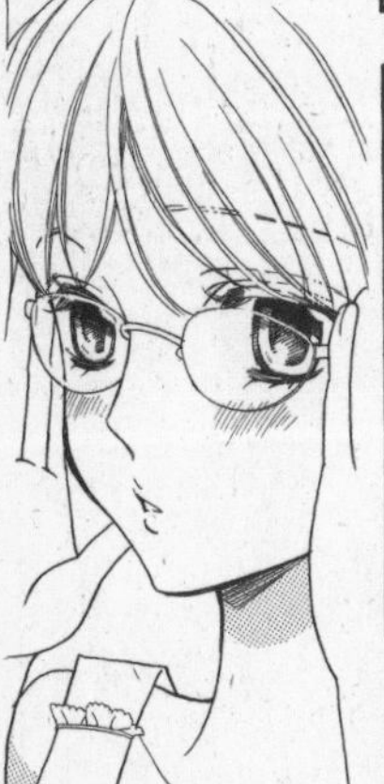

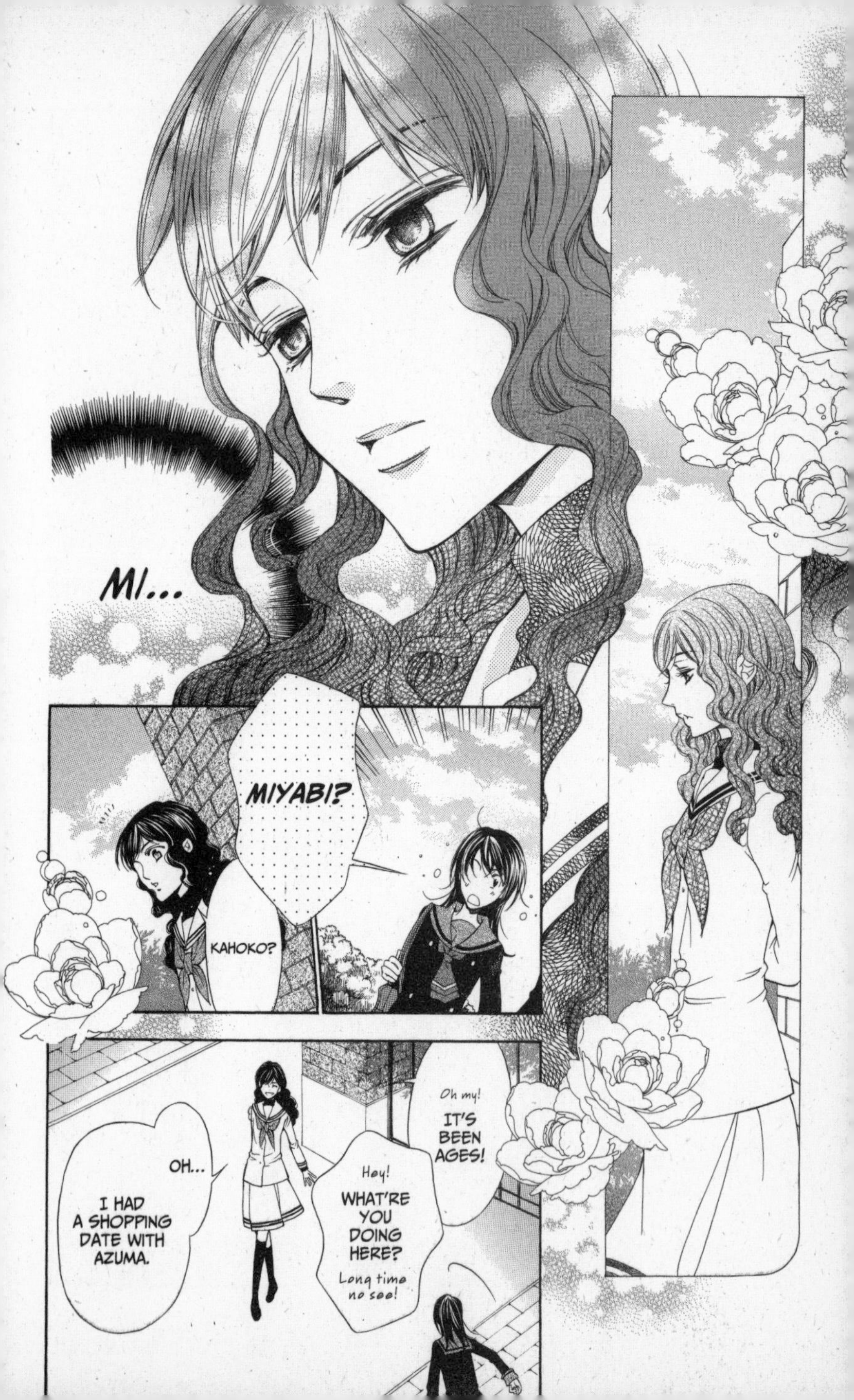
MI...
MIYABI?
KAHOKO?
Oh my! IT'S BEEN AGES!
Hey! WHAT'RE YOU DOING HERE? Long time no see!
OH... I HAD A SHOPPING DATE WITH AZUMA.

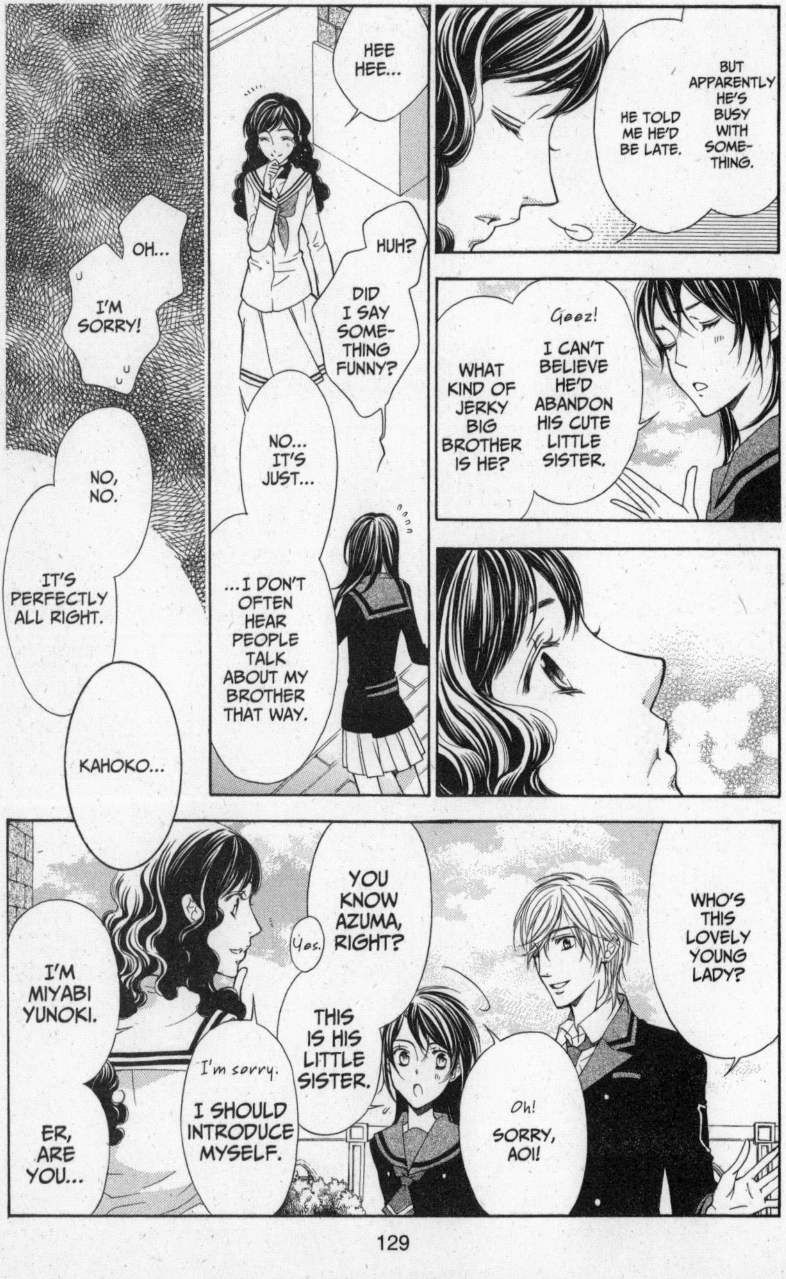
HE TOLD ME HE'D BE LATE.
BUT APPARENTLY HE'S BUSY WITH SOME-THING.
Geez!
I CAN'T BELIEVE HE'D ABANDON HIS CUTE LITTLE SISTER.
WHAT KIND OF JERKY BIG BROTHER IS HE?
HEE HEE...
HUH?
DID I SAY SOME-THING FUNNY?
NO... IT'S JUST...
...I DON'T OFTEN HEAR PEOPLE TALK ABOUT MY BROTHER THAT WAY.
OH...
I'M SORRY!
NO, NO.
IT'S PERFECTLY ALL RIGHT.
KAHOKO...
WHO'S THIS LOVELY YOUNG LADY?
Oh!
SORRY, AOI!
YOU KNOW AZUMA, RIGHT?
Yes.
THIS IS HIS LITTLE SISTER.
ER, ARE YOU...
I'm sorry.
I SHOULD INTRODUCE MYSELF.
I'M MIYABI YUNOKI.

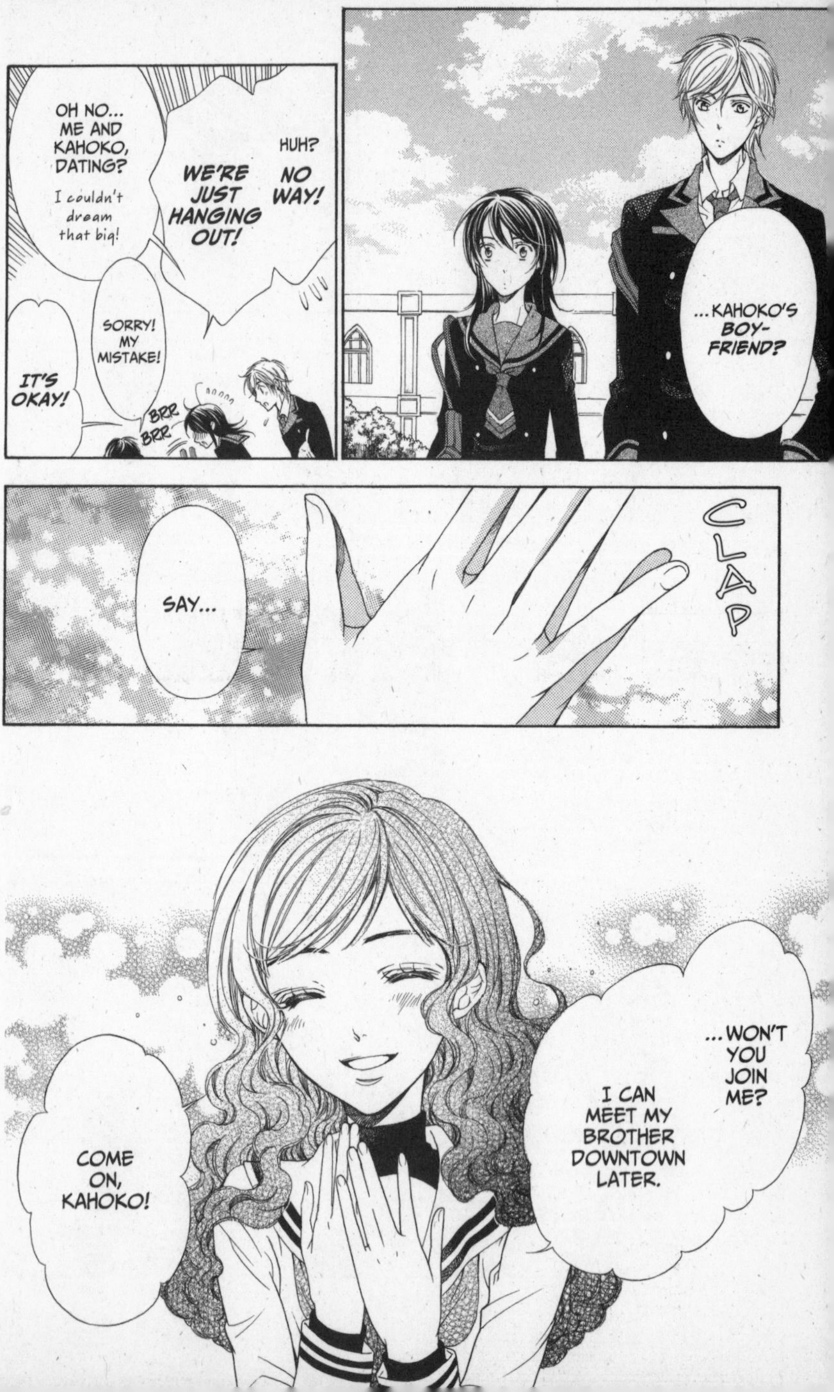
...KAHOKO'S BOY-FRIEND?
HUH? NO WAY!
WE'RE JUST HANGING OUT!
OH NO... ME AND KAHOKO, DATING?
I couldn't dream that big!
SORRY! MY MISTAKE!
BRR BRR
IT'S OKAY!
CLAP
SAY...
...WON'T YOU JOIN ME?
I CAN MEET MY BROTHER DOWNTOWN LATER.
COME ON, KAHOKO!

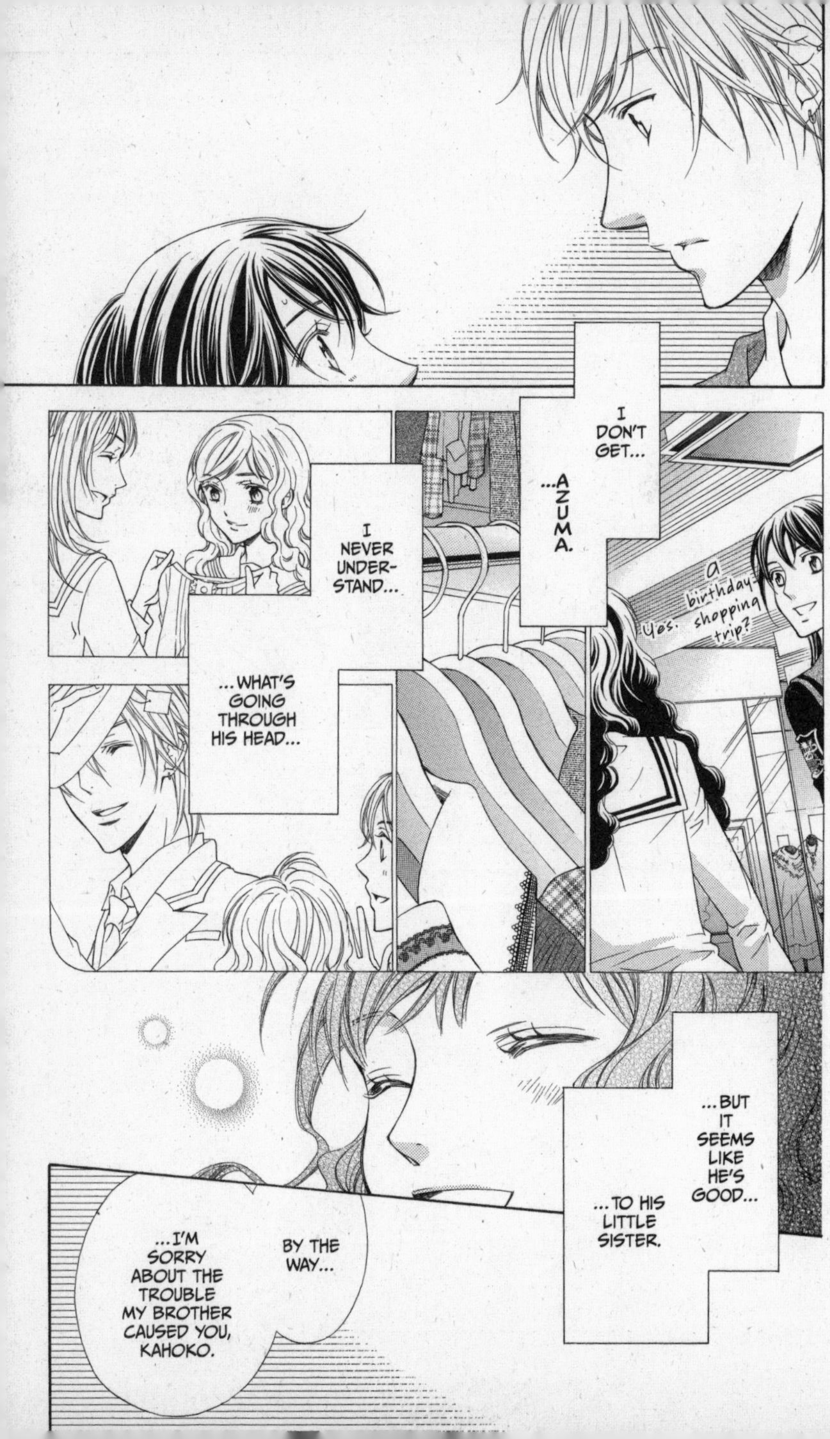
I DON'T GET...
...AZUMA.
a birthday shopping trip?
Yes.
I NEVER UNDER-STAND...
...WHAT'S GOING THROUGH HIS HEAD...
...BUT IT SEEMS LIKE HE'S GOOD...
...TO HIS LITTLE SISTER.
BY THE WAY...
...I'M SORRY ABOUT THE TROUBLE MY BROTHER CAUSED YOU, KAHOKO.

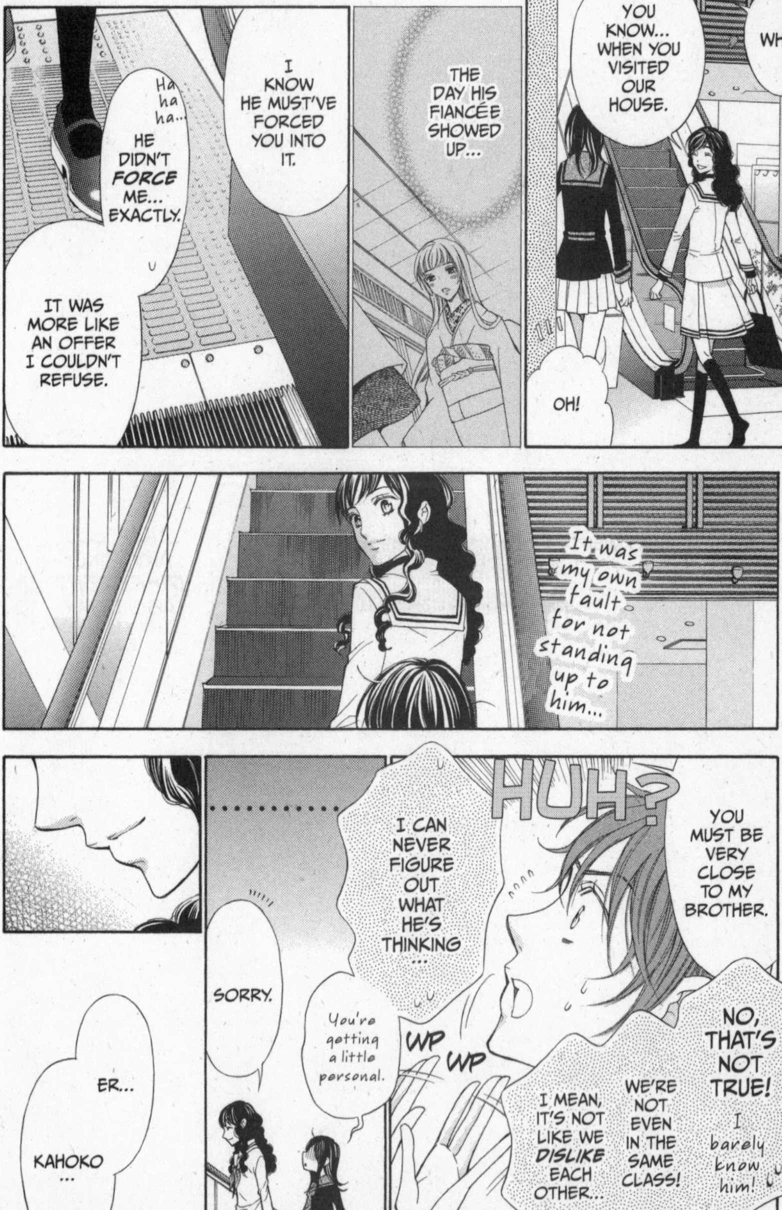
WHEN?
YOU KNOW... WHEN YOU VISITED OUR HOUSE.
OH!
THE DAY HIS FIANCÉE SHOWED UP...
I KNOW HE MUST'VE FORCED YOU INTO IT.
Ha ha ha... HE DIDN'T *FORCE* ME... EXACTLY.
IT WAS MORE LIKE AN OFFER I COULDN'T REFUSE.
It was my own fault for not standing up to him...
YOU MUST BE VERY CLOSE TO MY BROTHER.
HUH?
NO, THAT'S NOT TRUE!
I barely know him!
WE'RE NOT EVEN IN THE SAME CLASS!
I MEAN, IT'S NOT LIKE WE *DISLIKE* EACH OTHER...
WP WP
I CAN NEVER FIGURE OUT WHAT HE'S THINKING...
You're getting a little personal.
SORRY.
ER...
KAHOKO...

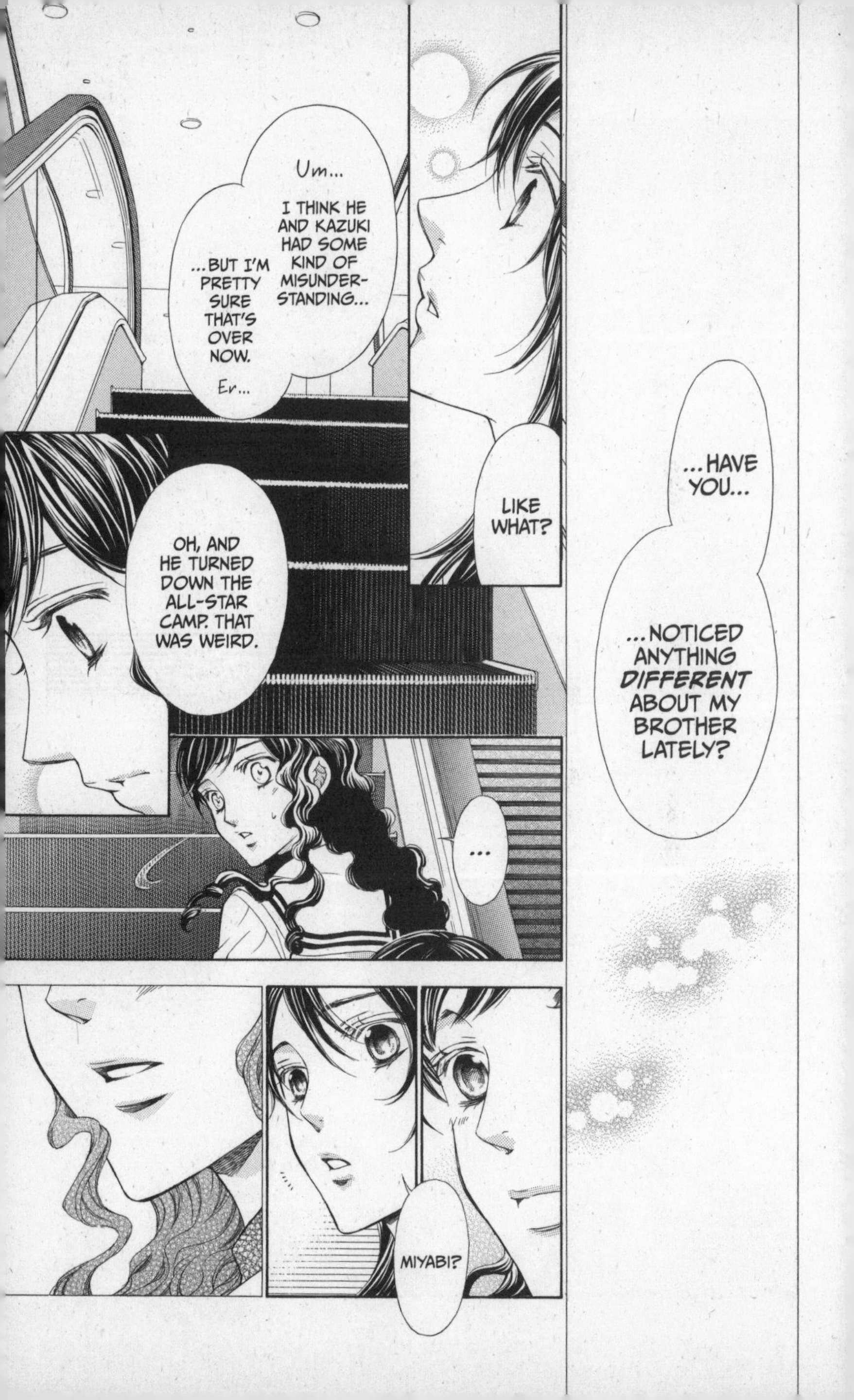
...HAVE YOU...
...NOTICED ANYTHING DIFFERENT ABOUT MY BROTHER LATELY?
LIKE WHAT?
Um...
I THINK HE AND KAZUKI HAD SOME KIND OF MISUNDER-STANDING...
...BUT I'M PRETTY SURE THAT'S OVER NOW.
Er...
OH, AND HE TURNED DOWN THE ALL-STAR CAMP. THAT WAS WEIRD.
...
MIYABI?

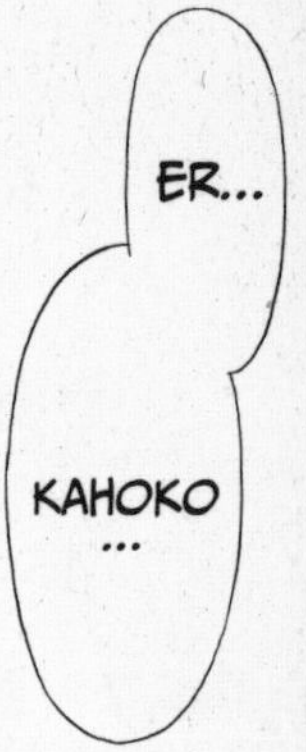
ER...
KAHOKO ...

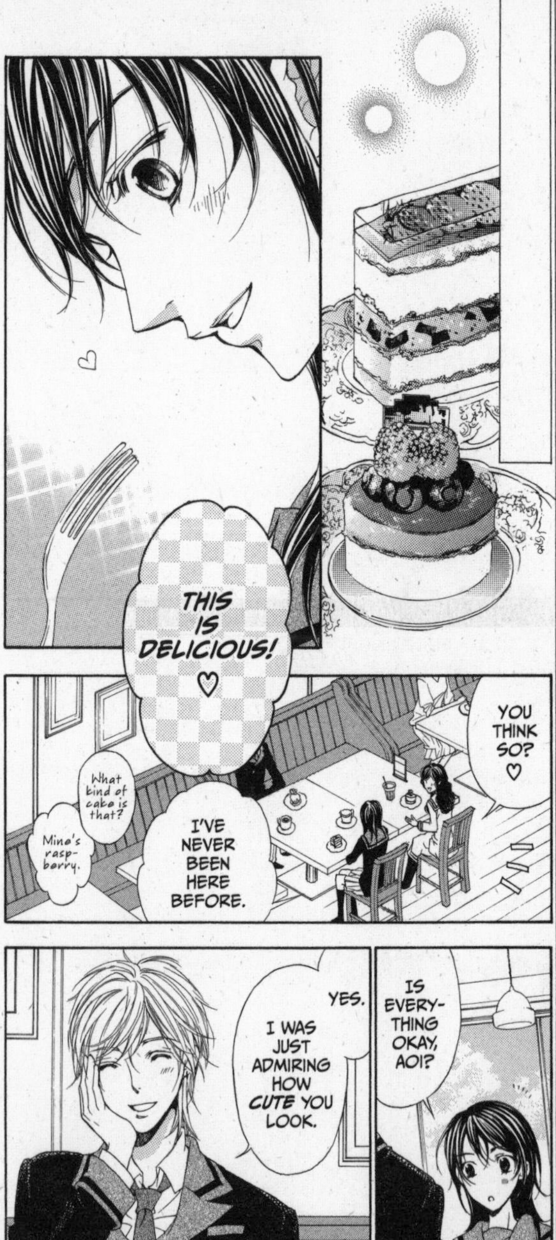
THIS IS DELICIOUS! ♡
YOU THINK SO? ♡
I'VE NEVER BEEN HERE BEFORE.
What kind of cake is that?
Mine's raspberry.
IS EVERY-THING OKAY, AOI?
YES.
I WAS JUST ADMIRING HOW *CUTE* YOU LOOK.

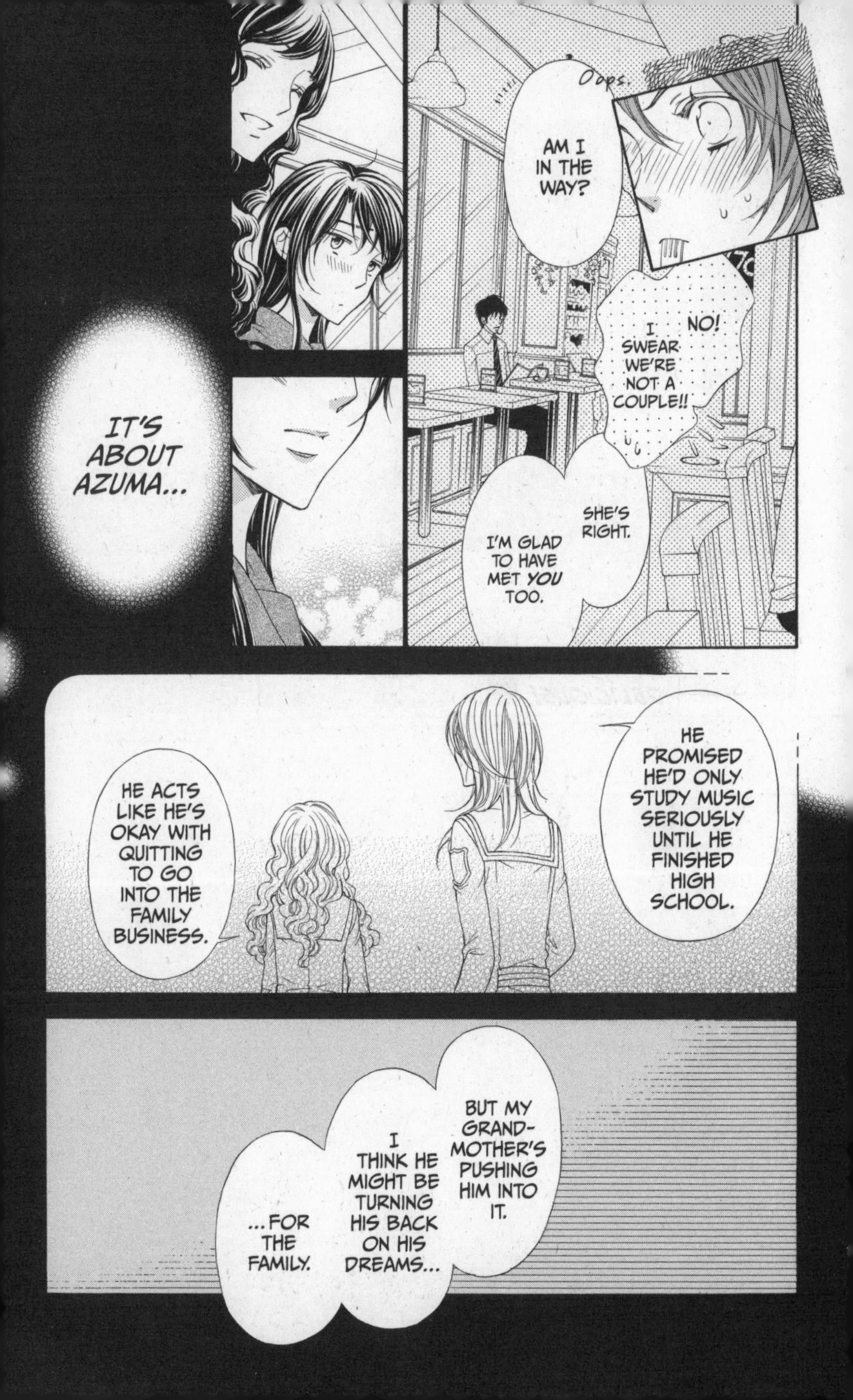
Oops.
AM I IN THE WAY?
NO! I SWEAR WE'RE NOT A COUPLE!!
SHE'S RIGHT.
I'M GLAD TO HAVE MET YOU TOO.
IT'S ABOUT AZUMA...
HE PROMISED HE'D ONLY STUDY MUSIC SERIOUSLY UNTIL HE FINISHED HIGH SCHOOL.
HE ACTS LIKE HE'S OKAY WITH QUITTING TO GO INTO THE FAMILY BUSINESS.
BUT MY GRANDMOTHER'S PUSHING HIM INTO IT.
I THINK HE MIGHT BE TURNING HIS BACK ON HIS DREAMS...
...FOR THE FAMILY.

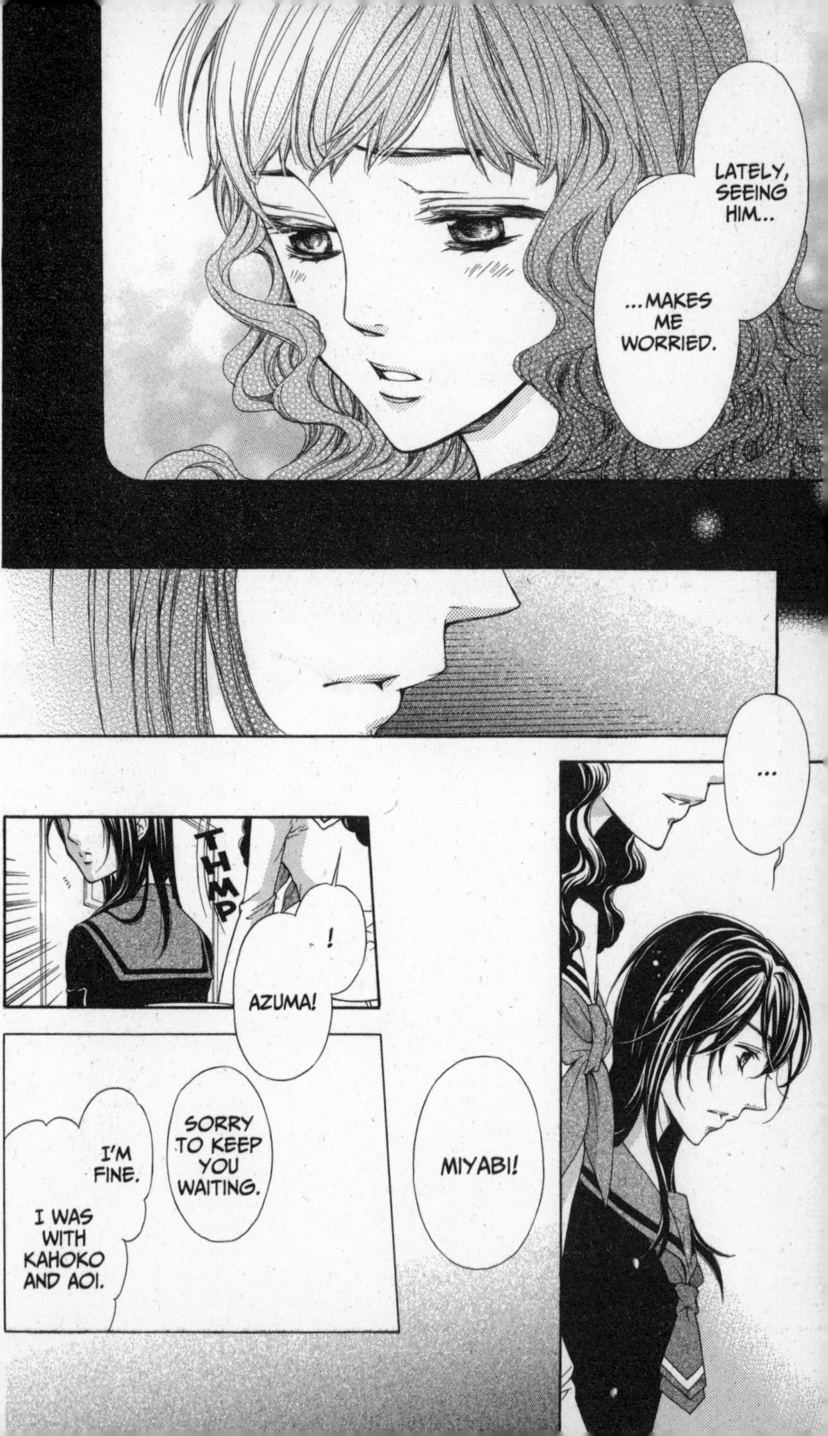
LATELY, SEEING HIM...
...MAKES ME WORRIED.
...
THUMP
!
AZUMA!
MIYABI!
SORRY TO KEEP YOU WAITING.
I'M FINE.
I WAS WITH KAHOKO AND AOI.

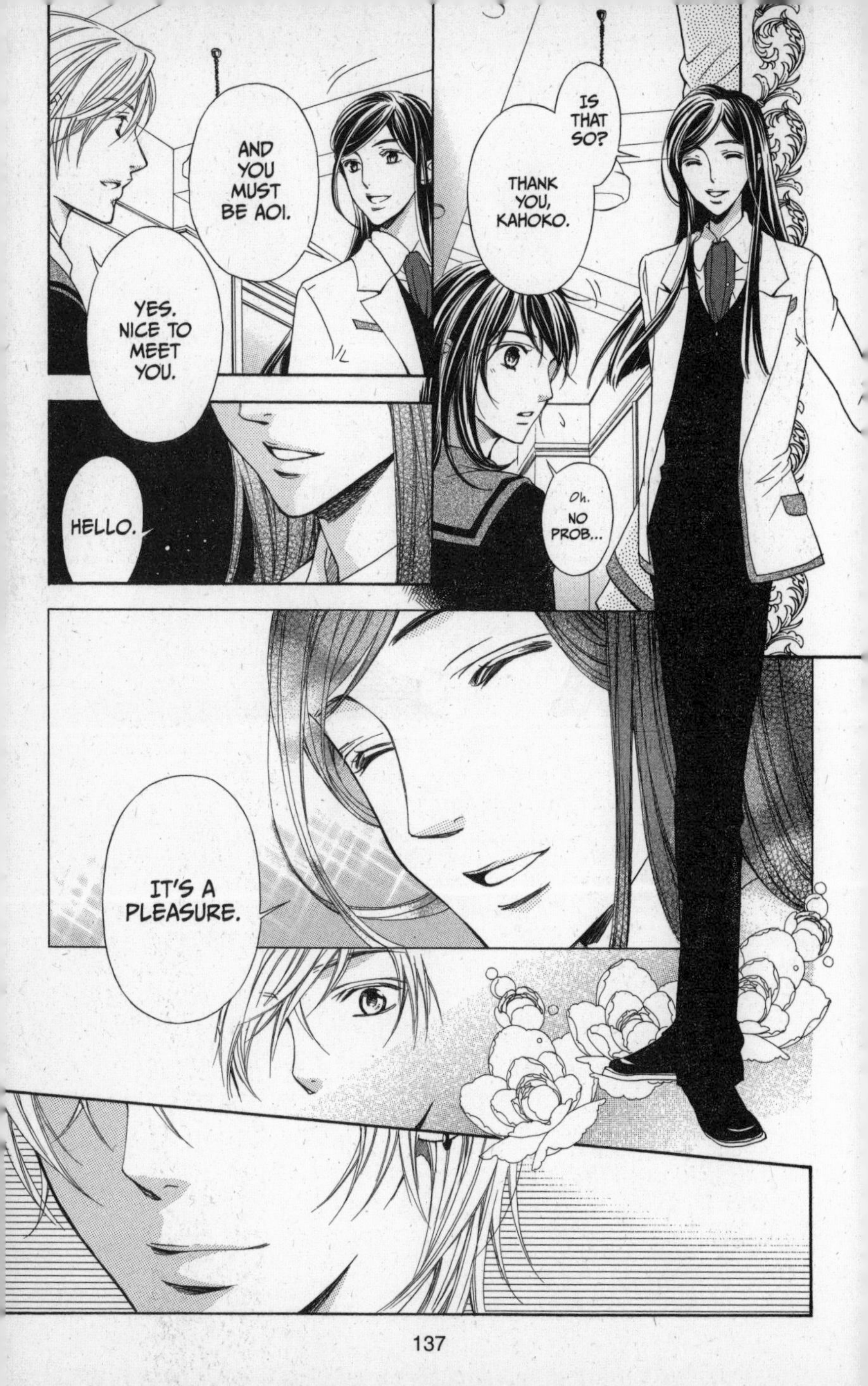
IS THAT SO?
THANK YOU, KAHOKO.
Oh. NO PROB...
AND YOU MUST BE AOI.
YES. NICE TO MEET YOU.
HELLO.
IT'S A PLEASURE.

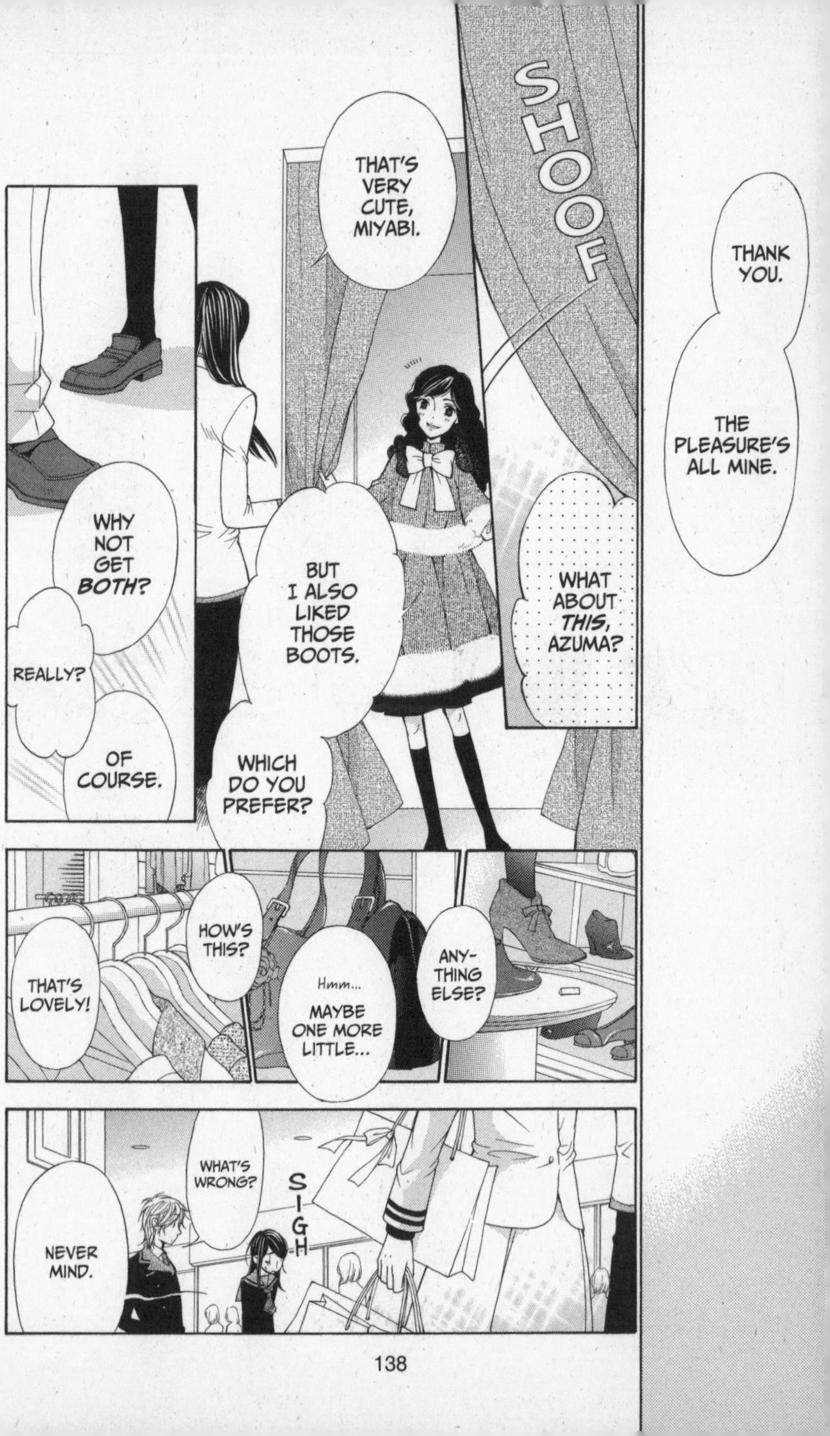
THANK YOU.
THE PLEASURE'S ALL MINE.
SHOOF
THAT'S VERY CUTE, MIYABI.
WHAT ABOUT *THIS*, AZUMA?
BUT I ALSO LIKED THOSE BOOTS.
WHICH DO YOU PREFER?
WHY NOT GET *BOTH*?
REALLY?
OF COURSE.
ANY-THING ELSE?
Hmm...
MAYBE ONE MORE LITTLE...
HOW'S THIS?
THAT'S LOVELY!
SIGH
WHAT'S WRONG?
NEVER MIND.

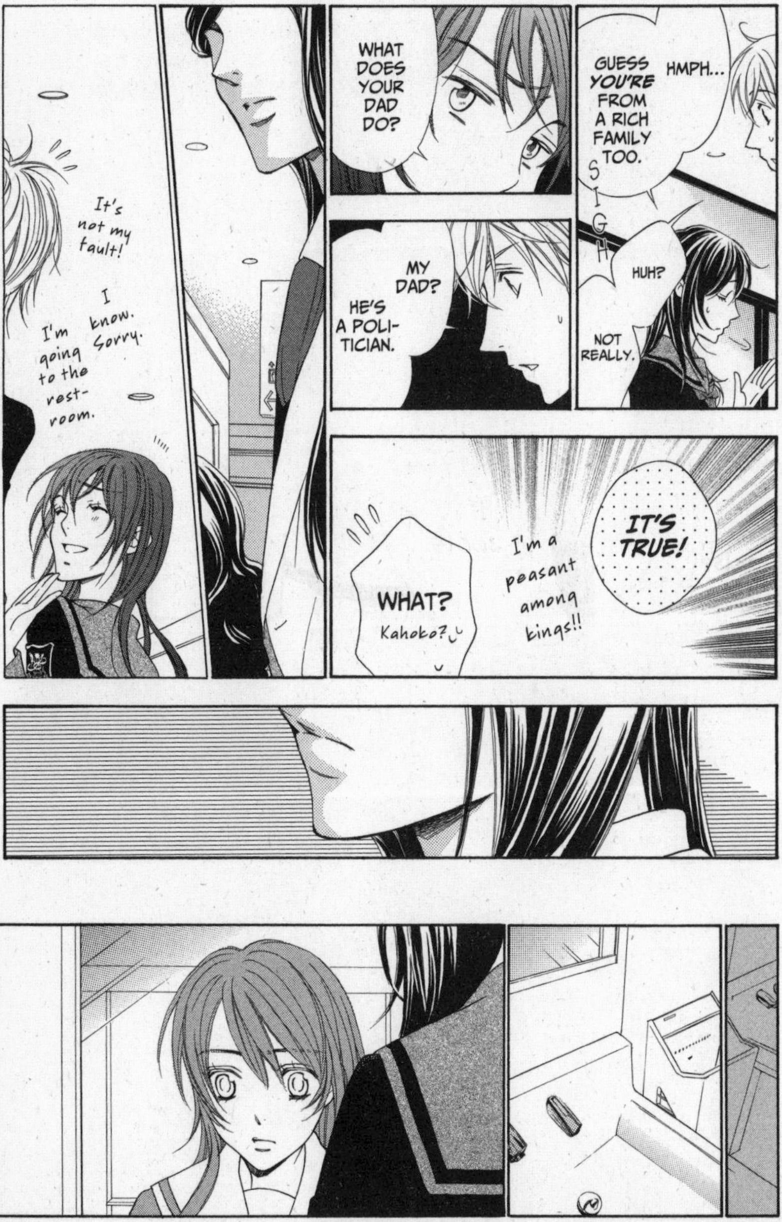
HMPH...
GUESS YOU'RE FROM A RICH FAMILY TOO.
SIGH
HUH?
NOT REALLY.
WHAT DOES YOUR DAD DO?
MY DAD?
HE'S A POLITICIAN.
IT'S TRUE!
I'm a peasant among kings!!
WHAT?
Kahoko?
It's not my fault!
I know. Sorry.
I'm going to the rest-room.

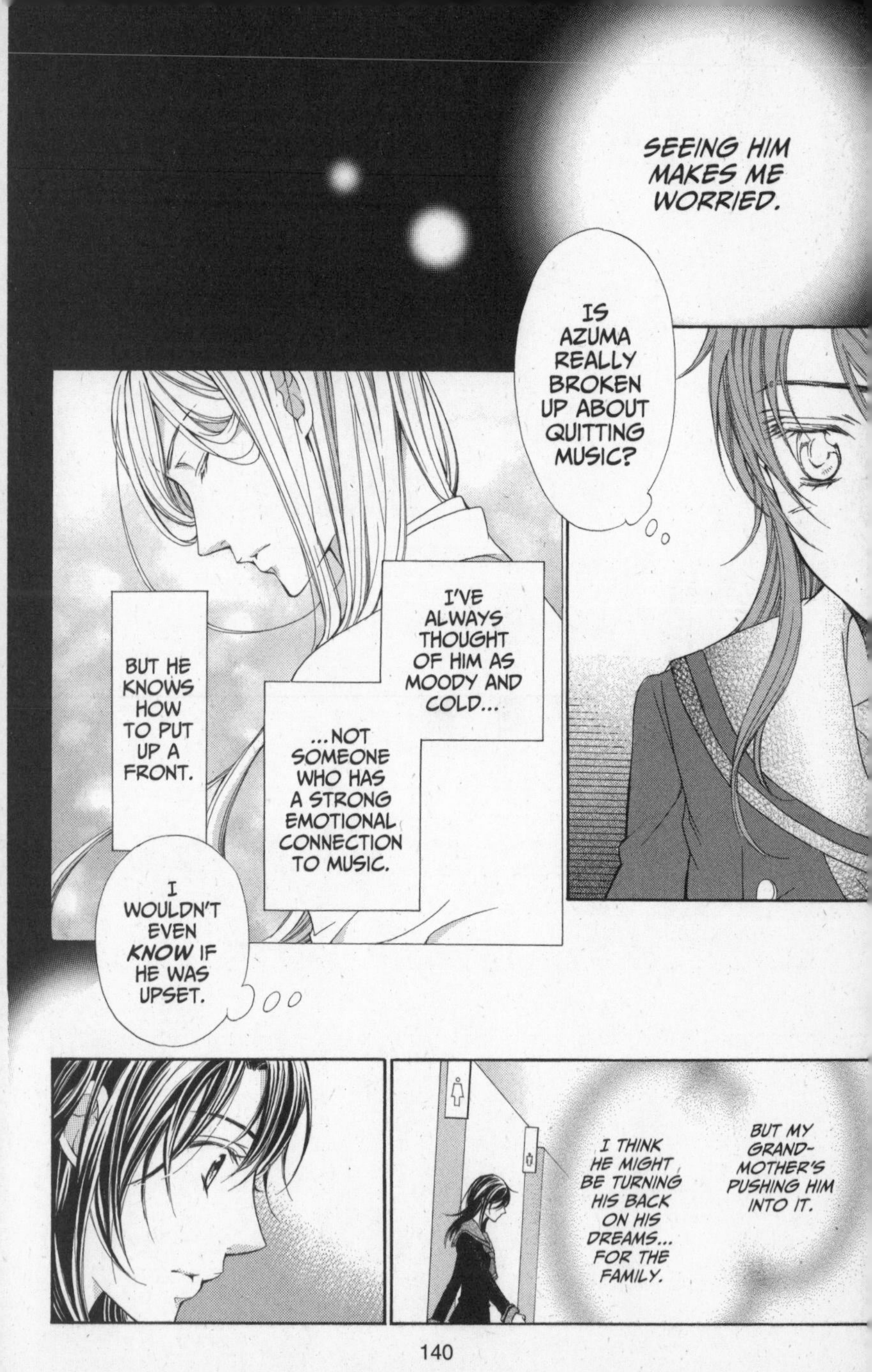
SEEING HIM MAKES ME WORRIED.
IS AZUMA REALLY BROKEN UP ABOUT QUITTING MUSIC?
I'VE ALWAYS THOUGHT OF HIM AS MOODY AND COLD...
...NOT SOMEONE WHO HAS A STRONG EMOTIONAL CONNECTION TO MUSIC.
BUT HE KNOWS HOW TO PUT UP A FRONT.
I WOULDN'T EVEN *KNOW* IF HE WAS UPSET.
BUT MY GRANDMOTHER'S PUSHING HIM INTO IT.
I THINK HE MIGHT BE TURNING HIS BACK ON HIS DREAMS... FOR THE FAMILY.

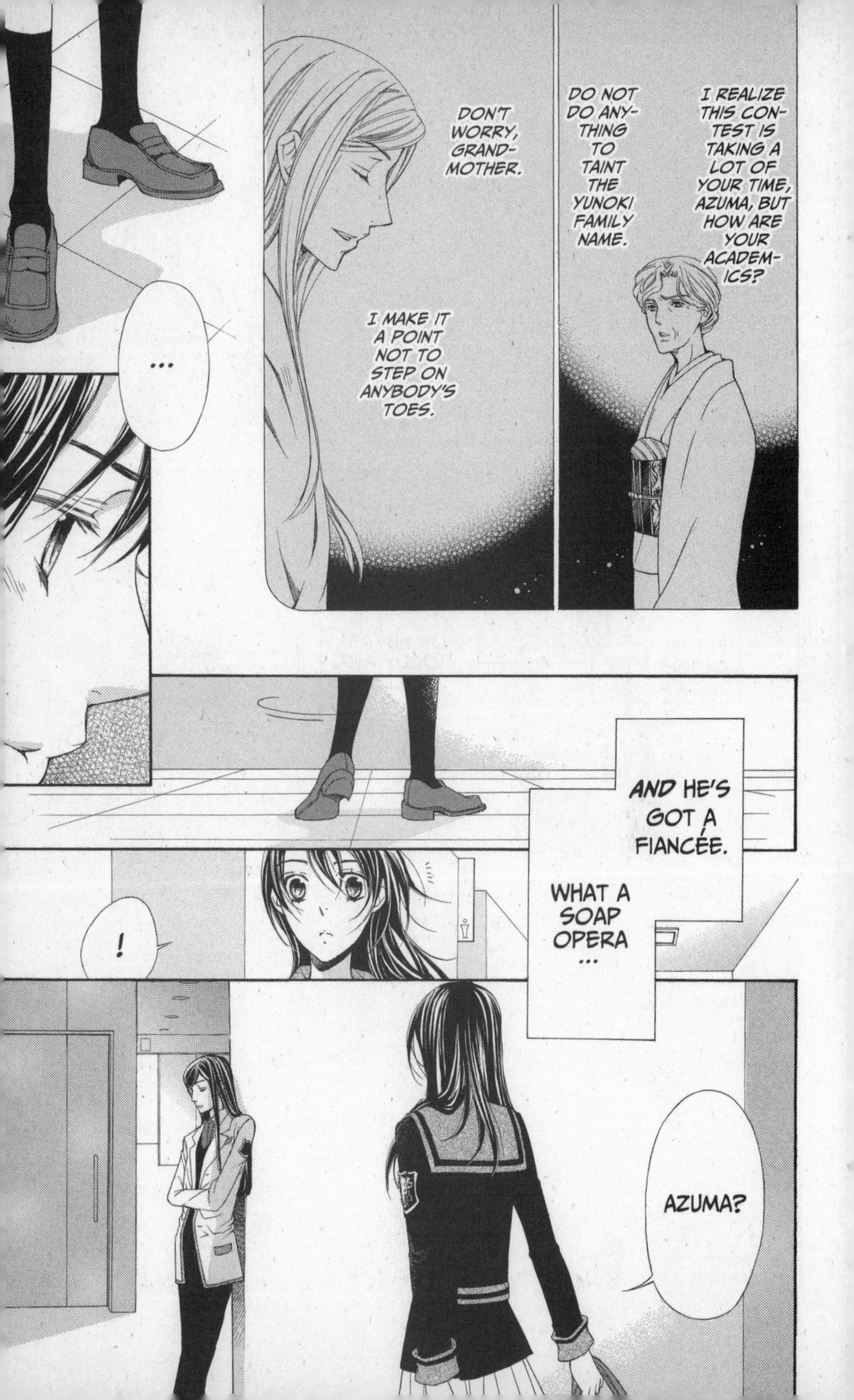
I REALIZE THIS CONTEST IS TAKING A LOT OF YOUR TIME, AZUMA, BUT HOW ARE YOUR ACADEMICS?
DO NOT DO ANYTHING TO TAINT THE YUNOKI FAMILY NAME.
DON'T WORRY, GRANDMOTHER.
I MAKE IT A POINT NOT TO STEP ON ANYBODY'S TOES.
...
AND HE'S GOT A FIANCÉE.
WHAT A SOAP OPERA ...
!
AZUMA?

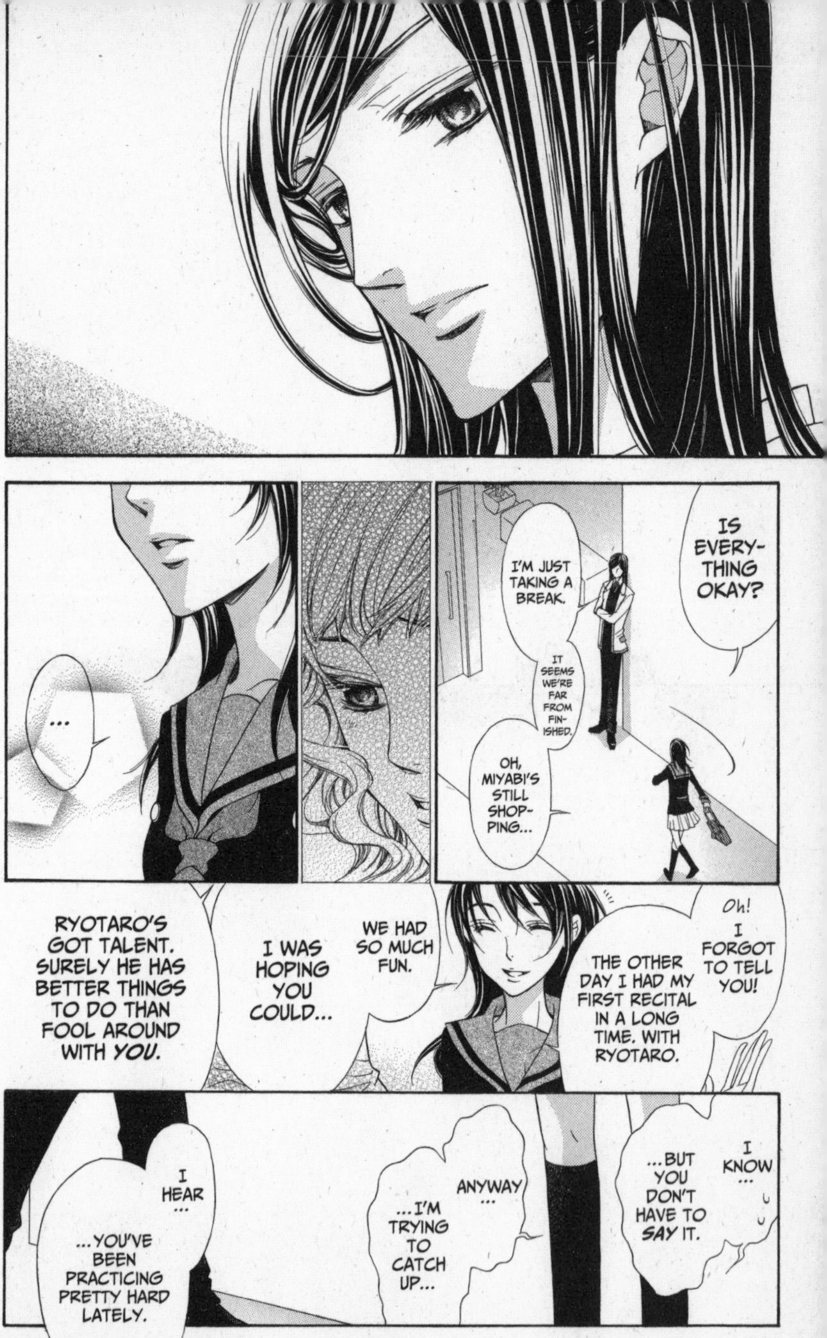
IS EVERY-THING OKAY?
I'M JUST TAKING A BREAK.
IT SEEMS WE'RE FAR FROM FIN-ISHED.
OH, MIYABI'S STILL SHOP-PING...
...
Oh! I FORGOT TO TELL YOU!
THE OTHER DAY I HAD MY FIRST RECITAL IN A LONG TIME. WITH RYOTARO.
WE HAD SO MUCH FUN.
I WAS HOPING YOU COULD...
RYOTARO'S GOT TALENT. SURELY HE HAS BETTER THINGS TO DO THAN FOOL AROUND WITH *YOU*.
I KNOW...
...BUT YOU DON'T HAVE TO *SAY* IT.
ANYWAY...
...I'M TRYING TO CATCH UP...
I HEAR...
...YOU'VE BEEN PRACTICING PRETTY HARD LATELY.

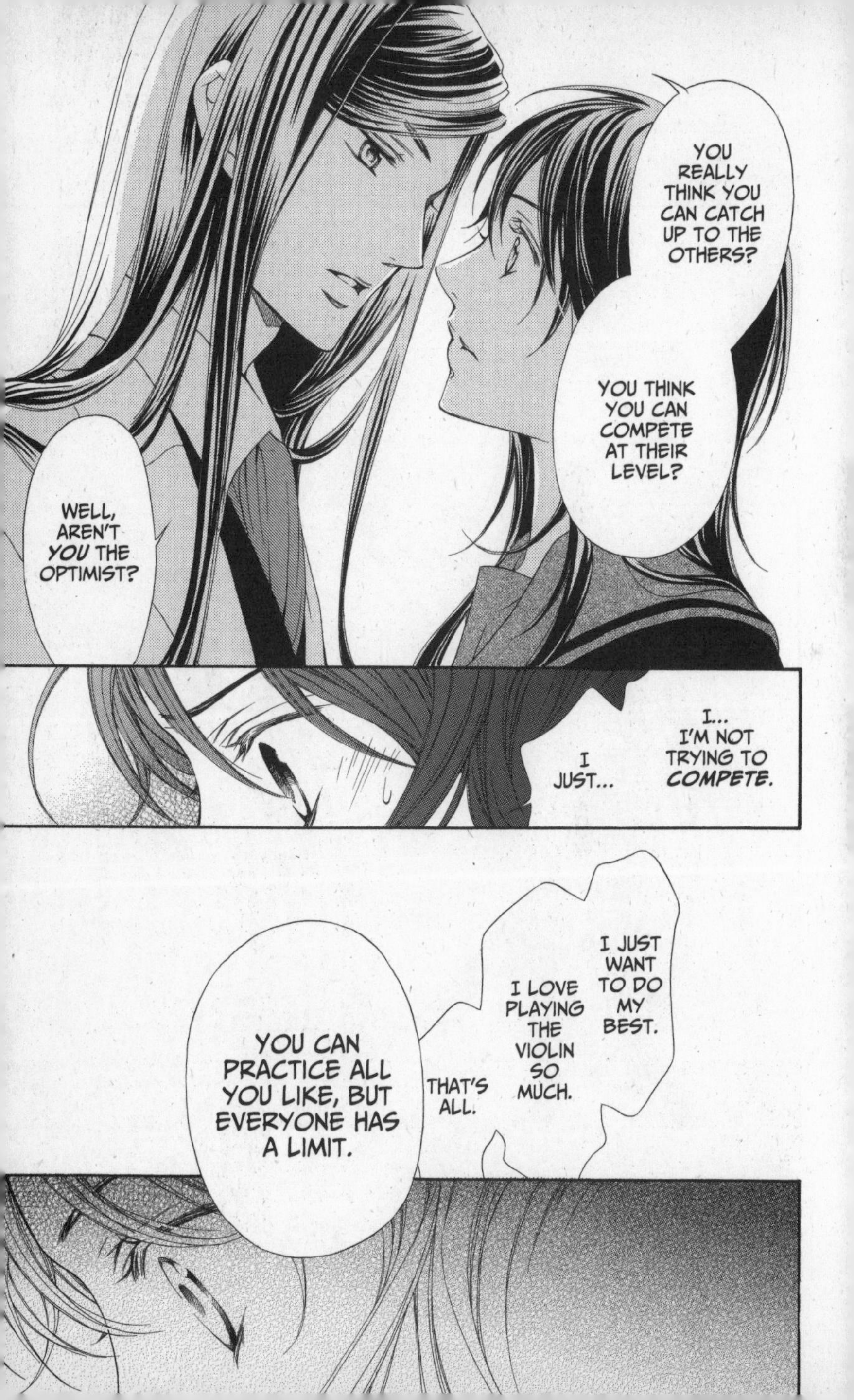
YOU REALLY THINK YOU CAN CATCH UP TO THE OTHERS?
YOU THINK YOU CAN COMPETE AT THEIR LEVEL?
WELL, AREN'T *YOU* THE OPTIMIST?
I... I'M NOT TRYING TO *COMPETE*.
I JUST...
I JUST WANT TO DO MY BEST.
I LOVE PLAYING THE VIOLIN SO MUCH.
THAT'S ALL.
YOU CAN PRACTICE ALL YOU LIKE, BUT EVERYONE HAS A LIMIT.

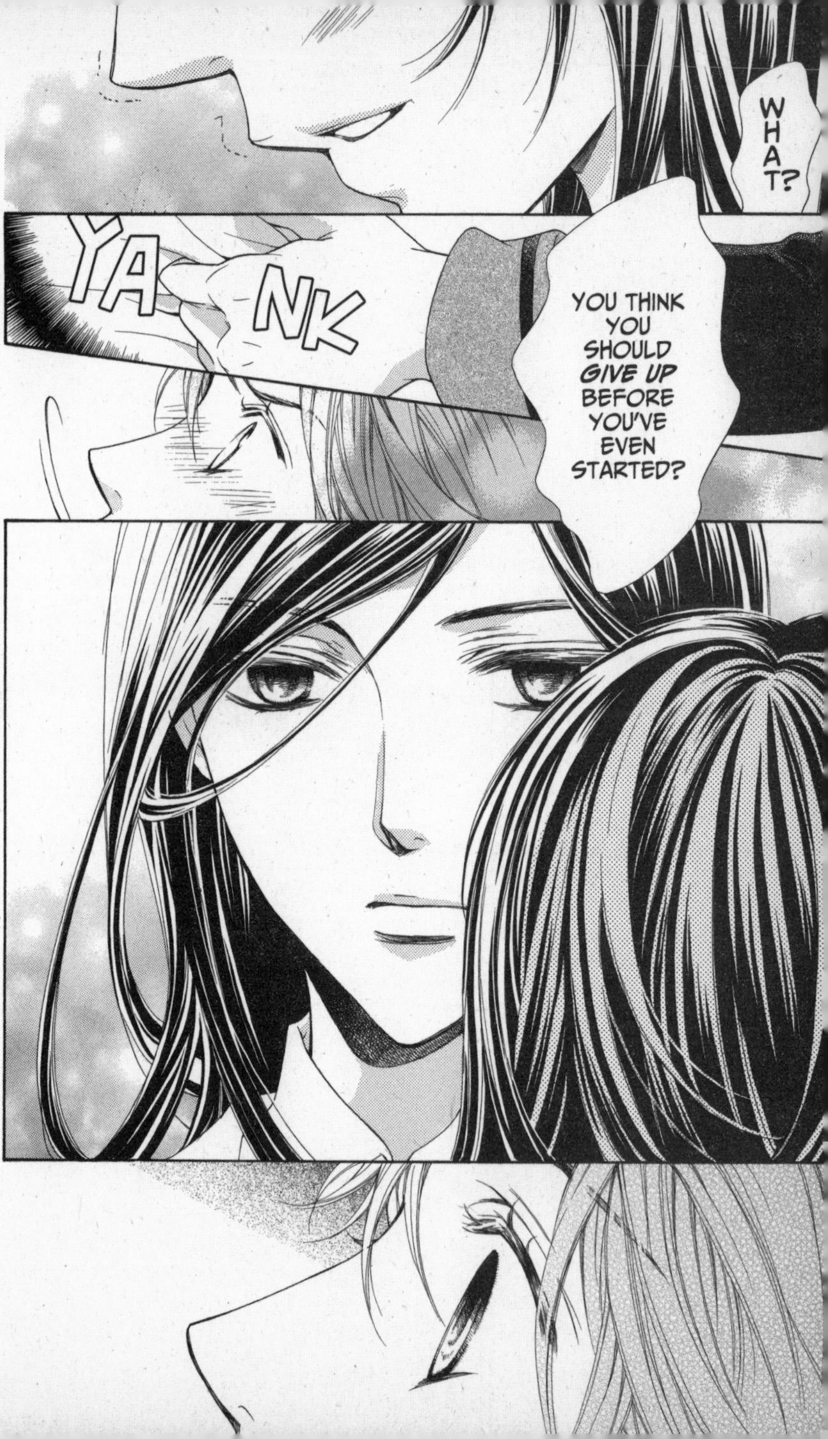
WHAT?
YANK
YOU THINK YOU SHOULD *GIVE UP* BEFORE YOU'VE EVEN STARTED?

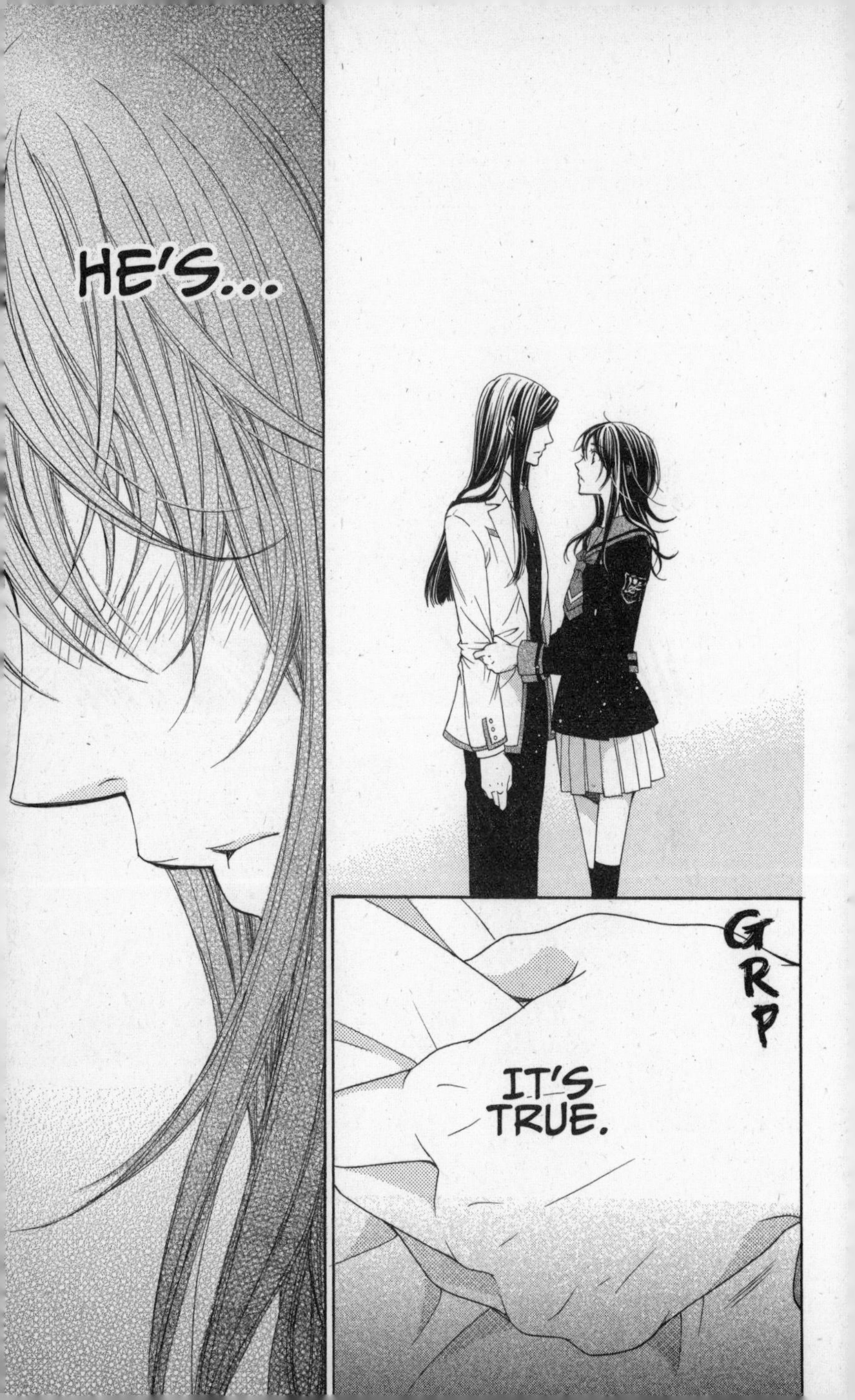
GRP
IT'S TRUE.
HE'S...

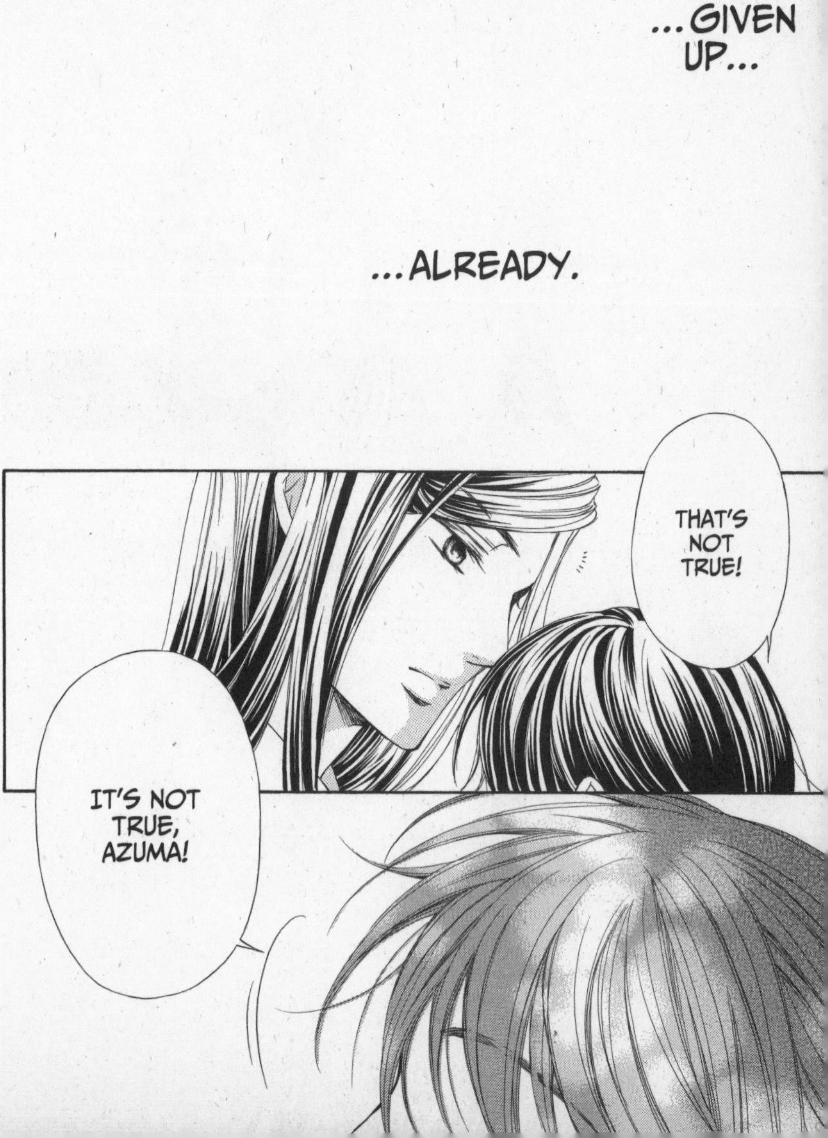
...GIVEN UP...
...ALREADY.
THAT'S NOT TRUE!
IT'S NOT TRUE, AZUMA!

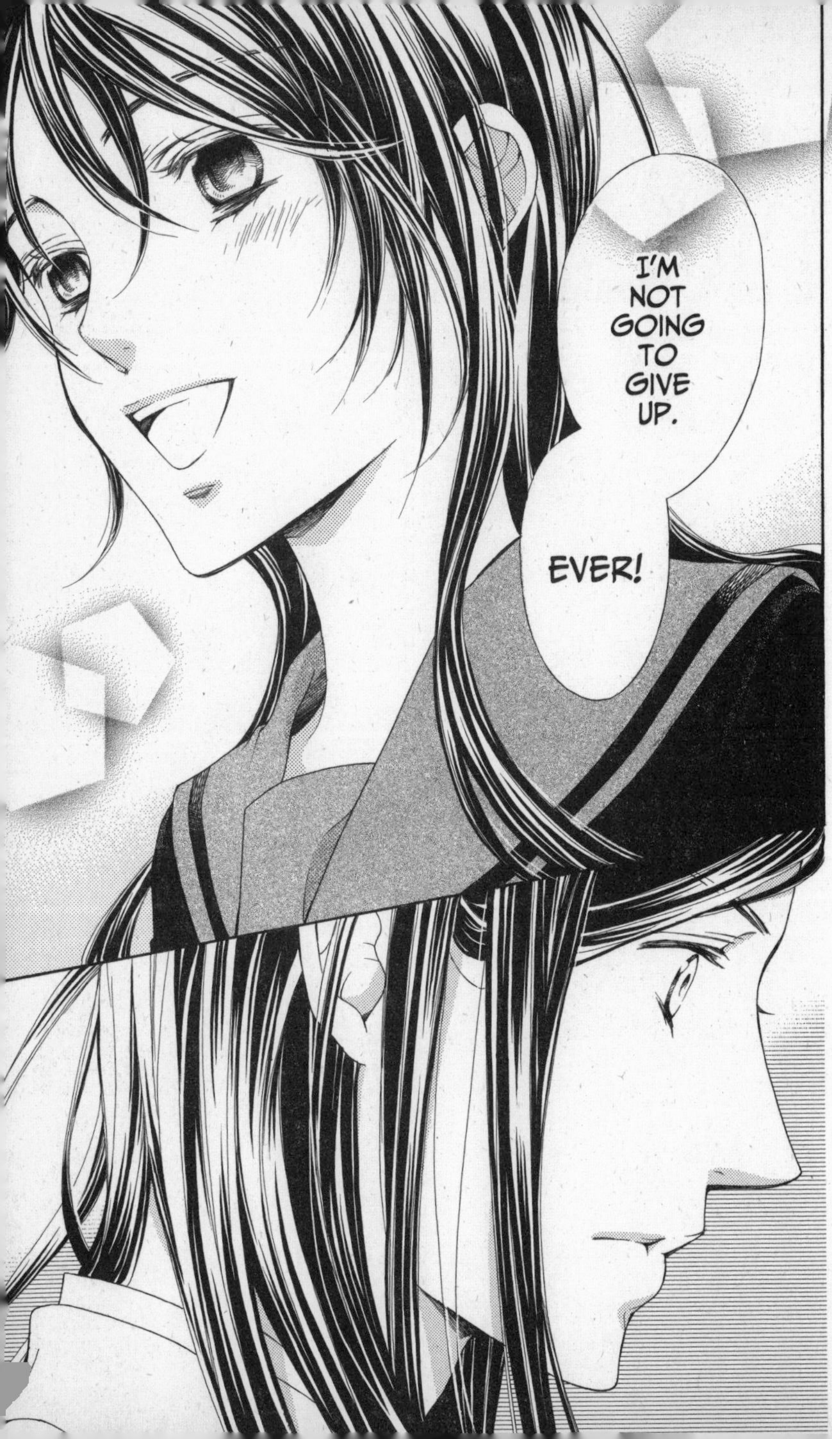
I'M NOT GOING TO GIVE UP.
EVER!

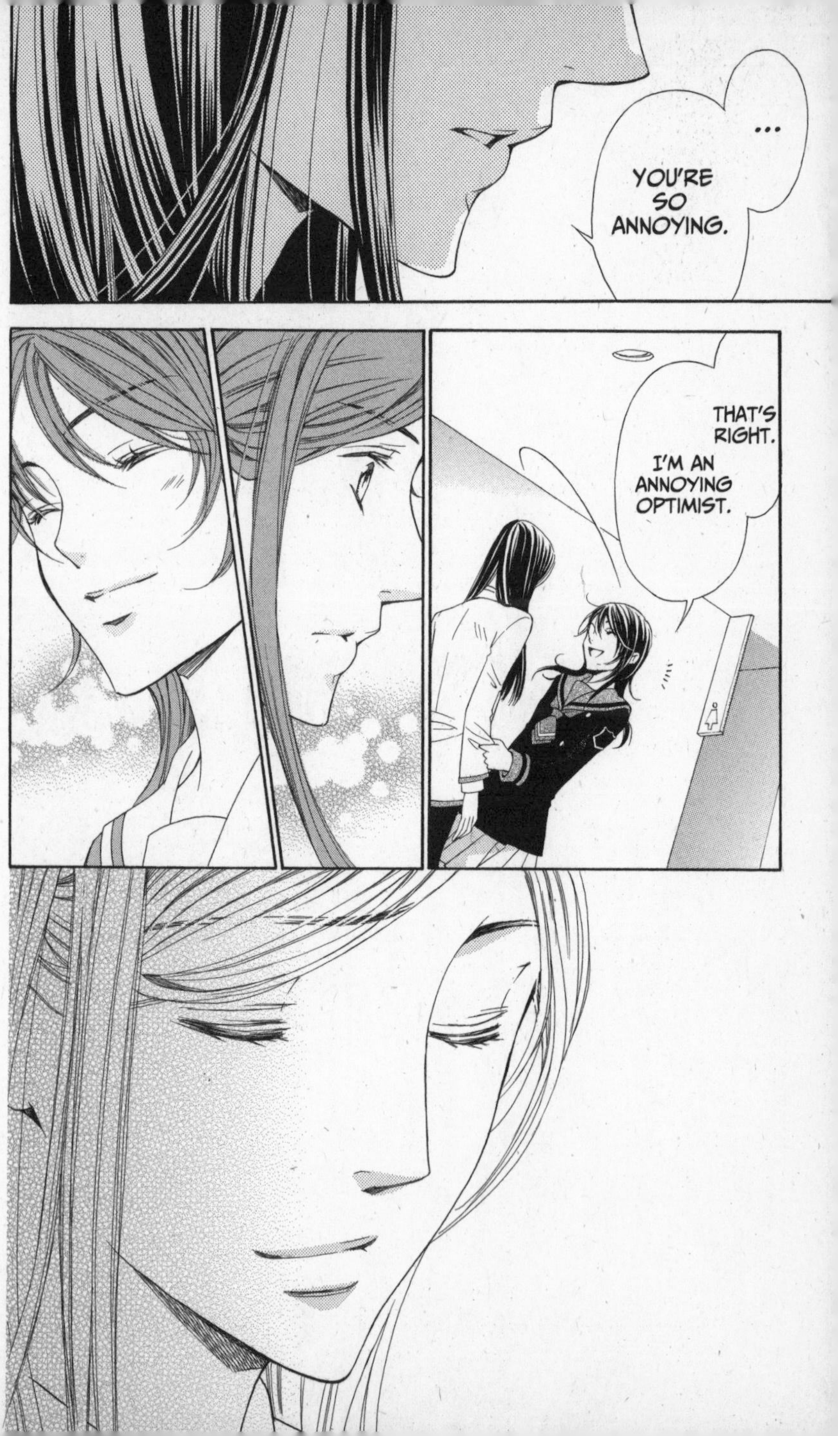
...
YOU'RE SO ANNOYING.
THAT'S RIGHT.
I'M AN ANNOYING OPTIMIST.

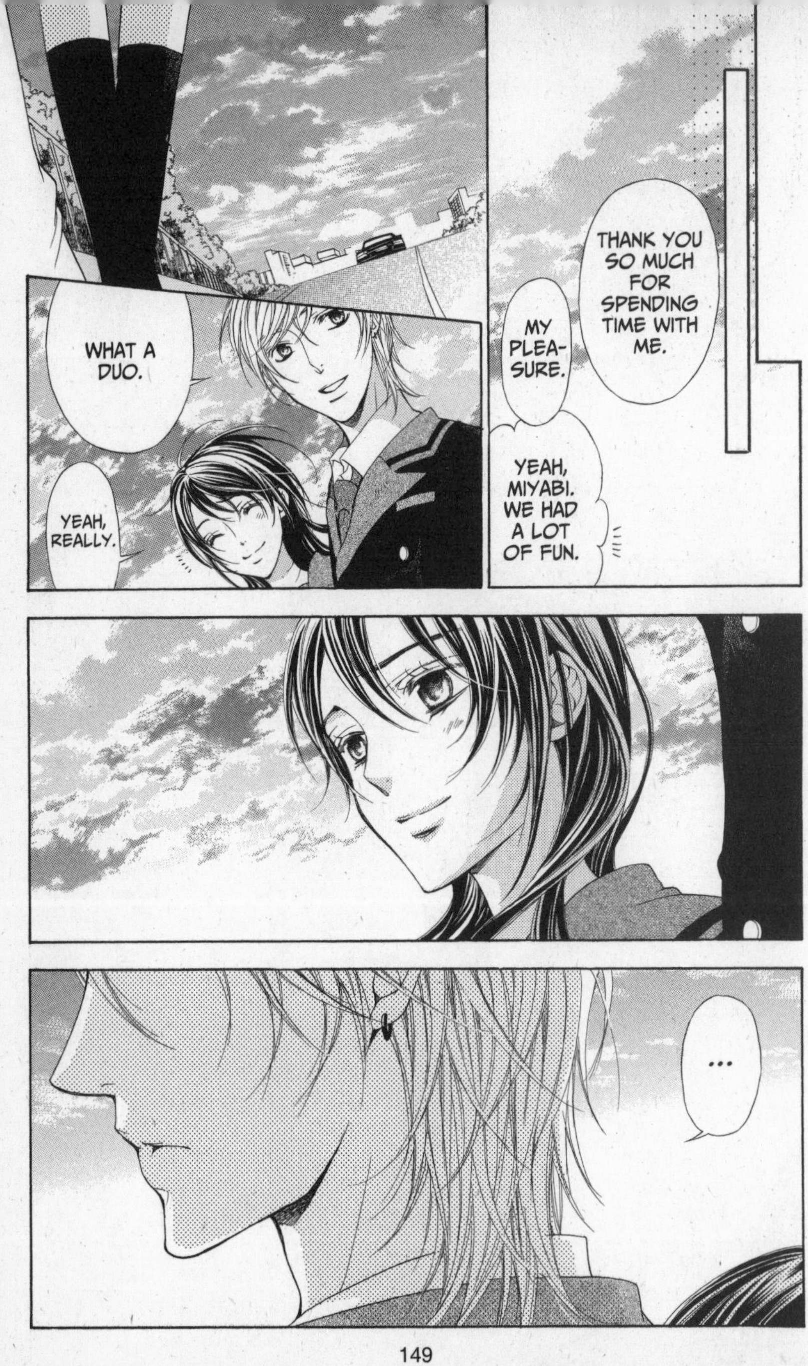
THANK YOU SO MUCH FOR SPENDING TIME WITH ME.
MY PLEA-SURE.
YEAH, MIYABI. WE HAD A LOT OF FUN.
WHAT A DUO.
YEAH, REALLY.
...

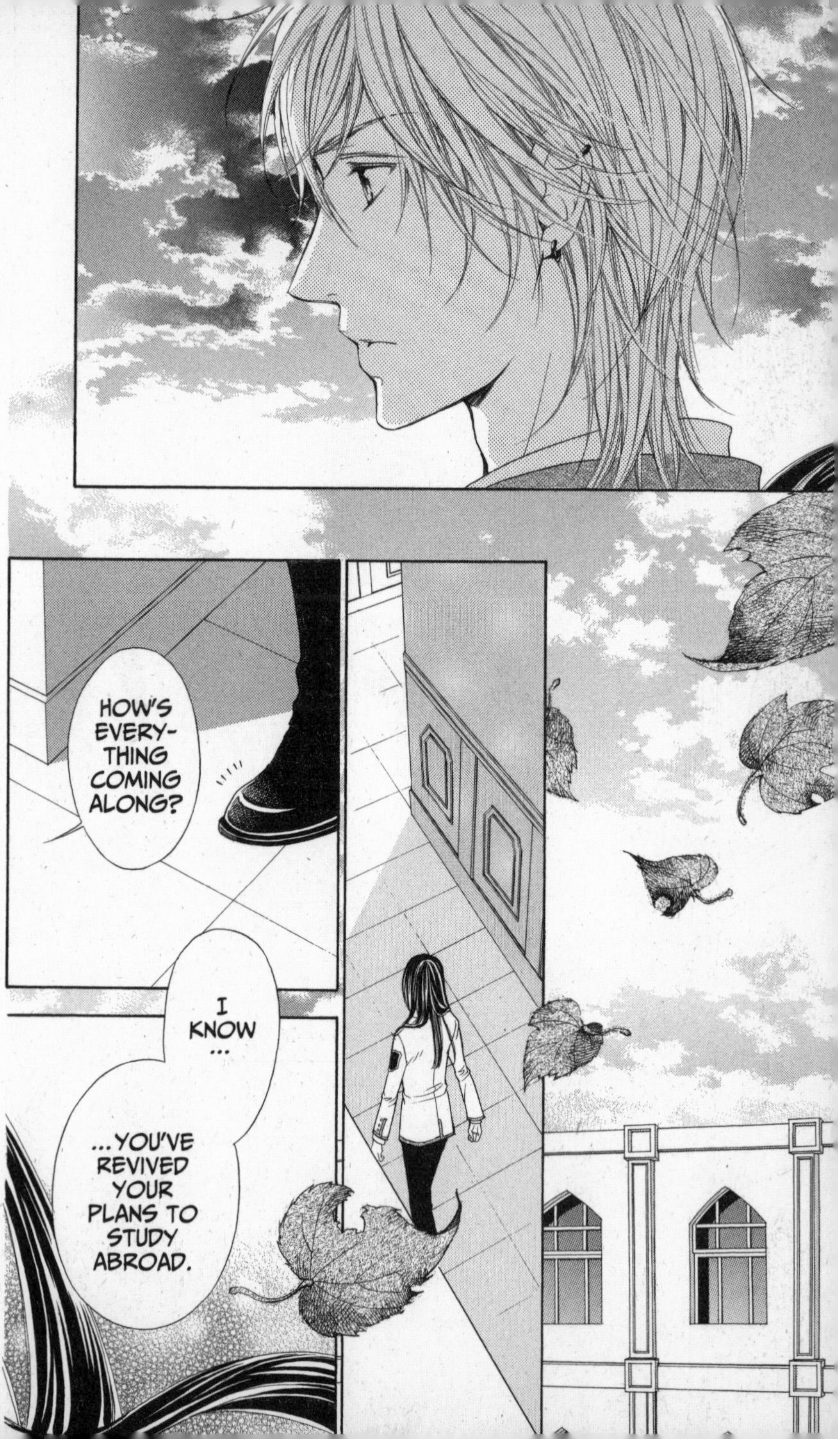
HOW'S EVERYTHING COMING ALONG?
I KNOW...
...YOU'VE REVIVED YOUR PLANS TO STUDY ABROAD.

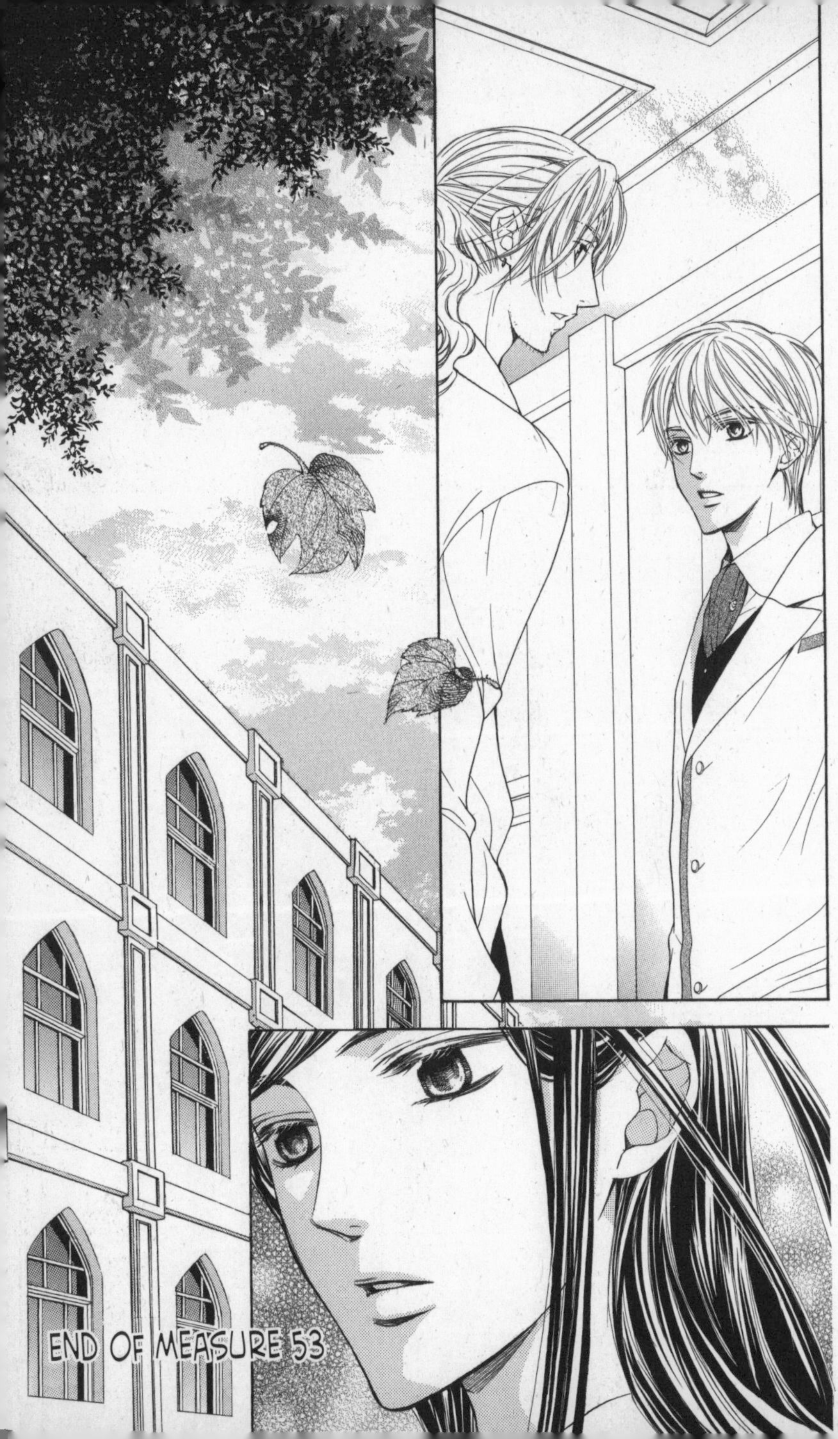
END OF MEASURE 53

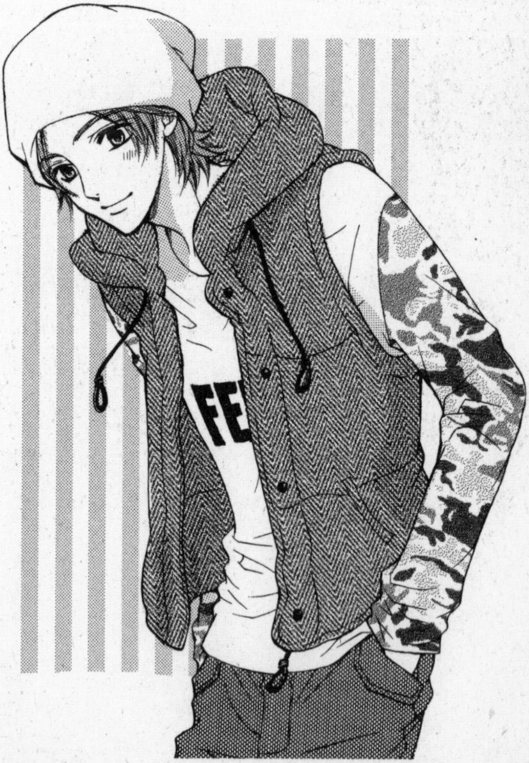
FE

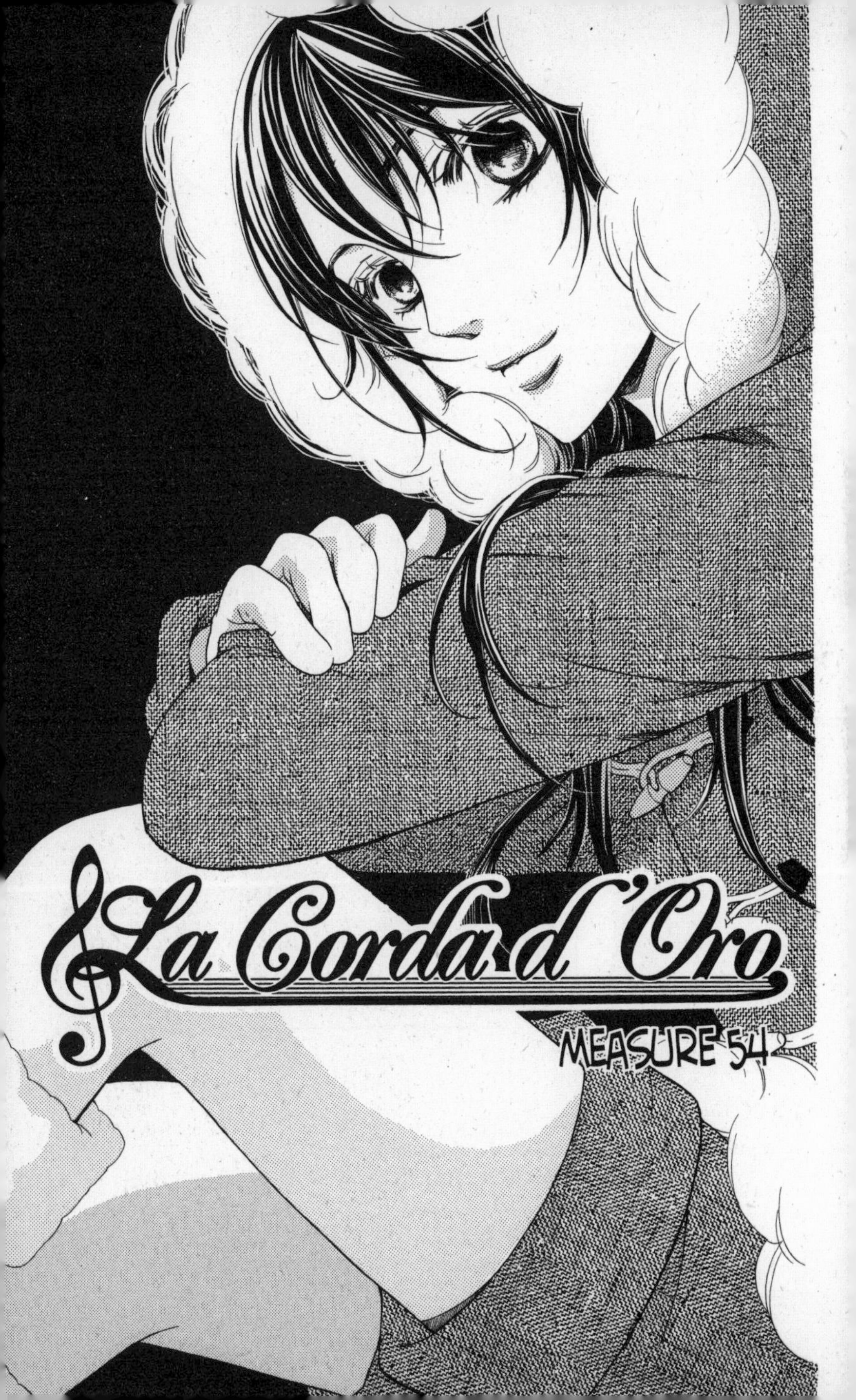
La Corda d'Oro
MEASURE 54

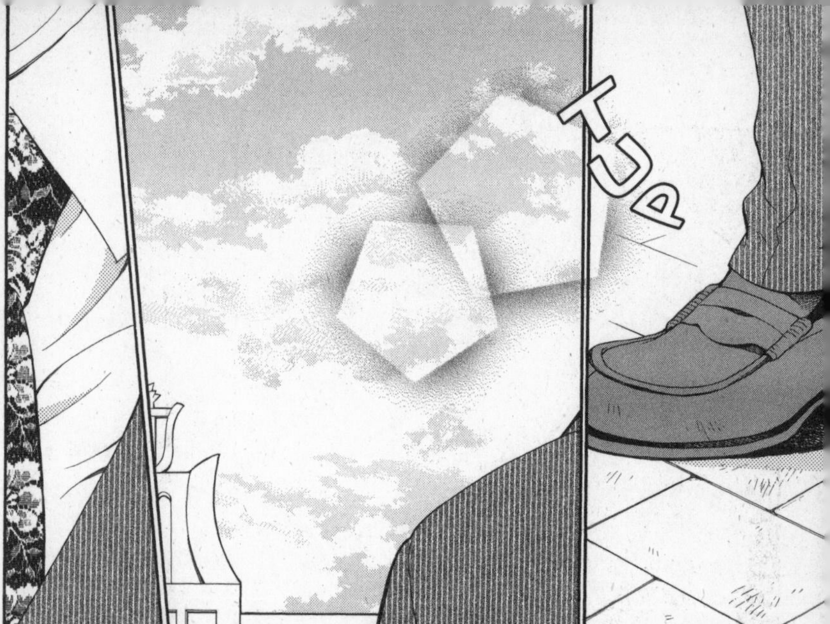
TUP
ALL RIGHT...

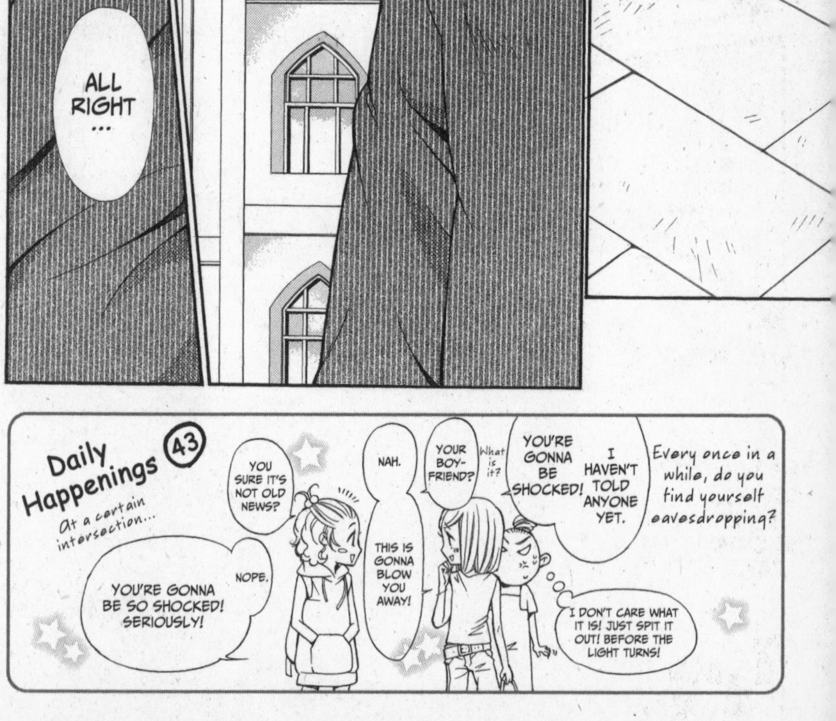
Daily Happenings 43
At a certain intersection...
Every once in a while, do you find yourself eavesdropping?
YOU'RE GONNA BE SHOCKED!
I HAVEN'T TOLD ANYONE YET.
I DON'T CARE WHAT IT IS! JUST SPIT IT OUT! BEFORE THE LIGHT TURNS!
What is it?
YOUR BOY-FRIEND?
NAH.
THIS IS GONNA BLOW YOU AWAY!
YOU SURE IT'S NOT OLD NEWS?
NOPE.
YOU'RE GONNA BE SO SHOCKED! SERIOUSLY!

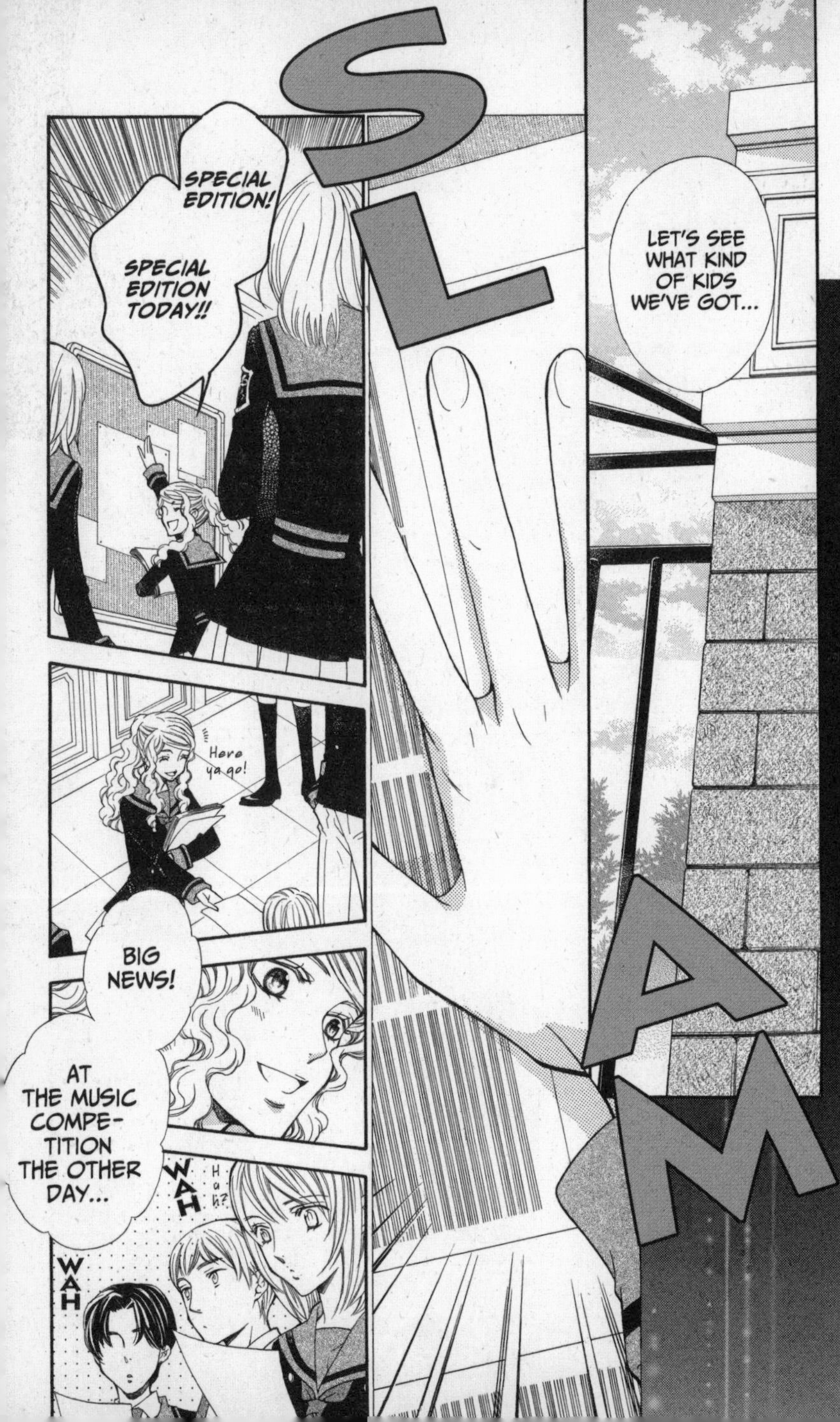
LET'S SEE WHAT KIND OF KIDS WE'VE GOT...
SLAM
SPECIAL EDITION!
SPECIAL EDITION TODAY!!
Here ya go!
BIG NEWS!
AT THE MUSIC COMPETITION THE OTHER DAY...
WAH
Huh?
WAH

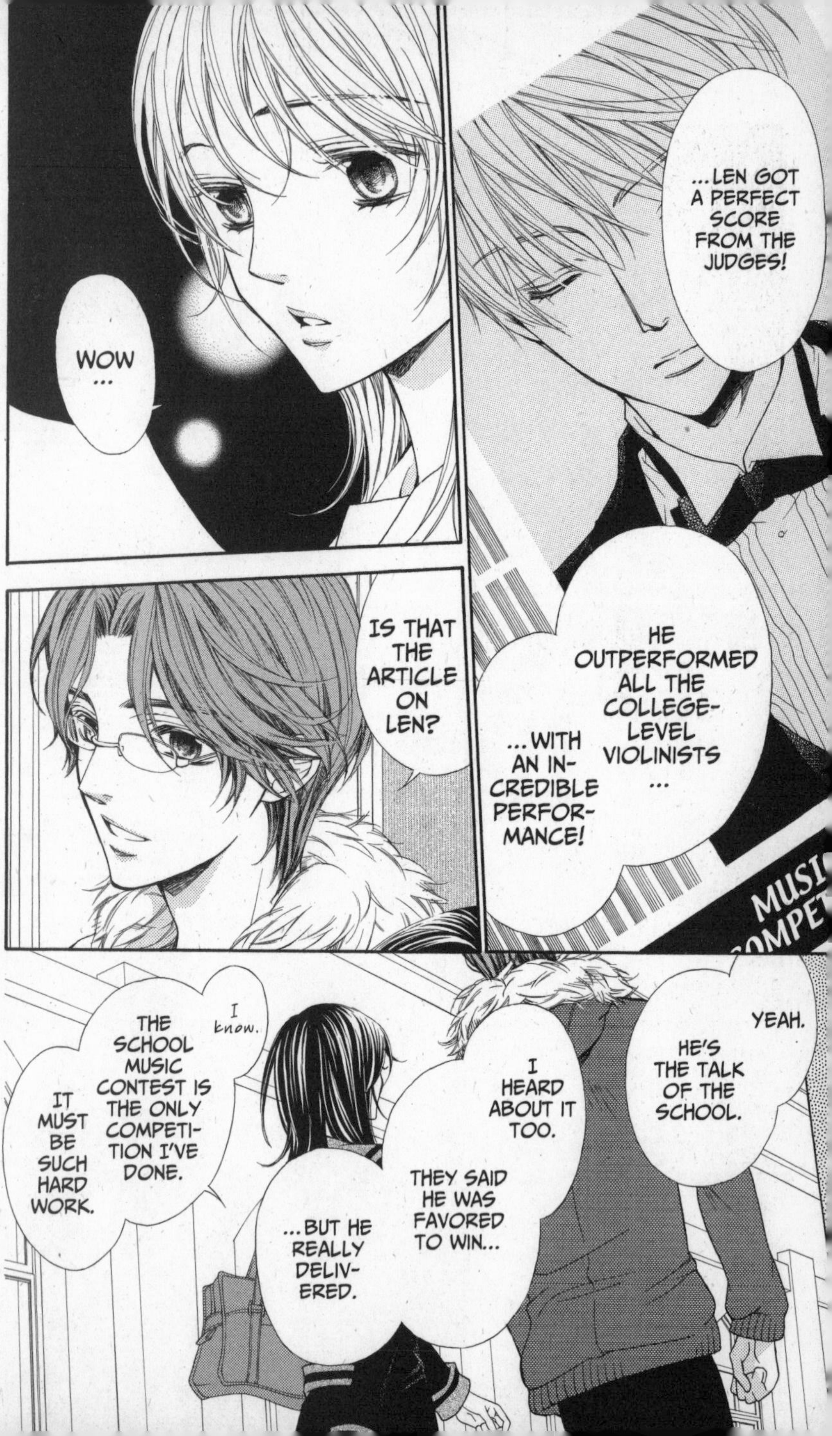
...LEN GOT A PERFECT SCORE FROM THE JUDGES!
HE OUTPERFORMED ALL THE COLLEGE-LEVEL VIOLINISTS...
...WITH AN INCREDIBLE PERFORMANCE!
WOW...
IS THAT THE ARTICLE ON LEN?
YEAH.
HE'S THE TALK OF THE SCHOOL.
I HEARD ABOUT IT TOO.
THEY SAID HE WAS FAVORED TO WIN...
...BUT HE REALLY DELIVERED.
I know..
THE SCHOOL MUSIC CONTEST IS THE ONLY COMPETITION I'VE DONE.
IT MUST BE SUCH HARD WORK.

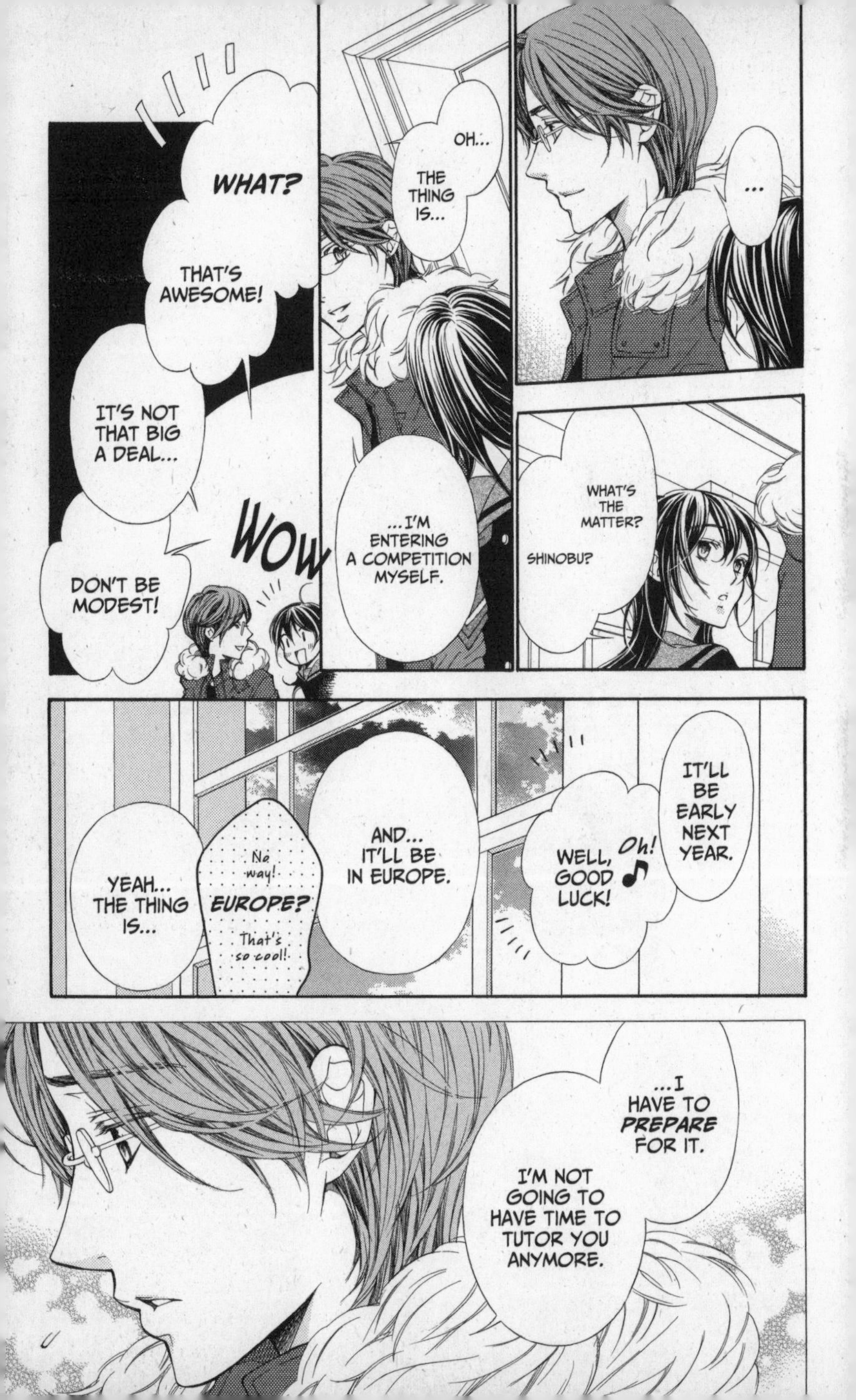
...
WHAT'S THE MATTER? SHINOBU?
OH... THE THING IS...
...I'M ENTERING A COMPETITION MYSELF.
WHAT? THAT'S AWESOME!
IT'S NOT THAT BIG A DEAL...
DON'T BE MODEST!
WOW
IT'LL BE EARLY NEXT YEAR.
WELL, GOOD LUCK!
Oh! ♪
AND... IT'LL BE IN EUROPE.
No way!
EUROPE?
That's so cool!
YEAH... THE THING IS...
...I HAVE TO PREPARE FOR IT.
I'M NOT GOING TO HAVE TIME TO TUTOR YOU ANYMORE.

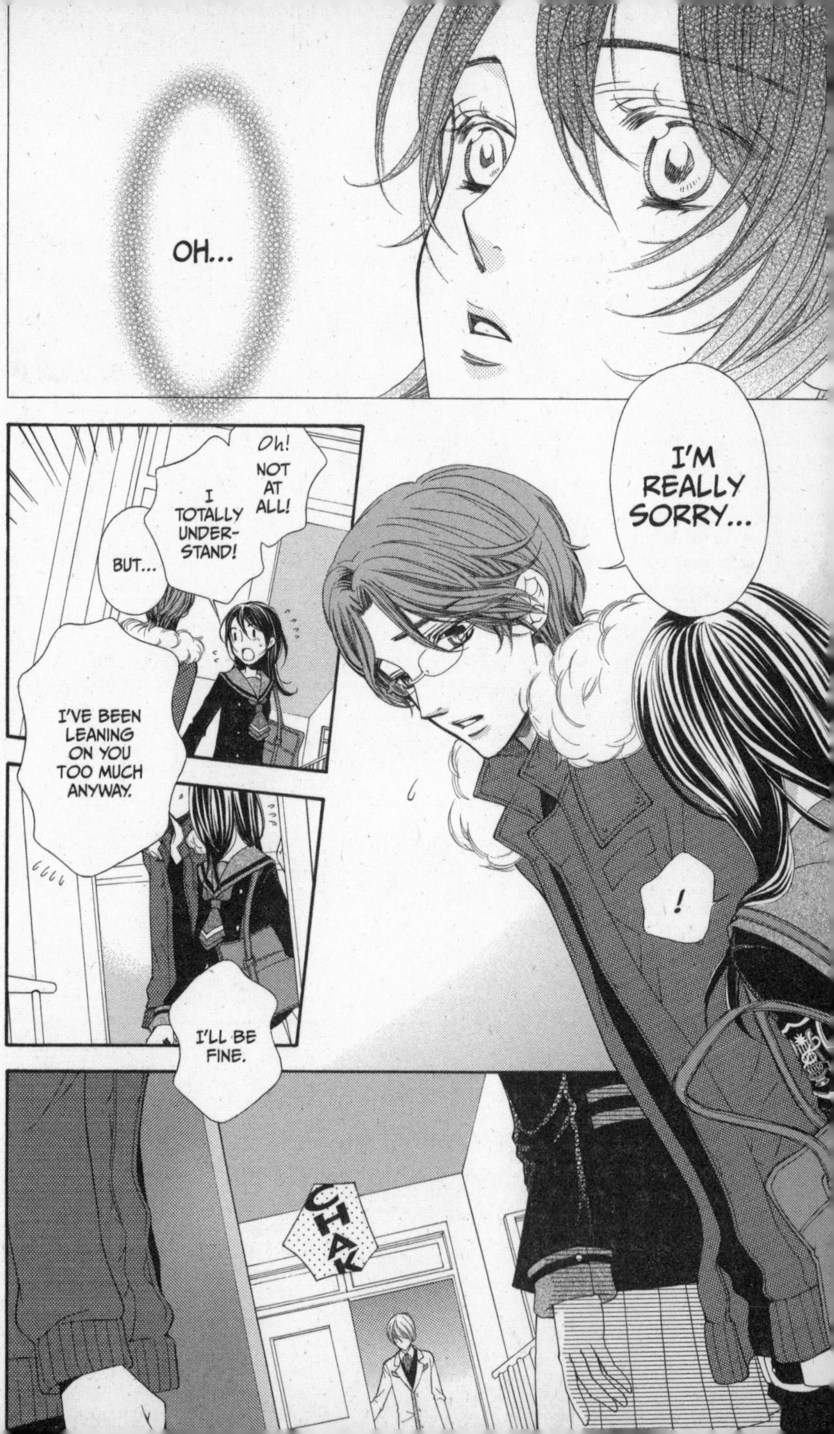
OH...
I'M REALLY SORRY...
!
Oh! NOT AT ALL!
I TOTALLY UNDERSTAND!
BUT...
I'VE BEEN LEANING ON YOU TOO MUCH ANYWAY.
I'LL BE FINE.
CHAK

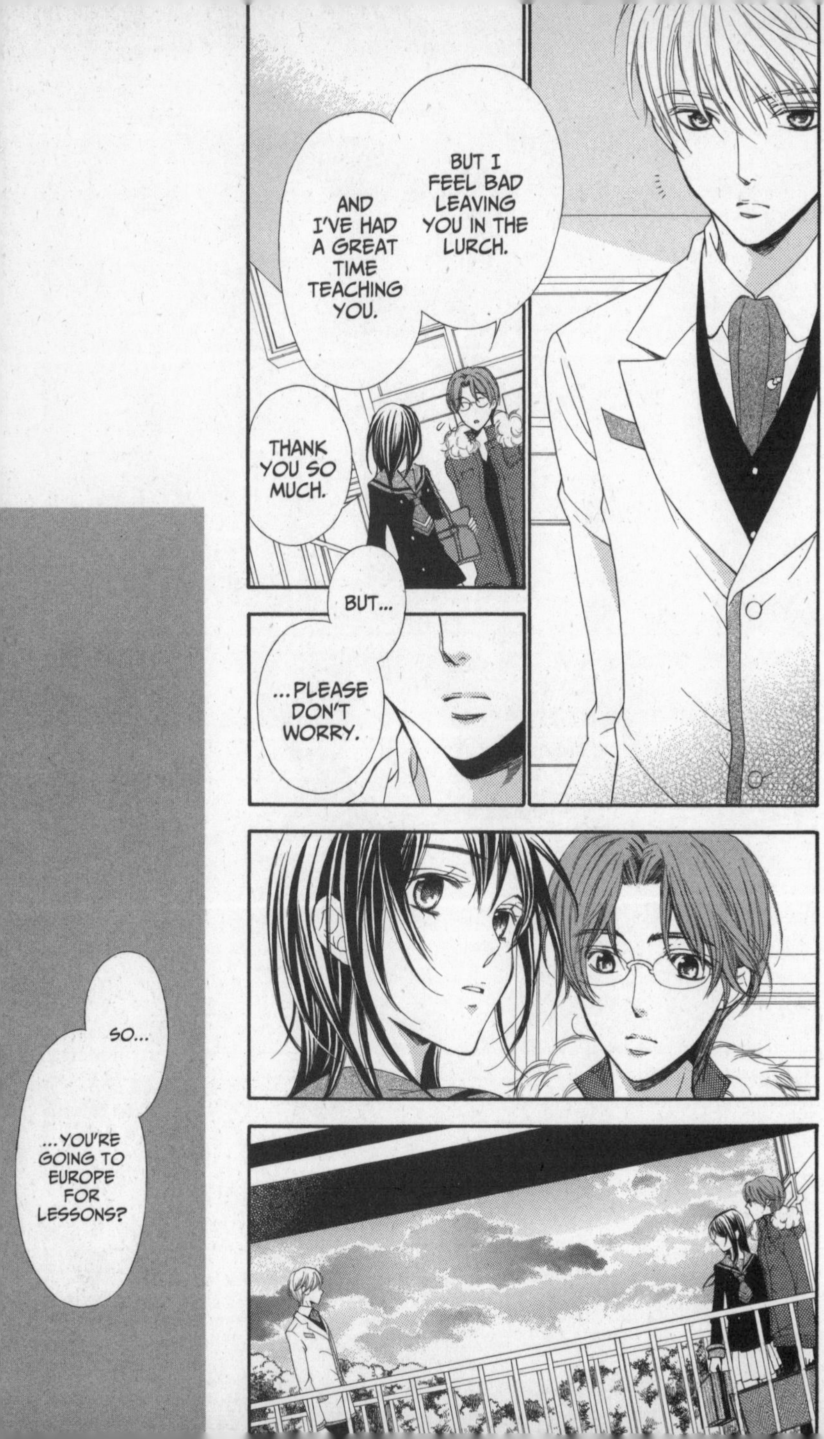
BUT I FEEL BAD LEAVING YOU IN THE LURCH.
AND I'VE HAD A GREAT TIME TEACHING YOU.
THANK YOU SO MUCH.
BUT...
...PLEASE DON'T WORRY.
SO...
...YOU'RE GOING TO EUROPE FOR LESSONS?

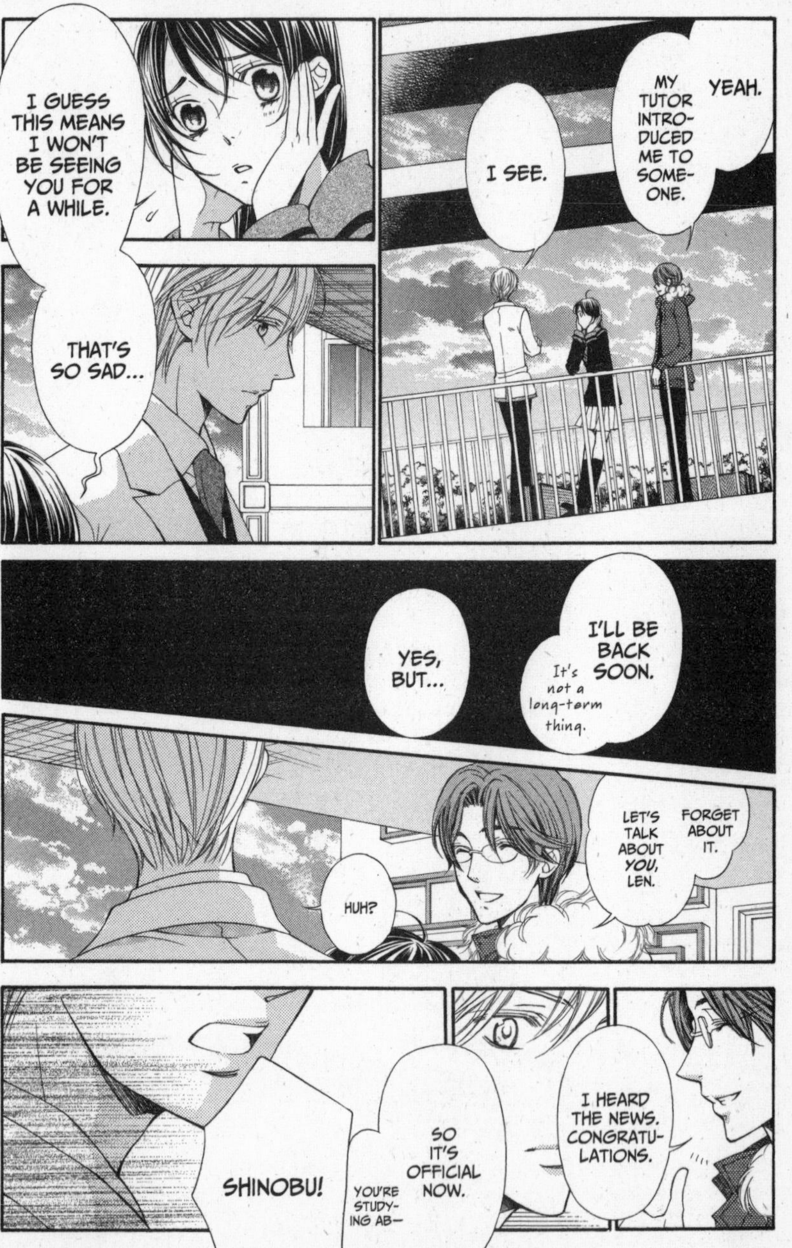
YEAH.
MY TUTOR INTRODUCED ME TO SOMEONE.
I SEE.
I GUESS THIS MEANS I WON'T BE SEEING YOU FOR A WHILE.
THAT'S SO SAD...
I'LL BE BACK SOON.
It's not a long-term thing.
YES, BUT...
FORGET ABOUT IT.
LET'S TALK ABOUT *YOU*, LEN.
HUH?
I HEARD THE NEWS. CONGRATULATIONS.
SO IT'S OFFICIAL NOW.
YOU'RE STUDYING AB—
SHINOBU!

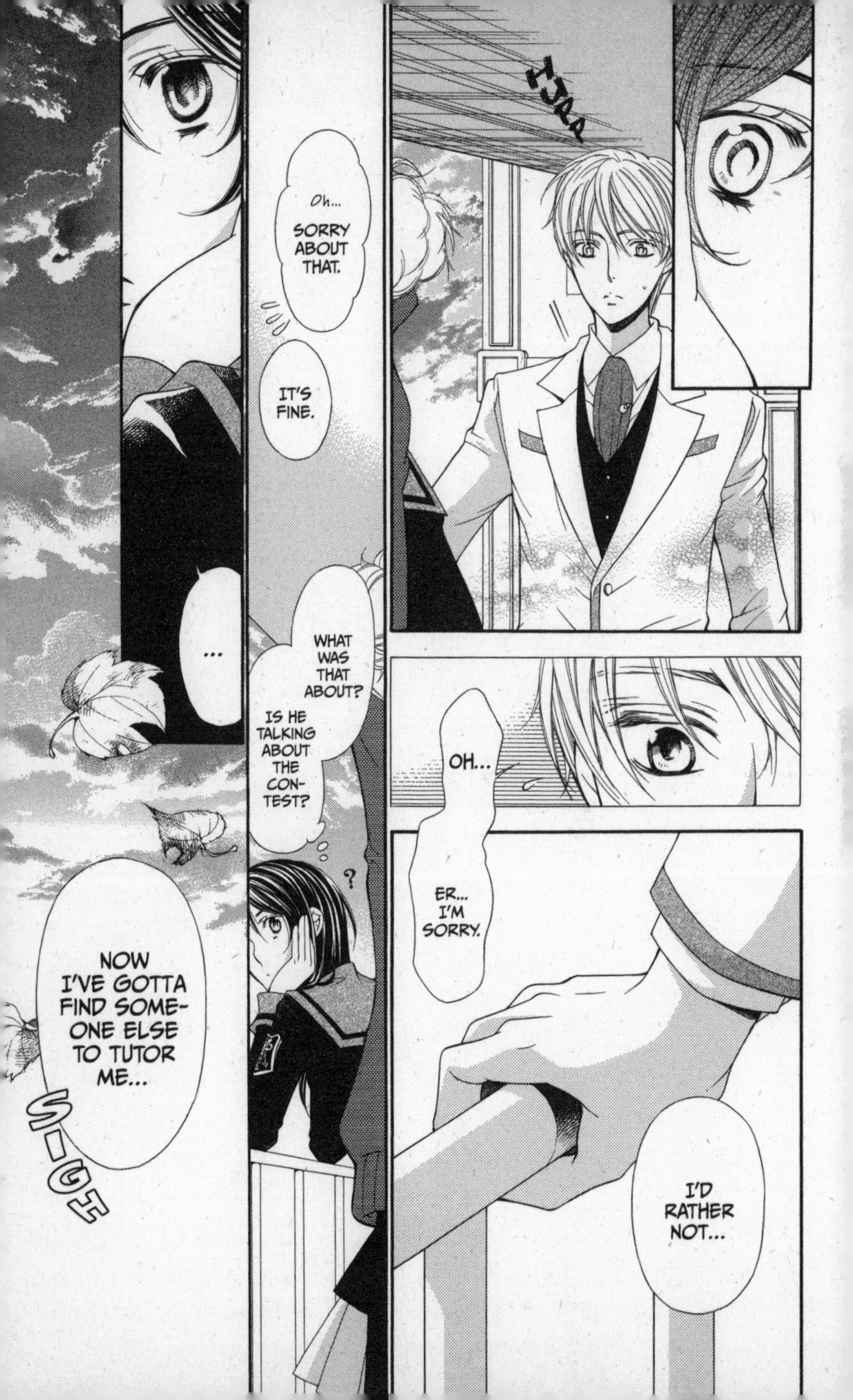
OH...
ER... I'M SORRY.
I'D RATHER NOT...
Oh... SORRY ABOUT THAT.
IT'S FINE.
WHAT WAS THAT ABOUT?
IS HE TALKING ABOUT THE CONTEST?
...
NOW I'VE GOTTA FIND SOMEONE ELSE TO TUTOR ME...
SIGH

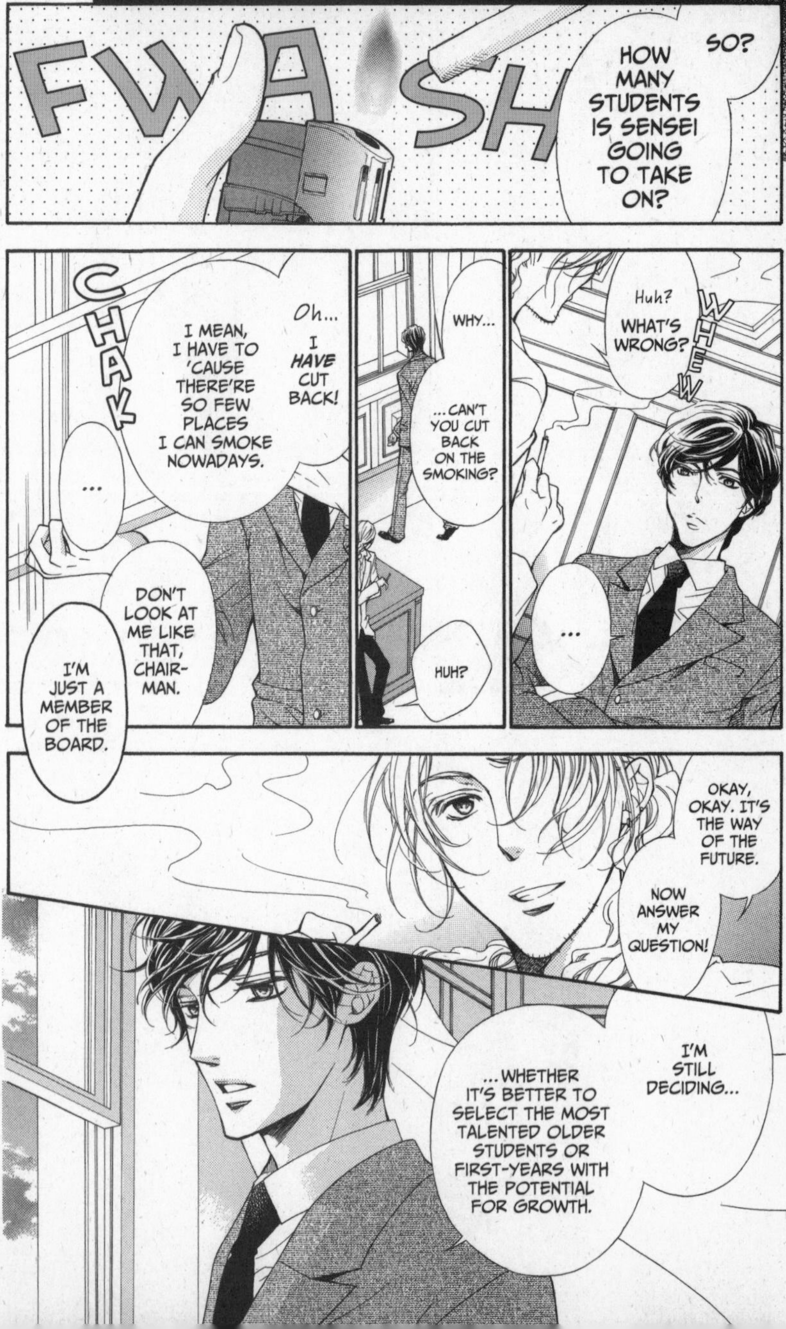

SO?
HOW MANY STUDENTS IS SENSEI GOING TO TAKE ON?
FWASH
Huh? WHAT'S WRONG?
WHEW
...
WHY...
...CAN'T YOU CUT BACK ON THE SMOKING?
HUH?
Oh... I *HAVE* CUT BACK!
I MEAN, I HAVE TO 'CAUSE THERE'RE SO FEW PLACES I CAN SMOKE NOWADAYS.
CHAK
...
DON'T LOOK AT ME LIKE THAT, CHAIR-MAN.
I'M JUST A MEMBER OF THE BOARD.
OKAY, OKAY. IT'S THE WAY OF THE FUTURE.
NOW ANSWER MY QUESTION!
I'M STILL DECIDING...
...WHETHER IT'S BETTER TO SELECT THE MOST TALENTED OLDER STUDENTS OR FIRST-YEARS WITH THE POTENTIAL FOR GROWTH.

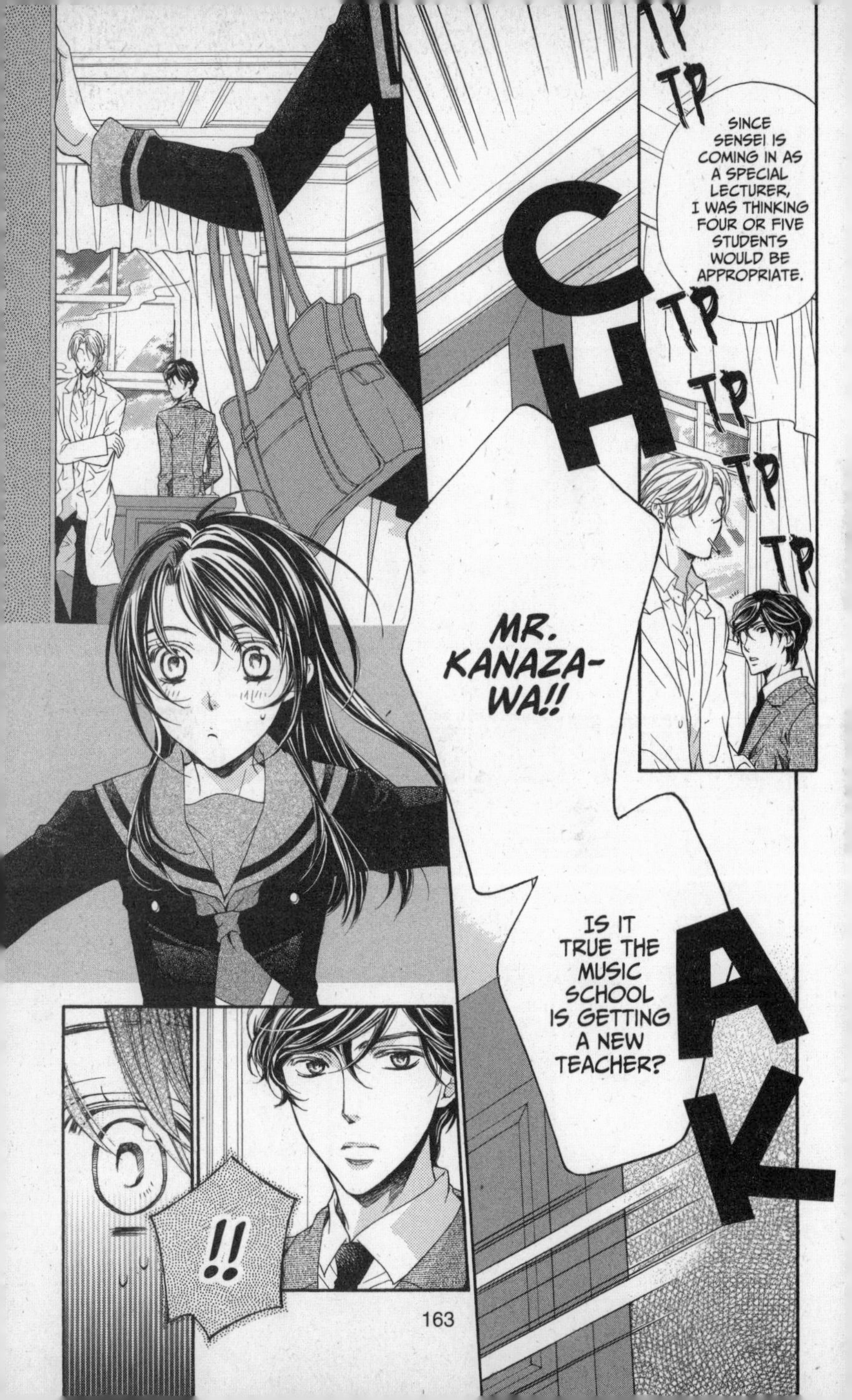
TP TP
SINCE SENSEI IS COMING IN AS A SPECIAL LECTURER, I WAS THINKING FOUR OR FIVE STUDENTS WOULD BE APPROPRIATE.
TP TP TP TP TP
CHAK
MR. KANAZA-WA!!
IS IT TRUE THE MUSIC SCHOOL IS GETTING A NEW TEACHER?
!!

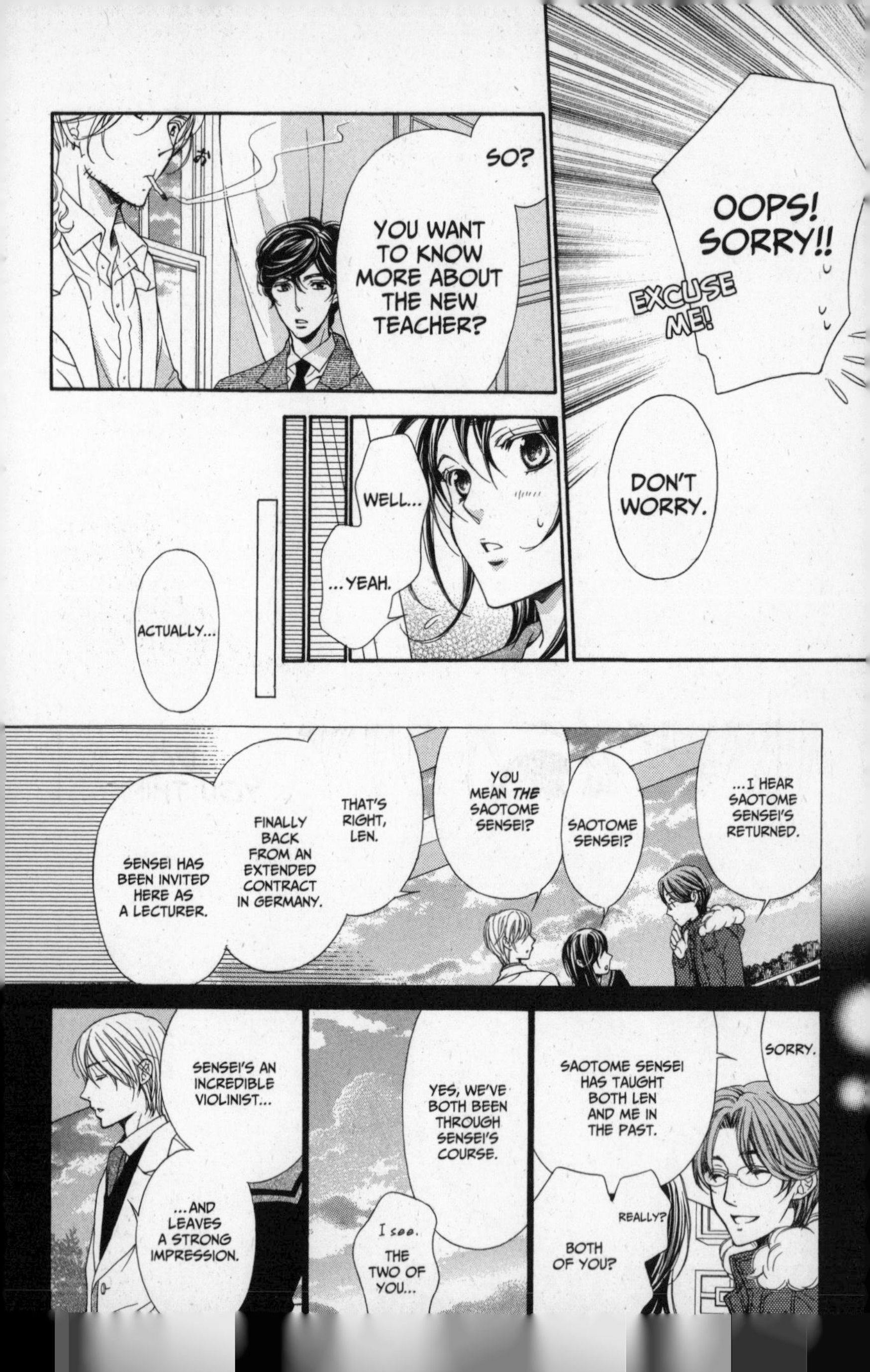
OOPS! SORRY!!
EXCUSE ME!
DON'T WORRY.
SO?
YOU WANT TO KNOW MORE ABOUT THE NEW TEACHER?
WELL...
...YEAH.
ACTUALLY...
...I HEAR SAOTOME SENSEI'S RETURNED.
SAOTOME SENSEI?
YOU MEAN *THE* SAOTOME SENSEI?
THAT'S RIGHT, LEN.
FINALLY BACK FROM AN EXTENDED CONTRACT IN GERMANY.
SENSEI HAS BEEN INVITED HERE AS A LECTURER.
SORRY.
SAOTOME SENSEI HAS TAUGHT BOTH LEN AND ME IN THE PAST.
REALLY?
BOTH OF YOU?
YES, WE'VE BOTH BEEN THROUGH SENSEI'S COURSE.
I see.
THE TWO OF YOU...
SENSEI'S AN INCREDIBLE VIOLINIST...
...AND LEAVES A STRONG IMPRESSION.

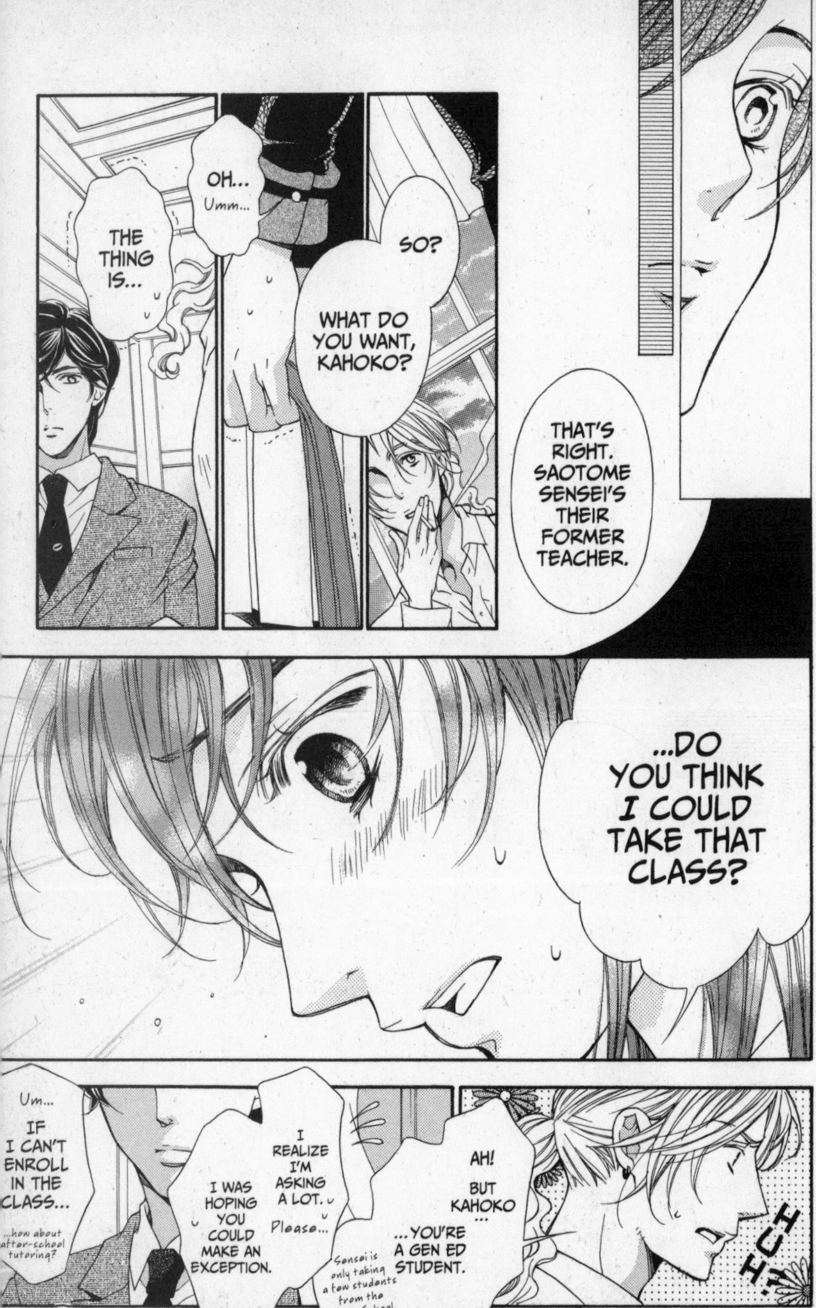
THAT'S RIGHT. SAOTOME SENSEI'S THEIR FORMER TEACHER.
SO?
WHAT DO YOU WANT, KAHOKO?
OH... Umm...
THE THING IS...
...DO YOU THINK I COULD TAKE THAT CLASS?
HUH!?
AH!
BUT KAHOKO...
...YOU'RE A GEN ED STUDENT.
Sensei is only taking a few students from the Music School.
I REALIZE I'M ASKING A LOT.
Please...
I WAS HOPING YOU COULD MAKE AN EXCEPTION.
Um...
IF I CAN'T ENROLL IN THE CLASS...
...how about after-school tutoring?

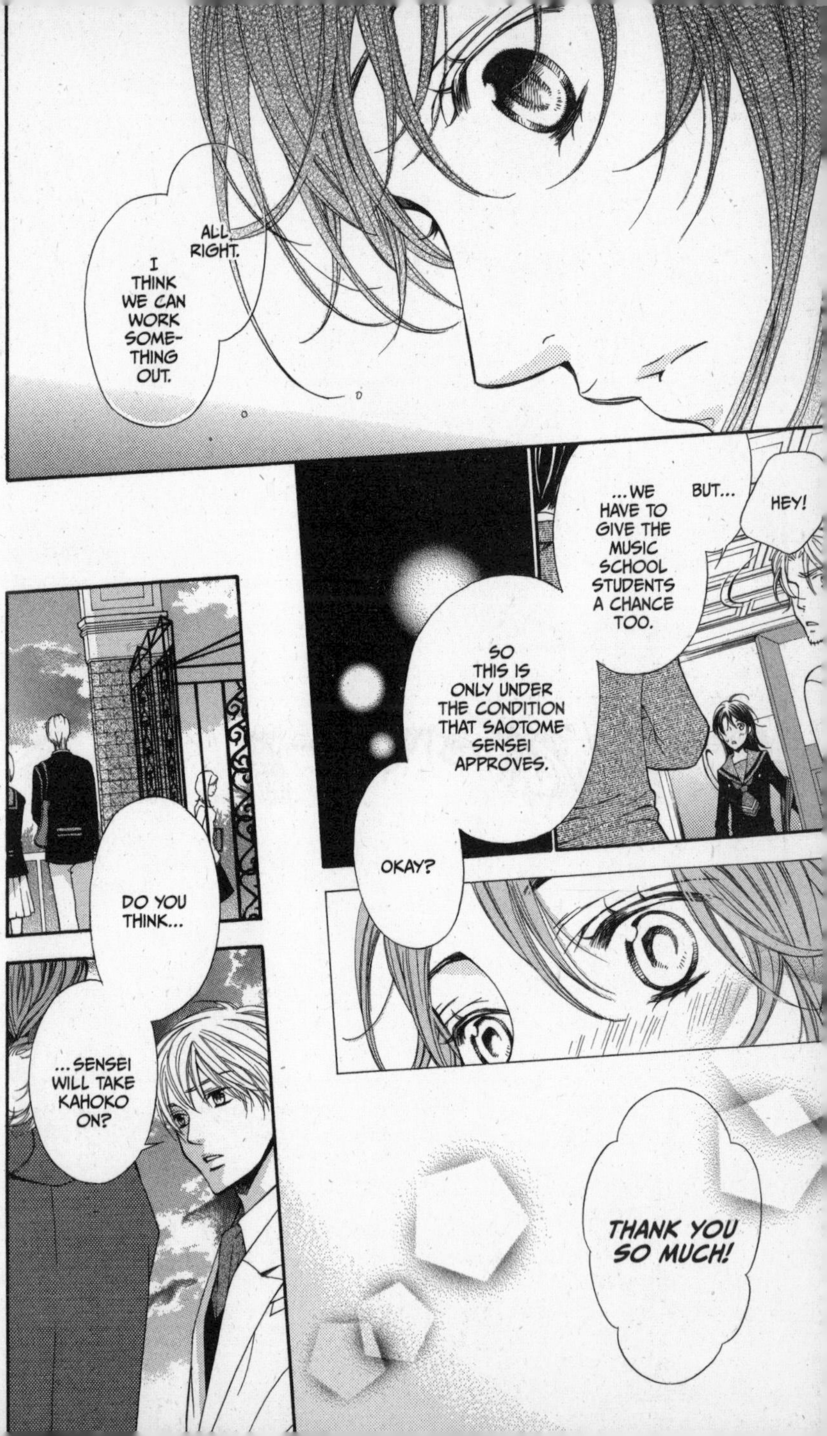
ALL RIGHT. I THINK WE CAN WORK SOMETHING OUT.
HEY!
BUT...
...WE HAVE TO GIVE THE MUSIC SCHOOL STUDENTS A CHANCE TOO.
SO THIS IS ONLY UNDER THE CONDITION THAT SAOTOME SENSEI APPROVES.
OKAY?
THANK YOU SO MUCH!
DO YOU THINK...
...SENSEI WILL TAKE KAHOKO ON?

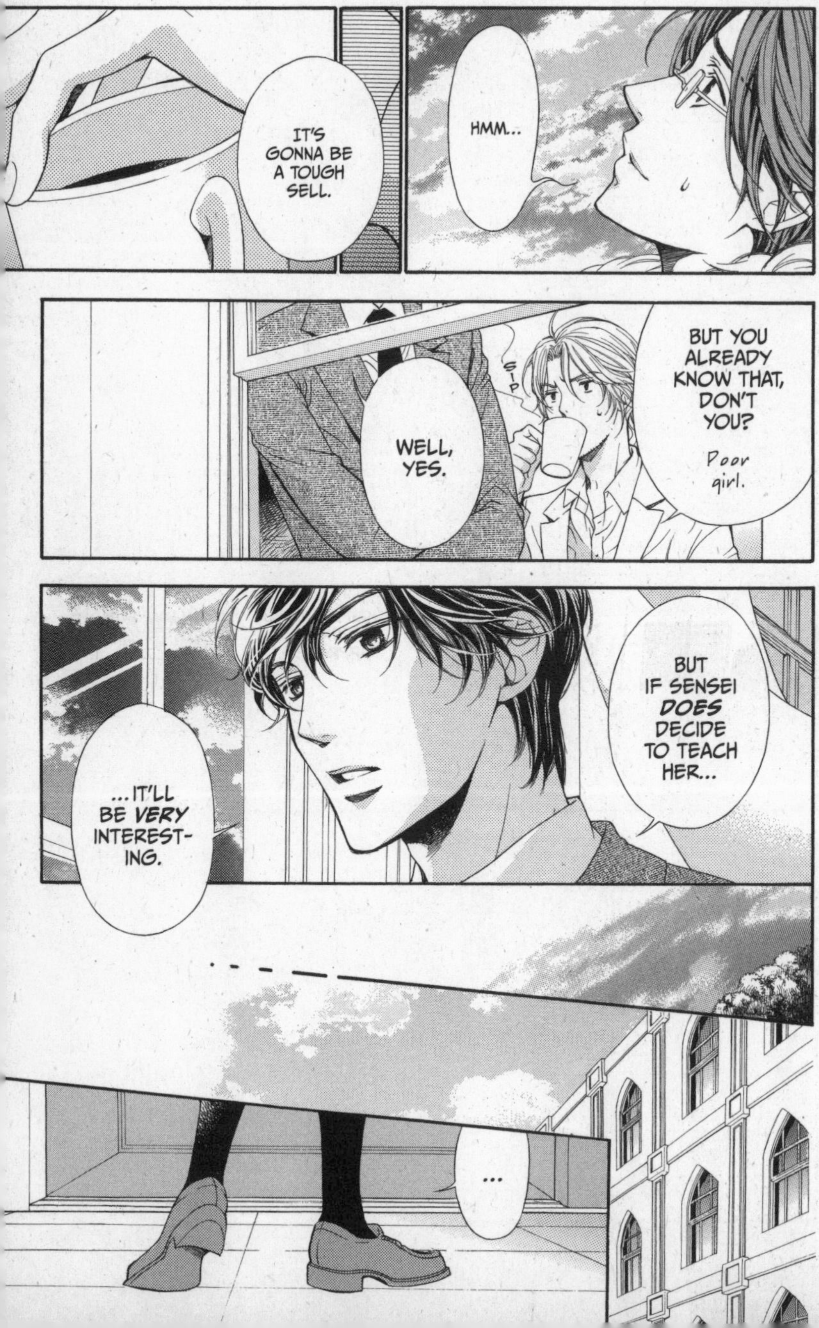
HMM...
IT'S GONNA BE A TOUGH SELL.
BUT YOU ALREADY KNOW THAT, DON'T YOU?
Poor girl.
SIP
WELL, YES.
BUT IF SENSEI *DOES* DECIDE TO TEACH HER...
...IT'LL BE *VERY* INTERESTING.
...

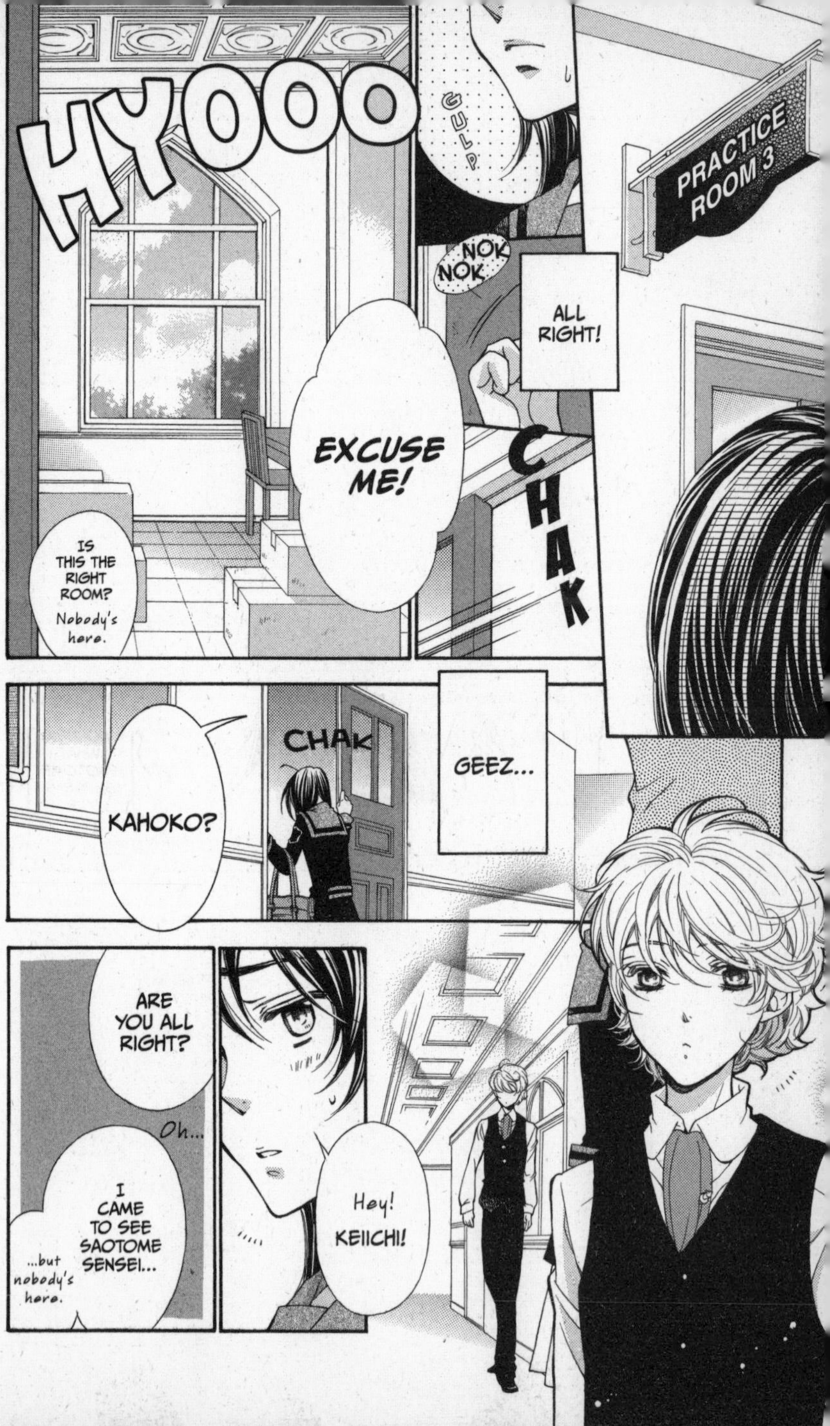
PRACTICE ROOM 3
ALL RIGHT!
GULP
NOK NOK
CHAK
EXCUSE ME!
HYOOO
IS THIS THE RIGHT ROOM?
Nobody's here.
GEEZ...
CHAK
KAHOKO?
Hey!
KEIICHI!
ARE YOU ALL RIGHT?
Oh...
I CAME TO SEE SAOTOME SENSEI...
...but nobody's here.

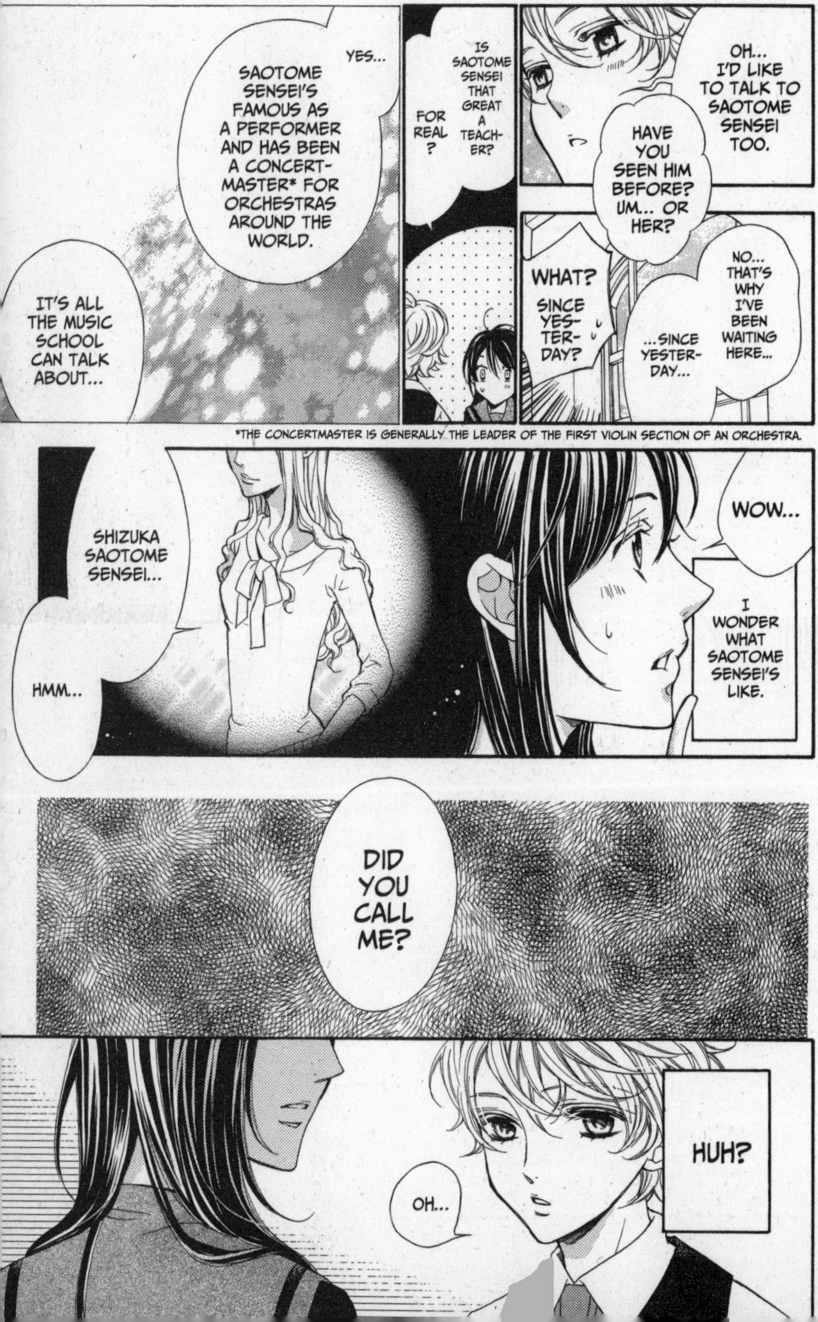
OH... I'D LIKE TO TALK TO SAOTOME SENSEI TOO.
HAVE YOU SEEN HIM BEFORE? UM... OR HER?
NO... THAT'S WHY I'VE BEEN WAITING HERE...
...SINCE YESTERDAY...
WHAT?
SINCE YESTERDAY?
IS SAOTOME SENSEI THAT GREAT A TEACHER?
FOR REAL?
YES...
SAOTOME SENSEI'S FAMOUS AS A PERFORMER AND HAS BEEN A CONCERTMASTER* FOR ORCHESTRAS AROUND THE WORLD.
IT'S ALL THE MUSIC SCHOOL CAN TALK ABOUT...
WOW...
I WONDER WHAT SAOTOME SENSEI'S LIKE.
SHIZUKA SAOTOME SENSEI...
HMM...
DID YOU CALL ME?
HUH?
OH...

*THE CONCERTMASTER IS GENERALLY THE LEADER OF THE FIRST VIOLIN SECTION OF AN ORCHESTRA.

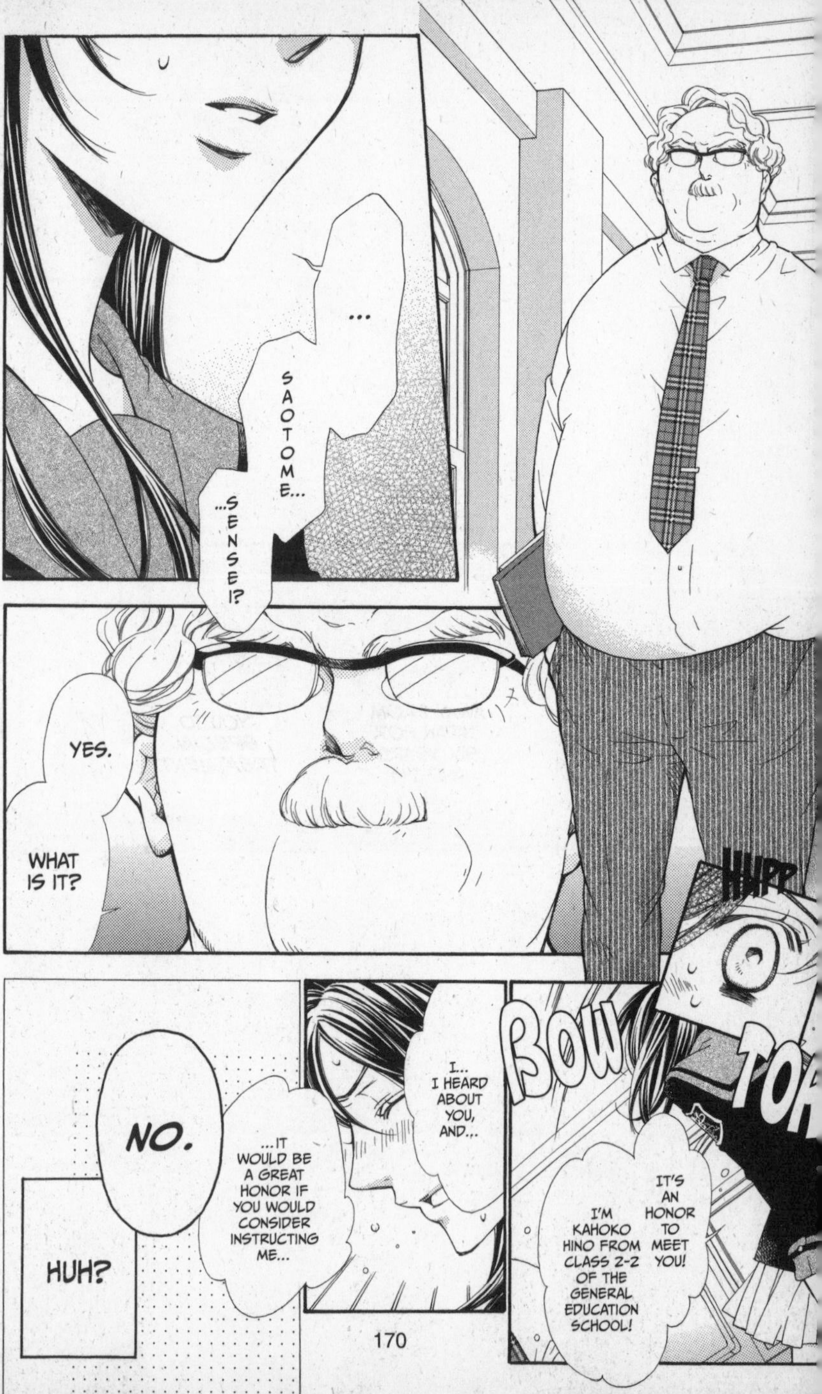
...
SAOTOME...
...SENSEI?
YES.
WHAT IS IT?
HHPP
TO
BOW
IT'S AN HONOR TO MEET YOU!
I'M KAHOKO HINO FROM CLASS 2-2 OF THE GENERAL EDUCATION SCHOOL!
I... I HEARD ABOUT YOU, AND...
...IT WOULD BE A GREAT HONOR IF YOU WOULD CONSIDER INSTRUCTING ME...
NO.
HUH?

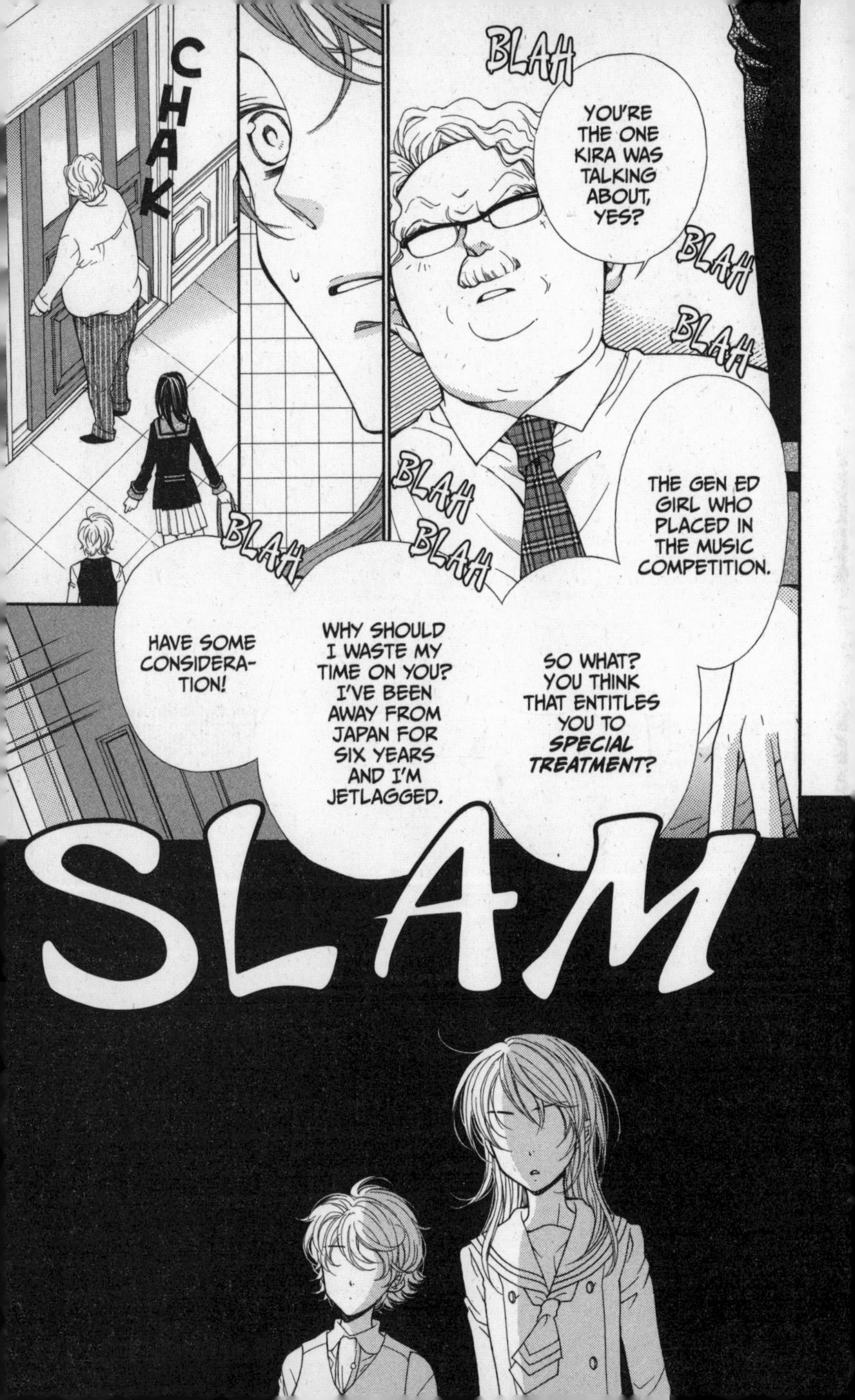
BLAH
YOU'RE THE ONE KIRA WAS TALKING ABOUT, YES?
BLAH
BLAH
THE GEN ED GIRL WHO PLACED IN THE MUSIC COMPETITION.
BLAH
BLAH
BLAH
SO WHAT? YOU THINK THAT ENTITLES YOU TO *SPECIAL TREATMENT*?
WHY SHOULD I WASTE MY TIME ON YOU? I'VE BEEN AWAY FROM JAPAN FOR SIX YEARS AND I'M JETLAGGED.
HAVE SOME CONSIDERA-TION!
CHAK
SLAM

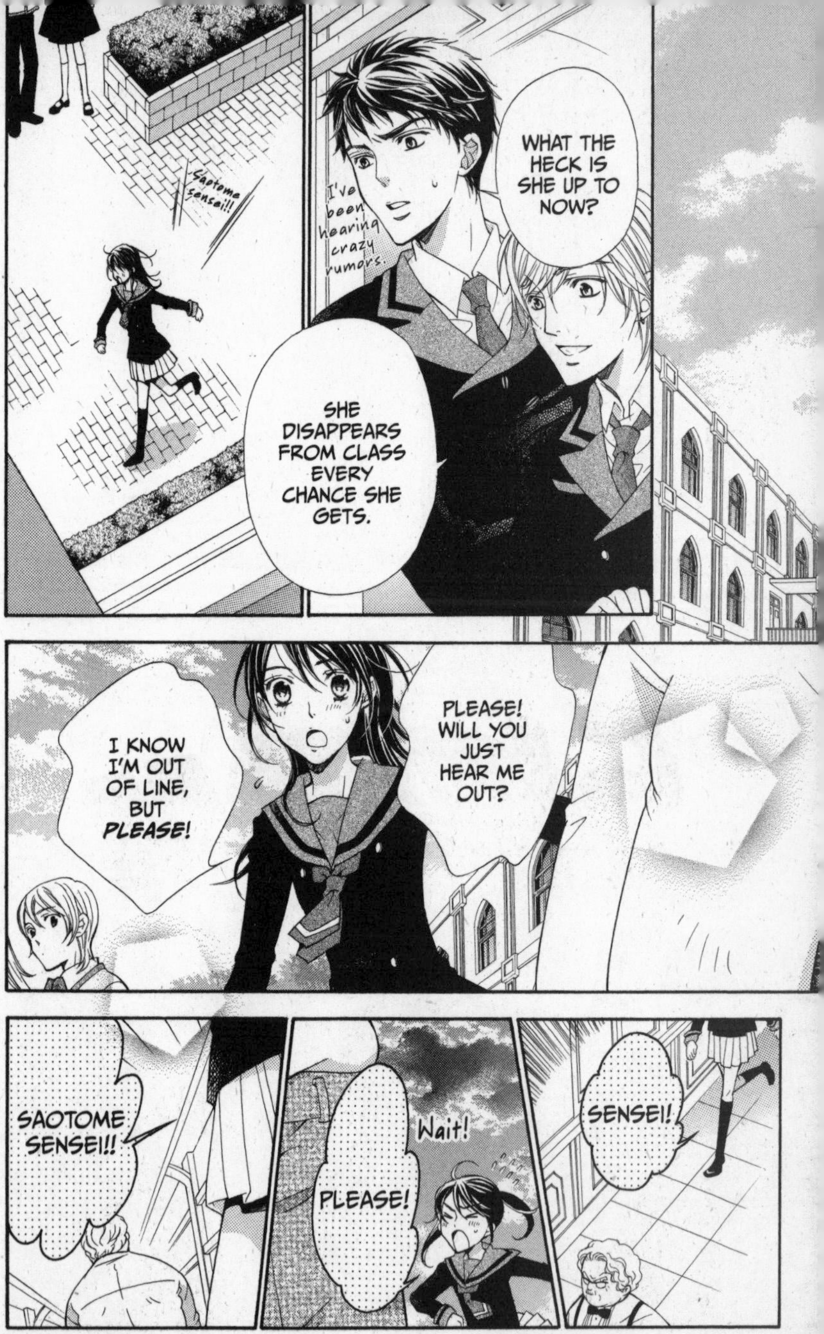
WHAT THE HECK IS SHE UP TO NOW?
I've been hearing crazy rumors.
SHE DISAPPEARS FROM CLASS EVERY CHANCE SHE GETS.
Saotome sensei!!
PLEASE! WILL YOU JUST HEAR ME OUT?
I KNOW I'M OUT OF LINE, BUT *PLEASE!*
SENSEI!
Wait!
PLEASE!
SAOTOME SENSEI!!

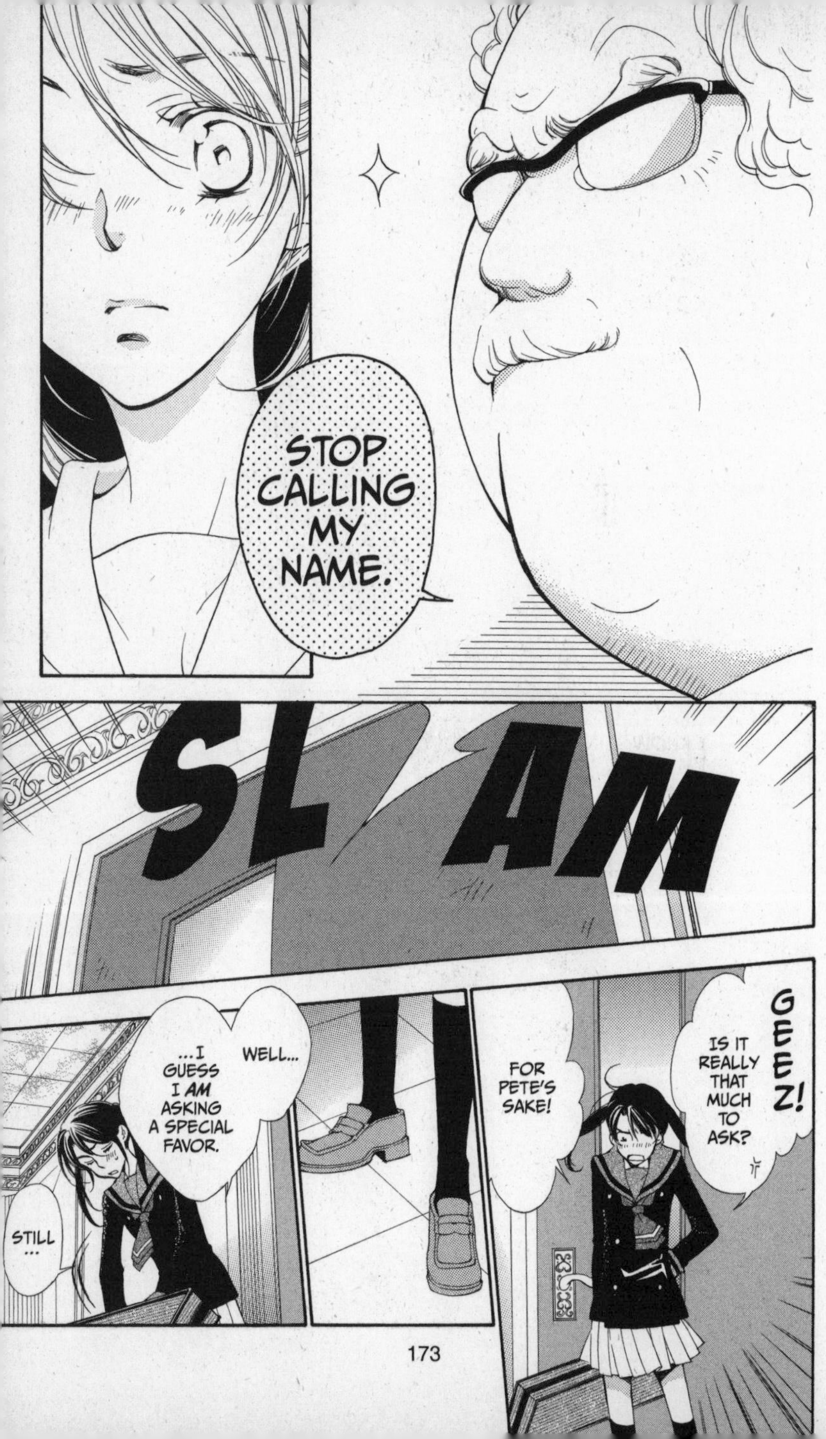
STOP CALLING MY NAME.
SLAM
GEEZ!
IS IT REALLY THAT MUCH TO ASK?
FOR PETE'S SAKE!
WELL...
...I GUESS I *AM* ASKING A SPECIAL FAVOR.
STILL...

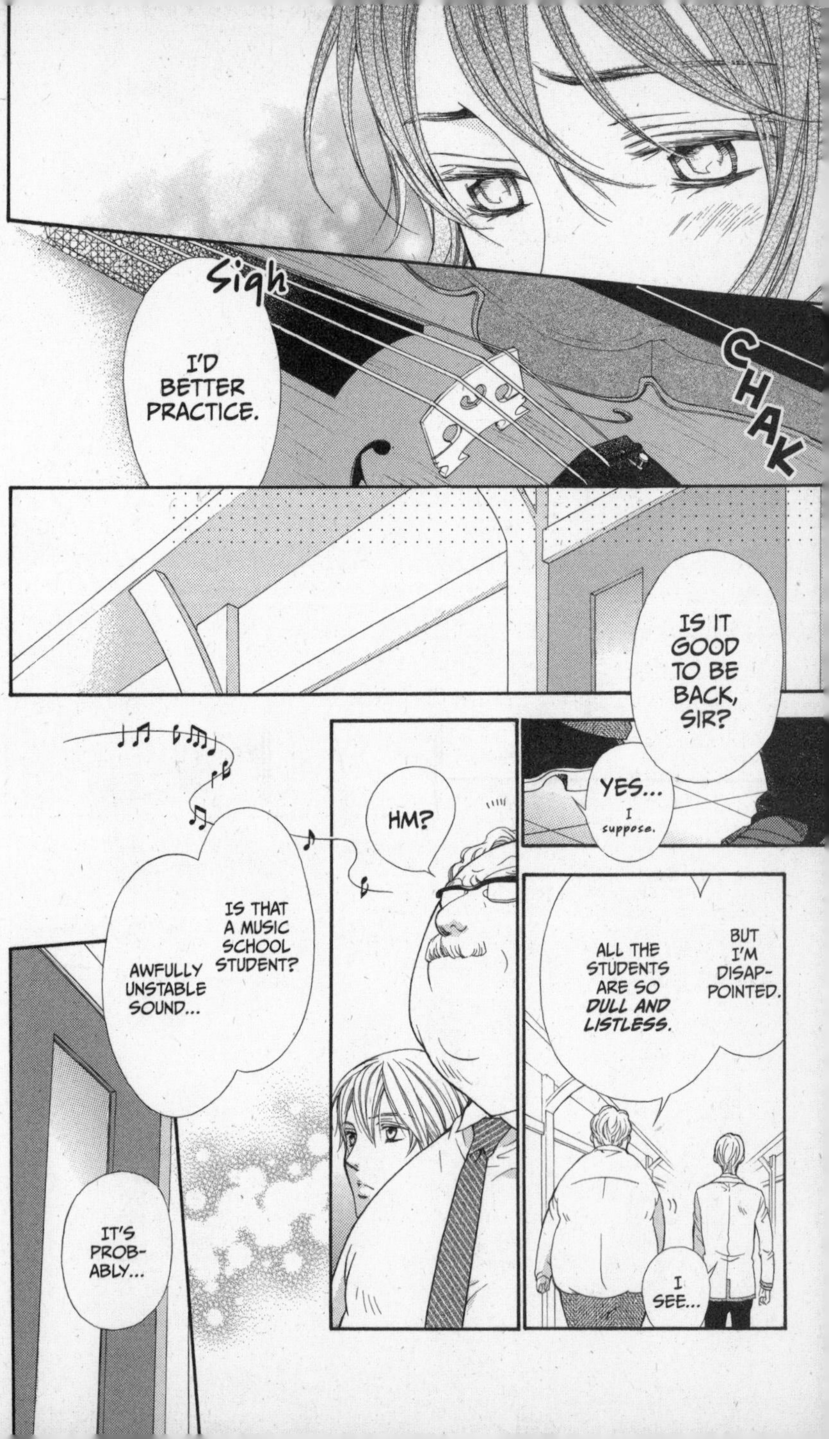
Sigh
I'D BETTER PRACTICE.
CHAK
IS IT GOOD TO BE BACK, SIR?
YES... I suppose.
BUT I'M DISAPPOINTED.
ALL THE STUDENTS ARE SO DULL AND LISTLESS.
I SEE...
HM?
IS THAT A MUSIC SCHOOL STUDENT?
AWFULLY UNSTABLE SOUND...
IT'S PROBABLY...

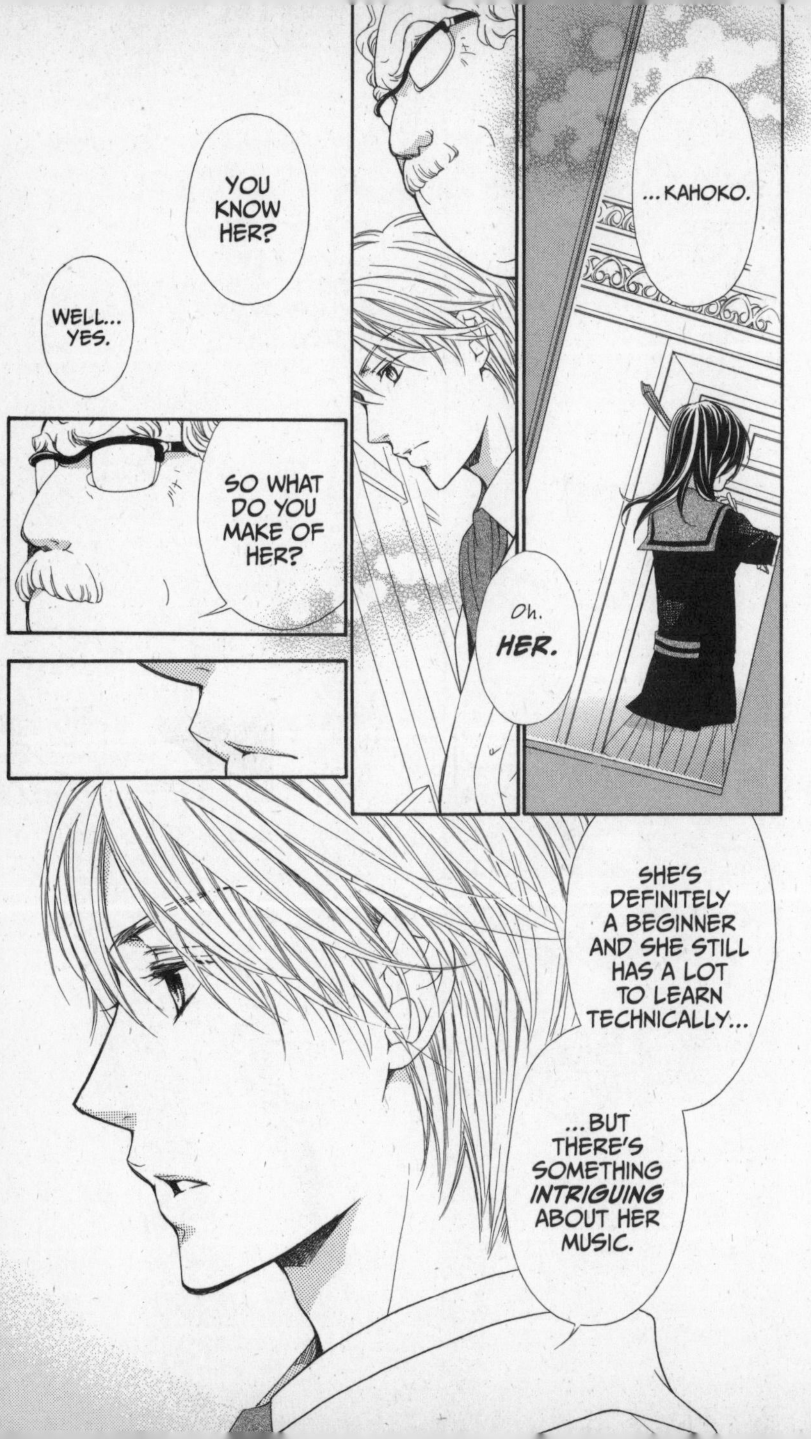
...KAHOKO.
Oh. HER.
YOU KNOW HER?
WELL... YES.
SO WHAT DO YOU MAKE OF HER?
SHE'S DEFINITELY A BEGINNER AND SHE STILL HAS A LOT TO LEARN TECHNICALLY...
...BUT THERE'S SOMETHING INTRIGUING ABOUT HER MUSIC.

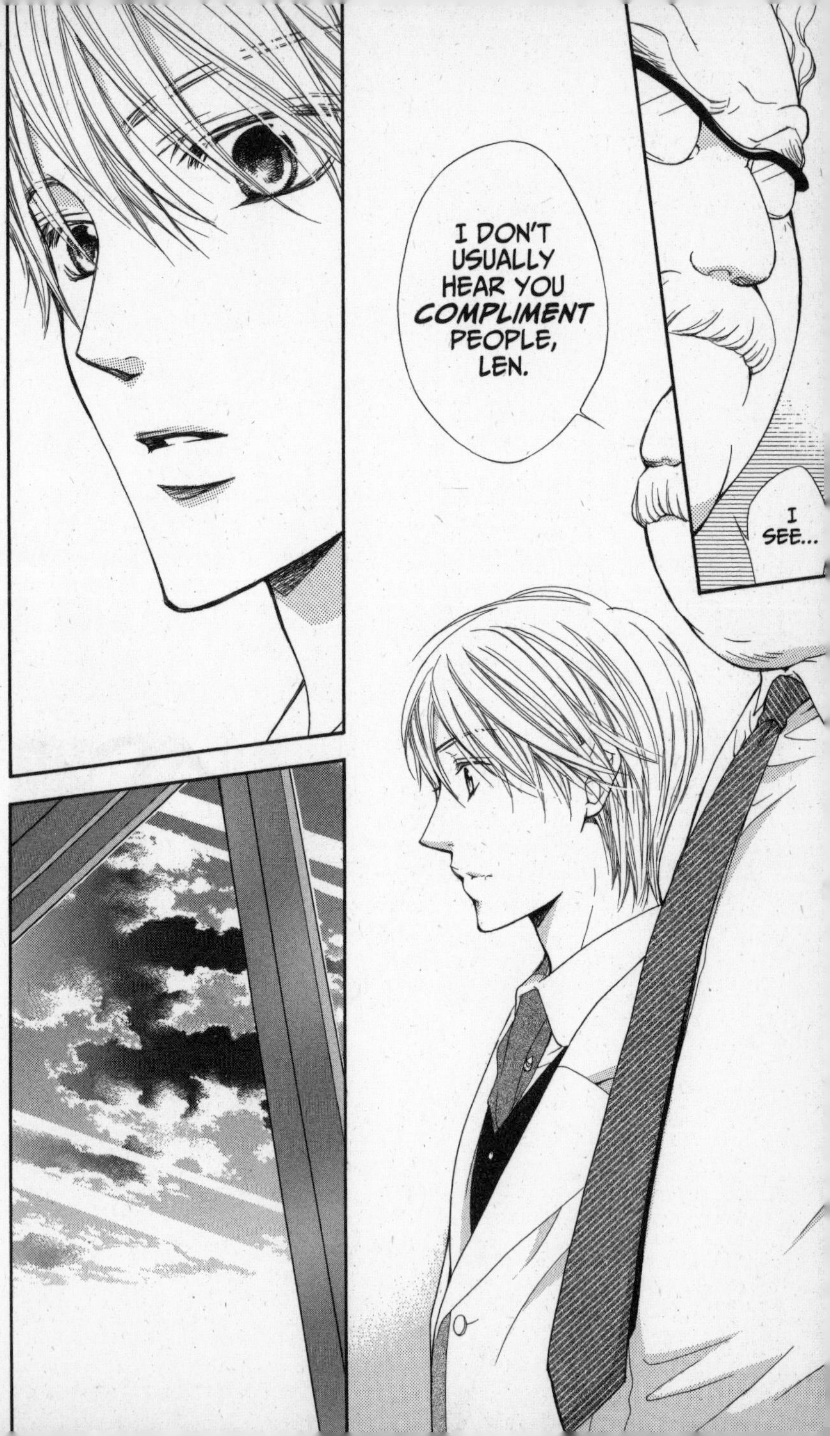
I SEE...
I DON'T USUALLY HEAR YOU *COMPLIMENT* PEOPLE, LEN.

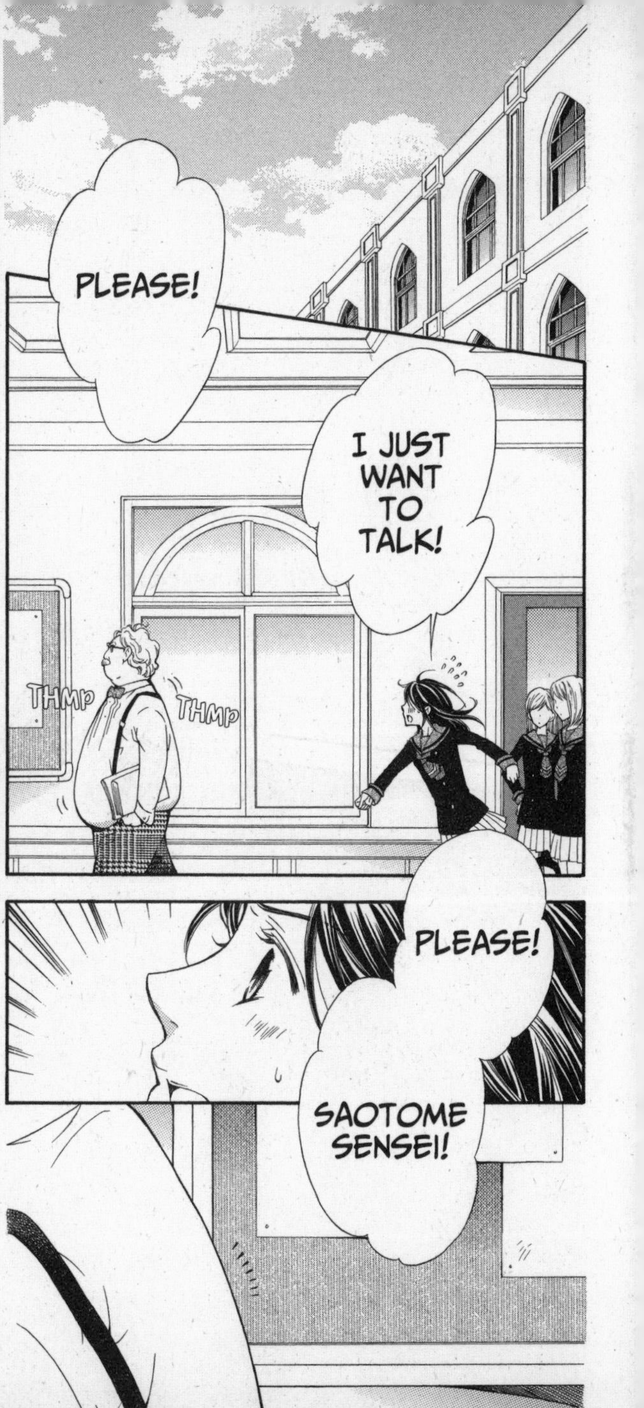
PLEASE!
I JUST WANT TO TALK!
THMp
THMp
PLEASE!
SAOTOME SENSEI!

Saotome Sensei finally makes his debut in Measure 54. My editor told me he shouldn't be handsome, so I had to decide between a scrawny guy or a big guy. I ended up with a big guy. I may have drawn him a little ***too*** big...

There's now a PSP version of the game with new characters. It's called *La Corda d'Oro 2f*. I've gotta get started on it. I'm really not much of a gamer...

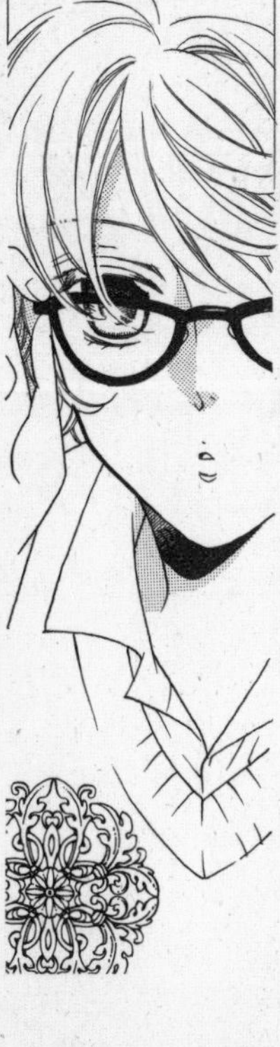

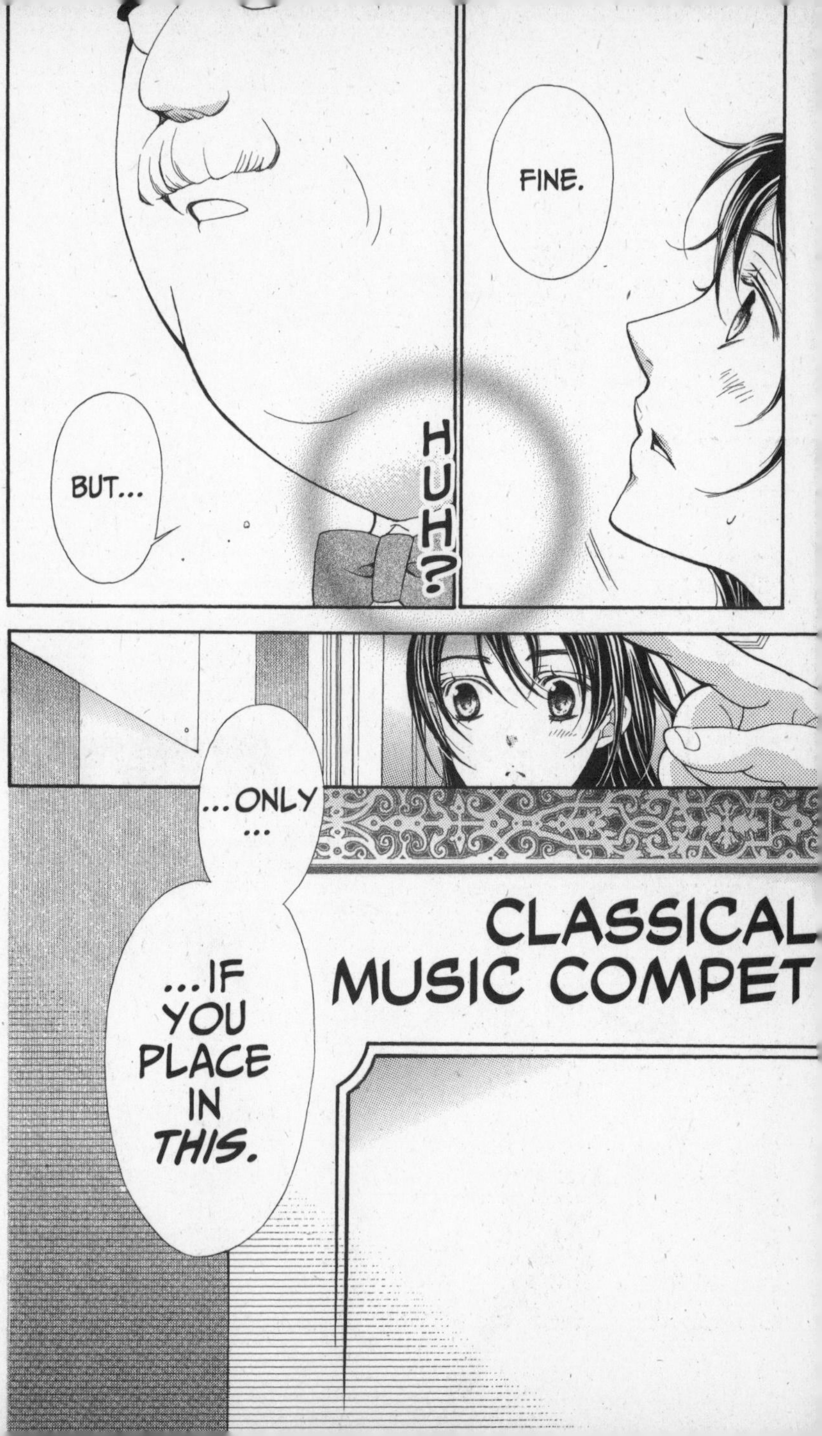
FINE.
HUH?
BUT...
...ONLY ...
...IF YOU PLACE IN THIS.
CLASSICAL MUSIC COMPET

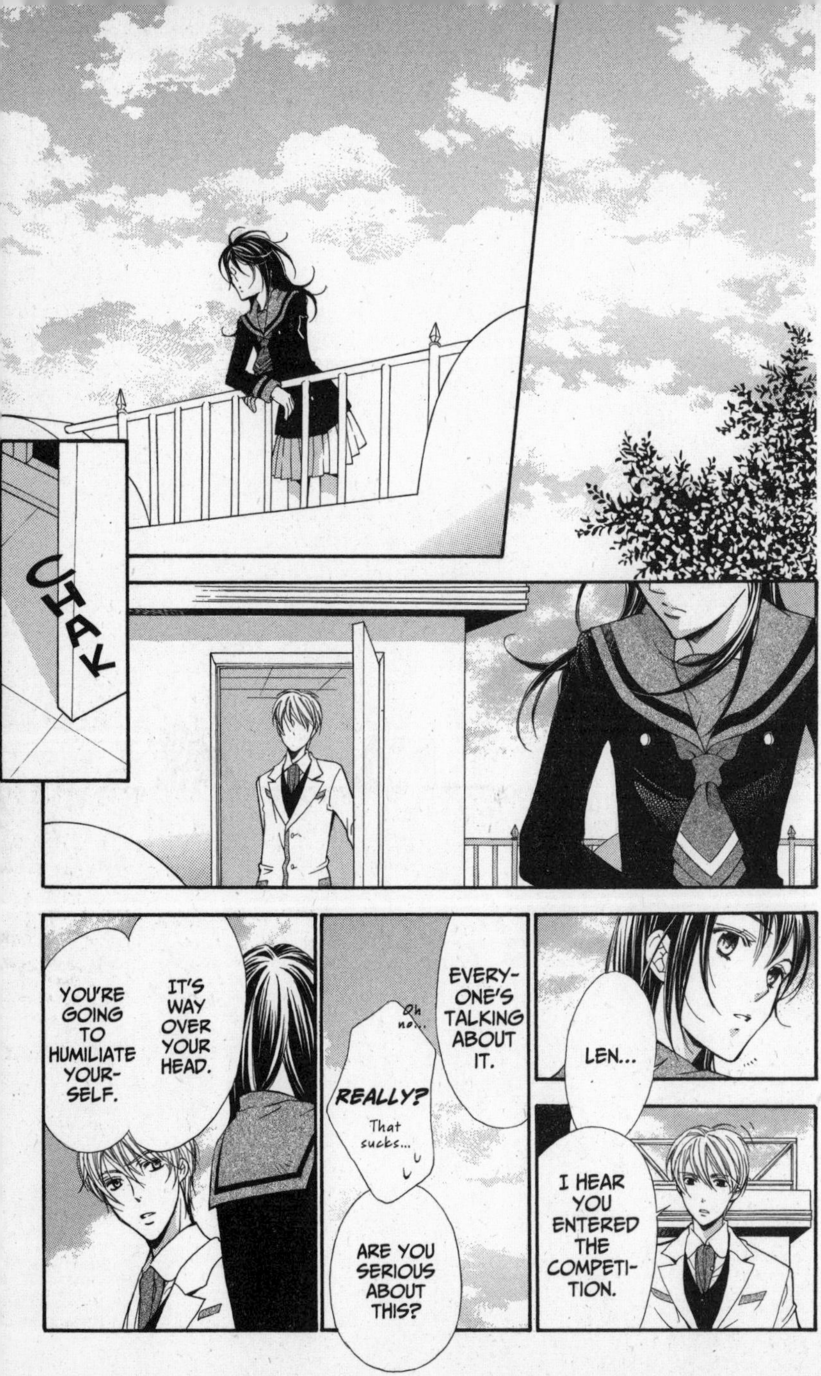
CHAK
LEN...
I HEAR YOU ENTERED THE COMPETITION.
EVERYONE'S TALKING ABOUT IT.
Oh no...
REALLY?
That sucks...
ARE YOU SERIOUS ABOUT THIS?
IT'S WAY OVER YOUR HEAD.
YOU'RE GOING TO HUMILIATE YOURSELF.

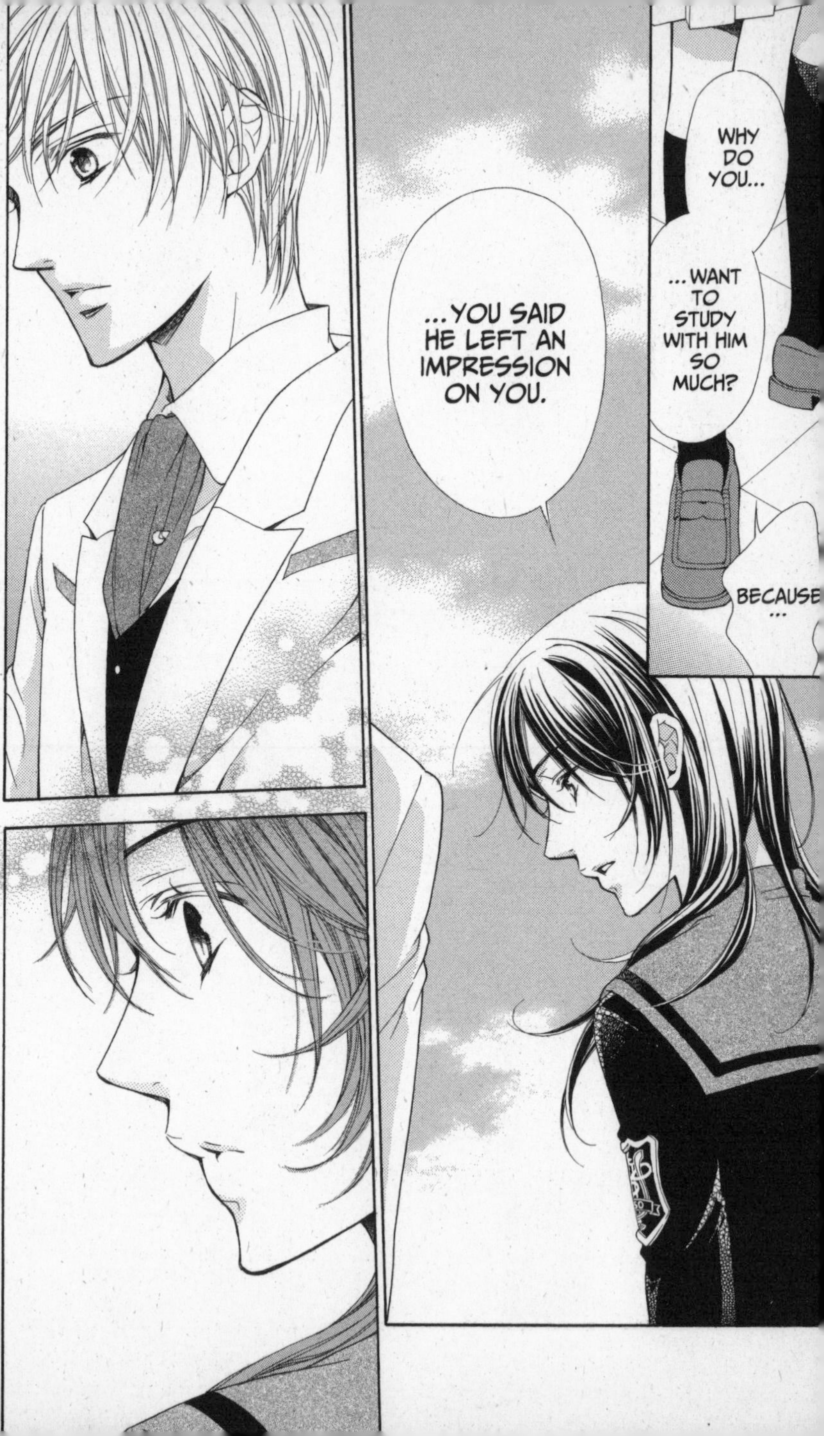
WHY DO YOU...
...WANT TO STUDY WITH HIM SO MUCH?
BECAUSE...
...YOU SAID HE LEFT AN IMPRESSION ON YOU.

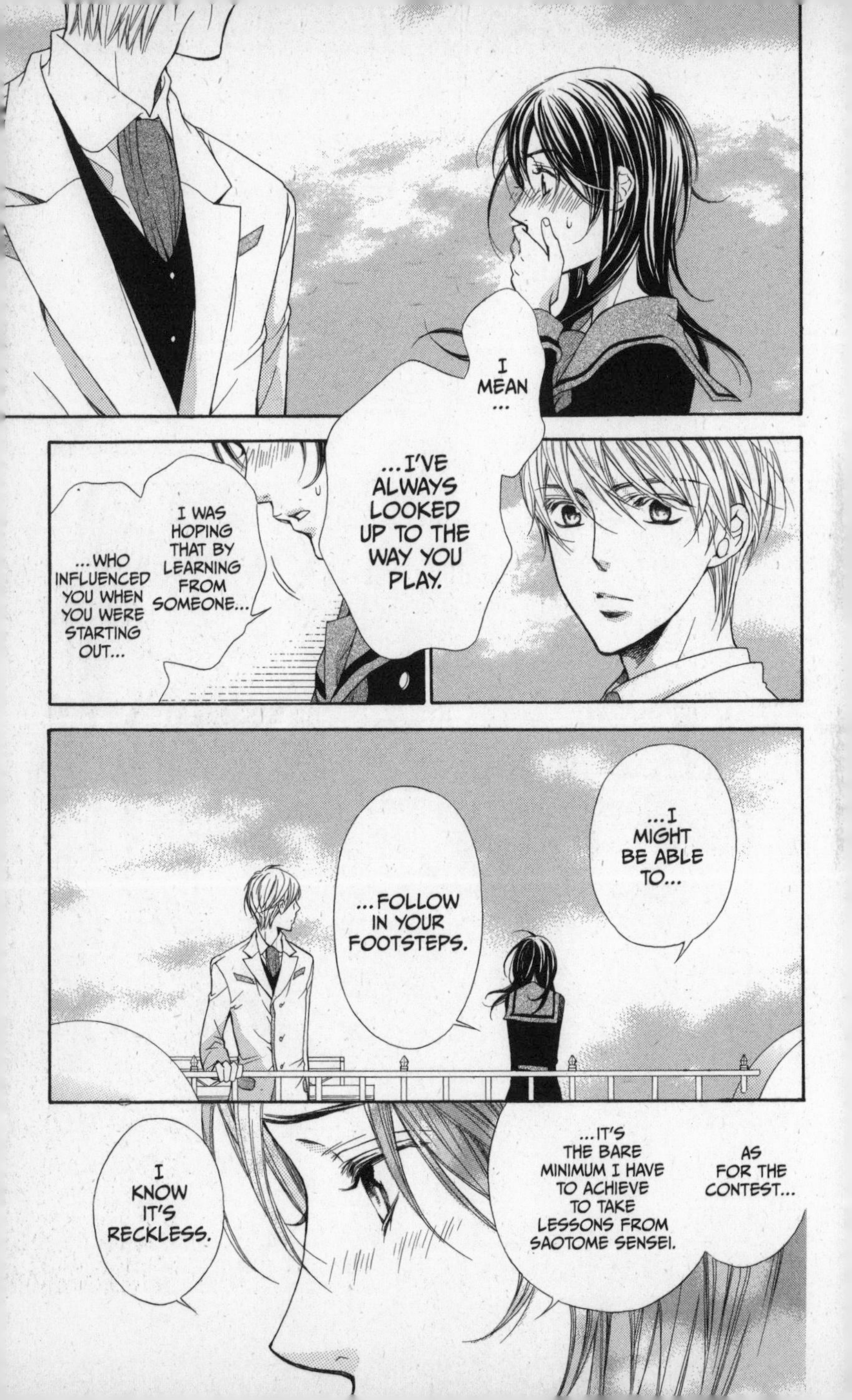
I MEAN...
...I'VE ALWAYS LOOKED UP TO THE WAY YOU PLAY.
I WAS HOPING THAT BY LEARNING FROM SOMEONE...
...WHO INFLUENCED YOU WHEN YOU WERE STARTING OUT...
...I MIGHT BE ABLE TO...
...FOLLOW IN YOUR FOOTSTEPS.
AS FOR THE CONTEST...
...IT'S THE BARE MINIMUM I HAVE TO ACHIEVE TO TAKE LESSONS FROM SAOTOME SENSEI.
I KNOW IT'S RECKLESS.

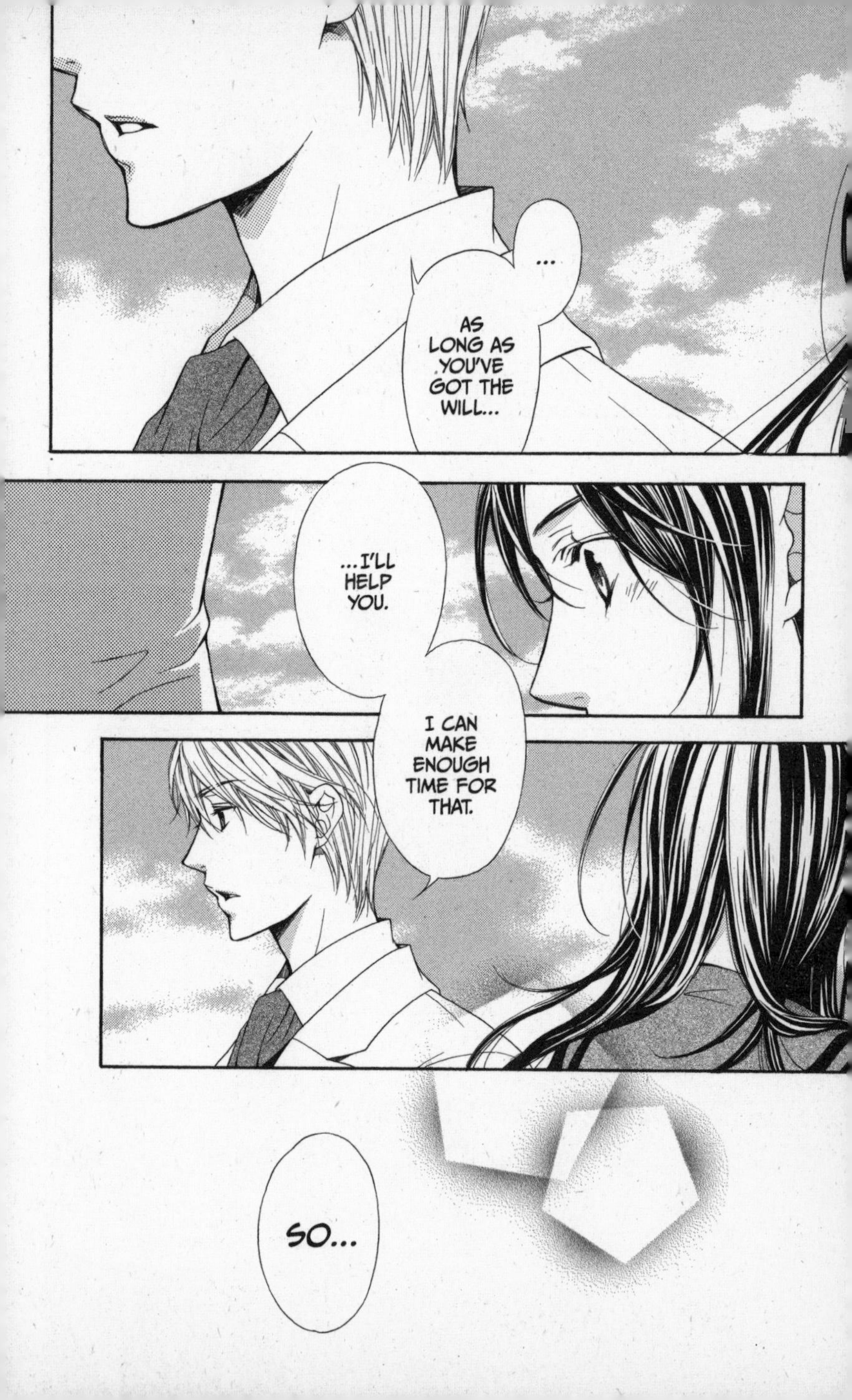
...
AS LONG AS YOU'VE GOT THE WILL...
...I'LL HELP YOU.
I CAN MAKE ENOUGH TIME FOR THAT.
SO...

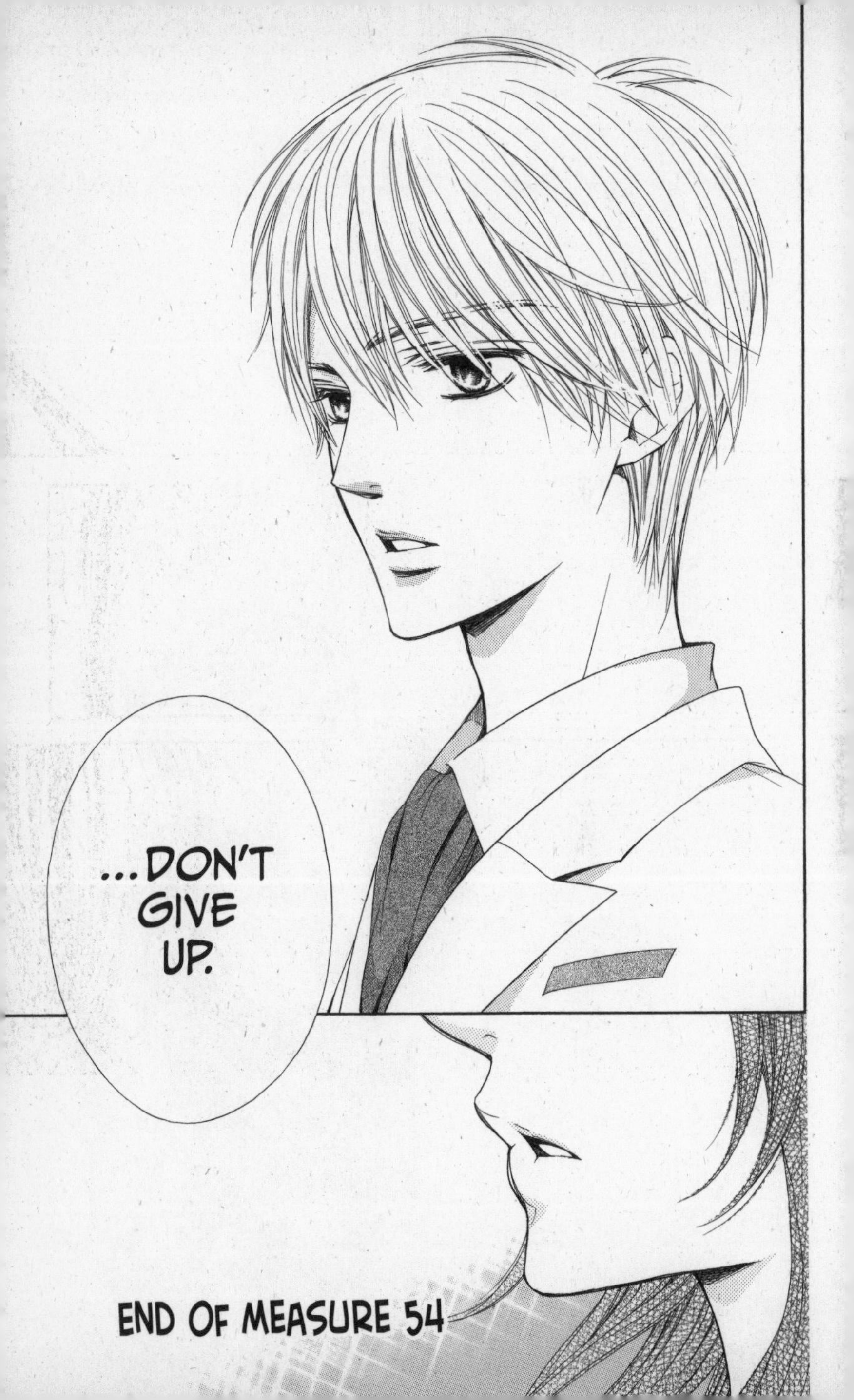
...DON'T GIVE UP.
END OF MEASURE 54

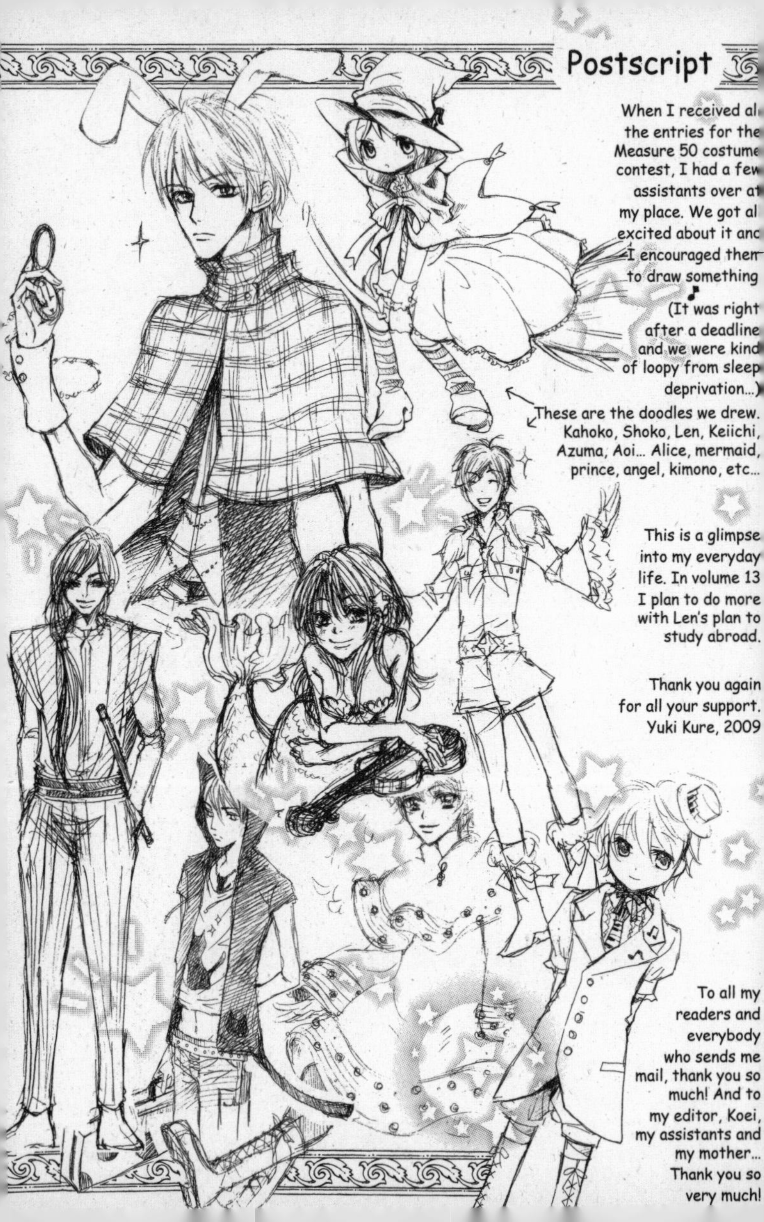

Postscript

When I received al
the entries for the
Measure 50 costume
contest, I had a few
assistants over at
my place. We got al
excited about it anc
I encouraged them
to draw something
♪
(It was right
after a deadline
and we were kind
of loopy from sleep
deprivation...)

These are the doodles we drew.
Kahoko, Shoko, Len, Keiichi,
Azuma, Aoi... Alice, mermaid,
prince, angel, kimono, etc...

This is a glimpse
into my everyday
life. In volume 13
I plan to do more
with Len's plan to
study abroad.

Thank you again
for all your support.
Yuki Kure, 2009

To all my
readers and
everybody
who sends me
mail, thank you so
much! And to
my editor, Koei,
my assistants and
my mother...
Thank you so
very much!

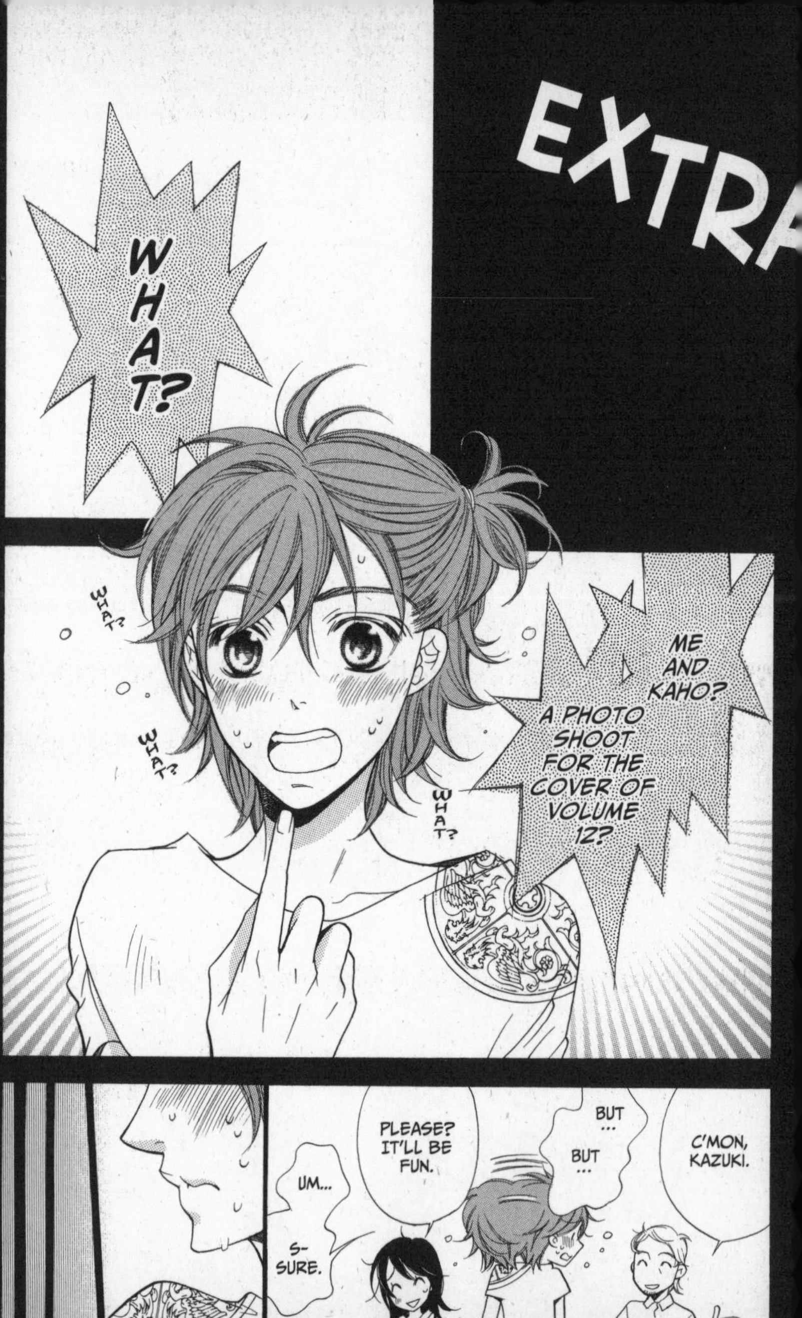
EXTRA
WHAT?
ME AND KAHO? A PHOTO SHOOT FOR THE COVER OF VOLUME 12?
WHAT?
WHAT?
WHAT?
C'MON, KAZUKI.
BUT... BUT...
PLEASE? IT'LL BE FUN.
UM... S-SURE.

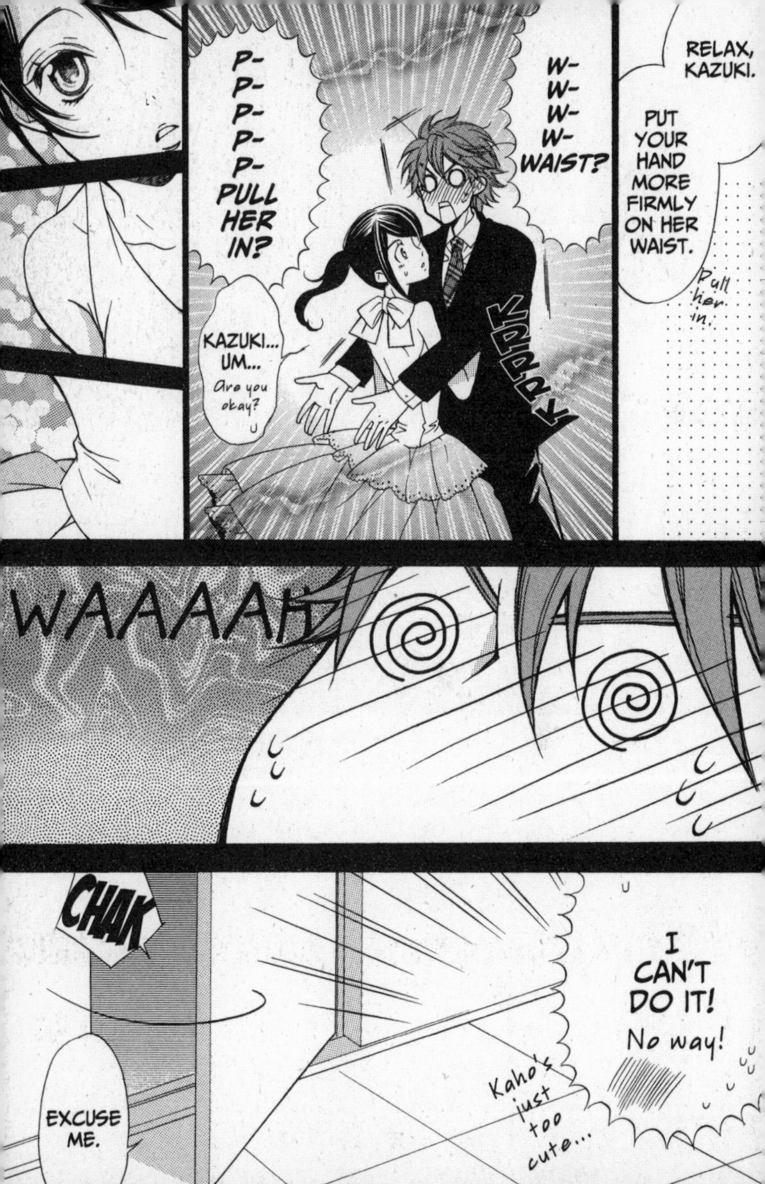
RELAX, KAZUKI.
PUT YOUR HAND MORE FIRMLY ON HER WAIST.
Pull her in.
W-W-W-W-WAIST?
P-P-P-P-P-PULL HER IN?
KRRRRK
KAZUKI... UM...
Are you okay?
WAAAAAH
I CAN'T DO IT!
No way!
Kaho's just too cute...
CHAK
EXCUSE ME.

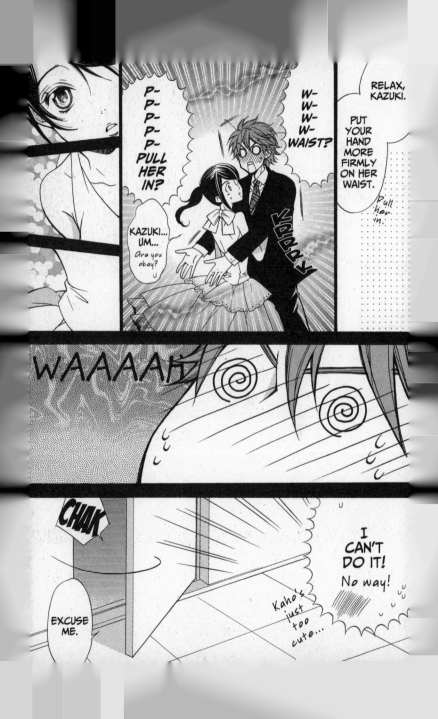

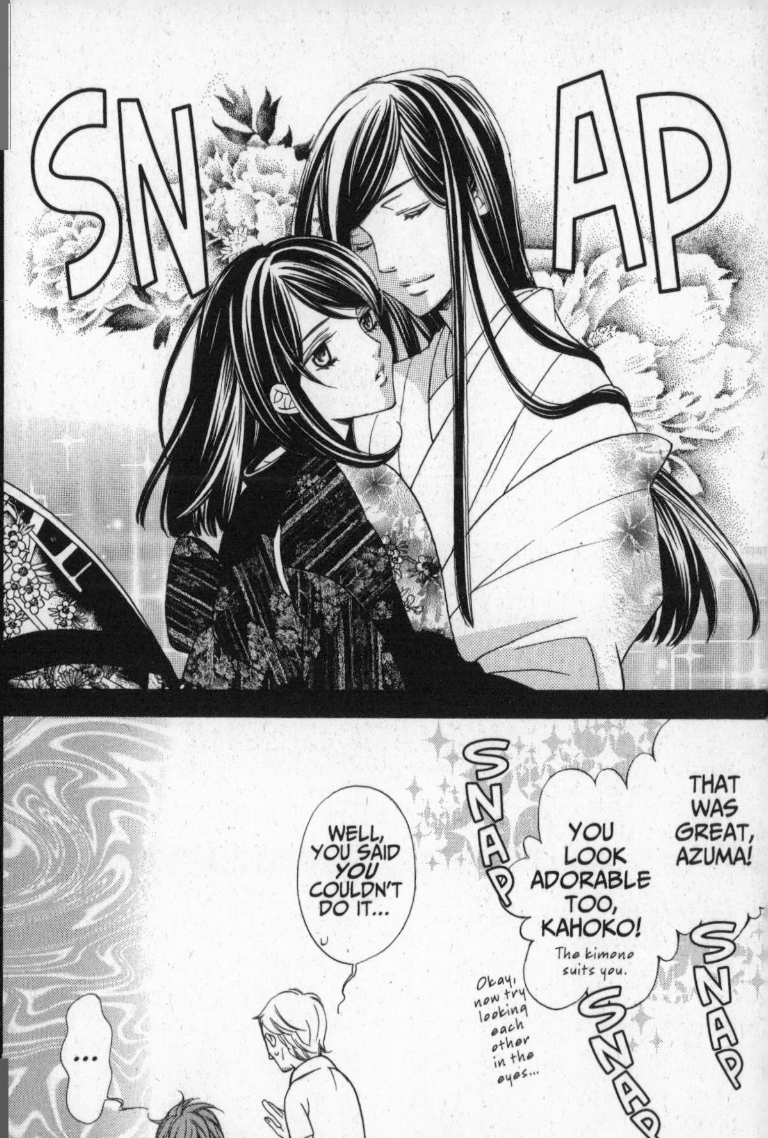
SNAP
THAT WAS GREAT, AZUMA!
SNAP
SNAP
YOU LOOK ADORABLE TOO, KAHOKO!
The kimono suits you.
SNAP
Okay, now try looking each other in the eyes...
WELL, YOU SAID YOU COULDN'T DO IT...
...

※ The cover for volume 12 was originally supposed to be Kazuki and Kahoko.

SPECIAL THANKS

M.Shiino
N.Sato
A.Kashima
S.Asahina
A.Uruno
H.Mizusaki

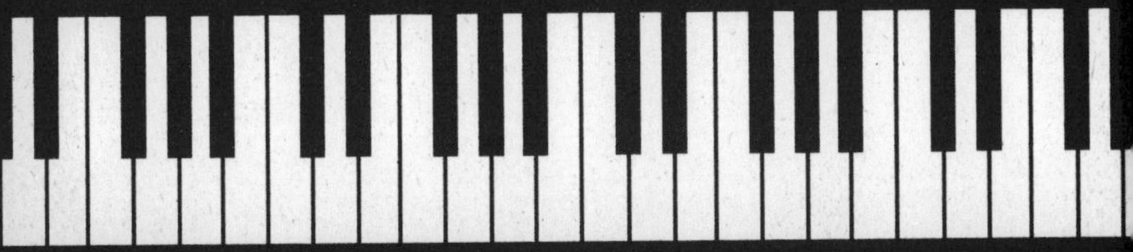

La Corda d'Oro End Notes

You can appreciate music just by listening to it, but knowing the story behind a piece can help enhance your enjoyment. In that spirit, here is background information about some of the topics mentioned in *La Corda d'Oro*. Enjoy!

Page 33, panel 6: 18,500 yen
About $185.00.

Page 94, panel 1: *Loath to Depart*
The piece is Chopin's *Etude*, Opus 10 no. 3, known in Japan as *Wakare no Kyoku* (Song of Parting). Kahoko played it in the First Selection. Ryotaro is also a fan of Chopin; the first piece Kahoko heard him play on the piano was Chopin's *Fantasie Impromptu*.

Yuki Kure made her debut in 2000 with the story *Chijo yori Eien ni* (Forever from the Earth), published in monthly *LaLa* magazine. *La Corda d' Oro* is her first manga series published. Her hobbies are watching soccer games and collecting small goodies.

LA CORDA D'ORO
Vol. 12
Shojo Beat Edition

STORY AND ART BY
YUKI KURE
ORIGINAL CONCEPT BY
RUBY PARTY

English Translation & Adaptation/Mai Ihara
Touch-up Art & Lettering/HudsonYards
Design/Amy Martin
Editor/Shaenon K. Garrity

VP, Production/Alvin Lu
VP, Sales & Product Marketing/Gonzalo Ferreyra
VP, Creative/Linda Espinosa
Publisher/Hyoe Narita

Printed in Canada

Published by VIZ Media, LLC
P.O. Box 77010
San Francisco, CA 94107

10 9 8 7 6 5 4 3 2 1
First printing, June 2010

www.viz.com

www.shojobeat.com

PARENTAL ADVISORY
LA CORDA D'ORO is rated T for Teen and is
recommended for ages 13 and up.
ratings.viz.com